THE GREAT
PERHAPS

Joe Meno is the author of four previous novels, and his
short fiction has been published by the likes of *McSweeney's*,
Witness and *TriQuarterly*. He is a professor of creative
writing at Columbia College Chicago.

OTHER BOOKS BY JOE MENO

THE GREAT
PERHAPS

JOE MENO

PICADOR

First published 2009 by W. W. Norton & Company, Inc., New York

First published in Great Britain 2010 by Picador

First published in paperback 2010 by Picador

This edition published 2011 by Picador
an imprint of Pan Macmillan, a division of Macmillan Publishers Limited
Pan Macmillan, 20 New Wharf Road, London N1 9RR
Basingstoke and Oxford
Associated companies throughout the world
www.panmacmillan.com

ISBN 978-0-330-51248-0

Copyright © Joe Meno 2009

All illustrations by Koren Zelek

The right of Joe Meno to be identified as the
author of this work has been asserted by him in accordance
with the Copyright, Designs and Patents Act 1988.

1 3 5 7 9 8 6 4 2

A CIP catalogue record for this book is available from
the British Library.

Printed in the UK by CPI Mackays, Chatham ME5 8TD

Visit **www.picador.com** to read more about all our books
and to buy them. You will also find features, author interviews and
news of any author events, and you can sign up for e-newsletters
so that you're always first to hear about our new releases.

For family, new and old

One of the great American tragedies is to have participated in a just war.

—*Kurt Vonnegut,*
University of Chicago graduate school alum

Where there is an unknowable, there is a promise.

—*Thornton Wilder,*
University of Chicago faculty member

THE GREAT
PERHAPS

One

ANYTHING RESEMBLING A CLOUD WILL CAUSE JONA-
than Casper to faint. Jonathan, a quiet, middle-aged professor, suffers from an odd form of epilepsy; seeing the shape
of a cloud—a cumulus, its appearance like a magnolia tree in
bloom, a stratus, as bleary as a pigeon startled to flight, or a cirrus, with its vague, ghostlike veil—and he will immediately collapse, his heart beating irregularly in perfect terror, his breath
slowing to a whisper, his arms and legs going weak. These
symptoms may only last for a few moments or up to several
hours, depending on a number of unknowable factors, such
as the size of the cloud, its color, and its height. The cause of
Jonathan's disorder—first documented in a 1961 article in the
New England Journal of Medicine entitled "The Boy Who Feared
the Sky"—was thought to be hereditary in nature, as other,
distant relations had been beset by similarly strange defects.
Jonathan's condition was later named as its own neurological
disease, *Casper-Cerebrovascularitis*, when he was eight. The medical community marveled at the shocking, undeniable effects
which could be duplicated whenever a doctor, medical stu-

dent, or neurological researcher showed the boy a picture of a "cloud" on a small flash card exactly like this—

Figure 1: A cloud

—the boy suddenly fainting, falling lifelessly from his seat. An antiseizure medication was introduced when Jonathan was ten, addressing all of his ongoing and awkward symptoms, allowing him to step outside without collapsing, as long as he remembered to take the unusual-looking silver pill each day. The antiseizure medication was such an astounding success that, afterward, the boy came to hold an unshakable belief in the infallibility of science. By then Jonathan had begun to prefer the relative safety of his schoolbooks. Discovering, by accident, the unlikely existence of the giant squid sometime during a sophomore biology class in high school—the giant squid, a creature who, like Jonathan, favored the solitude of darkness to the unsafe spectacle of the clouds above—the young man began to learn all he could about this gloomy animal and its outsized ancestors, finding at last a world unthreatened by the perils of an irregular sky.

As a PALEONTOLOGIST specializing in Triassic mollusks and a tenured professor at the University of Chicago, Jonathan, age forty-eight, is now able to ignore this strange medical problem, finding himself lost in a cloud of his thoughts—imagining the elusive, prehistoric giant squid, a world of wavering seaweed, of dark blue shadows, of ageless creatures armed with razor-edged beaks and endless grasping tentacles, leagues and leagues beneath the silent plane of the sea. Many, many moments in Jonathan's life are spent safely indoors, dreaming of the colossal invertebrate, studying his ink-stained notes, lost in a cloudiness of gray ideas. Rapt in his research lab, scratching at his bristly blond beard, adjusting his thick bifocals, staring down at the fossilized remains of what may or may not be the great mantle of *Tusoteuthis longa*, unaware of his two graduate assistants bickering nearby or, standing before his enormous lecture class, enduring his students' nearly intolerable and blank stares or, hiding in his office at home, listening to his wife and daughters as they argue, Jonathan finds this cloudiness is often caused by the antiseizure medication, phenytoin, which he is supposed to take daily.

TODAY IT HAPPENS when the family goes to the zoo. Behind the wheel of the ancient silver Volvo, Jonathan has forgotten to take his antiseizure medication, and because of this, the atom-sized world of his family will soon be upset. Madeline, his wife, doesn't seem to have noticed that anything might be wrong. She looks happy sitting there in the passenger seat, staring out the window, humming, her short brown bob held in place with a hairpin. Their teenage daughters, Amelia and Thisbe, are both silent in the backseat. The stereo plays a song by the Beatles, and because the Volvo is actually Madeline's car, it's always her turn to pick the music, even when she's not driving. The sun is bright and glorious, a lovely Sunday afternoon at the beginning of October, a month of indecision: though there haven't been any acts of terrorism lately, everyone is still doubtful about everything. The upcoming presidential election is a month away, while the war in Iraq continues on with-out much hope. There are billboards and ads with political slogans suggesting this uncertainty everywhere. A cobalt-blue BMW passes the family's Volvo on the left, a BUSH/CHENEY '04 bumper sticker blazoned on the rear bumper. Madeline, seeing it, immediately sighs.

Jonathan turns to look at her and sees the smooth sheen of his wife's bare legs. He glances at all the lovely freckles on her white skin and sees her dark hair blowing beside the open window and feels his heart strum a timorous chord. He places his hand on Madeline's knee and smiles. It is impossible that they are actually married. It seems that she is too pleasant to be his wife. He immediately forgets the secret deliberations of his unsteady scientific mind and smiles at his wife in wonder. She is still so girlish, so bright-eyed, exactly like her younger self, but even more so now, somehow. She is talking to him. She is telling him about something that has happened at work. Madeline is an animal behaviorist, also employed by the Uni-versity of Chicago, though her field is avian research. She is explaining how a test group of pigeons she's been studying have begun to commit murder.

"It's an incredibly difficult problem," Madeline says. "I've never seen anything like it before." Jonathan smiles, staring at a group of freckles on Madeline's shoulder. He has forgotten how pretty his wife is. He has forgotten how badly he would like to kiss her.

The Volvo, with its own innumerable bumper stickers—KEEP RELIGION OUT OF SCHOOLS and NO TO WAR IN IRAQ and ALL GREAT TRUTHS BEGIN AS BLASPHEMIES—GEORGE BER-NARD SHAW—speeds down Lake Shore Drive, the windows partly rolled down, the family hearing the music beneath the sound of the wind whipping past, the city of Chicago appearing brilliantly before them. *We are marvelous! We are amazing! We have won the war against nature!* Jonathan thinks. *We, this brave species, in our little indestructible cities, in our little indestructible cars, are much too smart, much too fast, much too happy to ever be harmed. We have somehow outsmarted the entire, cruel order of the natural world! We will live for one million years and then become marvelous, electric clouds of thought and nothing bad will happen to us or to anyone we know.*

"Dad? I was thinking," Thisbe, his youngest, calls from the backseat.

"Yes?"

"I don't think I want to see the lions. Or the tigers. They make me want to cry."

Jonathan raises his eyebrows, scratching at his beard, looking over at Madeline to respond. He glances in the rearview mirror and sees Thisbe, fourteen, in a plaid outfit and red sweater, her brown hair hanging in her dark eyes, looking sulky.

"We don't have to see any animals you don't want to," Madeline says, turning around in her seat. "But I bet you'll change your mind when we get there."

"I don't know if we should go to the zoo at all. I think it's cruel," Thisbe says, definitely moody.

"It's not cruel," Jonathan says. "It's educational. I used to go to the zoo with my father all the time. It's normal. It's what normal families do. They go to the zoo and tell their dads how lucky they are for being their daughters and then they make up songs about how great their dad is. Doesn't that sound like fun?"

Thisbe just huffs, turning back to pout, staring out the window.

"I don't think God likes the idea of zoos," she says.

Jonathan smiles. Beside him, his wife shakes her head, rolling her eyes. Thisbe, a high school freshman, raised without a religious background of any kind, has begun to make bold arguments on behalf of God. To Jonathan it only seems like a silly—though perfectly natural—thing for a teenage girl to do, struggling to find answers to the compromising mysteries of her young life. Madeline, a former Catholic, does not find her daughter's recent religious sentiments so very funny.

"I don't want to go to the zoo either," Amelia adds.

Jonathan frowns, glancing in the rearview mirror once more.

Amelia, a junior in high school, age seventeen, is wearing that awful black beret again. Amelia has recently declared herself a Marxist. Though she is white, and whiter than most, with her mother's pale skin, chestnut hair, and sad, haunting blue eyes, Amelia has begun to wear T-shirts featuring the likenesses of Che Guevara, Malcolm X, and others, with slogans like NO MORE PRISONS. Sitting at the dinner table, in their expensive little home, Amelia has begun to mention *revolution*, with strange facts like, *"Did you know the CIA totally admitted to killing members of the Black Panthers and nobody even cared?"*

"I think the zoo is totally bourgeois," Amelia says.

Jonathan smirks, silently pleased by his oldest daughter's growing political intelligence. He is also a little amused at her slight mispronunciation of the word. "Well, we're going to the zoo today, guys. It was your turn to decide what we did last weekend. Besides, I've heard they have a baby tree sloth. Wouldn't you like to see that? A baby tree sloth? It sounds pretty awesome. Or maybe you're afraid of doing something pretty awesome?"

"No," Thisbe says.

"No," Amelia says.

"We could go to the aquarium," Madeline suggests in a whisper.

"We're not going to the aquarium. We're going to the zoo today. That's what's been decided. We're not changing the plan now. We stick to the plan. That's what winners do. They stick to plans."

"This family is like some sort of oligarchy," Amelia grumbles.

"Great word choice," her mother says with a grin.

"This family is not an oligarchy," Jonathan adds. "It's a republic. Look it up."

"Thisbe, honey, that reminds me, how was your history test the other day?" Madeline asks.

"Awful," Thisbe mumbles. "I'm bad at history. And there's this girl that sits behind me who has bad breath. I think I should say something but I don't know if I should. I don't know if God would want me to."

"Oh, my God," Amelia sharply interrupts. "I forgot to tell you guys. I've figured out what I'm going to do for my science project this year. I've decided to try and make a bomb."

Jonathan does not know what to say to that. He turns and looks over at Madeline, who is also momentarily silent. Amelia keeps talking. "It's like to prove how easy it is to make an explosive device and everything. Like how there are all these instructions online and you can use like cleaning products and everything. I need you to sign a permission slip for me."

"Amelia, why don't you decide to do something a little more constructive?"

"It is constructive. I'm constructing a bomb."

"No," Madeline says, smiling. "Why not make something that isn't *de*structive? I bet it would be much more challenging."

"I'm already doing that. I'm making a movie for my history class."

"What's your movie about?" Jonathan asks.

"Capitalism, mostly. Like how there's all these different classes of people and how people need to overcome it."

"Well, that sounds like something," Jonathan says.

As the station wagon passes the exit for Thirty-fifth Street, Thisbe shouts, "Dad! We're going the wrong way. Isn't Grandpa coming with?"

"Not today. He said he wasn't feeling up to it."

"Oh," Thisbe whispers with a small, disappointed sigh.

"All he ever does is talk about airplanes," Amelia adds. "It's kind of embarrassing."

The family is quiet for some time after that, the Beatles playing "Yellow Submarine," the sound of the open windows and the city hurrying past. Madeline turns in her seat and sees Thisbe sitting there with her eyes closed, her hands held together like a tiny steeple.

"Thisbe? Are you praying back there?" she asks. Jonathan gives a look to his wife, who simply shakes her head.

"No. I was just listening to the music," Thisbe says, her face going red.

THE FAMILY STARES out the windows of the Volvo silently. Jonathan, oblivious to the afternoon traffic, imagines an explosion of applause. He is standing behind a great wooden podium, reading the conclusion to a stunning speech on the solitary nature of *Tusoteuthis longa*, the prehistoric giant squid. "I want to thank the National Academy of Sciences for their award today. I believe it speaks to the great scientific ambition within us all." Many, many hours are spent dreaming of this, while Jonathan pursues his work in the research lab at the Field Museum and within the smallish den of their Hyde Park home, which over the years has become an exhibit of drawings, maps, fossils, and charts marking the locations where remains of the prehistoric giant squid have recently been found.

As strange as it may seem, Jonathan is trying to prove that the prehistoric giant squid, one of the most isolated species in the history of the natural world, is still alive, hiding in the ocean's dark depths, and that—because of the squid's relative solitude and lack of interaction with early predators like the mosasaur and *Cimolichthys nepabolica*—it is the perfect case study for the theory of evolution. It is a theory that, of late, has come under considerable criticism. Jonathan's hope is that the discovery of this lost species will present new evidence that will inform a unified idea about why the world is the way it is, and where, as human beings, we truly come from. In his search for the prehistoric squid, Jonathan is looking for a single, uncomplicated answer to the mystery of human life: there must be one somewhere, he is sure of it. An article on *T. longa* published nearly a year ago in *Paleontology Today* quoted Jonathan as saying:

> *The prehistoric giant squid may be alive in our ocean's depths at this very moment because of its preference for isolation. If found alive, it will certainly represent the last opportunity to observe a living prehistoric organism and to closely study its behavior, its anatomy, and its genetic material—a perfect specimen for better understanding the evolution of heredity. Surely, the discovery of this remarkable creature will begin to provide answers to our most important questions. What might we learn about ourselves as human beings, about our capacities to live without struggle, and who we truly are? Is it not important to note that all living species were, at one time during our evolution, also ocean-dwellers? Perhaps the promise of our future will be revealed with a better knowledge of our quiet, unproblematic past.*

More strange than the object of Jonathan's study is the high level of competition within this particular field. Jonathan's scientific nemesis, Dr. Jacques Albert, of the FSA, the French Sédimentologie Association, recently discovered an important clue in this prehistoric mystery, an intact prehistoric squid pen—something like a backbone but not quite—dissimilar to the pens of other giant squids in its size and shape, that had washed ashore along the coast of southern Japan. Hour after hour, alone in the den, Jonathan will stare down at topographic sketches of the ocean floor near New Zealand or the Azores Islands or Japan, imagining that, at that very moment, the great tentacled beast may now be jetting backward silently through the cloudless water, in search of a darker spot to guard its secrets. Madeline, charmed by the sight of Jonathan mumbling to himself in wonder, will sometimes come and stand in the doorway, watching her husband work. He will not notice her, not until she has quietly stepped behind him at his desk and placed her freckled arms around his neck. He will smile, distracted, kiss her, and silently wait for her to leave. Jonathan will then turn back to his maps, circling a spot here, triangulating another position there, immediately forgetting the shape of his wife's lips upon his lips.

AT THE ZOO that day, the family is sad to discover that many of the animals have mysteriously begun to die. The glass cages echo with silent grief and blank sunlight. Placards have been placed along the display information in front of their cages that read UNDER QUARANTINE. Three elephants and two camels have quietly expired, and all of the zoo's pink flamingos have died as well. The rest of the animals look morose, some losing their fur, some with bright pink spots. The family walks from empty exhibit to empty exhibit without speaking. The jungle cats, perched low in their plastic trees, seem unaffected. Thisbe still refuses to go into the Lion House to look at the lions. She says she cannot stand watching the lions and tigers pace around in their tiny glass cages. Amelia rolls her eyes, yawning, bored by her sister's complaining.

"Well, I'd like to go see the lions even if nobody else does," Amelia says, glaring directly at Thisbe.

"Well, I'm not going," Thisbe mumbles. "I'll have nightmares."

"I'll wait here with Thisbe," Jonathan offers.

"We can meet you guys by the food court," Madeline says. "Maybe you guys can go get a snow cone or something."

"I don't want a snow cone," Thisbe whispers. "I'm going to pretend I'm not here."

Jonathan frowns. "I was hoping today we could maybe act like a family and walk around the zoo together. But I guess that's hoping for too much. Maybe I can join up with one of these other families. They look like they understand what being part of a family means."

"Dad, you're so gay," Amelia says with a sigh.

"I just want to go look at the groundhogs," Thisbe says. "That's all I want to see."

"We can go look at them and then the baby sloth," Jonathan offers, then adds, "If you like."

Why does he want his daughters' approval so badly? It makes him feel like a schoolboy. He immediately thinks of his own father, and the outings with him to the Museum of Science and Natural History in St. Louis, when he was a child. He wonders if his own father worried so much about what he, as a boy, thought of him; whether or not he always had to be having fun; whether or not he always had to approve of everything.

"Whatever, I don't care," Thisbe whispers, still in a huff.

"I'll go see the lions and tigers with Amelia," Madeline says. "And then maybe we can all meet back here at one-thirty and get some ice cream."

Jonathan scratches his beard. "If that's what you'd all like. But I just want to go on the record saying I think it's pretty pathetic that we all can't walk around together. I think whoever built this zoo would be pretty upset with us right now. I think whoever invented the idea of zoos would be pretty unhappy."

"We'll see you at one-thirty," Madeline says, and, grabbing Amelia's hand, she and their oldest daughter hurry off, rolling their eyes at him.

Jonathan thinks about maybe putting his arm around Thisbe's shoulder, but the way she is standing there, frowning, her shoulders hunched up, her chin sunk into her chest, he decides not to. He begins walking, Thisbe pouting beside him, glaring at the other families, at the kids running around, at the signs to each exhibit which Jonathan tries to read as they pass.

"How about the buffalo? Do you want to see them?"

"No. They're like all crowded in there. It's too sad."

"No buffaloes, okay. What about the seals? The seals are right over there."

"Fine. I don't care," she says in a snit and off they go, approaching the enormous seal tank. Inside, two slick-skinned seals pedal through the water, their noses skimming along the surface.

"They have spots on their heads," Thisbe whispers, pointing. "Like leopards." Jonathan glances over at his daughter and is surprised. Is she smiling? It looks like she's almost smiling.

"I never noticed that before," Jonathan says, staring at her dimples, which he has forgotten even exist. They both lean against the blue metal railing, staring down into the dark silver pool. Jonathan turns and sees Thisbe has closed her eyes. Her eyelashes are fluttering, and she is whispering something to herself.

"Thisbe?"

"Yes?"

"Are you all right?"

"Yes."

Jonathan nods, but does not say anything else. They silently stroll off toward the groundhog exhibit, Jonathan glancing out of the corner of his eye, watching his youngest daughter suspiciously. As they pass the elk and the ibexes and worried-looking mountain goats, Jonathan notices Thisbe is still whispering something to herself. They stop before the llamas, their woolen fur flecked with bits of wood and brambles, their great camel jaws working on some hay. Thisbe closes her eyes again, muttering softly spoken words to herself. She is staring at the llamas, saying something, and this time Jonathan speaks up.

"Thisbe, honey, what are you doing?"

"Nothing."

"What are you saying to the llamas?"

"Nothing. I was just praying for them. That they don't die."

"Thisbe, honey, you don't have to pray for them."

Thisbe nods. Together, they walk on. Jonathan glances up at the sun and suddenly feels faint. For the briefest moment, the lights of a conference room in New Jersey flash somewhere within his brain.

• • •

ONLY ONE MONTH before, at a paleontology conference, a threat was made against Jonathan's life during his presentation on the ongoing search for the prehistoric giant squid. Dr. Jacques Albert, of the FSA, the France Sédimentologie Association, with his awful accent shouted, "I should strike you dead, Professor Casper, for the ridiculous statement you have just made. I should strike you dead!" A color slide of *T. longa* was being projected behind Jonathan as he immediately began to panic, unsure what it was he should do, standing behind the awkward podium in the conference room of the Holiday Inn of Greater Newark. The lights above began to flicker, emitting a thin wisp of gray-colored smoke. Jonathan found himself beginning to go under, as if a great shadow had suddenly appeared over his head, *a cloud*, his legs quickly becoming numb and weak. *Oh, no*, he thought. *I didn't take my* . . . , and then the French scientist was yelling, "For it was I, with my team of excellent researchers, who discovered the intact prehistoric squid pen, not you. And it will be I, with my excellent team of researchers, who will discover the first living specimen." A moment later Jonathan collapsed exactly where he was standing: *The prehistoric giant squid jets quietly through the dark gray water. The prehistoric giant squid jets quietly through the dark gray water. The prehistoric giant squid jets quietly through the dark gray water. The prehistoric giant squid jets quietly through the dark gray water. Phylum: MOLLUSCA, Class: CEPHALOPODA.*

When he came to, Dr. Albert was kneeling above him frowning, and a petite blond German scientist with enormous glasses, Dr. Arzt, was cradling his head. Jonathan found he was mumbling, "I'm okay, I'm okay . . . it's no big deal." With the German doctor's help, supporting him as he limped down the hallway to his room, Jonathan soon recovered. The compassionate foreign woman held a damp washcloth to his forehead through the early hours of the morning, each of the scientists exchanging poorly worded admissions of inadequacy. Dr. Arzt, or Heidi, as she insisted, had recently lost an important research grant, her work with the prehistoric dragonfly all but ending. Lying beside her in the hotel bed, fully clothed, Jonathan admitted he was forty-eight years old and afraid of almost everything. It was as lovely and profound a secret as he had spoken in some time, and the confession sent something fluttering, like a delicate *Meganeura monyi*, in the German scientist's heart. When he awoke, however, Heidi was gone, maintaining her professional decorum. Jonathan, on the flight back home, decided not to tell his wife anything about the incident. He was also determined to keep the matter from his family doctor, who would, no doubt, feel compelled to report the episode to the Illinois Department of Motor Vehicles—the agency once again having to temporarily suspend his driver's license.

Only one day after returning home from the conference in New Jersey, Jonathan received a stilted though lovelorn email from the younger German scientist, to which he responded with what could only be called poetry. The online affair was an awkwardly postpubescent game, really, a fantasy to occupy his off hours, one other thoughtless mistake.

AT THE ZOO, the family does meet up at the aforementioned time, does get ice cream, and, all together, does head to the Reptile House. There Jonathan stands beside his oldest daughter, Amelia, both of them staring down at the crocodile pond. He is admiring *Crocodylus cataphractus, Pseudosuchia*, relative of so many land-dwelling dinosaurs, while Amelia is staring down into the murk. He glances out of the corner of his eye and looks at her. She is taller now, thin, has a beaded hemp necklace on. Jonathan has never noticed her wearing jewelry before.

"Dad?"

"Yes?"

"Can I ask you a question?"

"Okay."

"Do you ever feel like the rest of the world is totally stupid?"

"How do you mean, kiddo?"

"I don't know. Like everybody. Like people on TV and everyone at school. Like everybody. Everybody just seems so stupid to me," she says.

"Like who?" Jonathan asks.

"I don't know. Everybody. I started making a list of all the stupid people I hate."

"You did."

"Yeah."

"I see. Well, who's on the list?"

"Rupert Murdoch."

"Who else?"

"Donald Rumsfeld."

"Who else?"

"I dunno. Charlton Heston. Britney Spears. Madonna. Rush Limbaugh."

"How many people are on the list right now?"

"Forty-three."

"Who are all the other people?"

"I don't know. Just people I hate."

"Oh."

"Do you hate anybody, Dad?"

"No, of course not. I don't think so, at least."

. . .

BUT, OF COURSE, Jonathan immediately thinks of Jacques Albert of the FSA Dr. Jacques Albert the most incredible fucking annoyance Dr. Jacques Albert only thirty-three years old Fuck him Dr. Jacques Albert on the cover of *Modern Paleontologist* Dr. Jacques Albert blond with his small silver earring Dr. Jacques Albert at every panel at every presentation always in the audience always trying to provoke Jonathan always with some patronizing comment: "I noticed your new project barely received any new funding, Dr. Casper, that must be difficult," or "I don't know if you saw my feature essay in *Modern Paleontologist*, sir, but I think it might excite you to hear what kind of research the rest of the world is now doing," or "I heard your team is still looking for an intact squid pen from *Tusoteuthis longa*, can that possibly be true? How long has it been, Dr. Casper, ten years already? I feel like I was reading about you back in graduate school" Dr. Jacques Albert with his little blond goatee Dr. Jacques Albert with reporters from every paleontology journal hanging on his every word Dr. Jacques Albert standing above him with that frown Jonathan dazed dizzy his hands and feet numb staring up at the lights from the floor of the conference room of the Holiday Inn Dr. Jacques Albert Dr. Jacques Albert Dr. Jacques Albert.

AT THE ZOO, the family heads into the sweltering shadows of the Great Ape House. The building is dark and heavy with the stink of urine and fecal matter from the primates, who, lying in the corner of their enormous glass exhibits with their old-men expressions and sad eyes, stare back heartbroken. Thisbe and Amelia hurry ahead while Jonathan takes his time, watching a pair of chattering chimpanzees groom each other. He is thinking about the terrible presentation in New Jersey and fainting on the hotel floor. He is glancing at Madeline every few moments, wondering if he ought to tell her now what happened. All of a sudden his wife takes a step beside him and kisses his cheek.

"What was that for?" he asks.

"I don't know. Just felt like doing it."

"I'm glad."

"Are we going to talk about last night?" she asks.

"I don't know," he says. "What happened last night?"

"Where did you go? I woke up and looked at the clock and you were gone."

"I was in the den working."

"Looking for your sea monster, huh?"

Jonathan smiles and takes his wife's hand. They stroll quietly past the orangutans, then the mandrills, and stop before the enormous gorillas. Jonathan turns to his wife and says, "Thisbe was praying for the llamas. And the seals."

In a whisper, Madeline says, "She's so fucking weird. I don't even know what to do with her." She rolls her brown eyes as she says this and Jonathan immediately thinks of his two daughters, realizing exactly where they've gotten their eye-rolling from. "Okay, don't freak out: but Amelia and I were talking and she asked me about oral sex."

"What did she ask?"

"I don't know. When I first did it. How old I was. That kind of thing."

"What did you say?"

"I told her the truth."

"You did?"

"Yes."

"That's not what I would have said."

"I know that's not what you would have said."

"Well, has she done it yet or is she just making plans?"

"I think she's making plans."

"With who?" Jonathan asks.

"I don't think anybody in particular. I think she's just start-ing to think about it."

"Okay. Wow," Jonathan says. "I don't think I want you to tell me about those kinds of things."

"Too bad," Madeline whispers.

Jonathan nods, grabbing her hand. His wife looks so beauti-ful, so unfamiliar all of a sudden. Jonathan thinks about reach-ing out and grabbing her around the waist, to feel her body up against his. He does, grinning at her. "Hi, there," Madeline says, a flirt now, a woman he has just met, coyly winking. She kisses him again, this time on the mouth, right there in the shadows of the gorilla exhibit. Jonathan feels the soft pressure of his wife against his chest, and suddenly they are laughing. They stop and hear Thisbe and Amelia up ahead, in front of the baboons, arguing about something.

AN IMPORTANT NOTE: Jonathan and Madeline, though happy now, had been separated once, nearly eight years ago, at what Jonathan felt was a critical moment in his search for *Tuso-teuthis longa*, journeying to Norway to complete his fieldwork. It was all done rather academically, with Jonathan explaining the reasons he was leaving in a detailed presentation before their daughters, which at one point involved some kind of chart, and Madeline sending messages for Jonathan through the two girls, written as savagely polite memos: *From: Mad-eline, To: Jonathan, Re: Informing the girls of how sorry you are*. This brief separation only lasted ten months, although over the last two decades Jonathan has been absent more times than his wife or his daughters would care to remember. What Jonathan has missed while attending various academic symposia, speaking at notable scientific conferences, or voyaging to the most remote quarters of the ocean for critical research trips: Amelia's first tooth and first word, a number of Thisbe's piano recitals, Madeline's broken arm, Madeline's involvement in a serious car accident, Madeline's broken ankle.

AN ADDITIONAL NOTE: Jonathan has recently taken to driving alone to the many unoccupied lots adjacent to the lake, stopping to buy a racy magazine along the way, parking there before or after work, to masturbate. The girls in the magazines, with titles like *Swank*, *TOY*, and *Juggs*, are young, with impossibly fake breasts. Jonathan, even in this short panic of lust, is not fooled by his own weakness. Sometimes he will stare down at the glossy pictures and imagine what the young women would look like without any skin at all, how beneath their layers of downy hides, beneath their freckles and moles and hairless flesh, their organs are all quite similar to that of the prehistoric giant squid: heart, stomach, jaw, anus. The thought of this perfect, unacknowledged order, of this wondrous shared simplicity, even during his fantasies, gives Jonathan an inexplicable glow.

ANOTHER NOTE, in addition to the previous ones: there is the undemanding online arrangement with Dr. Heidi Arzt as well. This relationship, hardly an affair, consists of sixty-seven email responses, all written in lowercase, with poor spelling and erroneous punctuation. Rarely are the notes sexual in nature. Although, sitting in his office at the university, Jonathan knows that the words he writes in his amateurish ardor, like, *i am thinking of your outstandingly firm body and what it would be like to be alone with you again*, would do much harm if his wife ever happened upon them. He thinks he has been careful, however. He does not use the computer at home to respond. If he does, he is sure to erase his messages. He knows nothing will come of this relationship and so goes on enjoying it without much worry. But still, there is a feeling in his heart, an echo of fear, the future memory of some imminent defeat, considering what he has to lose, what his life would be like without Madeline or his daughters, and how he would ever go on without the complicated attentions of his family.

TODAY THE ZOO has not been much fun. As Jonathan is backing the Volvo out of its spot at a parking meter, Madeline is staring out the passenger window again, fiddling with her hairpin. She looks dreamy, as lovely as the day they first met. In the backseat, Amelia is complaining that the air conditioner is too cold and Thisbe is asking if they can please never go to the zoo again. Jonathan turns up the stereo, and it is another Beatles song. One of the girls immediately begins to complain about it. The Volvo pulls into traffic.

As the enormous brownstones of Lincoln Park rush past, only a flash of gabled history and fading light, a gigantic white SUV cruises around a double-parked car, swerving onto the wrong side of the street, speeding head-on toward the Volvo. At that moment, Jonathan stares at the blur of the SUV— small globes of sunlight flickering from the sky, the white sport utility vehicle rising inevitably before him—and then his brain promptly names it, though incorrectly: *a cloud.* As soon as he thinks he understands what he is seeing, he immediately begins to feel very strange, his heart beating terrifically loud, and then he knows it—he is having a seizure. His left arm feels stiff, then his right, then he is having a hard time breathing. His heart begins pounding even louder. His arms feel lifeless and heavy. He cannot hold on to the steering wheel. As the Volvo collides with the SUV, Jonathan tries to say something, to cry out or shout, but all he can do is whisper. Metal meets metal amid the sound of cracking glass. Thisbe screams in the backseat. Jonathan hits the brakes, then the gas, then the brakes again. His ears begin to ring, then everything goes silent. The Volvo is no longer moving. The family is completely quiet and then Madeline is turning around and asking if everyone is okay. Everyone says yes. Everyone except Jonathan. Jonathan opens his blue eyes, feeling his vision losing its focus, the world going hazy, an enormous cloud rising there before him. He begins to tremble and then he begins to convulse. Madeline is holding his hand, trying to keep him still, saying, *Oh, God, don't do this to me, Jonathan. Oh, God, don't do this to me,* and suddenly everything becomes bright and lovely

the prehistoric giant squid jets quietly through the dark gray water. The prehistoric giant squid jets quietly through the dark gray water. The prehistoric giant squid jets quietly through the dark gray water. The prehistoric giant squid jets quietly through the dark gray water. Phylum: MOLLUSCA, Class: CEPHALOPODA, Subclass: COLEOIDEA, Order: VAMPYROMORPHA, Suborder: MESOTEUTHINA, Family: KELAENIDAE, Genus: TUSOTEUTHIS, Species: LONGA. The particular history of the prehistoric giant squid is largely misunderstood. With the incredible dearth of genetic material for evidence, much is still unknown, as the chitinous gladius, or, more commonly, the pen, is rarely discovered intact. The prehistoric giant squid jets quietly through the dark gray water. The prehistoric giant squid jets quietly through the dark gray water. The prehistoric giant squid jets quietly through the dark gray water. The prehistoric giant squid jets quietly through the dark gray water

OUT OF THE CORNER of his eye, Jonathan looks up at his wife. He has been staring at her soft face for some time. He tries to smile, holding her hand. A bothered-looking paramedic with a blond mustache is taking his pulse. His daughters sit on the curb, holding each other, staring at him, terrified. Jonathan is sitting up, trying to think of something funny to say, but his head hurts very badly. His wife's eyes are red. There are black smudges of makeup beneath her eyelashes. "I'm okay," Jonathan finally whispers. "I'm okay," but his wife does not stop crying.

THE FAMILY DOES NOT go to the hospital. Jonathan says he is all right and refuses to get in the ambulance. He is more embarrassed than hurt, his face red with humiliation, shaded by his blond beard. When they pull into their garage, Madeline puts the Volvo in park and says, "Girls, I need to talk to your father alone for a minute." Amelia and Thisbe are uncharacteristically obedient, scared to death maybe, and hurry out, slamming the car doors behind them. Jonathan, anticipating an argument, grabs his wife's hand, trying to smile widely, trying to let her know that there is no need to worry, that everything is all right, but Madeline will not look him in the eye. Instead she stares straight ahead, still holding the steering wheel.

"I want to know the truth." She turns and looks at him, unsmiling, her eyes still red from crying.

"About what?" he answers quietly, the words stiff on his tongue.

"Did you take your medicine today or not?" she asks.

Jonathan must first think how to answer. He looks away, the words coming very slowly.

"Did you take it or not, Jonathan?"

"No, but, honey, it was a simple mistake. I was busy this morning looking at some data from Japan—"

"When was the last time you took it?"

Jonathan stutters, then murmurs, "I don't know. Two days ago, I think. I've been wrapped up in these sonar reports and . . ."

Madeline quickly looks away. Jonathan tries to take her hand, but she is unmoving.

"I was fine all day," he says. "It was just an accident . . . it could have happened—"

"You have no idea . . . no idea how it feels. You didn't have to call the ambulance, Jonathan. You didn't have to see the look on Thisbe's face. You promised me this would never happen again. You promised me."

"I only need to go to Martin and try some other pills. I've been taking those other ones for too long, I think."

"You promised me, Jonathan, you promised me."

"Honey. I—"

"I won't do this anymore," she says. "I can't."

"It was only—"

"I don't . . . I don't have anything else to say to you right now," Madeline whispers and hurries out of the car. Jonathan sits there, in the passenger seat, in the dark of his garage, holding his face in his hands.

"Damn," he mutters. "Damn, damn, damn."

THE ARGUMENT IS NOT resolved, will not be resolved, by the time Madeline goes to bed. Jonathan stands beside her in the dark, trying to summon some words, an apology, something appropriate, but all he can do is mutter her name. "Madeline," he says. "Madeline?"

Madeline does not answer him. She is a white pile of pillows and blankets. He nods, after some time, then grabs his pillow and the spare sheets from the closet and quietly steps down the hallway to the cramped, disorganized den—papers and maps and charts left scattered about the room. Laying the sheet over the cluttered sofa, Jonathan closes his eyes, listening to the empty sounds of the house settling around him—the drip of the kitchen faucet, the wind whining against the windows, the dishes settling in the sink. He lies there for a long time, holding his breath, waiting for the echo of Madeline as she tiptoes down the hall, for the sound of her bare feet against the tile, for the shaky warmth of her voice, for the touch of her kiss upon his forehead, but, for some reason, it does not come.

Two

A. Madeline Casper, age forty-five, does not like the way the world is going. She does not like the way things are at the moment—with Jonathan, with Amelia and Thisbe, with her ongoing dominance study at the research laboratory. Unlike her husband, unlike her two daughters, Madeline is not afraid of being direct. She is not afraid to admit that there are things she doesn't understand. She sits behind the vinyl steering wheel of the Volvo the next morning, wondering what is wrong with the world, listening to NPR, waiting for her two daughters to stumble into the backseat already unhappy, already bickering.

B. Madeline looks up quickly and sees a cloud, shaped like a figure, standing in the treetops, as she glances from behind the Volvo's windshield. Madeline glimpses at the oak tree beside the gray garage and sees something moving in the empty air. There is something quietly shifting. She squints upward and sees it, hanging in the open space just above the garage's flat roof, in the tentative morning light: it is in the shape of a man—arms, legs, head, hands, feet, but made of clouds, no face, no expression, just the shape—he is drifting above the treetops, as if he is stepping from the highest branch directly into the air. Madeline holds her hand above her eyes and sees the cloud is life-sized, the size of a person. It is slowly moving, expanding, somehow changing, like a blossom opening in place. Madeline stares up at it, her mouth open, as Amelia and Thisbe come hurrying from the house, the back door slamming behind them, the older sister referring to her younger sister as "an absolute savage."

C. Madeline does not know if either of her daughters notices the cloud. She keeps glancing in the rearview mirror at Amelia and Thisbe; Amelia has her headphones on and is adjusting her beret, staring at her own reflection in the window, and Thisbe has her eyes closed, trying to fall back asleep. Madeline looks through the dirty windshield as the cloud steps slowly from branch to branch. Then it is gone, hidden by the dark leaves, disappearing, one weird, early morning daydream. Madeline places the car into drive and the Volvo speeds away down the street.

D. Madeline drives her girls to school as often as she can because she wants to. Though they usually prefer to walk, since their high school is only a few blocks away—part of the University of Chicago's campus—Madeline likes to drive them, wishing them both a good day. Their neighborhood—shady, tree-lined streets, quaint-looking faculty homes, antique apartment buildings, collegial facilities of brick and mortar, modern-looking student housing of steel and glass—is really only a rectangle of a few blocks, extending from Fifty-first Street to Fifty-ninth Street, from the lake to Cottage Grove Avenue. Beyond the rectangle, everything is run-down,

depressed, a blight of black-populated subsidized housing—
dollar stores with cracked windows, ubiquitous liquor ads, an
El train station that looks heartsick, trash-filled street corners,
and sad, windowless buildings. Guiding the Volvo down the
street, glancing over her shoulder at her two daughters, speeding toward the girls' school, Madeline considers this—how the
university happens to have one of the largest private police
forces anywhere in the world, how a venerable institution of
thought, of higher learning, peopled with some of the most
intelligent, most privileged young students in the world, could
exist, blindly, in the heart of one of the poorest parts of the
city. What lesson are these young college students learning, or
Amelia or Thisbe, for that matter? Before the question can
be answered, Madeline is at the corner and her girls are hurrying out, slamming the doors closed, neither one of them
mumbling a goodbye or even a thanks. She wonders if she and
Jonathan have messed them up by talking to them like adults,
by always being honest, by not letting them watch more television. She stares at them as they cross the sidewalk, hurrying
into school, both of them now nearly as tall as she is.

**E. Madeline always feels like something terrible is about
to happen.** Driving down Lake Shore Drive, she always takes
the slow lane, the right lane. She puts on a CD by Bob Dylan
or the Beatles and sings along. When the traffic is lousy, she
will turn and sing to the people in the cars around her. Today
she is listening to NPR. "A *Washington Post* story revealed a
secret report from the Joint Chiefs of Staff that blames set-
backs in Iraq on a flawed war-planning process that limited
the time spent preparing for post–Saddam Hussein opera-
tions. The report also shows that President Bush approved
the overall war strategy for Iraq in August 2002, eight months

before the first bomb was dropped and six months before he asked the U.N. Security Council for a war mandate that he never received." Madeline passes car after car, stalled in traffic, staring at their bumper stickers, many of them touting BUSH/CHENEY '04. The Volvo exits the expressway, then speeds down Roosevelt, passing several newly constructed townhomes and high-rises, many with Bush/Cheney signs positioned in their windows. Seeing them, she sneers, shaking her head. She turns down a grim-looking side street and then parks in front of the enormous rectangular research facility.

F. At work, Madeline does not know what to think when she finds three more pigeons murdered in her experimental coop. She is even more disturbed to discover that the three dead birds are all female. She shoos the rest of the pigeons toward the back of their enclosure to further inspect the dead animals. They have been pecked to death, their throats slit by the reptilian claws of some other pigeon. She turns and stares at the rest of the birds scurrying about the wire cage.

G. Madeline does not know why, but she is fascinated by the hierarchy of dominance among these birds. In a very real way, they are a miniature version of the human world, complete with males and females that mate for life, a kind of ruling class, and now, unfortunately, murder. Her experiment with the pigeons is pretty simple, really: she has closely studied their social interactions, and has noted the rank of each male bird within the dominance hierarchy. In her notebook, Madeline has assigned the color red for the dominant males. After observing their social interactions for nearly a month, she has determined that there are three males of this strata and each has been banded with a red plastic cuff along its left leg. These dominant males, marked by the red plastic bands, are easy to distinguish: puffing up their chests as she opens the cage door each morning, bullying the other birds out of their way when it comes time to be fed. Madeline, quite unscientifically, thinks of these birds as smug little right-wing assholes, ruling the rest of the coop with physical intimidation, cruelty, and terror. These dominant birds, she hates to admit, demonstrate the worst aspects of human nature: loud, obnoxious, selfish, violent, needy, with an overpowering sense of entitlement.

To better understand the hierarchy of dominance, these three dominant males have been removed from the experimental coop, and are now being kept in their own separate cage, which is what makes the discovery of the dead females so puzzling. Staring at the rest of the birds in the experiment, the beta males, tagged yellow, and the females, tagged green, she wonders how this tragedy might have happened. Did she mislabel one of the males? Did one of the other females, having temporarily lost its mate, react in some radically barbaric way? With the most dominant birds in isolation, why were these three female pigeons murdered?

H. Before Madeline disposes of the three dead females, she makes another terrible discovery. They have been raped. Hurrying back to the indoor lab, she places the remains of one of the victims in a tray and inspects its cloaca, the opening through which waste and sexual fluids pass. The fleshy gland is irritated. She prepares a slide for the microscope, which reveals the presence of sperm. She checks each of the three birds and is saddened to discover all three of the dead females have been inseminated with the reproductive fluid of one or more male pigeons. Madeline does not tell anyone about what she has found. She is humiliated by the distressing results of her experiment and decides she needs to find out what is happening first.

I. Madeline does not like to think of herself as a bad researcher, but she is afraid she is. She has begun to treat her subjects anthropomorphically, which is a serious mistake. There is one female pigeon, tag-numbered 26, from Group B, with a striking purplish white coat of downy white feathers, that Madeline has, against all scientific and ethical norms, named Lucy. She has begun to remove Lucy from the coop at odd intervals, and, holding the frightened animal against her chest, she has started singing to it, usually random, nondescript songs, though lately she finds they have been all nursery rhymes. It does not take much of a researcher to figure out what is going on there, she thinks. She does not feel like she is doing much good as a mother. She does not feel like she is doing much good as a scientist either.

J. Madeline does not like to think about it, but she has been smoking cigarettes with Laura, an intern, and Eric, another researcher, almost every day on their lunch break. Together, they climb into Laura's awful Ford Escort, then secretly, surreptitiously, they all light up. Madeline is ashamed she has started smoking again but feels this may be the only way to get through her day. Today, sitting in the backseat, Eric, his large glasses shiny with the afternoon sun, lights Madeline's cigarette, touching her hand so softly. When her fingers meet his, she smiles, brushing the hair from her eyes, but he does not let go of her hand. She looks at him and immediately feels a jolt of panic, smiling wider now, nervous. He is staring deeply into her eyes and with his flickering irises he is saying: *In our minds, we are making incredible love together. Come be with me in* *my mind. We can be together. In our minds.* Madeline is still smiling, shaking her head, and he has now let go of her hand. Laura, in the driver's seat, is completely unaware of what is happening, the Kinks playing loudly on the stereo. Madeline decides not to look Eric's way again, not ever, because her heart is beating so quickly and somewhere between her thighs, something has begun to ache pleasantly.

K. Madeline does not like the way her husband has been kissing her. It is like he is afraid, like he thinks she is made out of brittle bone, like she is a fossil, like he is trying to preserve her for an exhibit of some kind. She wishes he would kiss her like he used to. With total, ridiculous abandon. Like he still had something to prove.

L. Madeline thinks about being separated from Jonathan again. She does not know if she likes her husband anymore. Really. She thinks she does, she believes she still does, but she is not sure of anything. She isn't even sure if love is anything more than some stupid song on the radio. A song like "Rocket Man" by Elton John. Or Lionel Ritchie's "Hello." Or "I Will Survive."

M. Madeline thinks about vanishing. She does not like to think about it, but she does. She does, a million times a day. Maybe not a million. But a lot. Why? She does not believe the kinds of things that she has begun to worry about. Like what kind of toilet paper to buy. (Recycled or two-ply.) Like what Thisbe will or won't eat. (Nothing brown or green.) Like why she does not feel bad that Jonathan slept in the den last night after their fight, both of them still not speaking. (He is as demanding as a third child, she thinks.) How does she try to forgive him? Should she even bother? She does not ever remember being so mad. She does not ever remember being so full of doubt about everything.

N. Madeline tries to ignore the pigeons she does not like. She really does. But it is very hard. She stands observing their interactions from the other side of the gray wire of their cage, recording minor conflicts, disputes, moments of affection. There are a number of young, beta males, only a few months old, all with yellow bands on their legs, that peck meanly at the other birds. When one of the beta males begins to mount a gray female who has already bonded with another, less dominant mate, Madeline, against her better judgment, intercedes, opening the cage door, kicking the animal away. Later, Madeline does not make a note of this interaction in her notebook.

O. Madeline does not like how often she swears. She runs to the grocery store before picking up her girls from school. The parking lot, unfortunately, is almost completely full. At the end of the last row, an enormous silver Hummer has seized two parking spots, a sticker of an American flag decorating its rear window. "Very fucking appropriate," Madeline curses, circling the parking lot again. By the time she makes it around a third time, a woman, talking on her cell phone, is climbing into the gigantic silver vehicle. Madeline is unable to stop herself. She hits the brakes, rolls down her window, and shouts, "Nice parking job!" The woman, lifting her sunglasses from her bright eyes, squints at Madeline, then flips her off, laughing to herself. Madeline, more furious now, does not see the lone shopping cart rolling aimlessly in front of the Volvo, and without slowing, she plows right into it. The cart spins wildly, scratching up the paint on the Volvo's passenger side, but Madeline does not stop driving until she has found a parking spot, far away on the other side of the lot.

As Madeline is about to switch off the car, she hears on NPR that there have been one thousand U.S. fatalities in Iraq since the war began. This figure haunts her as she tries to shop, the endless products marching up and down the grocery store aisles, their bright advertising echoing the number again and again: *one thousand, one thousand deaths for all of this*. Driving the Volvo an hour later, Madeline sees a flurry of red, white, and blue signs decorating several front lawns, some advertising President Bush, some the Democrat John Kerry. Madeline hits the brakes, shoves the station wagon into park, and— leaving the car running—leaps out. Murmuring to herself, she marches up the sidewalk, snatching a Bush sign out of the ground, kicking another one over.

Embarrassed, out of breath, her hands red and a little dirty, she sprints back to the Volvo and drives off, her legs still trembling.

P. Madeline does not like that she cannot remember the last time someone said something nice to her, even if they didn't mean it.

Q. Madeline comes home from a bad day and finds her husband daydreaming. The phone is ringing but Jonathan does not answer it. He is hiding in the den, staring down at a drawing of that stupid fucking squid. Madeline drops a bag of groceries, two avocados tumbling beneath the kitchen table, before she can grab the telephone. By the time she hits the talk button, the party has already hung up. Madeline, frazzled, slams the phone down, then stands in the doorway to the den, staring angrily at Jonathan.

"Hey. Um, why didn't you answer the phone?"

"I'm sorry, I just didn't hear it. We just got some big news. Someone found another intact giant squid mantle somewhere off the coast of Japan. Looks like a sperm whale got ahold of it. We're trying to decipher what species it is. This could go either way."

Madeline stares at him and wonders if he is stoned. She cannot tell. He is maybe too excited to be high.

"Jonathan?"

"Yes?"

"What planet are you on right now?"

"Earth. Why?"

Madeline shakes her head.

"Your hair looks really nice today," he says, looking back down at the diagram.

"Great."

He pauses, then looks up. "I'm sorry for what happened. Yesterday. Forgetting to take my medicine. It was stupid. I'm sorry I fucked up. It was irresponsible and terrible and I'm stupid."

"Great."

"Can we be friends again?" he asks. He stands, taking her hand in his.

"Sure. Sure, we can be friends again."

Jonathan kisses his wife's cheek. She does not respond, only stares straight ahead.

"But you're still mad," he says softly, angrily, upset that he hasn't been forgiven so quickly.

"Yes. Yes, I really am."

"About me fainting or something else?"

"That and a lot of other shit. Jonathan, you live in your own world. And you expect me to take care of the things you don't want to do."

"Like what?"

"Like . . ." She thinks, glancing around the messy room. "Like how much money do we have in our checking account right now?"

"I don't know," he says, smiling. "But that doesn't mean anything. I'm talking about real things here."

"That is a real thing. What about savings? How much money do we have in our savings?"

"I don't know that either."

"What about car insurance? Where do we get our car insurance from?"

"I don't know."

"What about food?"

"I get groceries, too," he murmurs.

"How much do we spend on food each month?"

"Jesus, Madeline, I have no idea."

"Exactly. Because you don't care. And if you don't care about something, then that means I have to do it."

"What's your point?"

"I am sick of having to be in charge. You have all the time in the world for your work, while I have to take care of you and the girls and everything you don't want to do. When am I supposed to do my work? When is that?"

Jonathan frowns. "Everything I've ever done, all my work, has been for you. And the girls."

"That is such bullshit. You do it for yourself."

"Is this about the Talbott grant again?" Jonathan asks.

"Jonathan, I swear to God if you bring that up . . . this has nothing to do with that."

"Nothing? You don't still feel bad about it?"

"Jonathan . . . you gave the grant to someone else. Big deal."

"It wasn't just me. It was a whole committee. You're my wife. How would it have looked if we awarded it to you?"

Madeline ignores his question. "How long are you planning on staying down here?" she asks.

"I don't know. Maybe forever. Maybe I'll just move down here in the den. Then you won't have to be constantly disappointed in me."

"That would be okay by me," she says, slamming the door behind her.

R. Madeline does not like that she has begun to get a little fat. She does not like to be naked anymore. She thinks her backside is out of shape. She might even use the word "atrocious." She takes off her work clothes and wonders how she ever became someone's mother, someone's wife, how did she ever become forty-five?

S. Madeline does not like thinking that she may be the worst parent ever. She passes the doorway to Amelia's room, where her oldest daughter is busily building an explosive device.

"It works on the principles of concussive force." Amelia points to the empty soda pop bottle. "Gas builds up inside until it explodes. This is the easiest kind to make. I'd really like to figure out how to put together a pipe bomb."

Madeline slowly closes the door, shaking her head.

T. Madeline does not like to think about the war in Iraq. She does not know if it is good or bad. She can see points on either side. She hates to mention this ambivalence to Jonathan, or Laura, her research assistant who sends an angry email to the White House every day. Everyone else seems like they can make up their minds up without having to think. Maybe the war really is a terrible mistake. Maybe it is an awful display of military power meant to threaten an entire religion. Maybe it is only for oil, after all. But maybe, in the end, it might make those peoples' lives a little better. Maybe it might bring some sense of order to the region. Maybe it's something awful right now that might become something astounding later. Madeline does not know and she does not like that everyone acts like they already have the answer. She thinks about this as she folds her daughters' laundry down in the basement, glancing at the small television, which is now on CNN. The anchorperson, a woman with dark hair and glossy red lips, is explaining that an American soldier, a PFC by the name of Daniel Harkins, has been kidnapped somewhere outside of Baghdad. He has been videotaped and his captors are threatening to cut off his head. The soldier is very young, nineteen or twenty at the most, and his face is dirty, his forehead lined with cuts and scratches. He is crying. He is blond and handsome and shaking visibly before the video camera. Madeline feels sick to her stomach. She switches the television off, closes her eyes, and tries to imagine the soldier being safely returned to his family. But she cannot. She tries and tries and all she can see are his soft, wet eyes.

U. Madeline does not like smug people who go around thinking they believe in God. God might be a million different things, and who knows what the answer might be? At dinner that evening, Madeline notices that Thisbe is once again praying. The idea is enough to make Madeline go absolutely nuts. Before dinner is served, while the rest of the family argue, detail the major hassles and minor triumphs of their day, pass their plates, Thisbe lowers her head, closing her eyes, going very still in a pose of contemplative prayer, her lips moving slightly as the words thought privately in her brain echo upon her lips. Madeline glances out of the corner of her eye at her youngest daughter, feeling something go tight in her chest. When, finally, Thisbe opens her eyes, smirking a little to herself, Madeline realizes that the person she is glaring at is her own daughter. She looks down at the food on her plate and wonders if she has lost her mind, giving her daughter a dirty look like that.

V. Madeline, that evening, putting away Thisbe's laundry, notices her daughter praying again, lying in bed, her eyes closed in serene penance, like a painting of a young nun from the Middle Ages. Madeline does not know why, but out of anger, she quickly piles her daughter's clothes at the foot of her bed and then slams the door.

W. Madeline picks Thisbe up at school the next day, after chorus practice, both of them running late. In the backseat of the Volvo, Madeline notices that her daughter's hands are folded carefully in her lap. Driving, she glances in the rearview mirror and sees Thisbe muttering to herself.

"What are you doing back there, Thisbe?"

"Nothing."

Thisbe opens her eyes and her small white face goes flush.

"Were you praying?"

Thisbe nods but does not say the word.

"Yes?" Madeline asks.

"Yes."

Thisbe glances down at her lap. When the car pauses at a stoplight, Madeline turns around in the seat.

"You've been doing that a lot lately, huh?"

"I guess."

"Is everything okay?"

"Why?"

"Because I worry about you."

"It's no big deal," Thisbe says. "It's just something to do."

"Oh," Madeline says, searching through the radio stations. "I think it's nice."

"No, you don't," Thisbe says, glancing out the window.

"Of course I do. I think it's fine. I think it's better than fine. I think it's great."

Thisbe's brown eyes meet her mother's in the rearview mirror.

"Well, it's no big deal. It's not like I'm doing drugs or having sex or something."

"Wow, that's a relief," Madeline says, trying to make a little joke. Her daughter barely smiles, turning back to glance out the window.

"It's not like it's anything. It just makes me happy."

"I'm glad to hear that," Madeline says, though she is not, not at all.

The station wagon pauses at a stoplight. Cars blur in different colors back and forth. Madeline switches off the radio and glances in the rearview at Thisbe again. Her eyes are closed but she is pretty sure she isn't praying.

"Thisbe?"

"Yeah."

"When you pray, what are you asking for?"

Thisbe's face goes red again. Her tiny eyebrows scrunch up. "I don't know," she says. "Different things."

"Like what?"

"Like I dunno, personal things."

"Is it about us? Your father? Or me?"

"No. I dunno. Sometimes. But it's not like supposed to be anybody's business."

"Do you pray because you're worried about something?"

Thisbe shakes her head. Her eyes begin to look cloudy, like she might start to cry. Madeline sees the light has turned green and accelerates through the intersection.

"I just want to be sure you're okay," Madeline says.

Thisbe does not nod or respond. She is looking out the window again.

"Are you okay?" Madeline asks. She glances into the rearview and sees her daughter has started to cry. "Thisbe?"

Thisbe nods. "It's fine. I'm okay. It doesn't matter."

"I know things have been a little weird at home. But your father and I are fine. I just want you to know everything is okay."

Thisbe nods, wiping the tears away with her fingertips. "I know. I'm not dumb," she says.

"I know you're not dumb. I just wanted to let you know you guys are still the most important thing in the world to me."

"Okay."

"And I just want to make sure you're not praying this much because you . . . because you think you have to worry about Dad or me or anything."

Thisbe looks shocked. Madeline can't figure out what she has said that causes such alarm in her daughter's face.

"Thisbe?"

"What?"

"Why are you giving me that look?"

"The whole world does not revolve around you guys," Thisbe says. "That's not why I'm praying."

"Oh," Madeline says, feeling her heart beating heavily. "I just. I just wanted to be sure . . ."

"I'm praying because I'm trying to come to an understanding with God. I'm trying to figure out how to see Him, like in everyday situations. Like at school and around people I don't like. I'm trying to be like thoughtful."

"Well, I think that's really wonderful," Madeline says, more flatly than she would have liked. Then adds, "I mean, I think that's incredibly mature of you."

"I don't even care about you and Dad right now. It's like not even on my radar," she says. "I'm just trying to get through high school without killing somebody."

X. Madeline pulls the Volvo into the garage. Thisbe races into the house, closing the back door behind her so quickly that Madeline can't even call out to her to finish the conversation. Madeline turns, grabbing her purse, then climbs out, locks the Volvo, and closes the automatic garage door. Standing there in the dark, Madeline feels as if she is going to cry. For no reason. Just because everything is so junky. She holds her hand over her eyes, feeling the soft moisture building there, trying to calm herself. When she steps out of the garage, slamming the door closed behind her, something catches her eye.

Y. The cloud-figure is standing in the treetop.

Z. The cloud-figure seems to be moving.

Three

AMELIA CASPER, AGE SEVENTEEN, IS DOING WHATEVER she can to overthrow the evil empire of capitalism, day by day. Mostly by writing long rants in her high school paper about how awful capitalism is. Mostly by only listening to French pop music. Mostly by wearing her black beret.

WHENEVER AMELIA IS ALONE, she may hear the sound of mass-produced objects crying. If she listens carefully, closing her bright blue eyes, holding her breath, pressing the soft, fleshy ridge of her ear beside whatever object is now screaming—a yellow pencil, a glowing lamp, a furry, stuffed animal lying on her bed—she will be overcome by the urgency of these foreign-made products weeping for her help. *Liberate me*, each of them will beckon. *Liberate me*. For this reason, one of her dresser drawers is nearly filled with a number of useless and consumable objects, objects that she has either found or stolen, each of them manufactured in a faraway place like Taiwan or Indonesia, all of them molded from a variety of plastic and metal—a key chain, a rubber doll, a miniature American flag, made somewhere in Asia, which she decided to steal from a nearby convenience store. She does not know what she is supposed to do with these things. But whenever Amelia is alone in her room, whenever she is trying to think about the future of the world and the end of the capitalist system, she will hear this deranged chorus, this unmistakable, otherworldly aria, resounding from the back of her bottom dresser drawer.

AMELIA GETS HIVES whenever she's nervous or afraid. The hives—which are medically known as urticaria—can occur at almost any time, but they most often appear whenever she has to give an oral report in school. On paper, she can say whatever she wants, the words are as familiar, as trustworthy as her hands and arms and feet. But in front of her peers, in front of the drooling stares of her troglodyte classmates and her ineffectual teachers, she will instantly break out in a formidable rash, the skin of her neck and forearms and stomach popping with bright red blisters. As an agent of agitprop, as a high school editorial-page dissident, she thinks she is amazing. As a Patty Hearst, as a Fred Hampton, in front of a cluster of imaginary microphones and a disinterested crowd, she is totally unconfident, a zero, an absolute no one.

AMELIA IS MAKING an anticapitalist movie for her history class. It begins like this:

EXT. BATTLEFIELD—DAY

A film clip from The Charge of the Light Brigade *(1936) featuring Errol Flynn shooting a turbaned Thuggee.*

NARRATOR V/O:

We are at war, whether you know it or not. Armies of factory workers have totally lost control over their lives and the products they produce.

CUT TO:

EXT. BATTLEFIELD—DAY

An F-4 Phantom jet drops a payload of bombs on a small Vietnamese village.

CUT TO:

EXT. WAL-MART—NIGHT

NARRATOR V/O:

These people are only cogs, expendable parts in the great capitalist machine. They have become totally alienated from their true natures and their relationships with each other. Human beings are not being allowed to be human beings. So none of us are truly free.

CUT TO:

EXT. DESERT—NIGHT

A hydrogen bomb explodes in the distance, shadowing the desert with its enormous gray cloud.

NARRATOR V/O:

How can we free another nation when we are imprisoned ourselves? Capitalism has to be destroyed if our society's liberation is to be real. While tyranny oppresses its people with politics, capitalism oppresses its people economically.

CUT TO:

INT. WHITE HOUSE—DAY

President Bush stands before the press corps, answering questions.

NARRATOR V/O:

If capitalism is the answer, if capitalism is so great, why is the world so miserable? Why are there still thousands and thousands of wars? Why are people still suffering all over the world? Why do we allow ourselves to be controlled by corporate interests? Why don't we do something to fight back?

CUT TO:

INT. MALL—DAY

People walk around shopping happily.

NARRATOR:

Because people are totally weak and dumb. Because most people are too ignorant to even notice. Everyone is still shopping and eating and going to movies and driving their cars everywhere like they don't

even care that people are being killed all over the
world right now.

CUT TO:

EXT. PARK—DAY

A close-up of a statue of President Lincoln.

NARRATOR:
The only way to establish peace in this world is to
create a society that isn't totally based on capitalism,
even if it's by force. Because as long as there are
people who have a lot of money and other people
who don't, there's always going to be wars.

CUT TO:

INT. MALL—DAY

Clip from Dawn of the Dead. *Zombies attack mall visitors, amid
screaming and shouting.*

NARRATOR:
We need to revolt now! Everybody free yourselves
from the chain of capitalism and learn to be happy!
Let the revolution begin!

CUT TO:

*TEXT flashing on-screen: CAPITALISM IS LAME ... CAP-
ITALISM IS LAME ... CAPITALISM IS LAME ...*

GEORGE BUSH IS A TERRORIST ... GEORGE BUSH IS A TERRORIST

Amelia, sitting in her room, stares at the computer screen happily. She adds the last piece of text to the editing program and then figures out how to make the text look like it's flashing. Then she starts the movie again from the beginning. She imagines the look on Mr. Anson's face and nods to herself, proudly, adjusting the beret on the top of her head.

AMELIA WEARS THE black beret everywhere, even to school, where kids think she is uptight and a lesbo and a bitch. Her mother warns her that wearing that beret all the time might cause her to go bald but she doesn't really care. She prefers to get to school one hour early. As the editor-in-chief of the school paper, the *Midway*, she has keys to the newspaper office. Mr. Wick is sometimes there by then, sitting behind his diminutive desk, in his dirty white dress shirt and yellow tie, his nose sniffling, quickly editing the last page of copy before handing it to Brice Jackson, a lanky senior in charge of getting the copy to the printer. The *Midway* does one issue a week, and Amelia must edit her fellow writers' work as well as contribute to the Campus Politics page. Here her main duty is to report on the student council's meetings and activities. She loathes the student council; she believes they are all incompetent babies whose only concern is racking up extracurricular activities for their lackluster college applications. The ideas of truth, of justice, of revolution, mean nothing to these kids. Amelia is not afraid to voice her disdain. Mr. Wick, the faculty advisor for the school paper, an old leftist himself, refuses to censor her, and takes a certain amount of joy in seeing the principal and other members of the administration criticized. Most of the time her columns are more than a simple report from the student council's last meeting; usually she issues strongly worded threats to William Banning, the effete, spineless student council president, such as:

Why do we need another walk-a-thon? Why do we need another car wash? What exactly does the student council plan on doing with this money they raise? Do they simply do it because last year's student council had a walk-a-thon and a car wash? Are they, like the awful student council administration before them, only raising funds for a student council end of year party with pizza and balloons, which only the student council kids get to enjoy? Who does the student council president, William Banning, think he is? Dick Cheney? President Nixon? When will other student voices rise up to demand a moratorium on student fundraisers that do not, in the end, serve the school itself? Who will exorcise the demons of these self-serving, teenage, capitalist politicians?

DURING LUNCH, AMELIA does not usually eat. Instead, she sets up a folding table protesting the lack of vegetarian options, the school's uncaring administration, and American imperialism in general. She has made a different pamphlet for each cause she is championing. The pamphlet about the lack of vegetarian options is green, the one criticizing the school's administration is purple, and the one describing the horrors of imperialism is red. At lunch, two seniors, passing a football back and forth between each other, look at Amelia—short, dark-haired, wearing her black beret—and call her a fag.

"I'm a woman," Amelia says, sighing. "I know it's hard for you two Cro-Magnons to understand, but it's not physically possible for me to be a fag."

"Whatever, fag," they say, laughing, walking away.

IF AMELIA SEES her younger sister, Thisbe, walking down the hallway of their high school between classes, Amelia will ignore her. If someone asks if she has a little sister in the freshman class, Amelia will say *no* without thinking.

AMELIA HAS NOT shaved her armpits in three months. The hair there is dark and wiry. Both of her legs are also covered in dark, wiry fuzz.

AMELIA IS INSULTED that a Starbucks has opened so close to their house. She has many, many different ideas about how and when she will blow it up.

AMELIA'S ONLY FRIENDS happen to work for the school newspaper as well. They are also honorary members of clubs that Amelia has started—Young Environmentalists Club, Young Socialists Club, Young Atheists Club. They do not actually attend any of the meetings because Amelia has elected herself president of each and would rather handle the business of these clubs herself. Amelia sometimes gets high with these friends from the school paper—Max and Heather—after school, hiding in the darkroom of the photo lab. Max is an eighteen-year-old white kid with long black dreadlocks who is planning on going to Yale next fall. Max wears a different Bob Marley shirt every day. He is the music and sports editor for the school paper. He supplies the marijuana, which he gets from his father, an entertainment lawyer. Heather may or may not be a lesbian, no one really knows. She wears overalls all the time and has been trying to start a Gay/Lesbian/Bi Club at the school for two years, but no one seems interested in joining. Her hair is red and short and she wears sandals throughout the winter months.

Amelia and her two friends sneak into the darkroom—ignoring the many signs warning of hazardous, combustible chemicals—to get high. Max is the first to speak, handing the joint to Amelia, who holds it like a princess, her pinky raised. She lights it using Max's stupid pot-leaf Zippo lighter, the spark a quick flickering of light reflected in all of their eyes.

"I heard they're cutting off people's heads in Iraq," Max says.

"What?" Amelia asks, coughing.

"I heard they're kidnapping people, like aid workers, and cutting their heads off. On videotape."

"They're being occupied by the world's largest and most powerful military force," Amelia hisses. "It's all they can do, trying to frighten their oppressors."

"Fuck that noise," Max said. "I can't sympathize with people who cut off other people's heads."

"Sometimes violence is the only answer," Amelia whispers.

"What?" Heather coughs, her white face turning red.

"Think of like all the great revolutions in history. They were all violent."

"What about the civil rights marches?" Heather asks.

"Besides those. Like the Revolutionary War and all those other ones."

"Gandhi. He wasn't violent," Max says.

"Besides him."

"Like who?" Max asks.

"Like I dunno, like the revolution in Cuba. Or like Malcolm X."

"Malcolm X got shot," Heather whispers, taking another drag.

"I think it's totally naïve to think that you can accomplish something that big, that important, without hurting other people."

"Wow," Max mumbles. "That's some serious shit."

"It's because people are like so afraid to wake up and see what's going on in the rest of world. It's like everyone is in total denial. That's why people take pharmaceutical drugs and everything. Everybody is like in this total fog. The opiate of the people. Except it's like actually like opium."

"I hear that," Max says, exhaling, laughing hard, his voice echoing from an empty cavern in his chest.

"Violence is like, it's like the only thing that frightens people anymore. It's like the only way to motivate people to change. Because everyone is totally comfortable with like rich white men being in charge of everything."

"Hey, what's wrong with white men?" Max asks, still laughing.

"White men have like ruined everything on the planet. They're responsible for everything bad that's ever happened. Like pollution and genocide, everything that's wrong in Africa. White men are totally the problem."

"Too bad we're all white," Heather says, sadly smirking.

"Well, I'm not," Amelia says proudly, taking the joint and then inhaling.

"Yeah, right," Max mumbles.

"No, I'm serious. I'm part Native American."

"Sure you are."

"No, for real. On my mother's side. I'm like one-eighth Cherokee," she says, completely and utterly lying.

"So?"

"So what? So nothing," Amelia says with a frown.

"So what does that mean? You're one-eighth Cherokee. Big deal."

"It doesn't mean anything. It's just my heritage. One day people of color are going to rise up and overthrow the white power machine. And I'm going to be part of it. And we'll create a new world, with one flag that represents everybody, in like total harmony."

"Except white men," Max says, smiling.

"Yeah. Except them."

AMELIA HAS ALMOST had sex three times with three different boys. Each time, she changed her mind just before the act itself. The last time was with Max, in his parents' enormous Lincoln Park home, while they were away for the weekend at some wedding, and at the last possible moment, when Max ran up to his parents' room looking for a condom, Amelia, lying with her black skirt shoved hastily up around her waist, decided she would rather not. She decided to give each of the three disappointed young men blowjobs instead. She did not let them cum in her mouth. She forced the first one to ejaculate on his pants, the second onto the car seat, and Max onto a bedspread. For some reason, Amelia believes giving someone a blowjob is less intimate than actually having sex, and also more mature, more grown-up. She imagines hardworking feminist journalists all over the world giving their lovers blowjobs. This is what she tries to tell herself. Amelia does not know why, but she just wants to get her first time over with. She wants it to be with someone she never has to see again. Ever.

ONE DAY, AMELIA writes a column in the newspaper about how stupid the American flag is and why every flag in the country ought to be burned. The next week, in her editorial, she states, *Anyone who shops at Wal-Mart is a coward.* Principal Stuart stares at the pulpy pages of the *Midway* in disbelief. He calls to his secretary, Angie, a cheery, overweight assistant with at least four different pens stuck in her red curly hair, shaking his head. "Tell Wick to get his ass down here. And pronto." He sits behind his desk and almost has a heart attack when he flips to an editorial page from last month, where, in black and white, Amelia Casper writes, *Historically, white men are the cause of most of the trouble in the world.*

AMELIA, STANDING BESIDE Mr. Wick, who is pale and shivering with sweat, agrees to print a retraction in regards to the white-men-are-the-cause-of-trouble piece. She does not argue. She stares down at her dark black shoes, unafraid. She decides for next week's paper to take up a new cause: the cafeteria workers' unjust treatment.

TODAY, WEDNESDAY, the thirteenth, Amelia is finally suspended from school for trying to incite the cafeteria workers to strike. In her latest school newspaper column, she has written:

*Why are all the cafeteria workers in this school black? Or His-
panic (Maribel)? What message is the school trying to send to its
students? That privileged people should be waited on by people
of color? I say to the cafeteria workers, who prepare our lunches
with such care, such attentiveness, the time for a change has come!
Demand better hours, better pay, new uniforms, and an end to
class segregation!*

When Amelia steps out of Principal Stuart's office, the suspension a yellow piece of paper clamped in her hand, she
expects the students in the crowded hallway to begin clapping.
She imagines Heather and Max will have constructed a ban-
ner celebrating her bravery. But no, no one has even noticed.
No one. Amelia watches the students hurrying through the
hallway and when she finally spots Max and Heather, they
stare at her, their heads down, slightly embarrassed for her.
A girl, some poor freshman with a purple headband, accidentally bumps into Amelia. The girl stumbles, tripping over her
own feet, and tumbles to the floor. The girl instinctively calls
Amelia a bitch. Immediately Amelia begins shouting. "You are
all savages! Why don't you go home and plug your brains into
your stupid computers and do whatever MTV tells you to do!"
She collects her things and is forced to wait in the lobby of the
principal's office while he makes a big deal out of calling her
folks. Her neck has begun to blister, a swell of red hives running up and down her throat.

WHILE SHE IS WAITING for what seems like a century, Amelia notices a silver digital wristwatch resting atop the receptionist's vacant desk. Its segmented band is coiled beneath its
blank-looking face as it sparkles desperately. *Free me*, the watch

quietly whimpers. *Free me.* Amelia stands, pretends to be wandering around the tiny lobby, glancing over at the principal's diplomas, which have been framed along the far wall, and then lunges for the tortured object, feeling its cold heft in her hand. Quickly, she slips it into her purse and returns to her seat with an enormous, self-satisfied smile.

MADELINE GETS A CALL on her cell phone from Amelia's school about her suspension. It's just after lunch and she still has another few hours to go, observing the birds' reaction to predatory stimuli, which are, after all, only a few tape recordings and a plastic owl. Madeline hears her cell phone ringing and quickly steps out of the enclosure to answer it. She does not receive the news of Amelia's suspension very well. She immediately calls home, and after the fifth ring, Jonathan answers distractedly.

"Jonathan. I need you to go get Amelia from school. She's in trouble for something."

"Oh, hell, what happened?"

"I don't know. They wouldn't say. I think she insulted the principal or something."

"Should I go right now or should I wait for school to end?"

"No, you need to go now," Madeline says.

"Okay. Do I need to talk to her principal, too?"

"Yeah, I'm sure he'll want to talk to you."

"Okay. I'm getting dressed. I should probably wear a sweater or something nice, don't you think?"

"Jonathan?"

"Yes?"

"You have to figure it out by yourself, okay? I have to go."

"Okay."

Madeline hangs up the phone and hurries back to the lab.

ANSWERING IMAGINARY QUESTIONS from the imaginary principal, Jonathan puts on a black sweater, then changes his mind, puts on a brown shirt that is much too small, then goes back to the black sweater. *As a matter of fact, yes, we are quite proud of her political interests. We only wish she would exercise some restraint, maybe learn to listen more? Yes, that's exactly what we think.* Jonathan brushes his teeth, still talking. *Maybe she does need to get involved in other activities. Lacrosse sounds great. We didn't even know lacrosse was an option. We love lacrosse. Yes, we're great admirers of people who play lacrosse.*

AS USUAL, HIS CAR, a rusted red Peugeot from his college days, will not start. He has to coax it, talking to it like an unresponsive friend, *Okay, pal, okay, buddy, come on, now, pal,* until it turns over. At his daughter's high school, Jonathan circles around for a parking spot, finds one, then stumbles out, searching for the principal's office. He sees his reflection in a trophy case and is astonished that his hair looks the way it does, blond, uncombed, standing up straight along his neck. When he finds Amelia in the principal's office, sitting in a powder-blue chair, her chin resting in her hands, he begins to feel angry. She starts to stand and Jonathan sees she has been crying. Are they real tears? Yes, they are. His anger immediately turns to something else as he pats her shoulder gently.

"What happened?" he asks.

"I got in trouble for writing something."

"Writing what?"

"I said that the school is racist because all the cafeteria workers are black."

"Oh." Jonathan looks around the tiny office, sizing it up. "Well, are they?"

"Yeah. Except Maribel. She's Bolivian."

"I see." He wonders what other questions he should be asking. He shrugs his shoulders and asks, "How long are you suspended for?"

"Like a week, I think."

"Okay, wait here. I think I have to talk to your principal or something."

"Please don't make this worse, Dad."

"I'll do my best."

Jonathan nods, itching his beard. He introduces himself to the red-haired receptionist who nervously picks up the phone and whispers, "Mr. Hearst is here." Jonathan gives her a dirty look, squinting hard. The receptionist blushes, hangs up the phone, and says, "He'll be right with you." Jonathan glances back at his daughter, trying to figure it all out. Amelia has always been the smart one, the mature one, the one who knows the answer to the question before you've even had a chance to finish asking it. Maybe she is a little too bossy. Maybe she is a little too quick to tell you what your problem is. Maybe she is a little too proud, a little too superior. Looking at her sitting there, Jonathan knows that she's going to end up being somebody great. Maybe she ought to keep her mouth shut a little more often. But look at this place, this awful dreary office, this awful dreary school, with its little wood-veneered desk and coffee machine and fax and absentee reports. *It would drive me nuts, too*, Jonathan thinks. *Maybe it's better that she's testing her limits than just following the same, simple-minded rules. Maybe it's better she make a few big mistakes than to never try and do anything big at all.* Jonathan begins to nod to himself as the principal, Mr. Stuart, steps out of his office, extending his hairy hand.

"I don't believe we've met before. I'm Mr. Stuart."

"Jonathan Casper, Amelia's dad. Thanks for calling me."

Jonathan follows the principal into his office and takes a seat at Mr. Stuart's urging.

"Well, I'm sure Amelia has told you what has happened," the principal whispers.

"She has."

"Good. We're all very upset by the incident. Has she also shown you a copy of the editorial in question?"

"No."

The principal nods, reaching for the school paper lying on his desk. He solemnly hands it to Jonathan, who quickly begins scanning it. Jonathan nods, trying to hide his smile, then decides not to bother.

"I don't see anything wrong with this," Jonathan says. "It's her opinion. She put her name right there next to it. She's not doing it anonymously or anything. I think she's pretty brave for saying what she did."

"Brave, or a little inconsiderate, perhaps."

"I don't know if I see a difference here."

"Well, perhaps Amelia will have some time to think about that."

"When can my daughter come back to school?"

"We expect to see her on Monday the twenty-fifth."

"That's more than a week."

"Your daughter called me a savage. And a dickwad, Mr. Casper. If it wasn't for her outstanding grades, we would be looking at possible expulsion."

Jonathan nods, scratching his beard. "Okay." He stands up and looks around the terrible little office. "I want you to know

I'm taking my daughter to get Chinese food right now. Cantonese. I think what she did was wrong but I don't think punishing her makes any sense at all."

"Well, we'll see her on Monday the twenty-fifth, regardless."

Jonathan nods, opens the office door, and stands over his daughter, frowning.

"We're done here. You got your things?"

Amelia nods.

"Did you talk to your teachers? You know what you're missing in your classes?"

She nods again.

"Let's go get some Chinese."

AT NICKY'S CHINESE FOOD Restaurant, Amelia orders lo mein and shrimp fried rice and shares it with her dad. Her dad always gets the same thing: two egg rolls, chicken kow, and an almond cookie. He refuses to try anything new. They sit in the same red vinyl booth, the one in the corner, and after switching entrees, Jonathan looks up and says, "Just because you're smart doesn't mean you can get away with things other people can't."

"What?"

"You heard me. Just because you're smart doesn't mean you can get away with certain things."

"Like what?"

"Like today."

"Dad, I knew what I was doing was right."

"Sometimes there's the right thing to do. And then sometimes there's the thing you do because the right thing is going to get you in trouble, when you really don't need to be in trouble. Being smart and going to school and being able to write for the school paper, those are all privileges."

"I can't believe you're saying I should like . . . be a sheep. All I did was write down my opinion—"

"I'm not saying you should be a sheep. But kiddo, you're still a student. You're still seventeen. Those people, that principal, is an adult. He's not your equal."

"Well, that's not what you and Mom taught me. You always said just because we're kids doesn't mean we shouldn't have an opinion. All I did was write down my opinion."

"Amelia?"

"Yes?"

"I want you to think about this."

"Okay."

"Do you think anything you did today, that column you wrote, do you think that helped anybody? Do you think that helped those ladies, in the cafeteria? Or do you think it was something you wrote because you knew you could put it in the paper and get away with it?"

"What?"

"On the outside it looked like it was brave, what you did, but you and I know it really wasn't. Don't we?"

Amelia sets down her orange chopsticks, sulking. "I'm done eating."

Jonathan nods, wondering if Madeline would agree with anything he has just said. He pushes his food around his plate, staring across the table at his daughter, who sits there looking haughty.

"Are you finished?" he asks, and she nods. He waves to the petite waitress, who comes to deliver the check. Jonathan reaches for his wallet and finds it's empty. He places his credit card down next to the bill. Spotting it, Amelia leans across the table, alarmed.

"Mom said not to use the credit card anymore."

"I know what she said. I don't have any money."

"You guys really don't communicate very well, do you?"

"Amelia. Give it a rest."

Amelia nods, laying her chin on top of her hands.

"Do you think you'll get separated again?"

"Do you?"

"It doesn't look good," Amelia says with a sigh.

MADELINE, IT TURNS OUT, is a lot less sympathetic to the whole Amelia/protest/Chinese food situation. She does not care what Amelia's motivations actually were. In the kitchen, when she gets home from work, she calls Amelia snotty. She calls Amelia totally spoiled. She tells Amelia to go to her room so she and her dad can talk in private.

"I am not eight years old anymore!" Amelia shouts.

"Really? Because this, this all sounds like something an eight-year-old would do."

Amelia storms off to her room, then stops at the top of the stairs to listen. Her dad does a good job of explaining the situation, but when he gets to the part about the Chinese food, Madeline begins to whisper angrily, "What is wrong with you? What kind of lesson are you trying to teach her?"

"I don't know," Jonathan says. "It's a pretty complicated situation. I thought you and I could talk about it and figure something out. As a team. That's what parents are supposed to do. Work as a team."

"Jonathan, I don't even know what I'm supposed to say to

you right now. I can't believe you're actually proud of her for writing that shit."

"She's a great kid, Maddie. She just did something stupid."

"So she shouldn't get rewarded for doing something stupid."

"Maybe she should. Maybe my way is not so bad. I let her know I was disappointed. Maybe your way isn't necessarily the only way to do things."

"You're an idiot."

"Awesome." Jonathan turns and begins to walk off, shaking his head.

"Where are you going?"

"Back to the den. It's quiet in there. Nobody's in there shouting all the time about nothing."

"Great. So how long is this going to last?"

"I don't know. I'm beginning to like it."

Madeline nods, hurt, her eyes already wet with tears. "Wonderful."

Amelia quietly creeps from the top of the stairs, then goes to lie in her bed.

AROUND MIDNIGHT, Amelia comes downstairs to eat some yogurt. She sneaks down the hallway and sees her father has indeed moved into the den—he has made a bed out of the tiny sofa and has his clothes hanging from the bookshelves. She peeks in and sees her dad holding a magnifying glass up to a large color photo, a photo of what looks to be a squid tentacle, and he is mumbling. "Not so fast, my old friend. You thought you could trick me with your seizing tentacles. But you can't. I now believe you may be an *Architeuthis*. Ha, ha."

. . .

AMELIA DOES NOT sleep much. Instead, she stays up, searching the Internet, trying to learn how to build various types of bombs. She has already figured out how to construct three different kinds: for her science project, she is trying to learn how to build a pipe bomb with a timer. Already she has plans. Already she is thinking of blowing something up—like the principal's office at her high school or the new Starbucks in her neighborhood or maybe an SUV dealership. Just like the Earth Liberation Front. Or just like the Weathermen. She will take every precaution not to injure anyone. It will be a spectacular show of force, a moment to remind people that they are alive and that their lives need to be more meaningful. They will see the dazzling explosion and reconsider what it means to live in a world with other people in it. Or maybe not.

Four

FOURTEEN YEARS OLD, THISBE CASPER HAS BEGUN RID-
ing her bicycle around Hyde Park looking for God. Before
each school day and after, she pedals up and down the street
in a gray skirt and blue sweater, ignoring her wheezy asthma,
searching for signs of providence in the miraculously trimmed
hedges and perfectly kept trees. When she does not find His
Holiness in person, she will often seek one of her neighbors'
pets for an impromptu baptism instead. This morning, holding Mrs. Lilly's small white cat, Snowball, to her chest, Thisbe
whispers a prayer of her own invention:

Please

Please

Please let there be a heaven for everything that is too pitiful to believe,
and then the animal hisses, scratching Thisbe's wrist. Thisbe
turns the poor cat loose, watching it hurry back to its spot
beneath Mrs. Lilly's shadowy porch. Thisbe grabs her wrist
and sees three red marks, already dappled with blood. She
retrieves her math notebook from her book bag and makes
a small tally mark, next to a dozen others, noting Snowball's
unsuccessful redemption.

. . .

THISBE PRAYS FOR a number of things each day, usually in this order: for her neighbors' pets, for her hair to look okay, for her asthma not to get any worse, for her sister not to make fun of her, for her sister to act like she knows her in school, and for all the homosexuals she sees on television—who she truly believes can be saved with the right kind of prayer. She also prays for her singing voice to become an instrument of God, something miraculous, something to fill the world with wonder. Finally, she prays for all the black people in her neighborhood. Black people terrify her. She does not ever ride her bicycle west of Cottage Grove Avenue or south of Fifty-ninth Street into the tired confines of the adjacent black neighborhood. She does not like the way the black people dress, she does not like their music, she does not care for the way they look at her, like she is an intruder in her own neighborhood. She does not like their worn-out-looking storefront churches. She thinks these churches are an insult to God. She does not like the boys, her age or younger, standing shirtless on the corner, wearing silver chains, drinking from bottles hidden in brown paper bags, calling out to passing cars. She hates that some of them wear crucifixes. She does not believe they want to be saved. She thinks they are where they are in their lives, in this world, because they are all lazy. She does not like to ride past their sad little houses. She does all she can to avoid the few black girls at her high school, all of whom, without trying, can sing better than her. Thisbe pedals past them all, hoping no one makes fun of her skirt, which has just begun to come undone at the hem. There are a few loose threads there that anybody could see.

. . .

AFTER SCHOOL, Thisbe has chorus practice, which she loves, though she spends most of the day dreading it. Thisbe is an awful singer, worse than awful, very, very bad. Her classmates are forced to stand beside her, listening to her wail without tone or melody. Mr. Grisham, the very weird chorus teacher, a man strangely fond of Cary Grant—a signed photograph of the famous star rests on his desk—a man with a passion for songs by Bette Midler and by Bette Midler only, does not believe in turning students away from the performing arts. His chorus, for the past eight years, has received no major awards and has failed to place in even the lowliest of regional competitions. In his soft tan suit, his bushy brown mustache covering his moist, thin lips, Mr. Grisham always manages to make Thisbe feel unwanted, moving her from first to second to third to fourth soprano. Mr. Grisham was relieved when he discovered Thisbe could play piano. Susannah Gore, a hulking senior with oily dark hair, had been the accompanist, and though her scratchy tenor was nearly unbearable, it was an obvious improvement over Thisbe's caterwauling. Mr. Grisham made the switch, vainly hoping the heavy, melodious tones of the piano would drown out Thisbe's harsh though earnest wailing. They have not.

TODAY THE CHORUS is preparing for its first recital of the year, which is to take place that very evening. Thisbe folds her skirt under her thighs and takes a seat in front of the out-of-tune, upright piano. The rest of the girls take their places, gossiping quietly. Mr. Grisham is paging through his songbook when the door to the recital room bangs open. A girl with short blond hair and a funny-looking smile enters. Thisbe looks up from the piano and watches as the girl, a girl whom Thisbe has never seen in school before, unbuttons her gray sweater and wanders into place beside Alice Anders, a soprano. The new girl looks a little mean, with green eyes outlined in arrogant-looking mascara.

"Glad you could make it, Roxie," Mr. Grisham says, nodding, adjusting his small-framed eyeglasses. "We're happy you've decided to return to our little family again this year."

The girl, Roxie, nods and when Mr. Grisham turns his attention back to his awful songbook, she immediately flips him off. Thisbe, at the piano, is shocked. The other girls all laugh nervously. Mr. Grisham announces the first number, "The Rose." Thisbe flips her music book to the correct page, studies the fingerings for the opening chords, and places her digits above the keys, waiting. Mr. Grisham gives a nod in her direction, and Thisbe begins, much too slow, then much too quick, Mr. Grisham tapping his foot to set the pace. When the girls finally begin to sing, Thisbe is struck by how beautiful the new girl's voice is; and although she is standing there in the back line, rolling her eyes, the sound appears effortlessly in the air around her dirty-looking mouth. Each note is like spun gold, each phrase echoing like a single prayer, the girl's perfect tone confirming the startling order of the world. Thisbe feels a sad sting of envy as she glances out of the corner of her eye; the girl Roxie is not even trying, the lilting voice becoming stronger and stronger, filling the recital room with a magnificent glow. Thisbe decides she hates this girl with the beautiful voice, hates her for having something she does not even seem to appreciate, standing there in the back line, chomping on a mouthful of gum, rolling her eyes. She hates her and at the same time she feels clumsy, awkward, hammering her fingers along the keys without the smallest bit of talent, that voice, that one particular voice like a song she has always wanted to sing, a dream of a sound that she has so often wished would arise from her throat. Thisbe, no longer looking at the musical notes, closes her eyes and immediately pretends it is her voice singing brightly. When she makes a terrible mistake, missing the last chorus of "The Rose," and Mr. Grisham begins shouting, she is reminded it is not.

THAT THURSDAY EVENING, minutes before the chorus's first recital of the year, Thisbe sits down at the piano onstage, looking over the polished black monstrosity at the nearly empty auditorium, searching for her family. The audience is noisy and wet from the rain. Part of her hopes that her family is not there, while the other part of her aches to see her mother's face. And her father's, and Amelia's, too, unless she's still pouting. She quickly scans the audience, and sees row after row of tired-looking parents, bored in business suits, their hair glistening from the downpour outside. There, in the third row, she spots her mother, who gives her a quick, secret wave. Thisbe smiles, nodding, placing her fingers just above the keys. She sees Amelia is there, her arms folded across her chest, chewing a wad of gum. Every so often, Amelia stretches the wad with her finger, disgusted at having to endure this tedium on her sister's behalf. Beside Amelia is an empty blue seat, where Thisbe's mother has stacked their coats. Her father is late again; but what's new? Thisbe frowns. Mr. Grisham, nervously pulling at his mustache, appears beside her and says, "Let's not miss the grace notes tonight, Thisbe," then touches her back with his creepy hand and hurries off once again.

As soon as the curtain is drawn, and the chorus, in their

awful taffeta gowns, steps forward, Thisbe begins playing, "Wind Beneath My Wings," her fingers cramped, her hands shaking. Mr. Grisham, at the head of the chorus, is giving her a terrible look, but she refuses to glance up at him. She follows the black notes across the lined pages with her eyes, listening for Roxie's voice to swiftly fill the room with burnished light. Susannah Gore has a cold and is like an anchor, the huskiness of her tenor chaining the rest of the chorus to the boards of the dimly lit stage. Thisbe misses two notes, still waiting for Roxie to really begin singing. She is standing there, in the back line, head down, her nose buried in her lyric book. She does not at all seem interested in being there. By the third song, "Boogie Woogie Bugle Boy," Thisbe realizes that Roxie is only mouthing the words. The rest of the chorus trudges on, their voices like dull, metal weapons falling down a stone staircase, until the final number, "From a Distance," lands gracelessly at the audience's feet. The curtain falls, Mr. Grisham has begun shouting, Susannah Gore is coughing, some of the other tenors are crying, and Roxie stands in the back row, looking down at her nails, totally unconcerned.

IN THE PARKING LOT, Thisbe chases after the girl, calling to her, then grabbing at the back of her ugly blue dress. "What's wrong with you?" she blurts out, flushed with anger and what she believes to be an appropriate degree of indignation.

"What?" Roxie mutters, thoroughly bored.

"Why? Why didn't you sing in there?"

"Why don't you fuck off?" Roxie asks, and Thisbe discovers she does not have an answer to that particular question. Roxie turns and cuts quickly through the parking lot, disappearing behind a crowd of disappointed-looking parents.

•   •   •

WHEN THISBE FINALLY finds her own sad relations near the Volvo, they are fighting, once again. Her father has appeared, looking like a mess, his tie untied, his jacket wrinkled. He is saying, "I'm sorry. I had to take a cab. I thought you said eight," while her mother shakes her head and says, "Seven. Seven. That's what I said. Seven. You never listen to me. You never listen."

"I do listen. You said eight."

"So now I have to be responsible for picking you up, too?" she asks.

Thisbe climbs into the backseat beside her sister, Amelia. "Nice screw-up in there," Amelia mutters, to which Thisbe does not reply.

THISBE PRAYS FOR an asthma attack on the way home. Her parents continue fighting in the front seat. The Volvo idles at a stoplight while her father—from the passenger seat, his blond beard uneven with wet gray hairs—whispers angry, though incredibly quiet words at her mother. When her parents fight, they do it in near silence. Thisbe has seen her mother wordlessly cry during her parents' spats, her father looking away blank-faced and ashamed—but these disagreements are almost always impossible to hear from the backseat. Thisbe tries to stop herself from breathing so that she can make out a word or two, but all she hears is her mother mutter, "I told you I will not do this anymore," before she smashes down the gas pedal, the Volvo lurching back into traffic.

Thisbe begins praying to herself, roughly the same prayer she has been repeating for months now. Her parents, Jonathan and Madeline, too busy in the front seat, do not notice. Without their disapproval, Thisbe begins:

Attention, God the Judge, God the Father, who Art in Heaven, give me one miracle, please. If You exist as I know You do, even if no one else in the world believes in You, please give me a brain tumor. Please tear my limbs from their sockets and let the backseat and my older sister be totally covered with blood. Please make me dumb and blind and deaf, please make me a martyr, please, dear heavenly Father. Tear my heart right from my chest. Drive spikes into my eyes and let hot lava shoot out of my mouth. Make me silent and thoroughly dead, but please hurry. Before we get home, before we reach the next stoplight, let the only sound be no sound, the silence of my death burning in the empty sky. If You are a mighty and true God, if You are not just a dream I have made up, please, before another hour, another minute passes, let the wire in my bra poke through my heart. Dear Lord, please, please, give me this one miracle. I have begged You every day, every evening, so please, let Your will be done, let Your will be done. Give me a gruesome death as fast as You possibly can. Thank you, God. Amen.

Beside her, Thisbe looks over at her older sister, Amelia, who is reading a book on Lenin. Amelia is wearing her headphones and seems not to notice her parents arguing, or maybe she is pretending not to notice. Thisbe taps her older sister on her shoulder, but Amelia ignores her, turning the volume up on her CD player. Thisbe cannot tell what she is listening to, only that it is incredibly loud and someone is singing something in French.

As the Volvo accelerates along Fifty-ninth Street, with the evening sky of the east reflected in the dark, choppy water of Lake Michigan, Thisbe hears her father say to her mother, "I don't know how you could ask me that." The station wagon turns and speeds off, their street getting closer each moment, the rest of Hyde Park rising high and sleek and wondrous, like a specter before them.

"I won't do this anymore," her mother says again, no longer whispering. It must be an admission, it must be something her mother has suddenly realized and so she can no longer speak it quietly.

"I don't know what that's supposed to mean," her father replies, no longer whispering either. "I don't know what you want me to say to that."

Thisbe turns to stare out the window, her brown eyes starting to burn with tears. Her heart feels invisible and soft and fluttery and she is having a hard time breathing. But she does not go for the white plastic asthma inhaler in her purse. She can hear herself wheezing and at first hopes her parents will turn around in the front seat and ask if she is okay, and when they don't, she decides she is going to let herself suffocate if it means shutting them up. She will be Joan of Arc. She will be a blood-smeared figure in a Renaissance painting. Her prayer will be her own silent death. Her lungs feel as if they will explode, the blood in her ears pounding. Her hands are grasping at her knees, the fingers momentarily awkward and empty, now tugging at the hem of her skirt for something to hold. She places her hands in between her legs and, when she notices she is still fidgeting, she then places them beneath her thighs. She is barely breathing at all now, her heart pounding fast and faster. She opens her eyes wide to stop herself from crying, her heart beating louder now, louder than her parents' voices. Beside her, her sister is reading her stupid book, uninterested, the music from her headphones vibrating. The air around Thisbe's head becomes anxious with electricity. She sucks in a breath to prevent herself from sobbing, the air filling her thin chest. Suddenly she is lighter than the air itself, like one of the clouds drifting in the sky. It is as if she has begun to float, imperceptibly at first, her legs feeling almost weightless, the vinyl stickiness of the car seat tugging at the back of her bare thighs, her head rising toward the roof of the station wagon, like a bubble or balloon. She feels as if she is rising for a second in the air, floating, hovering, flying, and then, letting go of the breath, she falls, dropping back into her seat, her heart beating more quietly now, her hands folded beneath the back of her thighs, her eardrums throbbing with panic, her knees tingling, then she is gone, then she is nothing. A few seconds later, she realizes she has almost caused herself to suffocate. When the blood stops thrumming in her ears, she hears her mother and father still growling angry, silent words at each other, she sees her older sister still shielding herself with her book, and none of her family has noticed anything.

THISBE IS LYING in bed that evening, saying her prayers, when her father knocks on her bedroom door. At once she realizes he has come to tell her that he and her mother are getting a divorce. Thisbe stops at her forty-fifth Hail Mary of the night, speeding through the final lines, *Now and at the hour of our deaths, amen.* Thisbe says one hundred and ten Hail Marys every evening, an activity she began last year, when her grandmother, a devout Catholic, died while visiting from St. Louis; Thisbe had been helping her wash the dishes when a white serving plate slipped from Grandmother Violet's soapy, wrinkled hands. A few moments later, her grandmother was dead. Thisbe now says a prayer for each year of her father, mother, and older sister's lives, thus secretly, and without their knowledge, keeping them alive. Her arithmetic looks like this:

Dad	48
Mom	45
Amelia	17

Thisbe does not say a prayer for her grandfather Henry. She does not see him all that often—only on Sundays—and that's really only since Grandma Violet died and he had to move into a nursing home here in Chicago. Also, she does not actually know how old he is. Thisbe says the number forty-five aloud to remind herself where she left off as her father knocks again. She is sure it is him. His knock is so soft, so unobtrusive. She feels her father standing outside the door there, holding his breath, listening for her response.

"Yeah, Dad?" she says.

"Thisbe? Hey, kiddo, are you sleeping?"

"No."

He opens the door and peeks his head in. "I think we might need to talk for a few minutes," her father says. He looks so nervous now, sitting on the corner of the bed, careful with his weight, as if she is made of glass. His face is hard to see, just the shape of his poorly kept beard, his left ear, his blue eye. She remembers when she thought he was the most handsome man in the world, when he used to wear the red T-shirt she made with the iron-on that said BEST DAD EVER. She remembers helping her mother attach it, the sound of the steam escaping from the iron, the shape of her mother's smile. She knows why he is standing there in the dark now, what he is going to say, duh. They are both so obvious. Why can't they just say it? Suddenly Thisbe is thrilled by the terrible drama of it, the sense that something is over and something else is beginning, that her world, as lame and awkward as it has been, is about to change. But then she is trembling with sadness and the tears are beginning to fill her eyes once again.

"I wanted to apologize to you for what happened tonight," her father said. "I misheard your mother and I . . . I wanted to apologize for missing your recital."

"It was really stupid anyway. I messed up pretty bad."

"It doesn't matter."

"Well, you can come see me next time."

Her father smiles, nodding, rubbing his hands on the knees of his pants.

"Okay. I'll be there, I promise."

Thisbe can hear the music from her sister's room next door. It is "Marie-douceur, Marie-colère" by Marie Laforêt, the same stupid French song she's been playing for days now. Duh. She is probably in there getting stoned. Thisbe hates her sister for not being as thoughtful as she is. She hates that she will have to remember this moment for the rest of her life with her stupid sister's French music playing in the background.

"Thisbe?" Her father hesitates now, wondering if he should put his hand on his daughter's arm before he says it. No. She watches him struggle, unsure what words to use, what tone of voice, his hand finally resting on her foot, which is curled up under her leg. When his hand touches her, she knows, and her heart goes totally blank.

"You guys are getting divorced," Thisbe blurts out. "I knew it."

"What?" he asks, startled. "No, no, of course not. Did Mom tell you that?"

"No."

"No. No, we are just having a hard time right now is all."

"But you're not getting a divorce?"

"No, we're just going to spend some time apart."

"What?"

"A separation, so we can figure things out."

"Again."

"Yes, again."

"Dad, that's so stupid. Didn't you guys do that already?"

"It's not stupid. We want to try and work this out."

"But why?"

"*Why?* What do you mean *why?*"

"I mean why not just get it over with?"

"Because we still love each other. It's just difficult right now."

"Okay."

Thisbe lowers her head, staring down at her father's slippers. They are dark blue and sad-looking. In fact, everything about him is sad-looking, his ruffled blond beard, his haircut, his blue eyes.

"Thisbe?"

"Yes?"

"Do you want to talk about this?"

"I thought that's what we were doing."

"Well, do you want to say anything to me?"

"I'd like to think about it awhile," she says.

"It's okay to be angry, hon. It's okay to be sad."

"I'm not angry, I just want to think about it."

"Okay," he says.

She scratches her nose and then asks, "Are you both going to live here still?"

"We don't know how that's going to work yet. For now we will. Any other questions like that?" her father asks.

"No."

"No?"

Thisbe shrugs her shoulders, then asks, "Dad?"

"Yes?"

"What do you think God thinks about this?"

"Excuse me?"

"Do you think He's going to punish you and Mom for doing this?"

"I don't think it's any of His business."

"I don't think God believes in divorce," Thisbe whispers. "I think it goes against the Bible."

"I think God has other things to worry about. Like war and endangered species and things like that."

"God worries about all of us."

"We aren't Christians, Thisbe. You've only been to church twice in your life. And both times that was for funerals."

"Well, maybe we could start going now."

"I don't think that's going to help, honey."

"Maybe it would."

"Maybe it wouldn't," her father says, pinching the space between his eyes.

"When does the separation start?" Thisbe asks.

"What do you mean, hon?"

"When does it start?"

"It starts tonight. Right now, I guess."

"Right now?"

"I'm afraid so, honey."

"We didn't even get a last meal together."

"We'll still eat together, if you want."

"It won't be the same."

"I guess not. I know you probably don't want to hear this

right now, but I'm sorry. Your mother and I, we, we always promised we would never put you guys through this again."

"It's okay."

"No, it's not," her father says. "But it'll be okay, I promise."

"Where are you going to sleep tonight?"

"I don't know. In the den."

"It gets cold in there with the air-conditioning."

"I'll be all right."

"Okay."

"Okay."

"Goodnight."

He touches her foot again, counting each of her toes.

"Dad?"

"Yes?"

"Did you tell Amelia yet?"

"No."

"No?"

"Your mother is talking to her right now. We decided we'd tell you guys at the same time. Your mom'll be coming in here to talk to you in a minute or two."

Thisbe smiles unexpectedly, surprisingly happy, the thought of them, her parents, coming up with this fair solution. Her father leans over and kisses her forehead, then quietly departs, gently closing the door behind him. Thisbe lies in bed, wondering what's going to happen to all of them. She decides she will accept whatever God wants, even if it is something she does not like, like her mother and father getting divorced and her having to share a room with Amelia. Even then, she will not complain, if that is His will. Thisbe stares up into the dark, continuing her bedtime prayers, the silence of her room interrupted by the soft muttering and movement of her own lips until a familiar howl echoes from the dark, moonlit backyard below. It is her neighbor's cat, Snowball, crying to be let in. Thisbe decides she will get up early tomorrow morning to capture the animal. Tomorrow she will finally make it understand God's love once and for all.

Five

AGE SEVENTY-SIX, HENRY CASPER, FORMER AIRCRAFT engineer, widower, father, and grandfather, does what he can to make himself disappear. Resting his silver transistor radio in his lap—the noise and melody of which announces his looming, watchful presence—he wheels himself down the blue-toned hallways of the South Shore Nursing Home, warily observing the second-floor security doors, noting the times when the desk attendant leaves them unguarded. Secretly, he keeps a list of when the staff dispenses medicine to other residents, noticing the precise moments when the glass doors must be propped open in order to accommodate the plastic trays of lukewarm meals that appear on rolling silver carts three times a day. In his yellow notebook, which he quietly retrieves from the breast pocket of his faded robe, Henry writes down any new useful information, detailing the odd hours with a few additional sketches, planning another escape. By now the notebook is almost completely filled with these furtive observations, along with a number of impracticable drawings of heretofore unrecognized aeronautical shapes—airplanes as thin as sheets of metal, jets as long and narrow as needles, helicopters as small as children's bicycles. When one of the nurses finally notices the quiet buzz of Henry's radio, when the muscular security guard looms directly above the old man to ask what it is he thinks he is doing, when, at last, the squeaky left wheel of his chair gives him away, Henry, overcome with fear, finds he is unable to speak. Henry suffers from a neurological condition known as verbal apraxia, a disorder that has afflicted him since childhood. His mouth becomes peaked and rigid, his remaining teeth chatter together without a sound, and his words simply fade away.

> *To Whom It May Concern,*
> *You had a wife named Violet. She was two and a half inches taller than you. She had a laugh like a musical triangle. Once, the very first time you touched her skirt, you thought she might float away.*

Each day, Henry does what he can to make himself vanish, removing any fingerprint, any trace of life that may have been left in the semiprivate room, in the recreation center, in the cafeteria, in the dull, looping conversations of the other unfortunate residents chattering around him. Each day, he uses one less word, counting down the remaining days until the moment he won't speak to anyone again, the moment when he has absented himself once and for all from the dreary hallways of the retirement facility. Each day, at breakfast, lunch, and dinner, Henry eats one slightly smaller portion of the dreadful beige turkey, the sadly yellowed mashed potatoes, the irregularly green mashed peas, leaving the rest among the divided sections of his plastic tray. Each day, he gives away another article of clothing, offering to his fellow residents another moth-eaten sweater, another pair of old black socks, another unworn undershirt. Out of sight, hidden behind the white radiator in his room, are the few things Henry has not been able to abandon—a single color Polaroid photograph of his wife and son, Violet and Jonathan, a number of smudged and faded letters from acquaintances and family members now long gone, an old metal toy airplane, and a few other curious objects from a childhood that he can almost no longer recall— a decoder badge from a science fiction radio program he listened to when he was eight, a paper flower he was given when he was fourteen, a drawing of an imaginary aircraft he made in his forties—these small, unnameable things, the only evidence of a man whose existence has now become a complete blank, the sum total of a life now lived anonymously.

To Whom It May Concern,
You were always afraid of the dark. When you were afraid,
you could not speak.

And soon, in only a few days, Henry will slip through the front glass doors of the South Shore Nursing Home, flag down a taxi, ask the driver to please hurry, speeding off toward O'Hare International Airport, where, among the lines of weary-looking people, among the badly damaged suitcases and the stewardesses in grim uniforms and the little children timidly holding their mothers' hands, he will buy a single one-way ticket, then board an unassuming plane, asking for assistance with his wheelchair only when he really needs it, and then, when the airplane's engines begin to roar and the disagreeable force of gravity shakes the cloth seat beneath him, when the plane has departed from the ground, hurtling itself through the blue and white sky, Henry will once again be happy, the aircraft becoming lost somewhere just over the cloudy horizon, and who he once was, who he might have been, or who he has failed to be, will have all but vanished.

To Whom It May Concern,
You were too young to fight in the Good War.

At the moment, Henry is as tricky to spot as a ghost. His transistor radio switched off, the squeaky left wheel of his chair now silent, he wheels himself past the nurses to the far end of the cafeteria, and stops in front of the enormous window in the recreation room, gazing out at the boundless blue sky, completely unnoticed. Once, only a few months before, Henry managed to follow a nurse named Leticia through the glass security doors, into an empty elevator, through the ground-floor lobby, and out onto the street, before being chased down by a bullnecked security guard, just as a taxicab had finally pulled up. A second time, only three weeks ago, Henry made it as far as the cab ride. But when answering the cabbie's questions he found he had said too much, and the cabdriver immediately pulled over on the side of the expressway to radio the police.

To Whom It May Concern,
You had a nervous breakdown in your thirties.

In the afternoons, when he is not busy counting his remaining words, Henry does away with his memories, disposing of them all, scribbling down his few remembrances. Once they are written down and sealed within a white paper envelope, once he has mailed them off, he considers these memories to be gone for good, one less thing to keep him from disappearing. With his right hand cramped from arthritis, having found a secluded spot in the rec room of the South Shore Nursing Home, as far as he can get from the other residents staring up at the droning television, drowsy with their anti-Parkinson's medication and their willy-nilly arts and crafts, he begins writing another short letter addressed to himself:

> *To Whom It May Concern,*
> *You were one of the designers of the F-4 Phantom airplane. You worked on the nose cone and the wings and were able to reduce the drag coefficient on both by almost sixty percent.*

Or:

> *To Whom It May Concern,*
> *You used to like music by Woody Herman and Glenn Miller and sometimes Artie Shaw.*

Or:

> *To Whom It May Concern,*
> *You used to be able to speak some German. Your father and uncle were both tailors.*

Or:

> *To Whom It May Concern,*
> *The only thing you ever stole was a comic book, when you were eleven years old. You had the money for it but you wanted to see what it felt like to steal and you didn't get caught but you wish you had and so you never even read it.*

Henry will then date the letter, slip it inside a plain envelope, write the address of the South Shore Nursing Home on the envelope, fumble for a stamp somewhere within the breast pocket of his shabby red robe, and hand the letter to a nurse to be sent out later that afternoon. When the mail arrives, he does not open the letters he has written to himself. Instead, he carefully places them in a box of personal effects he intends to leave to his son, checking the postmark on each envelope, filing each one in order by date. When evening comes, and his right hand has grown sore from writing, Henry will wheel himself back to his room and stare out the tiny window—the empty, regretful branches of a single oak tree the only sight he ever sees—trying to ignore the inevitable appearance of night, a vague reminder of the approaching certainty of his most unimportant death.

> *To Whom It May Concern,*
> *You had eyes that weren't brown or green but which your mother called hazel. Your mother prayed all the time.*

By the time midnight arrives, the moon settling outside Henry's small window, the old man has become lonesome, the oak branches etching odd-looking shadows along the tile floor; he feels afraid. He has always disliked the silence, the dreadful soundlessness of night. So when the shadows have crept to the middle of his room, to the edge of his wheelchair where his feet rest, Henry looks about his room for his silver radio and switches it on, searching among the AM stations for an old standard by Benny Goodman or a rebroadcast of a Lawrence Welk show, or maybe an episode of *Inner Sanctum Mysteries* or *The Airship Brigade* or *The Shadow*. He wheels himself to the room across the hall, where Mr. Bradley, eighty-seven years old, lies in bed, his papery skin covering a sunken-looking face, eyes taciturn and fully resigned. He is too weak to even smile, but his thin gray eyebrows move slightly, this small gesture the only sign that the older man has noticed Henry sitting beside him. Together, the two elderly residents will listen to the worn-out jokes, the worn-out radio stories, the worn-out ballads. And when the static begins to clear, when an excited voice hurriedly calls out from beyond time and space, Henry recognizes it as the brave tenor and pitch of Alexander Lightning, teenage commander of the adventurous *Airship Brigade*, a science fiction show Henry loved more than anything else as a boy:

ALEXANDER: Gee whiz, Doctor Jupiter. That was a close one. I thought for sure we were going to be crushed by that mysterious meteor belt!

DOCTOR JUPITER: My dear boy, I was hardly worried, knowing our spacecraft, the amazing X-1, was safely in your hands.

ALEXANDER: Now if our gyrometer would only tell us where we are.

DOCTOR JUPITER: It appears that we're on a direct course for the moon.

ALEXANDER: All we have to do is find somewhere to land . . . but what's that? It's a city, made entirely of silver clouds. And what now? Oh, no, they're firing at us with a strange ray of some kind. Everyone, take your crash positions in a hurry!

DARLA: Father, I'm afraid.

DOCTOR JUPITER: There's no need to worry, my dear. As long as Alexander is at the controls—

ALEXANDER: Oh, no, we're going down!

ANNOUNCER: *Will the Airship Brigade survive the awful radio ray of the mysterious city in the clouds? Stay tuned, listeners, and . . .*

WHEN THE ADVENTURES of that particular episode are over, and the clarinets and saxophones have played their final tune, Henry wheels himself across the hallway back to his room, glancing up through his window at the cloudy silver moon, the stars looking like pinholes poked in the dark fabric of night. He stares up at the sky and murmurs, *Enough, enough, enough*, and then he begins counting on his fingers the number of hours and days that remain until he will have made himself vanish. *Eleven more days*, he whispers. *Only eleven more days. Can't you wait that long? Can't you? No?*

No.

No.

No.

ONLY ELEVEN DAYS LEFT, and yet today, Monday the eighteenth, Henry has decided he will wait no more and that he must try to escape this very morning. He has written down the appropriate numbers in his notebook to help him remember. There. Just above a drawing of an elliptical zeppelin: *11-3-5*. At approximately 11:35 a.m., when Jeff, the tall, bearded orderly, props open the glass security doors to deliver the rolling metal racks of preheated lunch, Henry, only eleven days away from being completely invisible, will quietly sneak past, wheeling himself to the first bank of elevators as quickly as he can. Arriving at the ground floor, he will hurry through the front lobby with a dignity and confidence he has very nearly forgotten, proudly wheeling himself outside, where he will hail himself a cab, and then, speeding toward the airport, he will disappear once and for all.

To Whom It May Concern,
You had a sense of humor which you kept to yourself. You were
afraid of other people's laughter.

At the moment, Henry looks up and sees the clock above the television set: 11:33. He nods, gathering what little courage he has left, wheeling himself as quickly as he can toward the glass security doors. In the next moment, Jeff, pushing a large silver cart stacked high with tray after tray of prepared food, whistles past, running his plastic security card through the electronic card reader, swinging the heavy doors wide, propping them open with the small plastic doorstop. Sitting there, just before the glass divider, unnoticeable to almost everyone, Henry wheels himself forward, hitting his elbow against the doorframe, his bony fingers grasping the rubber wheels with all his might. Holding his breath, he wheels past Jeff and the racks of food, then forces the glass door closed behind him, trapping Jeff on the other side of the locked door. He pushes himself toward the elevators, his heart beating like a tin drum in his chest. Without thinking, already terrified and exhausted, Henry presses both elevator buttons, up and down, glancing over his shoulder, hissing to himself as he waits for the heavy elevator doors to slide open. Finally, the elevator on the right gives an electric *ding!* and Henry's heart begins to beat wildly, rebelling out of cowardice, out of fear, out of panic. His hands suddenly feel too tired, too weak. He gives himself one final shove, catching a wheel on the metal threshold, almost tumbling out of his wheelchair. He begins to hit all of the glowing yellow buttons, finally managing to get the elevator doors closed just as Jeff begins to bang on the glass.

When, unbelievably, the elevator has finished descending and the heavy doors open on the ground floor, Henry lets out a small sigh of joy. He wheels himself as fast as he can past the waiting families, the off-duty nurses standing beside the coffee urn quietly chatting, the enormous security guard busy reading a newspaper, then all the way across the lobby, swinging wide through the front doors, rolling outside onto the sidewalk beside the busy street. *Traffic! What is this?* the sound of traffic having been something Henry had forgotten to even begin to forget. A taxicab pulls up and the bearded driver helps Henry into the backseat, folding up the wheelchair, forcing it into the taxi's trunk. Henry can hear the buzz and static of the cabbie's CB, the odd snatches of voices like the thoughts and sounds of memories he has yet to dismiss, so that when the cabbie asks, "Where to, pops?" when he turns around from behind the steering wheel and glances at his passenger in the rearview mirror, Henry gives the response he has already planned, speaking six of the eleven words he intends to use today, his voice hesitant, gravelly, predictably weak, as unsure as it was when he was a boy, when his words first began to fail him. "O'Hare. I'm going on a trip."

Additional Remarks of a Historical Significance

A CLOUD HAS APPEARED WHERE IT SHOULD NOT BE. There it floats, quite mysteriously, as if having fallen from the open vastness of a blue and white sky, drifting in the middle of a marshy field, its gray shape unchanging, hovering only a meter or two above the muddy earth. The cloud has begun to cause some panic among the superstitious villagers whose sugarcane and potato farms lie just outside of Meerut, and so Lieutenant George Kasper has been dispatched to see what there is to see.

George Kasper—unwitting descendant of the London Kaspers, with family relations in England beginning in the fifth century, and with other crooked branches of the same family tree reaching from England to France back to Germany—would rather be drawing his maps. Instead, today, on this morning in the year of 1857, in the unvanquished colony of British India, the young lieutenant stands glaring at the shape of a single gray cloud, unmoving, uncelestial, the soft, wet-smelling sugarcane extending around him in all directions, distinctly marking how alone in this moment he truly is. Ishari, his sepoy scout, forever loyal, only a boy really, age twelve or thirteen, a Hindu by birth but more and more British each day, stands some hundred meters back along the dry road. He watches each of the lieutenant's gestures, trying his best to read George's thoughts through his physical expression, his every movement, his every twitch.

"Well, I must admit, Ishari, this is certainly something of a puzzle," the young lieutenant whispers. George, only thirty-two years old himself, thinks he ought not foul this up in front of the young Hindu. There has been trouble recently in Meerut: unexplained fires in colonial storehouses, and yesterday the British hanged another sepoy, Mangal Pandey, a Hindu private of the Thirty-fourth Regiment who attacked his British sergeant with a sword and wounded a nearby adjutant on his horse. George feels the young boy's eyes along his back and takes another step deeper into the swampy muck. The cloud looms closer, making a terrible aching sound. George blinks again. The sun cuts behind an acacia tree. George hears the low, heartbroken moan again, and holds his hand up, shielding his eyes. Suddenly he smiles, relieved, seeing the cloud is no cloud at all. It is a rhinoceros, magnificent and ancient and startling white, lurching there in the mud.

Figure 2: A rhinoceros

George stares a little longer and sees the poor giant is trapped in what may very well be quicksand, too old to struggle or perhaps just resigned to the fate that lies beneath the florid estuary. *Dear old man,* George thinks. *It seems your reign has come to an end. As a geographer for the British East India Company, it is my sad duty to inform you that we no longer have any use for rhinoceroses of any kind. From now on, you and all of these unpredictable rivers, these septic marshes, these troublesome plains, will all be redrawn, refigured on my map. These plundered kingdoms and useless villages will be made uniform and compliant to the thoughtful order of British rule.* The animal gives a low, melancholy groan again, sinking deeper. It will soon drown in the mud. George decides he will have to shoot it, that being the Christian thing to do. *A magical cloud? A magical cloud? The sooner these people learn of civilisation, the better off all of us will be,* George thinks. The young lieutenant raises his Enfield rifle, aims for the monster's enormous head, but finds he cannot fire. The brutish creature is staring directly at him now, its head bowed, its great horn radiant. The lieutenant places his finger on the rifle's trigger, but still he cannot shoot. There, stranded in the weeds and murk, white as carved stone, the rhinoceros looks like a god.

"Ishari, go fetch the largest rifle you can find," George calls back. "Ask the colonel if he knows where to find an elephant gun." Ishari nods, holding his helmet as he does, and hurries off, his knees stepping high, as he has been taught. George turns back to the rhinoceros and sees the sad monster rearing its gigantic head, its gray horn luminous, huffing once, a low, baleful melody that ends with a lilting, dirge-like whistle.

"Help is on the way," George says, taking a step closer. He reaches a hand out toward the rhino's soft, febrile hide. The animal's wrinkled white skin is covered in bristly brown hairs. The lieutenant changes his mind, and returns his hand to his hip. The rhinoceros sinks farther. A number of bubbles explode around its trapped mass as it quickly begins to descend. George lurches forward without thinking, but the rhino is much too dangerous, its enormous head lashing about in panic. All at once, the empty valley echoes with the report of rifle fire. George turns quickly, surveying the gray land, his stern hand shading the sun, and catches sight of Ishari hurrying back along the road. The young lieutenant curses, seeing the boy is empty-handed. He turns back to the rhinoceros, which has sunk even farther, its noble head the only thing remaining above the dark murk.

Ishari reaches the lieutenant entirely out of breath. He is so winded he cannot speak. The lieutenant, seeing the red in the young sepoy's cheeks, softens, impressed by the boy's exuberance, dedication, and loyalty. He places his hand on the Hindu boy's shoulder and notices the poor, trembling child is covered in blood. The boy opens his mouth to speak, but is still too overcome, too frightened. Ishari turns, pointing back toward the military cantonment. Another rifle shot echoes across the open field, then a second, then a third.

"Ishari, my boy, what has happened? What have you seen?"

But Ishari still cannot speak. He reaches his hand up, touching the young lieutenant's clean-shaven face, then collapses. Only then does the lieutenant see the young sepoy has been stabbed, a gaping wound left across his back. The boy clutches the lieutenant's ankle, sinking into the soft, wet ground. He gasps, coughing up blood, trying to untie the lieutenant's bootlaces. George kneels beside him, clasping the boy's shoulder, but sees it is already too late. The poor child is dead, his hand fast at the laces of his commander's brown boot. George looks up and sees a cloud of smoke rising steadily from the direction of the cantonment. Something is wrong. He leans over and gently folds the fingers of his fallen protégé away from the toe of his boot. He makes a perfect knot in each shoelace and then feels for his pistol. He finds it at his hip and then rushes off. The road is uneven and full of stones, and the lieutenant is out of breath before he reaches the outskirts of the military encampment. His heart pounds dreadfully with each stride, and once or twice he nearly trips. He can hear gunfire and the sounds of what must be screaming by the time the gray, bulky shapes of the barracks come into view. Moments later, his heart wrenched loose in his chest, his brow slick with sweat, he stumbles into the cantonment and sees the impossible: the other British officers of his regiment, the Eleventh, lie dead.

A foot, a leg, an arm, a face staring there wide-eyed in the mud, the barracks are a shambles.

Somewhere beyond the shadows of the cantonment are more shouts and more gunfire, and the lieutenant, stricken, brandishes his weapon nervously, still unsure what has happened. Certainly it must have been an ambush of some kind, the Thuggees perhaps, but there is no sign of any assailants other than spent rifle cartridges and the loamy, blood-smeared bodies of his fellow officers. Hurrying into the first barrack, the regimental headquarters, he sees it is empty, a wooden table and chairs smoldering with fire, papers and field manuals strewn about. The next barrack, the colonel's quarters, is untouched, signs of struggle strangely absent. The colonel's pajamas, blue-and-white striped, lie on the dirty ground, a bedpan overturned on the white sheets of the imperious-looking field cot.

The third tent is inconspicuously crowded. The lieutenant, lifting the tent flap aside, gags uncontrollably; the pungency of death—of recently moved bowels and emptied bladders—steams through the air with acrid corruptness. The lieutenant covers his mouth and sees his three fellow officers, lying beside one another in the mud, all of them empty-eyed. The colonel, his proud red mustache now creased with dirt and blood, looks stupidly content, smiling up from the patchy earth. The major, his eyes closed, seems pensive as if in prayer, a slit across his throat leaving little to keep his head attached. The sergeant, a bulky man, lies face-down, his cranium crushed by something heavy, the stock of a rifle perhaps. Outside the tent, someone is singing bravely in Hindi.

George reaches down and touches the dead colonel's hand. Another series of rifle shots ring out. Through the tent flaps, he can see that the cantonment is on fire now, great red and black flames leaping from the pointed canvas roofs toward the cobalt sky. He can hear someone running, many, many feet hurrying back in this direction. Someone shouts angrily in Hindi nearby, and George, without thinking, shoves the expired colonel aside, crawling beneath the field cot, pretending to be dead. Though the major's loaded rifle is near his feet, George does not try and reach for it. He does his best not to weep. The sound of angry feet approach. His heart beats recklessly now, pounding in his closed throat, his eyes shut tight. He feels his breath vacillating uneasily in his chest, as he hides beside the still-warm bodies of his three fellow officers, their open mouths rank with blood, their gruesome wounds already drawing flies.

Outside the small cantonment, the makeshift barracks echoing with rifle fire, George can hear the screams of what he guesses are the final pleas of English women and children. *The children, the colonel's daughters!* George thinks. *What will become of them?* Certainly the sepoys, the Hindu and Muslim infantry once loyal to the British East India Company, have all lost their minds. With their own swords and borrowed Enfield rifles, they move through the crowded streets of Meerut, murdering all the British they can find. George lies there beside the dead, wondering in his spinelessness if he will ever see his beloved London again.

When three Indians, their tan uniforms covered in specks of blood, storm into the tent, George cannot help himself from letting out a startled gasp. With their lustrous swords in hand, they glance about for survivors. And then the lieutenant begins to cry, the tears quickly running down the sides of his dirty cheeks. His heart starts to tremble uncontrollably: his heart beats as it did when he was a sickly child, *"Young George has a terrible heart condition, he mustn't run or get overly excited,"* it beats as it did when he was an inconsolable young man, his father asking, *"How do you expect to become a great soldier against all your doctor's prohibitions?"* and George's reply, *"There is a need for geographers, and geographers aren't expected to wield anything heavier than a map and pen. It will be with a map and pen that England will put the world to rights"*—suddenly his traitorous heart is no longer his own. *No, no, no,* he mutters to himself. *No!* Gasping for air, his heart pounding in his chest, he is overcome with fright, much deeper than the terror of the moment. His heartbeat echoes with thousands of years of secret cowardice, running all the way back along the deformed branches of his blighted family tree, thousands of years of hidden weakness having finally produced this most misshapen, most frail of all human hearts, *"The boy will be lucky to see his tenth birthday, and if he does, the noise of a slammed door or a bolt of lightning might do him in,"* the organ wholly defective in its diminutive size. And now the minuscule muscle in George Kasper's heart can do no more and beats its final beat. The sepoys searching the nearly empty tent find the three murdered officers and quickly hurry on. But already it is too late: Lieutenant Kasper is dead, his pusillanimous heart having failed. His perfectly ordered and thoroughly uncomplicated maps of a British India, a British India that will never be, lie in a small notebook, pressed tightly against his chest.

Six

A SECRET: THERE ARE HUNDREDS OF DIFFERENT KINDS of clouds, distinguished by size, shape, and height of the cloud base, which Jonathan has unwillingly, over the years, memorized. There is the cirrus cloud, the cumulus, the nimbus, the stratus, the cirrostratus, the altocumulus and altostratus, the nimbostratus, and the stratocumulus. Today Jonathan thinks about each of these different kinds of clouds as he searches for his antiseizure medication. The den, littered with bedsheets, his dirty clothes, and mountains of research, now resembles a child's fort. The light from the east-facing window is much too bright in the morning, so Jonathan has hung two bedsheets— one over the window and one curtaining off the sofa where he has slept. Moving aside three different large-scale maps of Japan, Jonathan finds his bottle of pills and swallows one down with a cold glass of water.

ANOTHER SECRET: at the Field Museum, where he does his research, Jonathan will sometimes walk down to the World Under the Sea exhibit to talk to the life-size models of underwater creatures. The models—a life-size humpback whale, a pair of male and female dolphins, a hammerhead shark, and an enormous purple giant squid—all stare back with sad eyes of black glass, silent, attentive, a thoughtful audience. The creatures do not stir. They float there, listening quietly. Jonathan will sit on a bench before the great squid and smoke a cigarette, wondering aloud why everything in his life seems to have gone to shit. The museum where Jonathan does his research is mostly empty at this time of the morning, and the World Under the Sea exhibit has been under construction for some three months now, affording the tall, sad-faced professor dressed in his wrinkly beige jacket a moment or two of absolute stillness.

Jonathan stares at the giant squid and smiles.

"And how are you today, old friend *Architeuthis dux*, younger cousin of *Tusoteuthis longa*?"

The purple tentacles gleam from the overhead lights.

"Well, I am equally awful. I'm afraid we're not going to find *Tusoteuthis longa* anytime soon. At least, not before the French. I'm not going to be able to keep my research lab here if they find it first. And I'm afraid that my wife is not in love with me anymore, if you can believe that."

The squid does not respond.

Jonathan stands, searching his jacket pocket for another cigarette. He does not find one.

"No, I don't know. I don't have any idea what I'm going to do."

He smiles, staring into the beast's great black eye.

"Maybe I ought to be more like you. Maybe I ought to get used to being alone."

From down the tiled corridor, Jonathan can hear footsteps and the jingling of keys. He stands, then leans forward past the inoperative security barrier, touching the great squid's sturdy tentacle. A security guard, Roger, pokes his head around the corner of the exhibit, smiling when he sees Jonathan standing there.

"Hey, Professor, what are you doing down here so early?" he asks.

"Just visiting these guys," Jonathan says.

Roger nods. His tattooed neck, a musical quarter note with flames around it, catches Jonathan's eye once again. Roger, glancing over his shoulder, digs into the front pocket of his blue uniform and takes out a joint. Roger lights it quickly and takes an unbelievably long toke, then hands it to Jonathan, who also drags deeply, closing his eyes, imagining he is underwater. For a moment, he is happy to be drowning, and then, feeling his hands and feet beginning to tingle, he lets out a breath. A strange, numb sensation begins to extend all the way down his left arm. He stares at his fist, opening and closing his fingers. It feels empty, his hand. It feels completely numb.

"You all right, Prof?" Roger asks, and Jonathan just nods.

"Yeah, I guess," he mutters. Then, shaking his head, "No. No, I'm really not. Not at all, actually."

ANOTHER SECRET STILL: Jonathan has been eating a lot of fast food lately. In the drive-through of McDonald's, Jonathan finds himself staring up at the cloudy sky, the sky so much like the unstill sea, imagining the shape of the giant squid rising from its depths to gorge itself on a school of silver prehistoric fish. When Jonathan blinks, he realizes it is only a dark airplane floating there, drifting through the threads of the choppy clouds. He glances over at the glassy drive-through window and sees that the teenage McDonald's employee, unnaturally overweight, with an explosion of purple zits on the dark skin of his forehead, is shouting at him.

"I'm sorry," Jonathan says. "I was just daydreaming."

"You're the one with the Big Mac and large Coke?"

"Yes."

"It's going to be a minute, man. One of our fryers is down today."

"That's okay. I was just thinking: Did you know that some giant squids spend years of their lives completely alone, only breaking their solitude once or twice every few years to mate?"

"It's $5.38. You can pull up to the second window."

"Of course."

STILL ANOTHER SECRET: in front of his Monday Paleontology 101 class, Jonathan does not remember what he was just talking about. His teeth feel hard, his mouth dry, as he tries to recall what he has just been saying. The blank, uninspired faces of the students in the lecture hall stare back at him glossy-eyed, spoiled, and impatiently confused. A girl with too much makeup on, wearing an unflattering pink tank top, blows a large bubble with her bubble gum, glaring at him with resignation. Other students check their cell phones to see what time it is. Jonathan, his face flushed with embarrassment, glances down at his notes. He clears his throat, sees something familiar in his handwritten outline, then looks up at the daunting faces again. The girl in pink blows another bubble and then pops it with her finger. The sound of her bubble-gum chewing makes Jonathan incredibly anxious.

"I seem to have lost my place," Jonathan says, scratching his beard. "I apologize."

He sees the girl in the pink top yawn. Obviously, she doesn't understand how difficult all of this is.

DISAPPOINTED AFTER HIS lackluster class, Jonathan returns to his cramped office and finds a small pink note on his desk. It's from Ted, one of his research assistants. It says: *The French have their boats in the water—they've been chasing some sperm whales and think they might have found It.* Jonathan's heart slowly breaks. He reads the words over and over again, shaking his head. He feels like crying. The French team of paleontologists, led by that unremitting asshole Dr. Jacques Albert of the French Sédimentologie Association, have been following a congregation of sperm whales—natural predators of various species of squid. Apparently, they have now triangulated the position of what may be the first known living specimen of *Tusoteuthis longa.* Jonathan crushes the piece of paper in his hand, collapsing into the chair beside his desk. He sighs, staring at the computer. A decision has just been made, something he has been considering all morning. He places his fingers on the computer keyboard and types a quick email to *Dragonflydr,* Dr. Arzt in Germany, telling her about the new developments concerning the French research team. He ends the electronic missive with this sentence:

and so i am afraid our correspondence must come to an end: i love my wife and as complicated as it is sometimes, i have realized this before any real damage has been done, and as terrific as you are, there is no point in continuing—i wish you the best in all of your scientific and romantic endeavors.

> *yours,*
> *jonathan*

p.s. your new work with model wing reproduction sounds amazing.

Jonathan rereads it once more and then hits *Send*. Just then his office telephone rings, its beige receiver vibrating in its plastic cradle, and Jonathan lets out a little shout, sure it is either Dr. Arzt with an angry response or news that the French have captured the first prehistoric giant squid. His hand trembles as he reaches toward the phone, slowly slipping it from its base. "Hello . . . ," he mumbles and is overwhelmed with joy to hear Madeline's soft, familiar voice.

"Jonathan? It's your father. He escaped . . . from the nursing home, again."

"What?"

"They found him. At the airport this time. They think he was trying to buy a ticket to Japan."

"My father was at the airport?"

"Jonathan, you need to go to the nursing home right now," is all Madeline says.

THE FIRST TIME Jonathan ever goes to a museum he is holding his father's hand. Before the antiseizure medication, phenytoin, is introduced, there is a series of bizarre, painful, experimental treatments to try and help the boy overcome his neurological dysfunction. One particularly agonizing experiment, prescribed by an avant-garde neurologist by the name of Dr. Roberts, involves aversion therapy, during which Jonathan, only seven or eight years old, suspicious in a powder-blue butterfly-collared shirt and brown corduroy pants, is ordered to look at book after book about clouds—staring at the drawings of stratus and nimbus within—forced to watch hour after hour of filmed footage about storm clouds and meteorology, fainting and waking, fainting and waking with each turn of the book's page or each flicker of the film's frame. His father, Henry, greatly terrified for his boy and following the advice of Dr. Roberts, decides to bring Jonathan to the meteorology exhibit at the Natural History Museum in St. Louis. Holding his hand as they stand before a glass-encased diorama—a replica of a gray storm cloud menacing a miniature midwestern farm—father and son try to address this strange malady together. Jonathan bravely stares up at the odd shapes, the faded, dusty world of meteorology, facing his condition with courage. The hall where the display stands is entirely quiet, interrupted only by the whispers of the father and son. Jonathan lets go of Henry's hand and reaches out, putting his palm against the glass, but then pauses and frowns, his body beginning to convulse, his eyelids twitching, his dark brown shoes turning in on themselves until the boy falls backward, his father awkwardly catching him. Though that particular experiment fails, Jonathan will never forget the feeling of being carried back to the car, still pretending to be unconscious, carefully huddled in his father's arms.

ARRIVING AT THE South Shore Nursing Home, a little less than a half hour from their house, Jonathan finds his father resting in his semiprivate room—incoherent, weakly mumbling, his thin face strained with frustration. His father does not seem to recognize him. His father's greenish gray eyes are wide and empty and blank. He is lying in his bed, holding his transistor radio tightly against his chest. Jonathan glances at the old man's hands as he slowly moves the dial back and forth, his mouth looking slightly frozen, the lips curled in a weak sneer.

Jonathan says, "Hi, Dad, how are you doing?" but he does not get a response. Jonathan takes hold of his father's hand and immediately the old man seizes his wrist, his grip stiff as a claw.

"I . . . was . . . lost," his father whispers aloud, his voice slow and garbled and gruff. The voice is foreign, the voice of someone just learning to talk.

"Dad, did the doctors tell you what happened?" Jonathan asks.

Henry nods. He mutters, "I'm okay," which are the final two words he allows himself today. He hopes that his son will somehow understand the blank spaces between these sounds, the significance of the pauses, all the words he happens not to be saying.

"Why did you go to the airport, Dad? Do you hate this place that much? Are you unhappy here? Do you want to find somewhere else? Because we can. I don't . . . I mean, well, it's okay now. Just take it easy. Just stay calm. Are you breathing okay? It doesn't sound so good. Are you breathing all right?" Jonathan asks.

Henry nods to himself but does not say anything. Just then, Jonathan notices his father's uncovered feet: they are swollen, purple, and caked in red sores. They are lying uncovered at the end of the bed, a strange, disgusting odor rising from them. Jonathan glances at the curled-up feet, then back at his father.

"Did they explain what you did, Dad?" Jonathan asks again. "You took off from here? And then they found you at the airport. Why did you try and leave, Dad?"

But Henry does not answer.

"Listen, I'm going to go talk to the nurse. I'll be back in a minute, all right?"

His father looks at him with bright eyes that seem unconvinced. Jonathan unzips his coat and places it in the chair beside the bed. "See. I'm leaving my coat. I'll be right back. I'm just going to go down the hall."

Henry nods as his son touches his hand and then slowly closes the door.

THE NURSE SAYS his father escaped around lunchtime and was found at a counter at O'Hare Airport about two hours later, waiting in line to buy an international ticket. He's been unresponsive since he was discovered and may have suffered a minor stroke of some kind, possibly a small infarction. She describes it as some sort of neurological storm that has passed but may have left his speech and reflexes slightly diminished. She tells him the old man refuses to eat or get out of bed. He refuses to be washed and the blood clots in his legs and feet are getting worse. He has been sedated because he was threatening the nurses, clawing at them angrily when they wheeled him back into his room. He has been throwing things, the nurse, a round-faced black lady named Rhoda, says, adding, "He threw his food tray right at me and I told him that was no way for a man his age to act."

Jonathan nods, not knowing what to say.

"I wanted to warn you," the nurse whispers, placing a hand on Jonathan's shoulder. "I think he might be getting towards the end here. If he had a stroke, it wasn't so bad, but a lot of the time they know they're reaching the end. They get sort of ornery like that. They won't get out of the bed. They start talking to their mothers and fathers and brothers and sisters who have all passed. I just want to warn you, Mr. Casper. If he's got other family, you ought to let them know."

Jonathan nods again and says thanks. He slowly walks down

to his father's room and stops in the doorway, watching the old man whispering something to himself, pulling the sheet tight against his chest. Jonathan smiles softly, holding his father's hand.

"Okay, Dad, I'll be back tomorrow afternoon to speak with the doctor. Maybe I'll bring the girls with me. How does that sound?" Jonathan asks, then leans over and kisses his father's wrinkled forehead. His father nods, momentarily appeased, his heavy eyelids fluttering, the narcotics slipping through his system.

"Okay, Dad, I'll be back sometime tomorrow. You hang in there. You listen to the nurses, okay? They want to give you a bath, you should let them."

Henry nods, opening his eyes, looking up at his son. He nods, then turns his head, staring out the window at the moonlit night.

ON THE RIDE HOME, even with the Peugeot stalling twice, Jonathan does not begin to cry. Not until he is near the house, thinking of his father, so tall, as sharp, as quick-witted a man Jonathan has ever known, lying there, muttering unintelligible nonsense. Thinking of his hands, cramped and clawlike, and his feet, purple and bruised, Jonathan softly begins to weep, just a tear or two, just enough to make him feel sad and slightly embarrassed.

WHEN HE FINALLY gets home, he finds Madeline on the couch asleep. Has she been waiting up for him? The thought makes Jonathan smile. The television is on and gives her face a soft blue glow. Her robe is bundled tightly at the waist, her eyelids are closed, her long eyelashes lightly fluttering. Jonathan stands above her, gently touching her cheek. In her sleep, she smiles. Jonathan decides not to wake her, switching off the TV. He leans over carefully and kisses her earlobe, pulling the small afghan up over her bare feet. Suddenly she is startled, and sits up, like a child, wiping her eyes.

"You're home?" she asks.

"Yes."

"What happened? How is he?"

"It doesn't look good. He can barely talk. His legs, his feet. He won't get out of bed."

"Do you want me to make some coffee? We have some decaf, I think."

"No," he says, frowning. "Go back to sleep."

"What are you going to do?"

"Maybe I'll try to work for a while."

"Why don't you come up to bed with me?"

Madeline touches his hand softly, so gently. He nods, his heart weak and folding. "Do you want me to?" he asks.

"I don't know. Just come up with me."

Jonathan nods his head slowly. "Okay, I will, in a couple of minutes." He lets go of his wife's hand and then shuffles quietly into the den, where he shuts the door. Jonathan finds his penlight at his desk and then climbs beneath the tent of sheets, feeling like a boy, small and young and lost. There, on the floor, is an anatomical drawing of the mysterious prehistoric giant squid. There is an empty dish with crumbs. There is a map of the world's oceans, folded in twelve sections. The lines and patterns, the underwater mountains and ridges, all different shades of blue, suddenly seem blurry. Jonathan holds the small light over the drawing of the squid, drawing an X through its three still hearts. None of this, none of this makes any sense to him.

Seven

A. Because Madeline does not want to go to sleep without Jonathan, she waits up for some time, then abruptly decides to take a look for the cloud-figure in the backyard. Amelia is upstairs on her computer, the muted echo of her fingers tapping on the keyboard. Thisbe is already in bed asleep, or maybe she is just lying there praying. Madeline mopes around the house for a few moments, straightening a picture here, pushing in a vacant chair at the kitchen table. That's when she decides to go looking for the cloud-man. She finds the flashlight in the mess of the utility drawer and slips on her gym shoes. *Outside*, Madeline thinks, *it still feels like it's summer*. There is dew already on the grass, the moon high like a white apple hanging from some invisible branch in the sky. Her neighbors on the west side, the Amberstans, are asleep, the noise of their air conditioner rattling from their bedroom window. Madeline steps into the rectangular shadow cast by their small garage and flashes the light around, poking holes of brightness into the dark air above her head. The outlines of the trees quickly flicker into view, the skeletal shape of a twig, the silhouette of a glimmering leaf. Staring through the opening of the trees, Madeline sees something glimmering faintly up there, it is rounded and nearly undetectable, the soft figure of the man-shaped cloud. Madeline is surprised by how close it seems, floating there just a few inches above the topmost branches. Stunned for a moment, she switches off the flashlight, lowering it to her side. She glances around quickly to see if anyone else is watching, but the entire neighborhood has gone to sleep. Madeline switches on the flashlight once more and points it directly at the center of the strange cloud, and this time the light makes the object hanging in the sky perfectly luminous and perfectly transparent. Madeline can almost see right through it. She can see the cloud's feet, which are pointed, shaped like shoes, she can see each of the cloud's fingers, she can see the shape of an ear. Madeline lowers her flashlight and the cloud becomes opaque once again. Then something wonderful happens. The cloud begins to glow, just for a moment, flashing a single time, then going dark again. Madeline opens her mouth, her heart beating fast, then points the flashlight at the cloud and switches it on and off, on and off, twice. When the flashlight's beam goes dark, the cloud glows in response, blinking with light, exactly twice. Madeline drops the flashlight in the grass, then, stumbling for it, she finds it and shines it up at the cloud again. "Hello?" she softly whispers. "Hello?"

B. The cloud does not respond. Madeline switches off the flashlight and hurries back into the house. Madeline does not sleep a wink all night. She waits the rest of the night for Jonathan to come to bed, panicked and excited, wondering what she is going to tell him.

C. Madeline decides Jonathan is an immature, selfish asshole and that she is never talking to him again. She decides she is not going to tell him about the cloud, not ever. She decides she will talk to him when she is good and ready. But not tomorrow. Definitely not tomorrow. Tomorrow night at the earliest and maybe not even then.

D. At work the next day, Tuesday morning, Madeline finds another two dead pigeons. Again, both of them are female, and after some quick lab work, she finds both of them have been raped. Checking their tag numbers, Madeline makes another gruesome discovery: the purple-hued female from the study coop, the bird which she has unprofessionally dubbed Lucy, is one of the animals that has been killed during the night.

E. Madeline's experiment is a complete and total disaster. She stands outside the pigeons' enclosure for two and a half hours observing the birds' interactions but none of the beta males exhibit any particularly violent behaviors today. Then, just about fifteen minutes before lunch, Madeline watches one of the beta males mount a submissive female. Madeline does not intercede. The submissive female tries to fight off the male's aggressive advances. The male, cornering the female, mounts her unsuccessfully again and again, his claws scratching at her puffy white and gray feathers. The female refuses to submit and the male refuses to acknowledge his failure. The male tears at the other bird's back, scoring her skin, until Madeline opens the gate, shouting, scaring the beta male away. *Why is this happening?* she wonders. The female certainly should have relented. The male is hard-wired to expect female sexual submission. But the female is completely unwilling to participate. What has gone wrong in this tiny, miniature world of hers?

**F. Today Madeline does not feel bad about smoking a ciga-
rette during her lunch.** Laura, the intern, has taken the day
off. With a certain giddiness, Madeline climbs into the driver's
seat of the Volvo, while Eric, the other researcher, fumbles for
the package of cigarettes inside his lab coat. He offers Madeline one, then fingers a cigarette from the pack for himself.
He then hands his silver lighter to Madeline, who, smiling,
lights the cigarette and inhales deeply. She closes her eyes and
imagines being a cloud of smoke, ephemeral, weightless, rising
higher and higher into the sky, until she is just air, until she is
absolutely gone. She absentmindedly passes the lighter back
to Eric. When Madeline leans over to turn the radio on, Eric
reaches over and places his large white fingers on the outside
of her gray sweater, his palm gently cupping her breast. Madeline does not say anything. She stares at him, shocked, and
maybe Eric can see the shock in her eyes, because he just nods,
then slowly lowers his hand.

"I'm so sorry," he says. "I just thought . . . I thought . . . ,"
he mutters, dropping his hand back to his side, staring straight
ahead for a moment.

"No, it's okay," Madeline mutters. "I mean, I . . . it's no big
deal," but Eric is already scrambling for the door handle, and
without a single word, he pulls himself out, stumbling back
inside the research facility.

"Wow, okay," Madeline whispers to herself. "Wow."

**G. The cloud-figure is still floating there when Madeline
comes home, which weirds her out even more.** Madeline
stares up into the sky, where the cloud-man continues to hover.
She taps her foot on the sidewalk, then crosses the yard, glancing up at its faint shape, its nearly dotted outline.

"Hello?" she says again, but the cloud still does not respond.

H. Of course, Madeline finds Jonathan still hiding in the den. He is sitting cross-legged beneath the tent of white bedsheets. Madeline stands in the doorway, staring into the small room, which is dark, other blankets and sheets covering the two windows. Jonathan is huddled beneath the fort, reading something with a penlight.

"Jonathan?"

"Yes?"

"What are you doing?"

"Thinking."

"Do you want to talk?" she asks, kneeling beside the opening. "The kids are busy. We can be alone and talk."

"I don't think so right now."

"What's going on in there?" she asks, opening the flap. She can see his dirty gym shoes, which were white once but now look gray, his blue sweatpants, but not his face. "What are you doing?"

"I just found out the French may have found *Tusoteuthis longa*. They think they may have it on their side-scanning sonar."

"Shit. I'm sorry to hear that," she says, frowning.

"Well, they had more money. Better support. We really couldn't compete."

"Are you going to want to come out and talk about what's happening with your dad? Do you want us to all go visit him tonight?"

"No. I was just there. I just can't deal with it right now."

"Jonathan?"

"Yes."

"What about me? What about you and me? Are you going to come back upstairs ever? I thought we were going to work to fix all of this."

"I can't," Jonathan whispers. "I can't fix anything right now."

"Great," Madeline murmurs and shuts the flap.

I. Madeline does not know what to do, so she flips through the channels to find out what has happened to the captured soldier in Iraq. There is no news. There are two car bombs, one outside Basra, the other in Baghdad. Thirty-six people are dead. Madeline switches from cable news channel to cable news channel and finally finds something about the missing soldier on Fox. They are interviewing the soldier's mother. She is standing on the front steps of her porch, partly hidden by a white screen door, and is telling the world that her son appeared to her last night in dream and she fears he is already dead. The anchorman reminds the audience that the coalition forces have two more days to comply with the insurgents' demands before they will decapitate the captured soldier. Madeline decides to turn off the television. Upstairs, she hears Amelia playing her music too loudly. She suddenly remembers that Amelia has been home all week because of her suspension. Madeline gets up and calls from the bottom of the stairs.

"What is it?" Amelia asks.

"Are you doing schoolwork right now?"

"No."

"Well, what are you doing?"

"Just listening to music."

"I need some help with the groceries. I want you to come with."

"But Mom—"

"Come on, let's go."

J. Madeline finds herself at the supermarket, grocery shopping with her oldest daughter, having a conversation she'd rather not have. Madeline is pushing the cart down the frozen food aisle when Amelia turns to her and asks, "Mom?"

"Yes?"

"What's happening with you and Dad?"

"Your father is living in the den."

"I know. But like I thought you were going to try and work things out."

"Well, to be completely honest, so did I."

"It seems exactly like the last time you guys were separated."

"It is. That's what's making me crazy. It is exactly the same thing. It's total bullshit."

"He seems pretty upset about Grandpa," Amelia murmurs. "I mean, so maybe it's not all his fault."

Madeline nods. "I know. But I want you to know there's a good chance this might be it for your father and me. I don't want you to mention it to Thisbe. But I just want you to know what might happen."

Amelia nods, trying to look both concerned and unafraid. "Is Dad going to be moving out?"

"Well, we're not moving," Madeline says. "If he wants to be an idiot, he can be the one who moves."

Amelia nods again, pushing the cart down the aisle. "But maybe you guys will change your mind again," she whispers, sounding exactly like she did when she was nine.

K. Madeline imagines the feeling of Eric, the other researcher's hand, on her breast. As they are driving back home, Madeline wonders if she should tell her oldest daughter about what happened. She considers it, then decides it might be inappropriate. She thinks it is something she wished her mother would have told her, when she was Amelia's age, and so, sitting at a stoplight, she turns down the radio and says, "Amelia. I want to tell you something. Not as your mother. But as a friend."

"Okay."

"This is really weird, but I feel like I can trust you."

"All right."

"This guy, this other researcher at work today. We were at lunch . . ."

"Yes?"

"And he, well, he touched my breast."

"Did you slap him?"

"No."

"Why not?"

"I don't know. It was the weirdest thing that's ever happened to me."

"Mom?"

"Yes."

"Why are you telling me this?"

"I don't know. I feel like I had to tell somebody."

"But I mean, is he like a creep?"

"No, no, he's this totally quiet, sweet guy. And he, I don't know. He just put his hand on my breast."

"That's creepy."

"I think it's really weird. It's kind of funny, too, don't you think?"

"I guess," Amelia says.

"Now, you can't tell anyone."

"I know."

"It made me feel like I was in high school or something. It was the strangest thing."

"Mom?"

"Yeah?"

"The light's green."

"Right."

Madeline begins to pull away from the stoplight, glancing over at her daughter, who is staring silently out the window. Madeline is worried how quiet Amelia has become. She leans over and asks, "What are you thinking about?"

"You don't want to know."

"Go on. Tell me. Seriously. It won't bother me."

Amelia plays with the seat belt, then looks up and says, "Sometimes I wish you and Dad were more like actual parents."

"What? What does that mean?" Madeline feels her heart immediately seize.

"Forget it. It's no big deal. It's just like I wish you didn't tell us everything."

L. Madeline immediately regrets mentioning anything to Amelia, about anything.

M. Madeline does not speak to her daughter for the rest of the car ride home. Together, they silently unpack the groceries. When they are done, Amelia darts up to her room, leaving Madeline in the garage, her hands trembling. *Dumb, dumb, dumb*, she thinks. *Why would I just do that?* She slams the rear door closed and steps slowly from the garage.

N. The cloud-figure is still floating in the tree.

O. The cloud-figure is still there floating.

P. Madeline looks up at it sadly, as if it is something she should be embarrassed of, like a bad birthmark or off-handed comment. She stands beneath it and waves slightly, then says, "Hello up there."

Q. The cloud, shaped like a man, begins to move. Madeline is shocked. She watches as the cloud slowly drifts over the tops of the trees from the spot where it had previously been fixed, crossing incrementally toward the west. The cloud appears to be walking in the sky. "Where are you going?" Madeline calls out. But the cloud keeps on walking.

R. Madeline does not know what to do.

S. The cloud keeps on walking.

T. Madeline thinks how Jonathan would laugh at her right now if she told him what was happening. So would her daughters. Both of them. All of them.

U. The cloud keeps on walking.

V. Madeline thinks how everything in her life is terribly, terribly complicated. The cloud does not seem to be. It seems to be stupendously obvious.

W. The cloud keeps on walking.

X. Madeline watches it drift farther west, hanging gently above an old apartment building, still moving.

Y. Madeline decides to follow the cloud, climbing into the Volvo quickly. She starts the car up, throws it into reverse, and begins to follow the cloud, its silvery shape faintly crossing the late afternoon horizon. Madeline says to the cloud, "Okay, okay, don't go so fast."

Z. The cloud keeps on walking.

Eight

AMELIA, ON FRIDAY, HER FINAL DAY OF SUSPENSION, finds she does not know what to do with herself. Because she has been suspended from the only thing that matters to her, because she does not have any lame homework to do or another stupid column for the paper to write, because she finished all of her schoolwork two days ago already, she is now bored to death. Worse than that, Amelia realizes that all she has in her life is high school, and the thought of that, the fact that she is just a dumb high school kid with a beret and not a young revolutionary, makes her extremely depressed. She prints out a large photo of Patty Hearst from the Internet and tapes it to her bedroom wall, just above her computer. She organizes her wardrobe and tries to get rid of anything that isn't monochromatic or military in color: blue, green, beige, brown, and black, she moves these clothes all toward the front of her closet. She switches on the television, then switches it off, and mopes around the house all morning until she decides to go surprise her father at his office, in the biological sciences building of the university. Maybe she will sneak into his lecture class and watch him teach. Maybe she will raise her hand and ask a question and maybe he will wink at her and later tell her he was glad that she came. Maybe she will meet a college boy or two who actually give a shit about something other than getting in her pants. Maybe.

FINDING HER BLACK BERET, affixing it to her head, Amelia then puts on her reading glasses and her smartest-looking outfit, a dark blue turtleneck and gray skirt, then grabs her book bag and rushes off to her father's building. She has never seen him teach before and smiles at the thought of her dad, up there at the front of the lecture hall, pointing, talking, gesturing, everyone taking notes on what he is saying. How weird! What a funny idea that is, her dad, like how could anybody take him seriously? She skips across campus to the sciences building, then finds the lobby, where a list of the current semester's classes and their respective rooms has been posted. She finds her father's name, checks her watch, and rushes to Room 201. The university's hallways are dark wood and marble, and Amelia is thrilled at the idea that someone might mistake her for a student. She searches the building, finds the lecture hall, and opens the heavy wood door as quietly as she can. She hurries inside, finds the nearest open seat, somewhere near the back, and sits down. The hall, a large room of one hundred seats, is mostly empty. Her father, in a brown sports coat and tie, is muttering something near the front of the class. His back is mostly turned and he is writing something on the board. "The Paleolithic era," he repeats. "That's what I asked you guys to study? Did any of you do the reading or not? Because we can go back to having quizzes if you want. It doesn't matter to me either way. Is that what you would like?"

The class does not seem interested enough to answer.

"I'll be honest," her father mutters. "I'm a little disorganized right now. I'm just trying to get through this semester. So it would really help if you could do the assignments. I mean, that would make a difference for all of us, I think. Unless you know all of this information already. Does anyone here have a doctorate in paleontology? No? Then maybe it'd be good if you all did the readings."

A girl sitting next to Amelia looks at the boy beside her. In her notes she has written, in a large, underlined script:

THIS GUY SUCKS

The boy nods, then scribbles in his own notes:

HE HAS LOST HIS MIND

"Did you guys ever wake up and just want to say, *Okay, Universe, that's it. I quit*? Because that's how I feel right about now."

Amelia is horrified: her father is an absolute mess. His shabby little suit coat and tie, his nasal voice, his unkempt blond beard, the incredibly bored students, some yawning right there in the open, now he is up there, scrambling through his notes, he is checking his watch and shaking his head, he is staring at the nearly empty lecture hall blankly, as if it is the first time he is seeing it, he is now mumbling, "Well, I think we're done for the day," he is turning and opening his attaché case, shoving his notebooks inside, the students sighing a breath of exaltation at being released half an hour early. Amelia, thoroughly embarrassed for her dad, ducks out, rushing through the doorway, exiting along with the other young people. She glances over her shoulder once and sees her father still standing at the front of the hall, pinching the space between his eyes. It looks like he is still talking to himself about something. Amelia, her face flushed, follows the flood of students away from the lecture hall, pretending to be invisible, an orphan.

. . .

UNSURE NOW of what to do with the rest of her day, Amelia ambles around the university. She watches the college girls, in sweatshirts and jeans, their books huddled loosely to their chests, or book bags slung lazily over their shoulder with one strap. They seem so demure, so freshly scrubbed, so intelligent and mature and indomitable. They are the former editors of their high school papers, the former presidents of clubs they themselves must have invented. They laugh and chat and smoke in groups of two and three and blink and giggle and talk in low voices when a college boy crosses the quad to join them. It is totally unfair. They are so sure of themselves, so effortless, arguing about Hegel or the ending of *The Stranger*. They are aglow, nearly incandescent with some secret knowledge, they are having sex and probably enjoying it. They are all lying in their dorm rooms, in their beds, a boy with bushy hair beside them, naked, sharing a Chesterfield, and talking about Woody Allen movies. There are no asshole Cro-Magnons crowding the busy hallways, standing around thinking their dumb thoughts, just waiting for someone to make fun of. Everyone on the quad is here because they want to be. And all of them look so vibrant and smart. These girls are all involved in protests, they must have all come close to being arrested. And they are all too stylish, all too confident to be caught dead in something as pretentious as a black beret.

AMELIA, FOLLOWING A GROUP of these mysterious girls, ends up in a general education class called the Historical Perspectives of Biology. The professor, a young fellow in his late twenties, is also in a brown suit coat, this one slimmer than her father's, corduroy, more becoming. He also wears a beard, though his is reddish and has been recently trimmed. The class begins promptly at one-thirty and the professor, winking to a few students in the front row, cracks some unheard joke. He claps his hands together and says, "Okay, guys, today's topic of discussion is one I am sure you have been recently contemplating yourself: the inevitable nature of war."

Amelia quickly sits up, realizing she has nothing to write on.

"Why is it that, no matter how prosperous our country is, we always find ourselves caught up in military struggle of some kind?"

Amelia looks around the room and sees the entire class is silent, hurriedly jotting down abbreviated words in their notes.

"Okay, guys, take me, for example. I was born in the early seventies, during the Vietnam War. In the eighties, we had the arms race and the final stages of the Cold War. In the nineties, the First Gulf War, then military intervention in Bosnia. Now it's 2004, and here we are again, this time caught up as an occupying force in a country most of us know very little about. So my question for you, ladies and gentlemen, is why? Why does this pattern keep repeating? What does it say about us, as a nation? Or about us, our collective human nature? What does it tell us about our instincts? The way we're made? Our biology?"

A boy with a goatee raises his hand first. "It's all about money. War is like good for the economy."

"Sure. There's some truth to that," the professor admits. "The Great Depression didn't end until we got ourselves involved in World War Two. Okay, okay," he says, scribbling *Money* on the blackboard. "But is money the only reason?"

"What about religion?" a girl asks, raising her hand high above her head.

"Religion. Good. Think of all the wars you know, throughout the history of humankind, how many of those were motivated by differing religious beliefs? A lot, right? Christians against Muslims, Muslims against Jews, Christians against Jews, Christians against other Christians. Not to mention the wars of indoctrination against millions of indigenous people, across Africa, Asia, and North and South America, in the name of some spiritual power."

The professor nods, taking a sip from a coffee cup, then adds *Religion* to the blackboard.

"Okay, but what about biology? How do you think that plays a part?"

The class is slightly puzzled.

"Okay, maybe it's just part of nature itself that we go to war. Maybe war is part of the way the natural world organizes itself. All right, for example, there are certain male, adolescent dolphins that will gather together as a group and go and hunt porpoises, in gangs. They'll find a porpoise and kill it. And the scientists who have studied this phenomenon have discovered that it has nothing to do with a struggle for food, because their diets are different. It just seems that these dolphins, this one species, this one group, wants to dominate another group. Can you guys think of examples of this happening in your own lives?"

Amelia nods, wanting to raise her hand, but she restrains herself. She leans forward in her seat and listens to each word of the lecture, captivated, staring at the professor, hypnotized.

•   •   •

AT THE END OF the class, Amelia waits for the students to file out so that she can hurry to the front of the hall and thank the professor for his lecture. But it is not so easy. There are two or three other girls, already waiting in a small line. They blink at him happily, twirling their hair in their fingers. Amelia is undaunted, or not daunted enough to ignore the odd excitement building in her stomach. She feels the certain itch of hives trembling along her skin and does her best to ignore the uncomfortable sensation. She waits her turn silently, adjusting the terrible beret, then staring down at her feet, listening to the silly compliments the other girls are making—"I really loved what you said about religion, Professor Dobbs, it really makes a lot of sense," or "I think your class should be required, Professor Dobbs"—until she is the last one in the room, and Professor Dobbs is carefully stacking his notes, sliding them into his briefcase. When he has finished packing his things, he searches through his jacket pockets, finds a small silver cigarette case, pops it open, selects a foreign-brand cigarette, and lights it using a single match from an elegant-looking matchbook. He sighs, the cigarette smoke darting severely from his two nostrils, as he slips the silver case back into his jacket pocket. Amelia takes this moment to notice how serious, how intense this young man looks before she builds up enough courage to interrupt the professor's few seconds of silent contemplation.

"Professor?"

"Yes," he says with a movie-star smile, all white teeth, perfectly aligned, glittering like an advertisement.

"I just wanted to say, well, how incredible it was . . . your lecture . . . I think it's great someone is like talking about issues like that. I mean, it's so different . . ." She wants to say *than high school*, but, catching herself, she mutters, "It's like so different than most classes."

"I appreciate that, thanks."

Amelia nods for no apparent reason. The beautiful professor has not looked up from his briefcase yet. She stalls, trying to think of something else to say, and notices a small bald spot at the back of his reddish brown head. The bald spot is not unattractive, there is something about it, something humbling, that makes Amelia believe the professor may be as shy as she sometimes feels.

"Well, that was it, I guess."

"Well, thank you for your feedback," he says, still shuffling his papers. Then, with a quick glance, his eyes meeting hers only for a moment, "I like your hat."

"My hat?" It feels like she might implode. *My hat. What hat? Am I wearing a hat?*

The young professor smiles, the smile revealing how young he actually is, twenty-seven, twenty-eight at the most. He says, "Your beret. It's very becoming."

Amelia immediately wishes she could die, right there. Oh, my, God. She blushes, touching the beret once, then again, nodding. "Thanks . . . I . . . thanks."

"I hate to admit, but I'm still learning everyone's name in class."

"Oh," Amelia says, fidgeting, running a hand through her hair. "Sure."

"I don't believe I know yours."

"It's Amelia," she gushes, then, remembering who she is, her own last name, she adds, "Hearst."

"Wow. Any relation to William Randolph?"

"Distant," she lies again, all too easily.

"Are you a freshman or sophomore, Amelia?"

"Um, sophomore," she mutters, deciding to commit herself to a lie as grand, as bold as she can imagine.

"What's your major?"

"Undeclared so far."

"Undeclared? Huh. Ever consider history?"

"Sure. I love history."

"What part of history are you interested in?"

"All of it."

"All of it?" he asks, smiling again, now just another boy Amelia has met.

"I like to look at revolutionary movements throughout history. The Soviets, the Chinese, Cuba, South America."

"A young socialist?" he says with a grin.

Amelia returns the smile. "I'm a Marxist."

"I see."

"I don't think people should be treated as products," she announces proudly. "I think it's everyone's responsibility to care for each other. The only way to do that is to tear down capitalist interests."

"Wow," Professor Dobbs says, impressed. "Bold words. Would it be too bourgeois of me to ask if you'd like to continue this discussion over some coffee?"

"As long as it's not Starbucks," Amelia says, without missing a beat, and begins smiling uncontrollably.

AMELIA GETS COFFEE with the young professor, then gives him a blowjob in the passenger seat of his brand-new Saab. She does not intend for it to happen. Neither does he, maybe. They are simply two young people excited about the world, what's wrong with it, and how to fix it. After two rounds of lattes at a noncorporate coffee house, after finding out that Allen also grew up with the heavy burden of privilege—the Saab a gift from his parents, given when he successfully completed his graduate degree—after the two of them share a small roach, driving through the park, Amelia suddenly finds herself with her face buried in the professor's lap—Allen's lap—which is moist and very, very hairy. His skin tastes like salt and there is a musky odor coming from his privates, not gross, but a little surprising, like an animal smell. She does not know what to do with her hair. She is holding it up with her hand, but then thinks that is a little weird, so she lets it fall into the older man's lap. Allen moans a little, then slowly runs his fingers through her dark locks, tucking it behind her ear, squinting down at her with a stoned smile. Amelia feels a pubic hair in the back of her throat and it almost makes her gag. She keeps her blue eyes closed and feels Allen's body begin to tense up. She opens her eyes and sees the streetlights and trees surrounding the park, both strange shapes in the Saab's windshield. She does not know if doing this will make him take her more or less seriously. She hopes it does not change anything. Allen is running his hand through her hair, then down her back. He slides his hand down the space between her skirt and underpants, following her spine, his fingers slipping inside her panties. She does not know how long to keep going. Does he intend to cum? Does he want to have sex in the car? Is he going to ask her to come home with him? What does she do now? His hand is now moving back up her spine, resting along the back of her neck. His fingers tighten there, as she bobs her head up and down, her mouth beginning to feel sore. The head of his penis strikes the back of her throat and she closes her eyes to keep from vomiting. She looks up at him but his eyes are now closed. The radio is playing a song by the Velvet Underground; has the radio been on all this time? He is holding her head down there now, pushing it against his crotch a little harder than before, which Amelia immediately understands is his way of suggesting that he intends to cum soon. She moves her left hand up and down the shaft of his penis, hoping to expedite things as her jaw begins to ache badly. All of a sudden he is grasping her hair, pulling at it, his legs tightening against the driver's seat, his whole body clenching. Amelia knows what this means. She lifts her head back, closing her mouth, but it is of no use. His hand is against the back of her neck and she cannot move in time. He seems to be holding her face there, maybe hoping she will take him in her mouth as he finishes, but she does not. A stream of hot liquid spurts against the side of her face, spraying parts of her hair. She makes a terrified sound, blinking, closing her eyes in disgust. Allen jabs his crotch at her as he endlessly climaxes. He is moaning, his moan exactly like Max's or any of the rest of them, timid, stupid, childish. He holds her head there until he is done, then zips his pants up quickly, and does not look at her again, not even when he says a somber goodbye in front of her house.

"I never thought any of this was going to happen," Amelia says, still hoping. "I mean . . . well, I'm still a little surprised, I guess."

"I think it's best if neither one of us mentions it," Allen whispers, staring straight ahead.

"Of course, I just meant . . . well, I guess . . ."

"It was wonderful being with you today, Amelia," the young professor mumbles blankly. "You are a wonderful young woman."

Wonderful? Amelia thinks. *You just blew your load in my face and all you can say is I'm wonderful?*

"Well, goodbye," she says, leaning toward him, hoping for one final kiss.

"Goodbye," he mutters, oblivious, already gone, at home, in bed, in front of the TV with his wife or girlfriend or some other coed already.

WALKING SLOWLY, sadly, her jaw sore, treading up the stairs, Amelia finds her younger sister sneaking around in her room, looking through her bureau drawers.

"Do you want to die?" Amelia asks, giving Thisbe a shove.

"No."

"Then what the fuck are you doing in my room?"

"I don't know. I was just looking."

"For what?"

"For some of your girl things."

"What girl things?"

"I don't know," Thisbe whispers. "Things that make you look nice."

"Stay the fuck out of my room or I will terminate you," Amelia hisses.

"You don't have to be such a b.," Thisbe whines.

"A b.?"

"You know what I mean."

"A bitch? Is that what you're trying to say?"

Thisbe nods.

"God, you are so retarded. You are like an infant. Why can't you be like a normal sister?"

"I am normal. Just because I don't like to swear and I happen to believe in things you don't doesn't mean I'm not normal."

"Duh. You are such a fucking freak. You know God doesn't actually exist, don't you?"

Thisbe looks down, her eyes shimmering with tears. "I'm not listening to you."

"You know it's all like this invention to get stupid people to like slave their lives away because they think something good is gonna happen to them even when it's not."

"I don't care what you say," Thisbe whispers. "It doesn't change what I believe."

"God, why are you so pathetic?" Amelia asks.

"I don't know why," Thisbe murmurs, then slowly steps out into the hallway.

SITTING ON HER BED, feeling the stiffness of her jaw, her throat still a little sore, Amelia finds she has stolen Professor Dobbs's cigarette case. She does not remember taking it, and yet there it is, hidden in her purse, gleaming and stylish, a few scratches marring its otherwise luminous surface. When she presses the tiny button along its side, the case quickly springs open. *You have saved us!* the cigarettes and matches happily wail. *We are so happy. We cry tears of joy as we are forever in your debt!* Amelia closes the case in a hurry and shoves it into the back of her bottom dresser drawer, along with the rest of her disposable items. She does not want to consider why she has stolen the professor's cigarette case. She does not want to think about what any of this might mean.

AMELIA, LATER THAT EVENING, sometime around nine o'clock, decides the anticapitalist movie she has been making for her history project is the most pretentious, most obvious, most immature piece of shit ever. She can't even watch it again. She tosses the DV tape in the garbage and decides to start from scratch. She lies in her bed and begins to think to herself out loud. "Okay, capitalism," she says. "Capitalism is about capital. Commerce. Products. Production. Factories. Consumerism. An invisible shadow corrupting everything." Amelia thinks of the lecture she heard earlier today, she thinks of Professor Dobbs's words, then his hands and his soft face, and just then she gets an extraordinary idea: what if it wasn't a film at all? What if it was an actual event, like instead of reporting about some historical issue, what if she actually affected history, what if she actually tried to change it? Like a political action. *Ambitious*, she can hear Mr. Anson saying. Amelia begins to search under her bed, then in her closet, then under her bed again, running down the stairs past her mother, who asks where she's been, then down to the basement, where she finds what she's been looking for: a large cardboard box, which she immediately begins to tear apart. Running back upstairs to her bedroom, she finds a pair of scissors and begins to cut a familiar-looking shape, tracing the round edges in a circular curve, holding the dismantled box up against her body, checking its size. When she thinks it looks okay, she finds a large black Sharpie and, uncapping it, sniffing its pungent chemical odor for a moment, she begins to color in the large, cumulus shape. It is a cloud: a large gray and black cloud, which, like a costume, fits over Amelia's head. And on it, she writes a favorite quote from Proudhon: "All property is theft."

Nine

THISBE OFTEN WONDERS WHY GOD DID NOT GIVE HER a good singing voice, when all she would like in the world would be to sing a lovely song to glorify His name. And to be in the actual chorus and not to have to play the piano all the time. And to do well in her audition for the fall musical, which, this year, is Mr. Grisham's original musical adaptation of *North by Northwest*. Thisbe is trying out for the part that Eva Marie Saint played. On the small recital stage, Thisbe waits for her name to be called, pacing back and forth behind the large red curtain. She closes her eyes and holds her breath, folding her hands together against her chest as she prays:

Dear God, who Art in Heaven, Who is the Great Redeemer and Seer of All Good Things. Oh, Lord in Heaven, Heavenly Father, oh, Heavenly Lord, please grant me this one prayer, this one wish. Give me the voice I deserve. Let my lungs sound like a trumpet, let the words ring from my voice like the bell tolling for judgment. Let all the girls and boys sitting here backstage be stricken with awe and confusion and envy. Let Mr. Grisham in his all-time meanness be smited like St. Paul before he was St. Paul. Let Mr. Grisham be knocked down from his white horse of self-righteousness. Let the whole theater turn to gold with the sound of my

*voice and everyone standing around who has ever said a mean thing to me
or ever rolled their eyes when I have tried so hard with all my heart to sing,
let them be made blind or deaf or dumb from Your impenetrable beauty.
Let their eyeballs implode or their eardrums explode or their brains catch
on fire. Let my voice cause the wicked to weep and kneel at the foot of Your
golden throne. I ask this through Lord Jesus Christ, amen.*

Thisbe does the sign of the cross, incorrectly, but earnestly
nevertheless. She stands, waiting in the wings, hoping her
prayer has traveled the incredible distance to God's all-power-
ful ears. When Mr. Grisham, anxious in his starchy blue collar,
announces, "Next . . . oh, we have Thisbe Casper . . . ," his face
a portrait of equal surprise and equal dismay, Thisbe leaps to
center stage, blinks into the two blinding spotlights, and nods
at Mrs. Peters, who smiles, sounding out the opening chords of
"There's No Business Like Show Business." As soon as Thisbe
opens her mouth, she imagines sunlight, glorious, immutable
sunlight pouring forth from her wavering lungs. She imagines
girls like Susannah Gore and Missy Plotz suddenly turning to
ash, the gum in their awful mouths becoming lead. She imagines the boys stunned by her unseemly beauty, the look of
astonishment appearing on their pimply faces, as they all fall
to a single knee, genuflecting. She imagines Mr. Grisham and
Mrs. Peters incapacitated by the sound of her tempestuous
voice, the notes curving in the air like jeweled birds, filling
their poor, withered hearts with a joy they have both long forgotten. She imagines the whole world falling silent, the whole
doubtful world, the world of narcissism and confusion, turning toward the radiant clouds overhead and nodding, all at
once, *Yes, I believe. That girl's voice, like a great golden instrument,
has forced me to believe,* before each of them, each agnostic, each
atheist, each unbeliever, falls to his knees. But that does not
happen. Thisbe, nervous, her knees shaking beneath her long

skirt, misses the cue for her first note, and when she finally does begin to sing, the sounds that issue forth from her mouth do not float. They do not hover. They do not turn anything to gold. Irving Berlin's words come crashing down at her feet, falling through the wooden stage, groaning like an old harpsichord being shoved off the top of a skyscraper. Thisbe opens her eyes and is surprised by the unkind cacophony, the terribly desperate noises she is now struggling to make. Her eyes dart about the small theater, as Susannah Gore and Missy Plotz do indeed fall silent, not from religious ecstasy, but from the awful disharmony now calling attention to itself at center stage. Mr. Grisham looks stunned, a single vein throbbing along the side of his pale skull. Mrs. Peters, at the piano, a dear heart, tries her best to play loudly, hoping to drown out Thisbe's awful, warbled soprano, but no, somehow it is impossible. Like a wounded dove, bloodied and disfigured, flapping against a vibrating windowpane, like a horse's whinny only moments before succumbing to the horrible machinery of a century-old mucilage factory, Thisbe's voice withers, her dreams of a lead part—any lead part—dashed, her solemn prayers going unanswered, for the moment at least.

AFTER SCHOOL, on that Thursday the twenty-first, after the utter disappointment of her failed audition, Thisbe rides her bicycle around the neighborhood, searching for Snowball, her neighbor's unrepentant white cat. Soon she spots the animal lurking beneath the Whitmores' thornbushes, and after circling around once more to be sure, Thisbe quickly hops off her bike and grabs the little white terror by its tail, dragging it from its shady hiding spot. Snowball is no doe-eyed angel. Thisbe has never been sure whether it is a he or she. But it wants nothing to do with God's love or Thisbe Casper. It lets out a loud hiss, clawing wildly at Thisbe's thin arms. She kneels beside the Whitmores' garage, with what she hopes looks like grace, closing her eyes, thinking of a new prayer, one that will offer redemption for a creature who has no interest in being redeemed. Thisbe mutters, "Let this poor animal know Your one, true, undying love. Let it find Your spirit in its small, empty world, and let a place be made in Your wonderful palace for its unkempt soul. Through Christ, our Lord, amen." As soon as the "amen" is uttered, Thisbe hears Mrs. Lilly calling for her cat, shouting from her backyard, clapping her hands, whistling, making soft kissy noises. Thisbe stares at the animal, look-ing deeply into its gleaming black eyes, searching for any sign of salvation. There is none. Snowball then lunges, scratching Thisbe's right hand with its dirty white forepaw, hissing as she turns it loose. It disappears in a small white flash back into the shade and safety of the Whitmores' thornbush. Thisbe holds her left hand to her right, trying not to cry, but the disastrous audition and the failed plea for the cat's deliverance are all too much. When she cries, it is quiet, tearless, almost completely imperceptible: one more unheard prayer.

THISBE RUSHES THROUGH the front door of her house, hurrying down the hallway as quickly as she can, so that she can be alone in her room. She crosses the threshold but stops as soon as her foot touches the first stair. Her father has built a fort in the den, with white sheets hanging like a kind of tent. The den is mostly dark, the window shades drawn, a single light glowing from inside the tent from a flashlight resting in her father's lap. Thisbe turns, slowly crossing into the room as quietly as she can. She can see her father sitting on the floor there, his silhouette unmoving on the white sheets. He looks like he is reading something. Thisbe leans over, near the tent's opening, and whispers to him softly.

"Dad?"

"Yes?"

"What are you doing?"

"Not much."

"Are you okay?"

"I'm okay."

Thisbe can hear something in her father's voice—a catch of some kind, like a window that has a hard time opening—and it makes her very worried. She leans over farther and pulls open the flap.

"What are you doing in there?"

"Just looking at some pictures."

Thisbe can see a big black photo album in her father's lap, the photographs glossy and dappled, their edges lined with dust.

"Do you want to look at them with me?" her dad asks, and Thisbe nods, shrugging her shoulders, climbing inside her father's small white fort. Her dad has not taken a shower today. His long face looks bristly and tired. He is wearing a dirty T-shirt and a pair of old running shorts, which are splitting along the seams.

"Why are you looking at these in the dark?" Thisbe asks.

"I don't know," her dad says. "I guess I felt like being in here alone."

"Oh, well, I have schoolwork to do if you want me to go."

"No, I want you to see some of these. Look here," he says, pointing to a small black and white picture, a single shot of an angled storefront, the sign above the shop window having just been bolted in place. TAILORS, the sign says. Beneath the sign are two middle-aged men, smiling, pointing up at the sign. Beside the two men is a small boy, nine or ten years old, skinny, in overalls, his front teeth missing as he smiles widely. "That's your grandfather there," Jonathan says.

"Who? The one with the dark eyes?"

"No, no, the little boy. The one with the dark eyes, he's your great-grandfather, Len. The other one, the skinny one, he was your great-uncle, Felix."

"The tailors."

"Yep, they were all tailors. Even Grandpa for a little while, when he was young. He used to work in the shop there. Before the war."

"Which war?"

"World War Two. When the war came, they had to close their shop. Then, at the end of the war, they all went back."

"Went back where?"

"To Germany. Your great-grandpa and your great-uncle. All of them except your grandpa."

"Why did they all go back?"

"They didn't like it here anymore, I guess. They were German and everyone was mad at the Germans, so they decided to head back over there."

"Oh. But why did Grandpa stay?"

"I dunno. I guess he must have liked it here. He wanted to build rocket ships. That's what he told everybody."

"I thought he made airplanes."

"He did. He designed them for a long time. Then he got tired of that. Then he tried a couple of different things, but none of them really worked out. So he was a consultant for a while and then lived off his pension. He wanted to design a plane you could fly into space but no one would give him money to build it. And then your grandma, well . . ." He pauses here, afraid to watch Thisbe's expression change. "Once she passed away . . . we had to move him up here. He's had a pretty incredible life when you think about it."

Thisbe looks at her dad's itchy whiskers and begins to get worried.

"Why are you looking at all these pictures, Dad?"

Thisbe watches as her father smiles, a smile that is not really a smile at all, but a frown struggling with itself.

"Your grandpa is not doing so good," he murmurs. "I think . . . I think we're maybe going to lose him. He seemed a little better this morning. He was up out of bed for a little while but he's not eating very much and he's stopped talking."

"That's why you're in here?"

Her dad smiles, scratching his nose. "Yep. I guess so."

"Dad, I'm sorry," Thisbe whispers, touching her father's hand. "But God is watching over him. And you. I know He is. He wouldn't forget you in a time like this."

"Thanks, Thisbe," her father says, smiling slightly.

"Can we go and visit him?"

"Sure. Sure we can. I think he'd like that. Maybe tomorrow night, how's that?"

"Okay. Well, I'll let you look at your pictures."

"Okay."

Thisbe touches her dad's knee with her knee and then, feeling very sad, she kisses her dad quickly on the cheek. She climbs out of the small makeshift tent, then makes her way upstairs to her room and closes her door. She decides to pray again, for as long as she can before dinner.

DURING CHORUS PRACTICE the next day, Thisbe day-dreams, wishing her voice were not the worst in the room. She wishes she could be at least as good as Mary Wesley, who can't sing anything but the most piercing notes, her voice spinning around the rehearsal space like a sharp-edged butterfly made out of tin. Even then, Mary Wesley is able to find a recognizable melody. As Thisbe considers this, playing the choppy chords to "When a Man Loves a Woman," and the rest of the girls do their best to follow Mr. Grisham's coaching—"Your voices need to really growl here, to really show some soul, now I know you girls have soul, some of you, at least, I am quite certain have soul"—she lets her fingers wander aimlessly, mangling the black and white keys. At the refrain, Roxie, looking bored in a blue sweater, opens her mouth and begins to belt out the words, the sounds rising through the small rehearsal room, echoing with confidence and obvious grace. Even Mr. Grisham looks up from his sheet music, while the other girls, Mary Wesley and Susannah Gore and Missy Plotz, all turn, dumbfounded, a little shocked by the petite blond girl's husky vibrato. Thisbe looks up as well, and sees Roxie is only joking, making fun of the other girls and their weak voices. Roxie's contempt does not matter. For the first time that afternoon, Thisbe plays the song as it was meant to be played, feeling her heart beating along with the tempo of the song. Roxie and the rest of the girls rush toward the end of the last verse, the last chorus, then one final note, like an exclamation point placed at the end of a very wonderful sentence. Done trying, Roxie stares down glumly at her feet. Mr. Grisham immediately begins clapping, pushing his glasses up, which have slipped during the musical fervor. He winks at Roxie once and then says, "Now, girls, that—that was something. That was sung the way it was supposed to be sung, with raw, exposed soul. Let's move on to the next one, 'Love Me With a Feeling,' and try to maintain some of that enthusiasm, shall we?" Mr. Grisham nods at Thisbe, who, flipping through her sheet music, finds the appropriate song and starts off, her fingers light, expressive on the keys.

But Roxie is no longer singing. She is standing in the back row, rolling her eyes again, chewing on a large wad of gum. The rest of the girls try to ignore her, doing their best, their voices adequate, not awful, not unpleasant, but certainly not glorious, certainly not the voice of our Lord Jesus Christ coming through the wan frame of a teenage girl. Thisbe stumbles through an A chord, then a second, and by the time the refrain arrives, she has completely lost her place. Mr. Grisham, equally upset, hastily shouts, "If you cannot keep time, Thisbe, I'm sure we can find someone else to accompany us!" Thisbe thinks of screaming back, of cursing him out, but does not. She simply nods, biting her bottom lip, and follows Mr. Grisham's orders to take it from the top.

THISBE LOPES TO where she has locked her bicycle up, embarrassed, trying not to think of how awful she was in chorus practice today. She unlocks the bike and slings her book bag over her shoulder, feeling sulky. As she begins to pedal off, she hears someone calling after her. She turns, almost falling off the seat, and sees it is Roxie, in her dark skirt and blue sweater, unlocking her own bicycle.

"Which way are you headed?" Roxie asks, and Thisbe immediately says, "Down Fifty-ninth Street." Thisbe stares at the other girl's face, so small and lovely, not a mark or blemish, not a single pimple. There is something in her haughty nose and green eyes that seems a little hard, a little bossy, a little petulant, but her mouth—wide, the lips large and animated, her voice hidden within, just behind her small white teeth—makes Thisbe feel both jealous and slightly smitten.

"Well, I'll ride with you, then," Roxie says, hopping onto her bike. Together, the two girls begin to pedal off, away from the shadow of the rectangular high school, down the Midway along Fifty-ninth Street, the grassy stretch rolling beside them, the world suddenly much more broad and forgiving. Thisbe tries to ride next to Roxie at first, but then Roxie pulls ahead, speeding away, laughing. Thisbe does not know if she should try to catch up and, feeling a little embarrassed again, she decides she should not. Roxie, still giggling, slows down beside her and asks, "You don't like to race?" to which Thisbe replies, "I do. I just didn't know we were racing."

"Oh," says Roxie, still grinning. "Next time, I'll say *go*, then."

"All right," Thisbe says, smiling.

"So do you always ride your bicycle to school?" Roxie asks.

"Sometimes. Sometimes my mom drives my sister and me."

"Wow, you're lucky. I wish my mother would drop me off."

Thisbe glances over and sees the other girl's cheeks are now flushed pink. Something comes unwound, some stitch somewhere. "Why don't you ever sing in chorus?" Thisbe quickly blurts out.

"What?"

"Why don't you sing? Like for real. Like most of the time, you're like only mouthing the words."

"So what? What do you care?"

"It just seems like you're not even trying."

"I'm not."

"Well, why are you in the chorus, then?"

"Because Mr. Grisham said if I was in chorus again this year, then he'd give me a good history grade."

"Wait a minute, you don't even want to be there?"

"No. I hate it. It's so stupid."

"Well, I think you should quit, then. It's not fair to the rest of us who want to be there."

"Duh," Roxie mutters. "I almost failed history last year. And since Mr. Grisham's my history teacher this year, he said if I sang, he'd help me get a good grade."

The two girls slow to a halt at a stoplight. Roxie looks over at Thisbe and smiles. "You really like it, huh? Chorus, I mean."

Thisbe is silent for a moment, then says, "I would give anything to be able to sing like you."

"Yeah, well, I'd give anything not to have to be there."

ON THEIR BICYCLES, the two girls pedal from the high school through the east part of the University of Chicago campus, the squat brick buildings rising up along Fifty-ninth Street, some surrounded by wrought-iron fences, some covered in ivy. Thisbe glances over her shoulder and wonders what her father is doing at that exact moment. Is he standing in front of a classroom or at home, looking through pictures in the den? Roxie pedals up beside her and whispers, "I love the way those old buildings look. Like they're haunted or something. They look like they're from some old movie. Like if you went to college there, there'd be like all these movie stars there or something. Like Gregory Peck and Angela Lansbury would be your teachers."

"Yeah," Thisbe mutters, still wondering about her dad.

"I'll never get into college," Roxie announces. "I just can't get myself to study hard enough."

"You could go. Anybody can go if they want to."

"I guess I just don't want to."

"Oh."

"So, do you want to ride down to the lake?" Roxie asks.

"The lake?"

"Yeah. That's where I go every day after school. I ride down there and just stare at the water."

"Okay, I guess," Thisbe says.

TOGETHER, THE TWO GIRLS ride past the tall high-rises and the Museum of Science and Industry, following the narrow sidewalk along Lake Shore Drive where it abruptly slopes downward, disappearing beneath the highway. The breeze blushes both of their faces as they pedal underneath the rumbling traffic, then reappear on the other side. The green fields of the lakefront seem to open up in all directions as they ride past the stone fieldhouse, following the curve of the lake farther south, winding above the glistening black rocks. The sun beats tiny freckles along their bare necks and noses. Finally the sidewalk seems to stop, and a thin dirt path extends through some high field grass and clover, where Roxie yells, "Go!" then hops off her bike and suddenly starts running. Thisbe begins to laugh, careful not to stumble, laying her bicycle beside Roxie's, before following her through the tall grass. The sound of the wind whispering through the field is a song, a simple poem, with one sustained note. Thisbe catches up with Roxie, finding her lying down on her back, staring straight up at the blue sky.

"Look," Roxie says, pointing. "Look how big the sky looks."

Thisbe nods, lying beside the strange blond girl, staring up at the cloudless field hanging above them.

"Sometimes I come here and lie on the grass and pretend

to fly," Roxie says. "I just lie here and listen to the wind and hold my hands out and fly off, like there isn't anything above or below me."

Thisbe blushes a little, happy to be taken into Roxie's confidence. She stumbles, trying to think of something to say, and then whispers, "When I was little, I used to wish I was a bird."

"Yeah?" Roxie sits up a little, tugging at the dry grass around her. "I used to wish that, too. I wanted to live in the trees and fly around all the time and never have to land."

"I used to wish I was a dove," Thisbe whispers. "So I could sing."

"You can sing."

"No, I can't. I'm not any good."

"You're fine. Grisham doesn't know what he's talking about."

"No, I really can't. I'm really awful at it."

"You can't be that bad. Go ahead and sing something," Roxie says.

"No, I can't."

"You just have to not care about what other people think. If you're afraid, you'll sound like shit. Go ahead. Try it."

"I'm just not as good as everybody else. I wish I was but I'm not."

"Here," Roxie says, leaning beside her. "Go ahead and sing something. I want to see how you do it."

"What do you mean?"

"I bet you're singing with your nose. Just sing something."

Thisbe shakes her head and says, "Fine. But don't make fun of me. Okay?"

"Okay, stop being so gay and just sing something."

Thisbe closes her eyes, holding in a breath, trying to concentrate. She opens her mouth and begins to sing "Ave Maria," but what comes out is discordant, harsh, lacking any melody. She opens her eyes and sees Roxie, kneeling beside her, smiling.

"You've got to sing from your diaphragm. Didn't Mr. Grisham go over that?"

"Yes," Thisbe says. "I am singing from my diaphragm."

"No, no, like this," Roxie says and holds her hand over her own belly, belting out the first few notes of "Ave Maria." What, only a few moments before, had sounded so much like heavy, leaden bricks, now seems easily turned to silver, floating up into the sky, whole and unreachable. Thisbe closes her eyes, placing her hand over her own stomach, and tries again. The notes give a little, bending slightly, as if they are really trying to find their spots in the air, but after a second or two, all of them come tumbling down awkwardly, not a single one taking flight.

"No, no, like this," Roxie says and places her hand over Thisbe's stomach. Thisbe immediately shudders, then relaxes, closing her eyes. The backs of her knees begin to tingle nervously. Roxie says, "Try it again," and presses lightly on Thisbe's belly. Thisbe opens her mouth and tries "Ave Maria" a third time, and all of a sudden the first note seems to ring out, like the sound from a peculiar and brilliant organ, the melody finding its way for a single moment, and then, blinking her eyes with excitement, Thisbe forgets herself and the rest of the phrase tumbles out hopelessly from her open mouth.

"See, you almost had it," Roxie says, smiling. Her hand is still on Thisbe's stomach and Thisbe does not know why. There they are, both of them still lying in the grass, the sky open before them like a still and bottomless lake. Thisbe's heart is beating hard, pounding with the joy of very nearly succeeding. The sound of the breeze rushes around her head, the other girl's fingers still pressing against her flat belly. Roxie's hand feels warm, the palm cupping the shape of her stomach, not moving, and then it is gone. Something flutters in Thisbe's chest. Roxie turns toward her and smiles.

"Pretend you're flying," Roxie whispers. "Pretend you're a million miles above the earth and you are as light as a feather."

"Okay," Thisbe says, grinning.

"No, go ahead and close your eyes."

"Okay."

Thisbe closes her eyes and feels Roxie take her left hand. It startles her and her heart immediately leaps, floating from her thin chest, as if gravity has forgiven itself. The wind whistling in her ears, the soft flutter of the field grass rising and falling like unhinged clouds, the remembered weight of the other girl's hand resting on her stomach, all give Thisbe the feeling she is flying through the sky, weightless, soaring. And then she is. She is sure of it. She is actually flying. She is a few dozen feet above the ground, drifting up into the sky. It is one of the most remarkable feelings in all the world, the feeling of having let go of the confines of the surface of the earth, of being happy, without order or meaning or regret.

"Don't open your eyes," Roxie says.

"Okay."

Thisbe has the sense that God is watching her, her hand in this other girl's hand, that she is somehow closer now, drifting near the cloudy reaches of Heaven, and His own unearthly love. The sunlight on her face feels like the certain warmth of God's grace. *He is watching me now*, she thinks. *He is really watching me.* Thisbe feels like singing again or shouting out her love of all things to the rest of the world. *He is real*, she wants to cry out. *His love is really real.* Thisbe feels the soft grass beside her, grasping it to keep herself from drifting off into perfect cloudless oblivion. *Of course He is here*, she thinks. *Of course He would live in a field like this, hidden but not so very far away. This is the place. This is the place where I can sing, where I can fly, this is the place where God lives.*

"We are drifting off into outer space," Roxie murmurs. "Wushhhhhhhhhhh."

Thisbe is unsure what to do now or what she should say, the other girl's fingers still gently gripping her own.

"We are like a million miles away," Roxie whispers. "More than a million."

"It's like heaven," Thisbe murmurs. "We are flying up into heaven."

"We are up, up, and away."

Thisbe laughs and opens her eyes suddenly. The two girls fall gently back to the earth and face each other, both of them unmoving now and lying in the grass. They are still holding hands for some reason. Slowly, the fingers of Roxie's left hand are moving along Thisbe's wrist. Thisbe finds she is no longer breathing. Roxie's fingers are sliding along Thisbe's palm, running back and forth over her knuckles. A spot begins to glow somewhere between Thisbe's legs. She realizes this and feels revolted and dizzy and sickly excited. Her heart seems to unfold, like a handwritten note, like a letter tumbling open. The contents of the note reads, *Please . . . please . . . don't move your hand away, please . . . please, I'd like you to please . . .* , but in her mind, Thisbe has no idea what else the note should say. She does not let go of Roxie's right hand. She does not know why she doesn't. She feels ashamed, then quickly ignores the shame, and feels more shameful, having done that. Roxie's breath is hot against Thisbe's neck and face, the field grass softly poking the back of Thisbe's legs. She feels like she is about to come apart, slowly disintegrating into one million pieces of brightly colored glass. Just then Thisbe begins to wheeze, her labored breath coming and going in tiny rasps. Roxie has opened her eyes, rimmed with black mascara, and is looking over at her, surprised at the awful sound coming from Thisbe's open mouth. Roxie draws her hand back and gives Thisbe a quiet, puzzled look.

"It's my asthma," Thisbe whispers, sitting up. "It's the grass . . . I . . . I don't have my inhaler. I . . . I have to go." Thisbe, feeling her lungs contracting, as tight as her nervous, beating heart, stumbles through the grass toward her bicycle. Then she begins pedaling off, the whole world spinning around her, as if she is riding her bicycle somewhere in the sky, as if gravity has finally just given up.

ONLY A FEW BLOCKS away and Thisbe is home. She dashes to her room, finds her asthma inhaler on her nightstand, and takes two quick pumps, breathing as deeply as she can. Falling into her bed, her breath returning to normal, she touches her own wrist, still feeling the other girl's hand moving there. She is disgusted, the shame trembling all across her body. Closing her bedroom door, she lunges to switch off the lights, and then nervously searches through her Bible for some relevant prayer. It has been a test, that's all. It was only a test, a test of silly thoughts and stupid, useless temptation. Like Job. Or Jonah and the Whale. They hadn't really flown. Roxie's hand had not lingered on her wrist all that long. It was all only in her mind anyway. Thisbe thumbs through the Bible, still searching for something, anything, to read aloud. All she can find is the "Act of Contrition," which she mutters aloud over and over again.

Ten

Or an airplane that could fly to the moon? Perhaps an aircraft made entirely of helium gas? Or a zeppelin that could fly as fast as a rocket ship? Henry sketches another idea in his notebook, outlining the shape of a compact-looking airship, then glances up at the gloominess of the recreation room. He has been wheeled here against his will by the nursing staff, abandoned to the worthlessness of Arts and Crafts. It is Friday, October 22. Only seven days left. Henry looks around the room, nodding with surety. A blond volunteer, a young woman with a lisp, is showing the residents how to knit. She holds a bundle of yarn in one hand and two long silver needles in the other. When she kneels beside Henry, offering him a collection of blue yarn, he shakes his head, reminding himself of the seven solemn words he has allotted himself today. Without uttering a sound, he wheels himself off toward the corner of the room, where he begins to summon his few remaining memories. From his pocket, he retrieves a small metal airplane, a toy from his childhood, an object no bigger than his hand. He stares at its wings, at its hollow cockpit, the sounds of its propellers echoing within his head. Oh, so very long ago, he thought he would fly. Sadly, he sets the toy down in his lap and then snatches up his notebook. One by one, he scribbles impressions from his nearly forgotten past down on the blank pages, tearing the pages out from the small notebook, slipping each one into an envelope, watching as they glow and then fade.

To Whom It May Concern,
Your father's hands were as small as a child's, smaller than yours were when you were five years old.

To Whom It May Concern,
What your father and uncle did was shameful.

To Whom It May Concern,
    The only time you believed in God was at night, because
you were afraid.

. . .

As a boy, Henry would lie in bed, terrified of the dark, unable to utter a single sound. Most of the time he would squint in the faint light from his windows reading *Adventure* comics or the latest issue of *The Airship Brigade*. If he was too frightened to do that, he would crawl into his younger brother Timothy's bed, waiting to hear the soft-throated songs of the birds echoing in the dawn, their whistles signaling the start of each morning. Then, as the sun had just begun to climb, Henry would hear his father, staggering about the tiny kitchen, the sound of the coffeepot slowly rumbling.

Henry's father Len was a tailor who owned a small shop near Lawrence and Lincoln Avenue with his younger brother Felix, their family name, CASPER, painted in gold letters on the glass window. Henry always fell silent when he was frightened, uncertain, or unsure, but he loved the noise of his father's shop: the sewing machines as they whirred; the steam press as it gasped; his father's voice, loud and brusque. Standing at his father's elbow, he would watch Len's tiny fingers as he worked a single thread through a long silver needle, shortening the cuff of a sleeve or taking in the hem of a serge pant leg. His father, tall, wide-shouldered, and dark-eyed, had been born with unbelievably small hands, which were a blessing in his chosen profession, though back in Nuremberg, where he had been born, they were a source of great embarrassment for him.

What Henry loved best about the tailor shop, which he and Timothy would visit each day, were the sheets of brown butcher paper his father would give him to sketch on, and also the loud static of the worn-out radio echoing along the counter, and most of all, his father's grand stories—tales of the

Brave Little Tailor and of old giants and of beautiful German fairies—which Len told with pins held in the corner of his mouth. As the little yellow clock on the wall approached four o'clock, Henry's father would stand, leaving his work at his sewing machine for a moment, and switch on the old honey-colored RCA radio. He would then light a cigarette, staring out the front window of the shop, as the announcer recited the grim news from London and Europe. Then he would switch the radio back off, return to his stool, and begin telling a story; the sound of his booming, excited voice was the exact opposite of the silent, dreaded night, a silence that gathered in the cobwebbed corners of Henry's tiny room each evening. Staring down at his sons, watching the sun slowly beginning to set, Len would wink at them both and begin to speak:

"Once upon a time, my boys, all the birds decided they would like one master. One of them would be made king. A meeting of the birds was called. They flew from the forests and the meadows and all the fields. And, yes, all of the birds came: the little sparrow, the robin, the owl, the finch, the eagle. The woodpecker came, too, and the vulture, and every other kind of bird, too many for us to name. And there was great noise from so many birds, every kind of song and whistle you can think. Then, after all the talking and the singing, it was decided that the one bird who was the bravest, the one who could fly the very highest, would be made the king."

Henry and his younger brother stared up into their father's face as he told them the story of the King of All Birds. His father, with his dark, expressive eyes, could be surprisingly meek, his extraordinarily small fingers deftly stitching the most minute seams, his voice becoming a whisper full of melancholy and splendid dreams.

. . .

ONCE, WHEN HENRY was four years old, the tailor shop was completely overrun with moths—moths: the dreaded pestilence of all thrifty, honest tailors everywhere. It had happened almost overnight—a widow by the name of Ansel had brought in a winter coat to be altered and two weeks later, the small brown insects fluttered about in clouds of feathery dust, while their offspring did serious harm to a number of furs, shirts, jackets, and trousers. Len, however, refused to kill a single one, scaring them from the inside sleeves of a rabbit-fur coat, urging them through the open tailor shop door. Chasing a particularly large, brown-specked intruder into one of the shop's corners, Len called Henry to his side and pointed, whispering in his storytelling voice: "*Nachtfalter.*"

Henry blinked, unsure of the word.

"A moth. We called them *motte*, in Nuremberg. They are magic creatures, did you know?"

Henry shook his head. His younger brother, Timothy, crept up quietly beside him. Len, their father, gently cupped his hands, capturing the moth in the prison of his fingers.

"They're messengers. They carry the souls of the dead, these do. At night, when everyone is sleeping, they do their work. They are the messengers. That is why you mustn't ever harm them. They are very important. Very special."

Henry took a step closer, staring down at the delicate insect, its gigantic wings flapping slowly.

"They tell us when someone will be sick or if a war is coming, and how long the winter will be, and how fierce, too. When they are worms, when they have the hair, you can look at them and know by how black their hair is how bad the winter will be."

The moth crept suspiciously over the knuckle of Len's small thumb.

"We are like this moth, Henry, no? They can do lovely things like tell the future and carry the souls, and they can do bad things, too, like eat up all our thread. Now they give us trouble. Look at this mess."

Henry turned then and saw his uncle Felix smashing a moth against the wall with the sole of his shoe. Henry's father began to shout until Uncle Felix slipped the shoe back on his foot. The next few days were spent chasing the moths from their hiding spots, Henry cupping them in his hand, against his chest, watching them take flight, nervously flapping their dusky wings in search of starlight.

PERHAPS THE APPEARANCE of the moths did mean trouble. Each afternoon following their arrival, some fellow German business owner would stop in the little tailor shop for a coffee: Mr. Kratz, who smelled of formaldehyde and who owned the funeral home down the street, a man who often needed suits and dresses altered for his recently departed customers, or Mr. Himmler, who owned a porcelain shop but grew tired of the lonely stares of his plates and dolls. Nearly every afternoon, someone would stop by and share a cigarette with Henry's father and discuss the terrible situation in Germany.

IN APRIL 1932, only a week or two after the incidence of the moths, Henry sat in the little tailor shop drawing a picture of a man riding a bicycle with metal wings like a bird. At the counter, Mr. Kratz, in a dark brown suit, whispered to Henry's father and uncle the latest news.

"They have passed a new law to stop these brownshirts from marching. I am proud to see them showing some spine."

"It won't do any good," Henry's father, Len, said. "If the people are mad enough to march, a law won't stop it."

"Maybe yes, maybe no," Mr. Kratz answered, his polite way of disagreeing. "They do not need any more trouble. What they need is work, I think. Let them put those men to work so that they can make money for their families. They need to be more patient with Herr Bruening."

"It's hard to be so patient when your children can't eat," Henry's father said. "My heart goes out to them."

Henry lifted his head from his drawing and looked at his father's face, which was stern and long and sad. Quickly, he drew the same expression on the minuscule man riding the flying bicycle, then a great black cloud gathering over him.

AT THE COUNTER of the tailor shop each morning, Henry's father would read the *Chicago Sun* searching for news from Nuremberg. In the late afternoon, Mr. Kratz would come in to share a cigarette with Henry's father, and ask him what he had read or heard.

"Nothing," Len would say. "And you?"

"Bloody Sunday. Three hundred wounded in Prussia," Mr. Kratz whispered. "My cousin has sent me a telegram saying it is very bad. They are killing communists now, with the police's help. I read a newspaper report from England saying the same."

"We must wait for the new elections in August," Henry's father said. "We must not get excited until we know what is happening there."

"Maybe yes, maybe no," Mr. Kratz said. "I am afraid those elections will be a fraud."

"We must wait," Henry's father said, poking the eye of a needle with the end of a piece of thread. "We will know soon enough."

ON JULY 31 OF that same year, 1932, their waiting came to a dreadful end. Mr. Kratz hurried into the little tailor shop with a telegram from his cousin in Nuremberg, the bright yellow paper still trembling in his hand.

"That madman has taken over!" he shouted. "My cousin has asked if we can find him a place to stay."

"That madman is the only man who is saying what needs to be said," Henry's father replied, standing beside the sewing machine. "If it comes to force to save the lives of a man's family, then that's what it takes."

Mr. Kratz only blinked, then stared down at the telegram again.

"But Mr. Casper, surely you see what is happening. There is blood on Hitler's hands already. What will become of a country with a leader such as that?"

"I don't know, Mr. Kratz. All I know is that I have this little shop. If I didn't have it, I couldn't keep my children healthy. I have a wife who is ill and a family to take care of. I do not know what I would do if I could not work. No, I do not agree with their ways, but we are not there. I think a man who puts his hand out to help another man is a hero."

"Maybe yes, maybe no," the old man said. "A man who calls out for blood so soon does not seem like the man to help anyone. I'm afraid he cares very little for the families you mention. I'm afraid this is only the ugly face of greed. I have seen it before, in Bismarck, and here, in this country. It is the root of all man's troubles, wanting more than he needs. Mark my words, Mr. Casper. That man is no hero at all."

Henry's father nodded.

"Your garment for the Lunt funeral will be ready by the end of the day, Mr. Kratz. Maybe around four."

Mr. Kratz nodded, stubbing out his cigarette.

"Then I will come for it at that time, Mr. Casper."

On his way out, the old man, his white hair slicked with pomade, a white flower in his lapel, stopped and looked down at Henry, busy at work, drawing steadily on his brown butcher paper in silence. The old man leaned down and smiled, patting the boy on his head, saying:

"Henry here is the wisest. One day he'll draw himself a flying machine and find a way to climb aboard and then he'll float away from us all." Then the old man gave the glass door a soft push and disappeared into the humid air.

WITH HIS LITTLE white flower reeking of formaldehyde, it was poor old Mr. Kratz who could not help but be right. By the beginning of December 1941, the world had changed terribly: Europe was a battleground of red and silver flames, while back in the States, the RCA radio sitting on the counter of the little tailor shop buzzed with the static of an inevitable war. Len, Henry's father, stared at the radio gravely, as it brought news of the Axis armies marching brutally across the Continent.

Henry, now thirteen, though not nearly as tall or as imposing as his father, worked in the shop every day after school: sweeping up, working at the counter when needed, making deliveries on his bicycle. Timothy, Henry's young brother, had no interest in the family business and stayed in the small tenement to care for Bluma, their mother, who lay prostrate in bed, muttering her vespers in German. That winter, she had lost another pregnancy, her third. Henry did not know how he should behave around her. He preferred the electric noise of the shop to the grim echo of her prayers reverberating about the graying apartment.

"Be careful with these garments," his father warned, as the boy set off on his bicycle. "This fabric is delicate. It is important that you do not pop the stitches."

Henry, older now, with his dark brown hair and hazel eyes, nodded, placed the packages—wrapped in the brown butcher paper—in the basket of his bicycle, and pedaled off. The boy often pretended that the garments were actually top-secret confidential messages being passed from one spy to another. As he rode along Lincoln Avenue to the first address on his list, he imagined he was being followed. The boy favored circuitous routes when he played the game, doubling back on his own path, crisscrossing from one delivery to another by the most complicated directions possible. There were his regular deliveries, all Germans: some were elderly resident aliens— who spoke in gruff tones and did not tip him at all. Others were younger, stylish, American-born Germans—who, receiving their tightly wrapped garments, sometimes offered him a nickel or a piece of hard candy. Then there was Mr. Miner, who seemed only as old as Henry's eldest brother, Harold, who, for all his hard work and study in high school was now only a grocery clerk. He no longer lived at home, and was hoping to one day become an assistant manager at the supermarket. Mr. Miner was the same age but wore expensive, terrifically cut black suits, his black hair pomaded and well trimmed. To Henry, he was as handsome and glamorous as a movie star, certainly as rugged as Clark Gable. Mr. Miner came into the little tailor shop nearly once a week with a different garment—a pair of slacks, a new suit coat, a jacket. Carefully, Henry's father measured the dapper young man's arms, waist, and chest with the yellow ruled ribbon, making the appropriate chalk marks on the fabric. Some two or three days later, Henry would pedal down Western Avenue to the small apartment Mr. Miner kept above an insurance office. A record would be playing inside the apartment when Mr. Miner would answer the door, something loud and brassy, like Jimmy Dorsey or Glenn Miller.

"What's the password?" Mr. Miner would say with a smile, holding up his first finger and thumb like a pistol.

Henry would smile and look down at his feet, embarrassed.

"What's the password, kid? Hurry up and spill it or there's gonna be trouble."

Henry would grimace behind his hand and then whisper, "Hound's tooth."

Mr. Miner would squint at him, then nod, and take the brown package from his hands. Then, flipping out his wallet, he'd slip out a crisp green dollar bill and plant it in the young man's hand.

"Don't tell your father where you got it from, okay?"

"Okay," Henry would say.

Mr. Miner would pat the kid on the shoulder, then slip back inside his apartment, slamming the door closed. Henry would stand there in the hallway, still smiling, his face flush with embarrassment as he stared down at the dollar in his palm.

MORE OFTEN THAN NOT, the dollar would go toward as many issues of *Adventure* comics as he could buy. The comic book featured the ongoing exploits of *The Flash, Hourman, The Green Lantern*, and Henry's favorite series, *The Airship Bri-*

gade. Standing alone in the alley behind the tiny tailor shop, Henry would finger the creased pulp pages, reading every enthusiastic word, staring for long moments at every panel, every drawing—the amazing golden zeppelin, code-named the X-1, the Airship Brigade's teenage commander, the dashing Alexander Lightning, the scientist Doctor Jupiter and his beautiful daughter Darla, Tor the herculean Man-Ape, and the lovable, bumbling Hugo—Alexander's boyhood chum—all of them busy at the mechanized controls of the airship, flying high above the glowing lights of some city—Henry memorizing every half-toned ink dot, every pulpy illustration. Standing in the near dark, in the snow-filled alleyway, Henry would watch as the empty skyline swiftly disappeared and became something spectacular, something unexplainable, something amazing.

OFTEN, RIDING BACK from Mr. Miner's apartment, with the dollar tucked securely in his back pocket, Henry would begin to narrate the latest episode of his favorite hero's adventures, having read and reread it so many times that the words had become a bright-sounding refrain in his head.

"Alexander Lightning, teenage boy, supreme commander of the Airship Brigade, has only his magnificent airship, the X-1, to rescue his friends, who have all been shanghaied by spies from the dark side of the moon. What will he do, dear readers, what will he do?"

Whizzing past the park on Western Avenue, Henry would glance at the clock on the Great American Savings Bank to see how long he had been gone on his deliveries.

"Flying the fearsome vessel through the cloudy reaches of outer space, our hero only has one hour before his fellow brigadiers meet their end at the hands of the menacing Lord of the Moon."

Henry, dashing down Irving Park Road, would squeal to a stop in front of the drugstore on Lincoln, leap down the aisle to the magazine rack in the back, and grab as many new issues of *Adventure*, *Airship Brigade*, *All-Flash*, or *The Justice Society* as he could afford. The clerk, some older lady in gray glasses or a boy roughly the same age, would watch Henry mumbling to himself as he approached the counter, glancing around the drugstore for a clock.

"Our hero only has twelve minutes left," he would whisper. "Only twelve minutes."

Then, grabbing wildly for his change, he would hop back on his bicycle, check to see if he was being followed by some Martian spy or rogue G-man, and pedal back to his father's tailor shop, slipping the comics beneath the long green bicycle seat. Throwing the front glass door of the shop open, he would clamber inside and ring the bell on the counter to signify that he had returned, looking up at the yellow clock that was hung above his Uncle Felix's sewing machine.

"The world is saved once again," he would whisper, nodding in victory. "With no small thanks to our hero, Alexander Lightning, teenage boy, supreme commander of the Airship Brigade."

ON MONDAY, December 8, the day after the attack on Pearl Harbor, Henry sat beside the honey-colored radio in the tailor shop, listening to the terrible exclamations about the sinking of the American fleet. At his sewing machine, Henry's father listened for as long as he could, before standing up and switching the radio off by turning its great golden knob.

"That is enough of that," he said.

Henry nodded, leaning over to sweep the dust into the dustpan with the end of the broom. Henry's father bundled up a pair of shiny black slacks in a sheet of brown paper, tied the knot tightly, and handed the package to Henry: a delivery.

"For Mr. Miner. Be careful not to drop it or to wrinkle it."

Henry nodded again, pulled on his winter coat and hat and mittens, then took the package and placed it in the basket of his bicycle. Glancing over his shoulder for enemy spies, he started off, quickly turning down a side street. Just then, he noticed a black sedan pull away from the curb. The sedan was beautiful, with a silver grille and bright hubcaps, exactly what Henry imagined a spy or enemy agent would drive. Behind the wheel were two stern-looking men in gray felt hats. Henry glanced over his shoulder and grinned, just as the sedan took the turn, slowly easing down the narrow street in pursuit.

"Our hero, Alexander Lightning, pursued by enemy agents, finds his radio-ring is suddenly not working. He is unable to contact his fellow brigadiers."

Henry popped a wad of gum into his mouth as he skidded along the snowy street.

"With two enemy spies hot on his trail, the young commander makes a bold move."

Henry hit the brakes, darting in between two parked cars, then up the curb and along the sidewalk to the opening of an alley. The black sedan veered speedily, hitting its brakes, its rear lights blinking red as it lunged in reverse. Seeing the car stop, Henry realized something was wrong. The sedan heaved backward, then stopped again, and turned down the alley.

"Our hero is in serious trouble."

Quickly, he pedaled along the narrow alleyway, past discarded cardboard boxes and overflowing garbage cans, the sedan moving swiftly behind him. The car began to honk, then flash its lights, and Henry—terrified of most strangers, let alone those following him so closely—let out a yelp. The sedan drew beside him, still honking its horn. The passenger, a man in a gray overcoat and hat, unrolled his window and shouted out to him:

"Hey, kid. Hey kid, we just want to talk to you."

But Henry, frantic now, was too frightened to speak. Small silver tears poured from the corners of his eyes. He flew out of the alley and turned quickly to the right. He double-backed the other way along the west side of the street and hurried back to Western Avenue, where he thought there would be more traffic. For a moment, hurtling back toward his father's shop, he grinned, thinking he had lost them, but then the sedan rounded the corner at the end of the block and flashed its lights twice in his direction. It quickly pulled alongside him.

"Okay, kid, listen, we just want to talk to you is all."

The guy in the passenger seat, big with square shoulders, opened the door and began to climb out. Henry let out a nervous peep and sped past him, darting down the avenue, past a woman with her groceries and some kids having a snowball fight on their stoop. The sedan was wheeling around now, cutting across traffic, its yellow headlights glaring angrily. Henry's bicycle slipped back and forth, careening over the wet snow.

"The Airship Brigade teen commander is in deep, deep trouble. Our hero is going to be murdered. Our hero is going to be put in those villains' trunk."

Henry slowed as he crossed Lincoln Avenue. He took a right, then another quick right, which he knew was a straight shot to Western Avenue, where Mr. Miner lived, where he hoped he would be safe. Pedaling slower now, his lungs tight in his chest, he glanced over his shoulder, past the rows of parked cars and drifts of gray snow. The street behind him was empty. He smiled a small nervous smile, his face red from fright and exertion, then pedaled down the alley behind Mr. Miner's apartment. Hurrying down the gangway to the front of the building, Henry bolted for the front door, holding down the door buzzer much longer than he normally did, as a signal to let Mr. Miner know that he was in dire trouble.

"Hello?" came Mr. Miner's calm voice.

"It's me, it's Henry," he said, pulling on the door, which was still locked.

"What's the password?" Mr. Miner joked.

"Mr. Miner, Mr. Miner, I'm in trouble," he whispered, still holding down the call button.

"Hold on, pal, hold on."

Suddenly the front door mechanism buzzed and swung open on its hinges. As he took the stairs one, then two, then three at a time, he thought he heard the footsteps of someone behind him, but he was too afraid, too full of cowardice to face those men again. With the brown package in his hand, Henry made it up to the third-floor landing just as Mr. Miner's apartment door opened. Mr. Miner was in a red robe, his hair as shiny as wet plastic, a long cigarette between his lips, looking collected, suave, his forehead unwrinkled, his narrow mouth a little smile of vague concern.

"What's the matter, kid? Who's after you?"

Henry was too scared to speak, his heart pounding so loud in his chest that he could not think. He fell to one knee, handing the brown package to Mr. Miner, who regarded it with a large smile.

"Okay, okay, kiddo, who's tailing you?" Mr. Miner asked, and then, as if they had been summoned, the two enemy agents from the black sedan marched up the stairs, their black shadows falling across Henry's red face. Seeing them, Mr. Miner frowned, the cigarette tumbling from his mouth, and slowly, gracefully, he backed into his apartment. But the enemy spies were out with their guns quick, both of them. From his spot on the floor, Henry gasped at the guns' bright, oiled certainty. Mr. Miner kept slowly backing into his apartment, raising his hands, as the two agents commanded him to be still. Henry could see Mr. Miner's red slippers move inch by inch until he had backed over the threshold of his apartment, and then, as quick as a nightclub magician, he saw Mr. Miner reach for something—was it a gun, too?—from behind the doorframe. Before he could raise his weapon, the bigger of the two thugs jammed his pistol hard against Mr. Miner's temple, then backed him with force against the shiny black door. A smallish, .22-caliber snub-nosed pistol, looking exactly as it did in the comic books, clattered from Mr. Miner's hand to the carpeted floor.

"We got it, Burt," said the other agent. "We got it, take it easy."

The agent reached down and grabbed the brown package, then, stowing his gun back in his holster, he began to slowly untie the white thread.

"What do we got?" Burt, the bigger man, asked. "What's it look like?"

"It looks like clothes," the shorter one said. "It looks like a pair of slacks."

The bigger man, Burt, frowned, and then gave Mr. Miner a shove.

"What's with the slacks? Spill it and maybe we can go easy."

Mr. Miner, a greased black forelock of his hair dangling

over his white forehead, only smiled, shrugging his shoulders. "Gentlemen, I believe there's been some kind of mistake," he said.

The two agents glanced at each other, then shook their heads. Burt pressed his pistol harder against Mr. Miner's temple, growling. "We know all about you and your pals, Silber. You might as well come across with what you know."

"I believe you have mistaken me with someone else."

The big agent laughed, nodding toward his partner.

"Pete, show him the credentials."

Pete, the shorter of the two, with gray hair and thin tired eyes, reached into his coat pocket and removed a leather wallet, which he flipped open to reveal his badge.

"Maybe you've heard of the FBI?" Burt asked.

Mr. Miner did not seem very impressed.

"I have done nothing wrong as far as I know of."

Pete looked down at the gray slacks again, eyeing the fabric, inching his fingers along the thread, checking all of the pockets carefully. He ran the cuff between his finger and thumb, nodding.

"Very fancy duds for a radio repairman. Where does a fellow like you get the money for a high-price item like this?"

Burt grunted a little at this and turned toward his partner.

"Maybe we give his place a once-over, what do you think?"

"Sounds wonderful."

Burt turned to Mr. Miner, knocking him in the head with the barrel of his gun as he spoke. He reached into his coat pocket, found a pair of silver handcuffs, and slapped them on Mr. Miner's wrist.

"Now, you don't try anything brave, Mr. Fancy-Pants, and we won't have to ruin your nice little robe there, how's that?"

Burt backed Mr. Miner into his apartment, pushing him toward a red velvet sofa.

"Take a seat and make nice."

He then turned to Henry, who was still kneeling, trembling, out in the hallway.

"You, the kid from the tailor shop? What's your name?"

"Henry Casper."

"You stand there and tell me if he moves, okay?"

Henry nodded, crossing into Mr. Miner's apartment. The apartment itself—which Henry had never seen before—was gloriously decorated with ornate statues of Greek nudes and lush oil paintings of pastoral scenes. Henry glanced around the place, his eyes moving from an enormous radio set, to a stack of books, to many, many rolls of unfolded blueprints. On the sofa, Mr. Miner smiled at him, sighing, moving a few inches to his right. As the two agents tore open drawers, upended the black wooden table, threw letters and papers to the floor, Mr. Miner only smiled, staring directly at Henry, who was fixed in terror beside the door. When the two agents holstered their guns to move a large piece of white antique furniture—some sort of curio cabinet—Mr. Miner winked at Henry, sliding as far as he could to the other end of the sofa.

"What do we got here?" Burt asked, staring at a large gaping hole in the plaster wall. "Look's like Mr. Silber here has been keeping secrets."

"Maybe he didn't know working for the Germans was against the law," Pete said with a grin.

"Maybe he forgot which country he was living in."

Henry did not make a sound, only watched in horror as Mr. Miner, glancing out of the corner of his eye, flung himself up from the couch toward the shiny white-paned windows. By the time the two agents noticed what was happening, Mr. Miner had lifted open the window closest to him, his handcuffed hands shoving the latch upward, and had gotten one of his red slippers up onto the ledge. Henry stood watching, his heart beating wildly, his mouth open, but unable to make his tongue and teeth work.

"Silber, my God, don't move," one of the agents shouted.

The last thing Henry saw was Mr. Miner's black eyes, as he winked just once, and then disappeared into the cloudy air, the red sash from his robe flapping like the tail of a kite as he flew decisively from the ledge. In his heart, Henry hoped that the man had somehow flown away, but he knew it was impossible.

By NIGHTFALL, a gang of federal agents had surrounded the Caspers' little tailor shop, and had torn the place apart from floor to ceiling—wrecking their old twin sewing machines, cutting up newly stitched garments, smashing the honey-colored radio. Henry, watching it all from atop his bicycle in front of the shop, saw his father and his uncle Felix marched out in shiny silver handcuffs, the yellow measuring ribbon still in his father's vest pocket. His father's face did not look outraged: only ashamed, his dark, wrinkled eyes small, his mouth weak-looking with embarrassment. While Felix, younger, full of fight, shouted and shoved at the empty-faced agents in their matching gray hats, Henry's father Len looked down at his feet as he was led past neighbors and customers. The shop—the thing Len had been most proud of in his life, even more than his ailing wife and his three children—was in ruins. His son, with his bright, questioning eyes and quiet, piercing gaze, sat atop his green bicycle, watching its destruction from outside.

"Tell your mother what has happened," his father said as he was led past. "Tell her I am not a spy. I did not do what they say I have done."

But as he stared at his father's long face, while the agents shoved him through the December snow into the backseat of a black sedan, Henry knew he had seen that same look on countless men, in serial films and in the final pages of dozens of *Airship Brigade* comics. It was the look of a guilty man, a villain, a crook. Henry's father was one of them—the black-hearted enemy. Having seen Mr. Miner step from the ledge of his own window, Henry did not wonder if his father and uncle were lying. Why else would the FBI be arresting them? No, it was becoming clear now. There was no longer any doubt in his mind. His father *was* guilty—of what, Henry wasn't exactly sure—but by Len's dull, weak-lipped expression, it was obvious he had been caught at something. Maybe he was a villain and, worse, a traitor, a spy—the most cowardly villain of them all. And now, having been captured—as spies in comic books never succeed, always crumbling at the feet of the hero in the final panel on the final page—his father was gone, abandoning Henry and his family, and for what? What do spies in comic books ever hope to gain? Money? Secrets? Power? All of it was useless now. And worse, without his father, without Uncle Felix or the tailor shop, how would the family live? A deep hatred began to glow silently within the boy's chest as the first sedan pulled away, then the others, all disappearing into the wintry light. Watching them go, Henry climbed from his green bicycle, then crept into the ruined shop, his heart beating hard in anger and shame.

Henry could barely look. Bolts of linen, silver tools, spools of thread, had all been upturned along the front of the shop. The stores of fabric strewn about, the recently mended garments had been trampled upon by wet, dirty shoes. Looking around the tiny shop until his shoulders began to tremble, Henry climbed behind the counter, then through the black curtain into the back of the store, searching through the unmended clothes that had been tossed about in mismatched piles. Leafing through the yellow claim tags one after the other, then moving to another pile, then another, he finally came upon what he was looking for: hidden beneath an inconspicuous black suit coat and white dress shirt was a yellow paper tag marked *Nachtfalter* in his father's writing. Henry tore through the plastic cover and found a pair of gray slacks, hemmed in the style Mr. Miner preferred. The waist needing mending, or so the note on the tag said. Henry moved his fingers along the waist and saw that the hem there was perfectly intact, the white thread as steady and unbroken as any he had ever seen. Moving his finger along the stitches, he felt what he had been searching for against his fingertips: there was an almost identical hem, all around the waist, but broken, in short lines and dashes. Holding the pants up to the fading winter light, Henry could see the thread was not stitched to hold the hem in place. It was a message, a secret code of some kind, left in his father's infinitesimally small stitches just a few millimeters below the real hemline, the evidence hanging there in his grasp: his father, with his cunningly small hands, was a spy, a traitor, a coward. Henry ran his finger along the message and felt his small heart shrink in his chest. He stormed from behind the black curtain, found a pair of scissors on the floor, and began to tear the false stitches apart, splitting the pants at the same time, until they no longer resembled a garment of any kind.

One by one, he searched through the other clothes in the narrow back room, flinging them from the shelves. At once, a tiny brown moth flittered from its hiding place, frightening

Henry as it swooped to an empty spot on the bare wall. He stared at the small creature for a moment, and then squinted his eyes, before he slammed the palm of his hand against the insect, watching the delicate-winged moth drift heavily toward the floor. He did not bother to lock the door of the shop behind him as he climbed onto his bicycle and pedaled the three blocks back to the tenement, overcome by the terrible feeling that the world, like the little tailor shop, like all of the garments within, had suddenly come undone.

> *To Whom It May Concern,*
> *You did not forgive your father for what he did or did not do.*

When Henry has finished scribbling this new letter, this last memory of his fading childhood, he folds the note inside the envelope, licks the seal, scrawls down the address, licks the stamp, and wheels himself toward the front desk. Without a word, he hands Nurse Rhoda the letters, then rolls himself forward, pausing before the glass security doors.

"Keep moving, Mr. Casper," Nurse Rhoda calls out, glancing suspiciously over the counter at him. Henry does not respond to her command, not immediately. Instead he stares at the smudgy glass divider, memorizing its exact shape, already planning his next escape: "Once I'm gone," he mutters, "please don't remember me."

Eleven

As Jonathan finds his way back from the research lab to the unlit den late that Saturday evening, tired from visiting with his father all afternoon, he pulls off his double-knit sweater, unbuttons his shirt, and, on his hands and knees, crawls beneath the white sheets that hang like long tent flaps. He is startled to find Madeline there, in her white nightgown, bare shoulders freckled and glowing. He starts to mutter something, but his wife puts her narrow finger to his lips and then helps him unbutton the rest of his shirt, and soon they are kissing, their tongues exploring each other's mouths, and Jonathan cannot remember the last time they kissed like this: they are like grad students all over again, making out in the stacks of the university's library or in her tiny apartment afraid that her ditzy roommate might stumble in at any minute. Off come his pants, off comes her nightgown, and soon they are having intercourse, her limbs pressed against his limbs, their bodies tensed and moving in one delightful motion, Jonathan staring deeply into his wife's brown eyes, wanting to say something, to thank her for waiting here for him, for knowing everything, but as soon as he opens his mouth to speak, she shushes him again, closing her eyes, a narrow smirk across her face. When they are done a few minutes later, Madeline pulls down her nightgown and crawls away through the flaps of the fort. Jonathan reaches out for her shoulder and asks, "Wait, where are you going?"

Madeline smiles and says, "We're still fighting."

"What? We are? Why?"

"Why? Why do you think, Jonathan?"

"I got to be honest, I really don't know."

"Well, for one, because you are totally in your own world. For two, you expect me to take care of you and the girls and the house and the bills but you're not willing to do the same for me."

"But you just had sex with me," he mutters.

"It doesn't matter. We're still separated," she says, then disappears into the darkness of the poorly lit house.

THE NEXT DAY is a Sunday, and in his office on campus Jonathan searches through the long list of his electronic correspondence. There is a response from *Dragonflydr*. Jonathan clicks on the miniature white electronic envelope and begins to read:

> *Jonathan Casper,*
> *You are a coward. You do not have any bravery in your blood and like the animals you study you will hide in the dark and be doomed to a life of the most mediocre kind. With regrets,*
> *Heidi Arzt*

Sighing, he deletes the message and tries to finish his notes for tomorrow's lecture, which is supposed to be about the evolutionary connection between physical traits and emotion. When the dull beige phone on his desk begins to ring, Jonathan, apprehensive, glares at it and lets it buzz once, twice, a third time, before answering.

"Hello?" he mutters.

"Jonathan? It's Ben Brandt. From the Hausman Institute."

Jonathan cringes. "Hello, Ben." He pinches the spot between his eyes and begins to shake his head. "You're calling me on a Sunday?"

"I wanted to try to get ahold of you today before you got the bad news from someone else tomorrow morning."

Jonathan sighs.

The Hausman Institute is a benevolent, though not very imaginative scientific organization, and the major funder of Jonathan's stalled prehistoric giant squid project.

"It's about your grant. We . . . we've had to pull your funding for next year."

"Why?" Jonathan whispers. "Why are you doing this to me?"

"Jonathan, we just wanted to let you know that we think you are doing incredibly important, really sophisticated work. But because of financial constraints and the sheer number of new applicants this year, we're unable . . . well, we've had to make the hard decision to no longer continue your funding."

"What am I supposed to?" Jonathan hisses, his teeth clicking against the phone. "What am I supposed to do now? This is my life. This is the only thing in the world that matters to me and you're cutting me off at the knees. You're fucking—" and, promptly remembering himself, his voice, his tone, "You're fucking castrating me."

"Jonathan, I know you're upset, but I'm sure there'll be other funding opportunities for you. I was speaking with Laura Hamlin, from the Manguson Foundation—"

"Laura Hamlin is an evangelical Christian. Those guys, those guys don't want anything to do with evolution. They'd like us to spend our time searching for Noah's ark."

"Jonathan, I hear your frustration, but the last thing I want to do is give you the impression that we don't believe in the work you've been doing. We're just not able to fund it any longer."

"Ben?"

"Yes?"

"Fuck you."

Jonathan slams down the phone, holding his hand over his face. Fuck, fuck. Fuck. Fuck. Fuck.

WHEN JONATHAN PULLS the Peugeot into the garage that evening, he notices the Volvo is missing. He crosses the small backyard, pushes open the back door, which is unlocked, walks down the hall to the family room, and collapses into his gray chair. Amelia and Thisbe are lying in front of the television, watching some drama about teens in southern California. Jonathan glances around and asks, "Where's your mom?" but the girls only shrug.

"Did either of you guys eat yet?" he asks.

They both mutter a depressed no without turning from the TV.

"Does anybody know what time it is?" Jonathan asks.

Amelia sighs and looks at her wristwatch. "It's like eight-thirty."

"How long have you been watching TV?"

"An hour," Amelia lies.

"Then you're done after this show."

"Fine," she whispers.

"Well, do either of you guys want something to eat?" he asks.

"No," Thisbe says, staring expressionlessly at the TV.

"No," Amelia says, turning over on her back.

"Well, I'm going to go make myself something to eat."

"Good," Amelia mutters.

"Good."

Jonathan sucks in a breath and pulls himself out of his chair. He putters around the kitchen, opening and closing the cabinets, the refrigerator, not interested in anything he sees. He finds a half gallon of milk and drinks a long draught, then caps it and places it back in the fridge. He sniffs around again, opening and closing the same cabinets. Why is there no junk food anywhere in the house? Why not a Ding Dong or a Twinkie? Why not some hot dogs or frozen pizza? Where the fuck is Madeline? It's eight o'clock on a Sunday night. What is happening to them? Does she still love him? Is she getting fucked by some dude with enormous biceps right now? Why can't they just be unhappy together? Why can't they just live like regular miserable people?

Glancing down the hallway at his two daughters, both of them lit up like zombies from the blue glow of the television, Jonathan skulks off to the den, where once again he switches off the lights, climbs through the opening of his fort, and pulls the sheet over his head. With the flashlight resting in his lap, he imagines he is at the bottom of the ocean, the sandy silt of silent, undisturbed civilization far above him. He starts to cry, the sound bursting like bubbles of dismay, rising through the air.

• • •

ASLEEP LATER THAT EVENING, beneath the shadows of the white sheet, Jonathan is awoken by the sound of the telephone ringing somewhere beneath the rubble of the den. He crawls through the opening of the fort, searching frantically for the phone, finding its cord, then follows it to the receiver itself. On what may be the third or fourth ring, Jonathan answers it groggily.

"Hello?" His voice sounds like he's still underwater.

"Dr. Casper?"

"Yes. Hello?"

"Dr. Casper?"

"Yes, this is him. Who is this?"

"This is Ted," and then some mumbling on the other end. "And Catherine is here next to me."

"Who?"

"Your grad students, Dr. Casper."

Jonathan nods, though there is no one around to see him do that.

"Ted?"

"Yes?"

"Do you have any idea what time it is?"

"It's about two in the morning, sir. Two-twelve actually."

"Why are you calling me at two-twelve in the morning, Ted?"

"Sir, we didn't know if it was appropriate to phone you but we both felt it was important."

"Okay."

There is more mumbling on the other end.

"Catherine wants you to know she did not think it was appropriate to call you."

"Okay."

"But we both agreed that we thought maybe you'd like to know."

"Know what, Ted?"

"It's the French, sir."

Jonathan then realizes he is standing. He is standing and sweating all of a sudden.

"The French?" His heart is beating hard now, his hand clenching the phone tightly. "What about the French?"

"Sir . . ." He can hear the grad student thinking, the sound of his lips parting and his tongue against his teeth. "Sir . . ."

"Just say it, Ted."

"They found it, sir. *Tusoteuthis longa.* They think they got one. It was just on CNN. Catherine saw it and then came over and woke me."

"CNN."

"That French scientist, Albert, he was on TV. I guess they found it near Japan."

"Japan."

"It was in international waters. That's how they got it so fast. Do you want to meet or something, sir? Catherine thought maybe you'd like to discuss a— "

"No," Jonathan murmurs. "No."

"Well, we can be at the lab as early as you need us, sir."

"Ted?"

"Yes?"

"Go back to sleep." Jonathan hangs up the phone, setting the device back on the carpeted floor where he found it. Staggering, he stumbles through the dark, down the hallway, and finds the television remote. He switches the TV on and then begins flipping through the channels, finally finding CNN. There behind the anchor desk is a bright-eyed woman, finishing up some news story about the latest tragedy in Iraq. Then the camera switches angles and she turns, her expression changing, softer now, pleased to introduce something less awful, less dreadful, a pixelated photograph appearing in a box above her shoulder announcing: SEA MONSTER DISCOVERED!

Jonathan, leaning forward, turning the volume on the television set up and up and up, stares in both wonder and a wretched sense of sadness as the news anchor announces, "And now some breaking scientific news: a few hours ago, researchers announced the discovery of a species of giant squid thought to be extinct for millions of years. An international team led by Dr. Jacques Albert of the French Sédimentologie Association made this surprising scientific find off the coast of Japan. Considered by many as the leading expert in the field of evolutionary science, Albert has been searching for this particular species of squid for more than a decade . . ."

Jonathan switches off the television, his face falling into his hands. All of his work, all of his work is nothing now, completely useless. Gone, gone, gone. He is too upset to even cry, to even make a sound, though he hears himself gritting his teeth. He looks up, staring into the darkness of the television room, wishing he were dead. A glow, a glimmer of light suddenly catches his eye. He turns and stands, staring out the curtained windows. There is something standing in the backyard. There is someone standing in his yard at two in the morning. Slightly panicked, Jonathan carefully parts the curtains and sees it is Madeline, in her white nightgown and robe, staring up at the trees. She is holding a flashlight in her hand and she is looking up at something.

Twelve

A. Beginning that Monday, Madeline follows the cloud in her Volvo every day after work. The cloud seems to follow the same general route, stepping northeast toward the open expanse of the dark blue lake, standing in the air for an hour or more. Madeline will park in the emergency lane to watch it, listening to NPR or the Beatles. Then the cloud will start moving north toward downtown, like some celestial commuter, momentarily disappearing in the windows of the highest skyscrapers, then reappearing, silently circling back to its spot just above the family's garage. Perhaps it is waiting for something. Madeline does not know. Sometimes the cloud-figure will veer from its normal path, heading way off course to the north, stopping over a particular row of trees along the lake. It is in these moments, uncertain as to where the cloud-figure might be going, that she feels strangely content, suddenly sure of life, of everything, the front seat littered with Diet Coke cans and candy bar wrappers, the Volvo swift and unsteady, swerving happily in and out of traffic.

B. Madeline decides to make a map of the cloud-figure's movement in one of her research notebooks. The map, drawn in erasable black pen, describes a large ellipse, a flattened-out circle. The cloud always heads northeast, then north, then west, then south, ending in Madeline's backyard. Madeline does not think about anything while she is driving, not Jonathan, not his father, not her awful failing experiment—the birds are still murdering each other—not her daughters, who have become distant and obnoxious, not the incident between her and Eric, the other researcher, not the war in Iraq, not the president, not the poor captured soldier who is waiting to see if he will lose his head, not anything other than the cloud-figure itself.

C. Night after night, Madeline hurries home from work, rushes into her backyard, and begins the long circuitous path through the city, wondering exactly where the cloud will go next, following the cloud-figure late into the evening. In the backseat of the Volvo, Madeline has even packed a suitcase with a few days' worth of clothing: work attire and makeup and even a toothbrush. She has slept in the car these last few nights—following the cloud to where it hovers doubtfully above the lake—parking in one of the lakefront lots and climbing into the station wagon's backseat to try and get some sleep.

Tonight Madeline listens to the radio while she sits in the driver's seat, waiting there alone in the dark, parked near the great blue lake. It is already one o'clock in the morning. The cloud-figure has not moved for the last two hours, drifting along an empty span of gray water and black rocks. Bored, Madeline switches the radio on, tuning it in to NPR. In the darkness, she hears a rebroadcast of the third and final presidential debate between George Bush and John Kerry, their voices distant and trebly. Bob Schieffer, the moderator, asks, "Will our children and grandchildren ever live in a world as safe and secure as the world in which we grew up?"

John Kerry responds: "I believe that this president, regrettably, rushed us into a war, made decisions about foreign policy, pushed alliances away. And, as a result, America is now bearing this extraordinary burden where we are not as safe as we ought to be."

George Bush: "Yes, we can be safe and secure, if we stay on the offense against the terrorists and if we spread freedom and liberty around the world."

Switching the radio off, Madeline then climbs into the backseat. She lies down on top of the uncomfortable vinyl and folds her arms under her head, staring out the windows at the nighttime sky, thinking, *When did we get so used to having to always fight somebody? When did we get so used to the idea of war? How come no one's really talking about how terrible the idea really is? How come no one's asking any questions? And how come there are no protests? How come there's no rationing? No rubber drives? How did war become such a distant, everyday thing?* She thinks of what her parents had to go through during World War Two, and what it was like growing up during Vietnam, she can still remember girls in her class crying during the Pledge of Allegiance each morning. She remembers her older brother shouting at her father, and a few friends and boyfriends her own age hoping the war would end before they would be eligible for the draft. She remembers watching a protest, somewhere downtown, and all the people involved were all just kids, only a few years older than she was. *How come my own girls aren't more upset by what's happening? Why doesn't it seem more important to anybody? And how come no one's affected by anything like they used to be?*

Thirteen

WITH THE BLACK BERET ATOP HER HEAD, HER WEEK
and a half of suspension served, Amelia walks into school
that Monday morning dressed as a cloud. The cloud outfit
is made out of cardboard and has been painted shiny black
and gray. Amelia waits to be sure her mother is gone and her
father has left for school before she carries it out of her room,
through the kitchen, and out the front door. Amelia has come
up with a new plan for her history project: she will prevent
the further spread of capitalism by making the world aware
of how far-reaching the influence of soulless corporations
already extends.

During her lunch period, Amelia takes a confident position
in front of the Coca-Cola machine in one of the corners of
the cafeteria. She holds her hands out when a young freshman
tries to get herself a soda pop, bravely announcing:

"Do you have any idea of how many third world workers
have died just so you can have a can of Coke? Hundreds. Maybe
thousands. Do you know Coke has its own death squads in
Central America? Do you know they won't let their workers in
Colombia have a union?"

The girl, shy, with enormous silver braces, shakes her head. "I didn't know," she says.

"The storm cloud of capitalism casts its shadow over everything," Amelia declares. "But communism is on the march. We can overcome corporate greed if we all just work together."

The girl nods and stumbles off, unsure of what has just happened, staring down at the unspent change in her palm. A few minutes later, another student, a lanky boy wearing silver headphones, approaches the soda machine, counting out the shiny quarters in his hand. Amelia leaps in front of him, her cloud costume awkwardly chafing her neck.

"Did you know that last year an independent study was conducted by the Center for Science and Environment in India and they found that Coke had thirty times the legal amount of pesticides in their drinks, pesticides which lead to cancer and totally destroy the immune system?"

The boy is silent, trying to understand what she is asking.

"Did you also know that Coca-Cola is made with high fructose corn syrup, which has links to obesity and type two diabetes, and that Coca-Cola knowingly uses this ingredient instead of something else because it's a lot cheaper?"

"Why are you telling me all of this?" the boy asks, looking from the sparkling change in his hand up to Amelia's shiny face.

"I'm telling you all of this because I'm trying to keep you from making a terrible mistake."

"Don't you have something better to do?" the boy asks quietly. He forces his change into the pop machine, grabs his Coke, and then walks off without glancing back.

A few minutes later, a third student, a surly-looking senior with a wadded-up dollar bill in his fist, approaches the soda machine. He pushes past Amelia with such force that he bends a large corner of the cloud outfit. "Nice potato costume," the large boy mutters, quickly inserting his dollar bill.

"Excuse me?" Amelia asks.

"I said nice potato costume."

"It's supposed to be a cloud, dipshit."

Amelia sneers at him, but the boy ignores her, snatching his can of soda pop, happily strolling away.

After an hour of this, of the self-centered guffaws, of the mediocre wisecracks, of the unintelligent answers, Amelia gives up and finally removes the cloud outfit. She forces it inside her locker, irreparably crushing it—the cloud now looking more like a misshapen fruit or malformed rock—before she rushes off to her English class.

WHEN AMELIA STRIDES into the school newspaper's office after fifth period, she expects to be greeted as a journalistic hero, like Woodward or Bernstein, or like somebody else famous for standing up for something, but instead she finds she has been summarily demoted to "Culture Vulture," the lowest of the student newspaper's ranks. Mr. Wick tells her this without looking her in the eyes once.

"I think, with your intelligence, you will be able to add a new level of scrutiny to the assignment."

"What am I supposed to be covering, Mr. Wick? Football games? Pep rallies?"

"Well, there's popular music. And also television."

"Television? Are you serious?"

"You might find it a great challenge."

"Well, who's going to be the paper's editor if I'm not?"

"Well, Mr. Stuart, he, well, he insisted on finding someone that better represented the personality of the school."

"Who? Who is it?"

"William Banning."

"William Banning? He's the president of student council. How can he be the editor of the school paper? Don't you understand anything about checks and balances?"

"Amelia, I know you're upset, but you have to understand this is only a small school paper, after all."

"Maybe to you. But I don't believe there's such a thing as a small revolution. You fired me and put someone totally unqualified in my place. And now you want me to write about TV shows. This, this is a complete joke. William Banning? You got to be fucking kidding me," she shouts, storming out of the *Midway*'s office, her neck turning red, a prickly sensation beginning to rise. She can feel it happening, the intolerable itching, a formation of pinkish hives spreading all along her bare arms, her neck, her wrists. Amelia tosses her books on the ground, holding her speckled hands over her face. Two seniors, Bret Standler and Mickey Dupre, stare at Amelia as they pass. One of them whispers what Amelia thinks she hears as "Lezbo." Amelia glances up at them and hisses, "I will fucking destroy you!" The surprised boys, like two frightened animals, quickly hurry off.

HAVING SKIPPED lunch in order to challenge the empire of American capitalism, Amelia decides to ditch her sixth-period class so she can buy an enchilada. She sits alone in the rear of the rectangular cafeteria with the wormy little freshmen. As she's unhappily eating, someone takes a seat beside her. It is a boy, a tall, skinny boy with blond hair, wearing a blue sweater. Amelia glances at him out of the corners of her eyes and feels her whole body tighten. It is William Banning, the student council president, the new editor of the school paper, and her greatest arch-nemesis of all time.

"Amelia?"

She ignores him.

"I just . . . I just wanted to say how awesome it's going to be working with you. I think . . . I think your stories are really good. I mean, the last one . . . the one about the lunch ladies— "

"Cafeteria workers," she corrects, still refusing to look his way.

"Right, the cafeteria workers, well, that was, I mean, that was really insightful and like everyone was talking about how great it was."

"Wonderful," she hisses, shoving another forkful of enchilada in her mouth.

"And, well, I thought . . . I was hoping, you know, that it would be cool . . . I mean, I'm really excited to have . . . the opportunity to be working with you."

Amelia slams down her fork and faces him. His nose is crooked, she realizes. His eyes are gray and he is not as handsome as she had thought he was. She stares at him, narrowing her eyes and clenching her teeth. "The only reason they asked you to be editor of the paper is because this school is just like this country. It's full of cowards. You and I are not going to be friends or buddies or whatever you had planned. As far as I'm concerned, you don't even exist. And if you even try editing my work, I will totally emasculate you." She sighs, then turns again, lifting up her fork.

"Oh . . . okay, well . . . I just wanted to . . . I just wanted to try and make sure things were, you know, cool."

"William. I think you are a total imbecile. Someday soon, like in college, or whatever, you're going to find that nobody cares that you were a track star or were on the stupid student council. This place, this place has nothing to do with the real world. Until then, just leave me alone, okay?"

"You really don't like yourself very much, do you?" William asks, then stands and quickly walks off. Amelia sets down her fork and stares down at the miserable food on her plate, then throws it in the trash with an inaudible scream. As she does this, she sees the backs of her hands are now covered in bright red spots.

AMELIA DITCHES MOST of her last-period class and heads over to the university to find Professor Dobbs. She waits at the back of the lecture hall, a gaggle of bright-eyed girls surrounding him, batting their stupid eyelashes, gushing like cheerleaders. Professor Dobbs, seeing Amelia there, smiles, and in one silent move he winks his eye at her, revealing his disdain for the noisy, girlish exuberance around him. Finally they are alone, and, placing his hand on her shoulder, he says, feigning disappointment, "Amelia, I would love to spend a few moments with you but I've got a four o'clock meeting with the dean. Maybe sometime later this week?"

Amelia nods, looking away, "Sure, I mean, it's not like . . . a big deal. I just thought . . ."

Professor Dobbs checks his watch and then, glancing around, he leans close and says, "Okay. We've got ten minutes."

AMELIA FINDS HER FACE in Professor Dobbs's lap again. In the faculty parking lot, behind the questionable cover of the Saab's tinted windows, Amelia sighs, closing her eyes, bobbing her head up and down. She hides her spotted skin from him, gently pushing his hands away from the hives that have appeared all over her body. When he ejaculates, it ruins her dark gray blouse.

AFTER THAT, Amelia sulks in her room, playing her French music much too loudly. She switches CD after CD, from Edith Piaf to Brigitte Fontaine to Air. Anything foreign, anything sad, anything that suits her shitty mood. After a half hour of this, her sister, Thisbe, knocks at her door. When Amelia doesn't answer, Thisbe slowly opens it, poking her head in.

"Amelia? Hey. Um? Are you sleeping?"

"There's a reason my door's closed, asshole! Stay the fuck out of my room or I will waste you!"

Amelia rears up out of her bed and shoves the door against her sister's head, locking it closed. Amelia's hives have not gone away. She has taken like a hundred Benadryl, she has put clear calamine lotion all over her arms and neck, she has tried to lie in her stupid bed and just relax, but nothing is working. She falls back onto the mattress, closing her eyes, pulling the pillow over her head, but her sister keeps knocking. Amelia, furious now, leaps to her feet and rips the bedroom door open. Thisbe, wide-eyed, takes a step back, cowering a little.

"Why don't you leave me the fuck alone! Or are you too stupid to understand English?"

Thisbe backs away toward the staircase, looking at her sister with trembling lips. "I didn't do anything wrong . . . Dad told me to come get you . . ."

"What?"

"He said we're all going to visit Grandpa now."

"Well, tell him to fuck off. I'm not going."

"He said we both had to go."

Amelia slams the door, pulling at her hair, throwing herself on the bed.

"I am not fucking going," she whispers, starting to cry, the sores on her arms beginning to shine and blister. "I refuse to fucking go. I am sick of being pushed around. I am not going to go." She rolls over and switches the CD. Searching through her stacks of jewel cases, she finds a Sylvia Vartan album and pops it in, turning the volume up as loud as it will go.

Moments later, there is another knock. It is Thisbe again, now wearing her gray jacket. She is holding Amelia's black coat in her hand. "Dad said to stop pouting. And he wants you to bring your radio."

AT THE FAR END of her grandfather's hospital bed, Amelia does her best to avoid his sunken face. He does not look like her grandfather anymore. He is not smiling. His eyes are weak-looking, only flicking open every few moments. His body seems to have shrunk. He looks like he is made of twigs. Finally Amelia has to look away, glancing anywhere but at his feeble shape, her eyes darting from the television set—which is on, though muted—to the plastic cafeteria tray beside her grandfather's bed. And in doing so, Amelia catches sight of something sitting on top of her grandfather's dresser. Almost at once, she sees it: a small silver airplane, an old metal toy, just about the size of her open hand. *Help me*, the airplane calls out to her. *I do not belong here. I could be something more than what I am. Make something useful of me.* It is perfect. It is the perfect addition to whatever it is she is supposed to be building. Amelia quietly marches over to inspect the toy plane and, looking over her shoulder to be sure her father or sister are not watching her, she stealthily slips it inside her purse.

When Amelia turns around again she sees that her stupid sister Thisbe is holding her grandfather's hand. Thisbe is brushing his thin white hair with a black comb and kissing his forehead like a newborn baby. "There, now you look handsome," Thisbe says. Amelia rolls her eyes. No one notices. Their father is busy plugging in Amelia's CD player. Finding an open outlet behind the hospital bed, he turns it on, adjusting the volume carefully.

"Look what we brought you, Dad," Amelia's father says, placing the radio beside the old man's bed. "Listen." He opens the CD tray and puts in an unlabeled disc, then hits play. Immediately the tiny white-tiled room is filled with the warm swell of violins and trumpets, a slow bass beat tapping along with muted drums. Thisbe claps, then, taking her grandpa's hands, she pretends to dance with him.

"It's Glenn Miller, Dad. You always said you liked Glenn Miller."

Amelia's grandfather nods. He measures his words carefully, already down to four. "I'll miss you all," he says, his eyes momentarily bright again.

Amelia frowns. She doesn't say anything. She watches her dumb little sister trying to dance with her crippled grandfather, detached, disconnected, uninterested in any of it. Her father takes a seat beside the bed, holding the portable player in his lap. "I brought some Woody Herman, too, Dad. The girls here, they thought it would cheer you up."

Their grandpa nods, his face expressionless.

"You're not going to die, Grandpa," Thisbe chirps. "We've been praying for you."

Their grandpa does not seem impressed by that. He closes his eyes as Thisbe continues to move his hands about, still pretending to dance. Amelia sighs, glancing out the small window at the top of a line of trees. She stares down at her watch, then out the window at the trees again.

"Amelia, tell your grandpa about what you've been doing. Dad, Amelia is writing for her school paper. She's doing very well."

Amelia rolls her eyes.

"I don't know, it's just stupid stuff. About school and stuff."

"Maybe we can take him for a walk," Thisbe suggests.

"I don't think he's strong enough yet," their dad explains. "Maybe in a couple of days."

"Maybe never," Amelia says to herself under her breath.

"How about some Woody Herman, Dad?" Amelia's father asks. He pops open the CD tray and exchanges the discs. "Listen to this, Dad, do you remember this one?"

Her grandpa closes his eyes, smiling, maybe nodding off.

Amelia shakes her head, standing up, anxious. Her father frowns at her. "What's the matter, kiddo?"

"It's really depressing being here. I mean, he doesn't even recognize us."

"He recognizes you guys."

"No. It's like we're totally bothering him."

Her father nods. "Okay. Well, why don't you go take a little walk or something?"

"Where? It's all like old people out there."

"Well, I don't know what to tell you, Amelia. Your grandfather's not doing so well. He might not be with us for much longer. You need to be a little more considerate. If you want to go wait in the car, you can. But I think you ought to say goodbye to him for now at least."

Amelia crosses her arms in front of her chest. Her hives, still itchy, are now dull and fleshy. She stands beside her sister, leans over her grandfather, and kisses his wrinkly cheek. "I'm sorry," she whispers and then rushes out, taking the car keys from her father.

ON THE RIDE HOME, Amelia stares out the passenger-side window, watching as the dark skyline flashes by. Without looking at her father, she suddenly asks, "Did Mom move out?"

"I don't know," he says without heat. "I think she's taking some time for herself right now."

"Well, I think it's ridiculous that you guys aren't getting divorced. I mean, like why do you guys keep acting like everything is going to be fine?" She looks over at her dad, but he is pretending to be busy driving and does not answer. When the Peugeot nearly stalls at the next stoplight, her dad glances in the rearview mirror at Thisbe, then over at Amelia, and whispers, "Amelia. Someday you're going to have to learn that being nice is much more important than being able to say everything you think."

BUT THE VOLVO is parked in the garage when they arrive home. Amelia, in the passenger seat, almost smiles seeing it. Then she actually does, turning away from her father, the slightest grin appearing on her face. The family stumbles lifelessly into the house and Madeline, sitting before the television, says hello. That is all. No one asks her where she's been. No one asks how long she is going to stay. No one tries to talk. The family, for one brief moment, all glance at each other, then cross silently into their separate worlds, Amelia and Thisbe climbing upstairs, Madeline returning to the television, Jonathan closing the door of the den, all of them disappearing without another word.

. . .

Amelia, finally alone in her room again, hunches over the nearly finished explosive device lying on her desk. The dresser drawer of stolen and found items hangs open across the room, the tragic voices of these disposed and disposable products no longer crying. Instead there is only an odd metallic hum, as if each object is quietly vibrating. Amelia hardly notices this strange sound, however. In front of her on the desk is the silver digital watch stolen from the principal's secretary. There is the cigarette case from Professor Dobbs. There is the old metal airplane belonging to her grandfather. She will use them all. She will take these mass-produced, insignificant objects, the detritus of a rampant capitalist system, and make something meaningful out of them. The silver watch will be the bomb's timer. The matches from the professor's cigarette case will be torn from their matchbook, their flammable heads will be carefully clipped off from their paper necks, and then they will be refashioned as the bomb's main explosive. The old metal toy itself—once hollow—will become the bomb's container, the vessel, once it is packed fully with the match-heads and mixed with some black fireworks powder, which Amelia thinks she still has somewhere in her room, the remnants of a failed science project from last year. Carefully, Amelia will insert the lead wires through the plane's cockpit—the object's only opening—and then she will close up the cockpit with several passes of black electrical tape. Before she does any of that, though, she has to get her hands to stop shaking. She glances from the three newly liberated objects to the spools of tiny red and black wires, comparing these components to the diagram on her computer screen. With her hands still trembling, she begins snipping off the match heads with a small pair of scissors. She holds her breath with each cut, until there are enough match heads to begin to place inside the silver airplane. One by one, she slips them through the cockpit's opening, trying to avoid any sort of friction. And somehow the amateur pipe bomb does not explode.

Fourteen

THE VERY NEXT DAY, TUESDAY AFTERNOON, FINDS Thisbe singing with Roxie in the Caspers' garage. They have decided to start a band. Now is the time for such bold moves, while her father has retreated to his fort in the den and her mother has all but vanished. Each of the girls sits on an orange milk crate, Roxie playing a bright pink guitar that is covered in Magic Markered words Thisbe is unable to read. Roxie is strumming the guitar wildly, playing a song Thisbe does not recognize. Already, like chorus, this is not going so well. First of all, the girls are not allowed to use Roxie's amp. Thisbe's dad has already said no, in a rare moment of actual fathering. "Bob Dylan did not need an amp until after he was famous," her dad argued. "Same with Joni Mitchell. Both of them didn't need amps." Thisbe, unfamiliar with the works of either musician, had no choice but to agree. But now it all seems kind of stupid. Roxie says so anyway. "This is kind of stupid. I mean, how can we be a band if we don't use amps?"

"Maybe we should make some songs up first. Then we can practice them and when we're good maybe we can play them with amps."

"Okay, fine, whatever. Do you have any songs?"

"No," Thisbe says. "What about you?"

"No."

"Well, maybe we can write one now," Thisbe suggests.

"Okay, I don't care."

"Okay, so should we write the music first or the words?"

"I don't know. The words."

"Okay," Thisbe says. She reaches into her book bag and finds her math notebook, the back of which is filled with her failed attempts to redeem the neighborhood's pets. Thisbe ignores these numerous tally marks and retrieves a ballpoint pen. "Okay," Thisbe says. "What should our first song be about?"

"I don't know. Elephants."

"Elephants?"

"Yeah. Like how they have their own graveyards and everything."

Thisbe taps the pen against the page, unsure.

"What?" Roxie asks, strumming the guitar again.

"Nothing. It's just that I don't think people sing songs about stuff like that. It seems kind of like a joke."

"Well, that's what makes it cool."

"I guess."

"Well, what are your big ideas?" Roxie asks.

"I don't know. Like about Love and Heaven. That kind of stuff. Like the songs from musicals. Important songs."

"Listen, this is just supposed to be fun, right? Why are you making it all serious?"

"I'm not," Thisbe whispers, though she knows she is.

"You are."

"We can write our first song about elephants, I don't care. It's fine."

"Well." Roxie nods, then gives the guitar another strum. "You start it."

"Okay. Um. How about like . . . *Elephants don't forget you when you leave the room . . .*"

Roxie smiles, clapping her hands. "That's good. Write that down." She strums the guitar again, making a C chord.

"They don't ever forget you, remembering is what they do . . ."

Roxie slowly switches her fingers, making an awkward G.

"I wish you were an elephant, I wish I knew how you feel . . ."

Thisbe closes her eyes, smiling, holding the pen before her open mouth like a microphone.

"I'm getting tired of trying to find you because you don't even seem real."

"Wow, cool," Roxie says, giving Thisbe a gentle shove. "You're like a poet. You're totally like a good singer when you don't try."

"I don't think so," Thisbe whispers.

"No, you totally have like a good talking voice."

"Wow, thanks," Thisbe whispers. "You were good, too." She shoves Roxie back, her hand touching the other girl's shoulder, the feeling momentary, electric. Before she can begin to feel awkward again, or guilty, the garage door lurches open, and Thisbe sees her dad behind the wheel of his car, dreary-eyed, his beard uncombed and blond and gray, as he begins to pull into the open space.

"Dad!" Thisbe shouts, standing up.

Her father shrugs his shoulders, then honks, motioning for his daughter to move.

"Okay, okay, God!" Thisbe hisses, sliding the orange milk crates aside. "It's my dad," she announces, sadly defeated. "He's okay, but he's been weird since him and my mom got separated."

"My dad is in Guam. He's in the Navy. I haven't seen him in like ten years," Roxie whispers.

Thisbe's father climbs out of the car with a distracted frown.

"Dad, this is Roxie," Thisbe says, humiliated.

"Hello there," Thisbe's dad murmurs, opening the backseat of the rusty Peugeot. An enormous stack of papers and maps tumbles out, Thisbe's father sighing as he leans over to scoop it up.

"What is all that stuff, Dad?"

"It's from the museum. I had to clean out the research lab."

"Oh."

"But it's okay, I think, well . . . your mother's not home again?"

"No."

"Okay. Well, your friend is welcome to dinner. I'm making microwavable mac and cheese. Do you guys want some?"

"No, thanks," Thisbe groans. Her father stares at her, perhaps equally embarrassed at the sight of himself, and then, arms full of scientific data, he stumbles off toward the house.

"Wow, what does your dad do?" Roxie asks.

"He's a scientist. He looks for squids."

"Cool."

"Not really. So what do you want to do now?" Thisbe asks.

"I don't know. I have to be home in like a half hour. My mom totally freaks if I'm not there when she gets back from work."

"Yeah," Thisbe says, sympathizing, though it's almost impossible for her to remember either of her parents freaking out about anything, other than themselves.

"We could go to the field for a while. By the lake," Roxie suggests.

"I guess. If you want to," and then Thisbe's heart begins to beat madly.

AS THEY PEDAL toward the hidden field, the secret field, Thisbe starts to pray, a prayer unlike any other she has whispered to herself: *Dear God in Heaven, who is Holier than Holy, dear God, please, please, please do not punish me for my wicked, unhealthy thoughts. Do not let a car hit me or a bus run me over or an airplane fall out of the sky and crush my pathetic heart. Do not let acid rain or a hailstorm or one of your terrible plagues destroy me. Do not let the arrows of Your most Holy light pierce my breast or snakes or falcons come and smite my traitorous heart from my chest, not until I have held Roxie's hand again.* Waiting for brimstone, waiting for a flash of lightning to cleave her from existence, Thisbe pedals with one eye open, following Roxie, the flick and float of the other girl's skirt the only thing she sees.

ON THEIR BACKS—leaving their bicycles twisted atop each other at the end of the trail—Thisbe stares up into the shocking blue sky and does not feel like she is flying. Instead, it is like she is falling off the face of the earth. She grasps at the tall green grass around her, the clouds drifting silently at her feet. She closes her eyes and feels her heart racing in her chest, her breath unsteady, ragged. She is aware of the wind as it brushes over her bare face and feels as if she is falling from some unimaginable height. She opens her eyes in panic, then turns her head and looks at Roxie, her short blond hair like a halo above her tiny ears, her snub little nose, her pink lips. Roxie smiles and takes her hand, both of the girls shutting their eyes. In that moment, they begin to fly. Their two bodies drift silently above the field, the sunlight streaking their faces as the clouds begin to swell around them. Thisbe feels like crying. She has never been so happy. But this time it is much shorter. For just as soon as she feels herself becoming weightless, just as soon as she's left the ground, Thisbe opens her eyes and sees they have already descended. She is only lying there, stretched out on her back. Beside her Roxie is humming, her green eyes still closed tight, pulling at the grass near her small hands. A strange, unfamiliar thought races through Thisbe's brain—*How would it feel if I suddenly climbed on top of her?*—and, immediately ashamed, Thisbe looks away. Roxie, opening her eyes, turns and drops a handful of grass on Thisbe's stomach. Thisbe smiles, picking the blades off one by one, and finds Roxie's hand moving along the waist of her skirt. Thisbe closes her eyes, feeling like she might start crying. *No, no, no, no*, she thinks. *Please don't touch me. Please don't touch me*, but the thoughts are only thoughts and have nothing to do with the feeling that has begun to vibrate all along the bottom part of her body. The other girl's fingers are warm and inch along her skin like a spider, creeping along the waistline, back and forth, as if she cannot make up her mind. Thisbe hears her breath coming and going quicker now, the rasp in her lungs beginning to catch, a spot somewhere in the back of her knees starting to tighten, and then Roxie's face is above her own, her face is floating there, her face is the sun, the moon, it is the entire horizon, her green eyes flickering with a question that Thisbe does not know how to answer. Roxie has placed her hand in Thisbe's hand and is looking down at her and neither one of them is laughing now or making any kind of sound at all, they are just staring at each other, the question beating in the air around them, the only sound the sound of a perfect collision of thoughts, like birds' wings, Thisbe thinks she now understands the question being asked but is too afraid to answer, how can she even begin to answer? The other girl's hand is against her own, their palms forming a perfect dark universe, Roxie's smile disappearing, replaced by something else, some new expression, something not quite serious, though by this look it is clear that this is not entirely a game now either. Thisbe does not get up. She does not run away. Even though her lungs have begun to burn, even though she is aching to be alone, in her room, on her bicycle, safe, her feet planted back on the ground where they belong, not pointed upward toward the sky, where nothing is at all clear, Thisbe does not know why she doesn't just go. When Roxie moves closer, kissing her on the corner of her mouth, then her nose, then her chin, then her neck, Thisbe closes her eyes and pretends it is the kiss of something else, something blessed, something she does not know by name, something she's sure she'll never quite understand. Thisbe lies there, happy for one moment, though she does not try and kiss the other girl back. She is content to be floating, adrift in that autumn sky, caught among a cloudy heaven and earth, sun and grass, fixed somewhere between what she thought she most wanted and the sound of this other girl's lips.

BY THE TIME the kissing episode is over, Roxie, uncharacteristically embarrassed, her face flushed bright red, afraid to look Thisbe in the eye, mumbles a weak goodbye and pedals off, leaving Thisbe there alone in the field to wonder what she has done. What *has* she done? She doesn't know but she is sure of the gravity of her sin. She knows God has seen what has happened and is terribly, terribly disappointed in her. She murmurs ten Hail Marys and a dozen Our Fathers, one for each place she let herself be kissed, her mouth, her neck, her cheek. She decides to go visit her grandfather, hoping to find forgiveness in dutiful service to the elderly. Pedaling away from the lake, down the wide boulevard, she does not bother to pray. She closes her eyes and imagines a sky full of locusts sweeping down, tearing her arms from their sockets. When she opens her eyes and the sky is still blue, and there are no scalding clouds of brimstone, what she feels then may be the worst disappointment of her life.

Fifteen

AT THE RETIREMENT HOME, LATE THAT TUESDAY AFTER-
noon, Thisbe sits beside her grandfather, praying for a quick,
merciful death for the both of them. She closes her eyes,
whispering a single prayer over and over again, holding his
tiny white hand, ignoring the noise of the recreation room,
which is now being used for an impromptu checkers tourna-
ment. Thisbe looks over and sees the frustrated expression
on her grandfather's face, she can tell that he is upset about
something, sitting there in his wheelchair so meekly, his teeth
and gums sadly sunken into themselves. His mouth, wrinkled,
blue-veined, small, perfectly weak, does not open to speak,
not at first. He only has three words left, and after that, he
will be done with words, just as he will be done with food
and done with remembering. These last utterances, these three
remaining sounds, must be carefully considered. When he
has made his decision, Henry leans over, placing his mouth
next to his granddaughter's ear, and asks in a solemn whisper,
"Help . . . me . . . escape."

Thisbe, surprised, turns to look in her grandfather's eyes.
He is not joking. There, in the gray-green flecks of Henry's

eyes, Thisbe can suddenly see the truth. Her grandfather is just as lonely and just as desperate as she is.

"But how? And where could you go?"

Henry doesn't answer; his fingers scramble into the breast pocket of his robe and produce his wallet, unfolding it in his lap. Thisbe can see a number of twenty- and one-hundred-dollar bills folded inside. Her grandfather glances down at the money and smiles.

"What will I tell my dad?"

Henry shakes his head and without speaking, only using his eyes, he seems to repeat the question.

Thisbe looks up, staring at the pairs of elderly residents distracted by the black and red squares of their game. There is no nurse or orderly on duty at the moment; the glass security doors that lead to the elevator are only twenty or thirty feet away. She turns to her grandfather and nods once, pulling herself to her feet. She slips behind his wheelchair and begins to push him toward the glass security doors. She loses her nerve when she sees a serious-looking nurse sitting behind the front desk, paging through a tabloid magazine. Anxiously, Thisbe pushes her grandfather past the desk, past the glass doors— the old man grabbing at the wheels to try and stop her—then back to his room, where she quietly closes the door behind them, already apologizing.

"I'm sorry," she whispers. "But there was a nurse. We couldn't have gotten past her."

Her grandfather shakes his head angrily, his eyes squinting with bright annoyance. He grabs her hand, pulling it toward the open door. But Thisbe is too afraid of the nurse at the front desk, too frightened by the idea of what her father might do or say whenever he finds out, which, of course, he eventually will.

"I'm sorry," she says, sitting down on the bed. "But I don't think it's such a good idea anyway."

Henry hisses his displeasure, then slowly wheels himself into the far corner of the room. Ignoring his granddaughter, he searches the pockets of his red robe for his notebook. When he finds it, he flips to a blank page and then begins to write angrily.

To Whom It May Concern,
You had a son named Jonathan and two
granddaughters, Amelia and Thisbe.

To Whom It May Concern,
You were not much of a father or grandfather.

To Whom It May Concern,
In this way, you were exactly like your own father.

. . .

WHETHER IT WAS only Henry's imagination or the sad, strange truth—that his father and uncle were indeed guilty of treason, their secrets hidden in the lines and stitches of the clothes they mended—was never officially proven. For within a day of the bombing of Pearl Harbor, President Roosevelt's Presidential Proclamations 2525, 2526, and 2527 had been issued, granting the federal law enforcement agencies the power to arrest and detain resident aliens of Japanese, German, and Italian descent for engaging in subversive activities. Immediately the federal agents of the Chicago Field Office quickly had their hands full.

December 8, 1941

FEDERAL BUREAU OF INVESTIGATION
UNITED STATES DEPARTMENT OF JUSTICE
To: COMMUNICATIONS SECTION

Transmit the following message to:

CBC:CSH

TO ALL SACs: MOST URGENT. SUPERSEDING AND CLAR-
IFYING PREVIOUS INSTRUCTIONS RE: GERMAN AND
ITALIAN ALIENS. IMMEDIATELY TAKE INTO CUSTODY
ALL GERMAN AND ITALIAN ALIENS PREVIOUSLY CLAS-
SIFIED IN GROUPS A, B, AND C, IN MATERIAL PREVI-
OUSLY TRANSMITTED TO YOU. IN ADDITION, YOU ARE
AUTHORIZED TO IMMEDIATELY ARREST ANY GERMAN
OR ITALIAN ALIENS, NOT PREVIOUSLY CLASSIFIED IN
THE ABOVE CATEGORIES. IN THE EVENT YOU POS-
SESS INFORMATION INDICATING THE ARREST OF SUCH
INDIVIDUALS NECESSARY FOR THE INTERNAL SECU-
RITY OF THIS COUNTRY. ABOVE PROCEDURE APPLIES
ONLY TO GERMAN AND ITALIAN ALIENS, AND NOT
TO CITIZENS. ABOVE PROCEDURE DOES NOT IN ANY
INSTANCE APPLY TO DIPLOMATIC OR CONSULAR REP-
RESENTATIVES OF THE GERMAN OR ITALIAN GOVERN-
MENT. BUREAU MUST BE ADVISED TELEGRAPHICALLY
AT EARLIEST POSSIBLE MOMENT CONCERNING INDI-
VIDUALS ARRESTED PURSUANT TO ABOVE INSTRUC-

TIONS. THIS TELEGRAPHIC INFORMATION TO BUREAU SHOULD SPECIFICALLY DESIGNATE, WITH REGARD TO EACH INDIVIDUAL MENTIONED, WHETHER THE ALIEN IN QUESTION HAS BEEN PREVIOUSLY CLASSIFIED ON THE A, B, OR C LIST, OR WHETHER HE IS BEING ARRESTED AS AN ALIEN CONCERNING WHOM INFORMATION JUSTIFYING HIS ARREST IS POSSESSED, ALTHOUGH NOT PREVIOUSLY CLASSIFIED IN THE ABOVE CATEGORIES. AS TO ALIENS IN LATTER CATEGORY, SPECIFY CONCERNING EACH INDIVIDUAL WHETHER CUSTODIAL DETENTION DOSSIERS PREVIOUSLY SUBMITTED BY FIELD OFFICE INVOLVED CONCERNING INDIVIDUAL IN QUESTION. AS TO GERMAN OR ITALIAN ALIENS CONCERNING WHOM INFORMATION IS POSSESSED INDICATING THEIR ARREST NECESSARY FOR INTERNAL SECURITY OF THE COUNTRY, ALTHOUGH NOT PREVIOUSLY CLASSIFIED IN A, B, OR C CATEGORIES, AND ON WHOM PREVIOUS CUSTODIAL DETENTION DOSSIERS NOT SUBMITTED. BUREAU MUST BE FURNISHED IMMEDIATELY COMPLETE SUMMARY OF INFORMATION POSSESSED CONCERNING INDIVIDUAL INVOLVED, JUSTIFYING ARREST. ALL INDIVIDUALS ARRESTED MUST BE TURNED OVER TO NEAREST REPRESENTATIVE OF IMMIGRATION AND NATURALIZATION SERVICE.

HOOVER

December 13, 1941

From a Department of Justice Press Release:

Attorney General Francis Biddle today announced that, under proclamation issued by the President, the Department of Justice and the War Department have apprehended a total of 2541 Axis nationals in continental United States and Hawaii who were regarded as dangerous to the peace and safety of the nation.

Mr. Biddle said that a report from Director J. Edgar Hoover of the Federal Bureau of Investigation showed that, from December 7 through December 11, FBI agents have taken into custody 1002 German aliens, 169 Italian aliens, 1370 Japanese aliens . . .

In addition to the enemy aliens, Director Hoover reported that FBI agents in Hawaii . . . have taken into custody 19 American citizens of German extraction, 2 American citizens of Italian descent, and 22 American citizens, most of whom are of Japanese extraction . . .

December 15, 1941

MEMORANDUM FOR THE FILE

Yesterday Dr. Prendergast furnished the undersigned the following data of the number of alien enemies for whom warrants of arrest had been issued in the United States, the number of warrants executed by the FBI, and the number of aliens arrested without warrant by the FBI:

GERMANS:

Warrants Issued	1757
Warrants Executed	374
Arrested Without Warrant	500

ITALIANS:

Warrants Issued	223
Warrants Executed	41
Arrested Without Warrant	85

JAPANESE:

Warrants Issued	700
Warrants Executed	437
Arrested Without Warrant	628

W. F. Kelly, Chief Supervisor of Border Patrol

. . .

HENRY'S FATHER and uncle were now both gone, his mother almost a phantom. Henry would stand beside her bedroom door and listen to her strange, brutal prayers. Closing his eyes, he would do his best to mutter along. Henry's little brother, Timothy, was as small and as frightened as ever. He refused to leave their apartment to go to school, preferring to stay at home with their mother. Henry, thirteen years old, continued to hope that his father would be released soon. Without Len and the little tailor shop, the family had no income, no way to buy food, clothes, to pay the rent for the residence where they all sat huddled in disbelief.

By the spring of 1942, with the United States now at war, Henry did odd jobs in the little shops around the tiny German neighborhood—sweeping up at the porcelain shop, repainting the viewing rooms at Mr. Kratz's funeral home, restocking the shelves at the small grocery store where his older brother Harold—now in the United States infantry—had worked. But a cloud of suspicion hung above the young boy, and many sympathetic store owners, fond of Henry but fearing for their livelihoods, felt they had no choice but to refuse his services. When he could not find work, Henry would crouch in the back row of St. Benedict's Church on Irving Park Road, staring up at the broken body of his mother's Lord and Savior, muttering his prayers in English, asking for help and guidance. More often than not, he spent the evening watching the flickering candles near the altar, imagining that their movements held a secret message. Outside, walking home, in the rain or snow, each raindrop became a note, each snowflake a code, a missive telling him not to be afraid. *Be brave*, the snowflakes would read: *Be brave*.

• • •

BY THE WINTER of 1942, after a year, with no news of his father's case, the family was living on credit and the rent hadn't been paid for many months. One night, Henry's mother finally crept from her room and, having brushed her hair and dressed in her best gown, crossed the hall to ask their neighbor Mr. Holz for help. On behalf of the family, Mr. Holz—the only one in the tenement building who owned a typewriter—wrote to the FBI, demanding to know the status of Len Casper's imprisonment.

After another two months without a response, Henry's mother once again crossed the hall to Mr. Holz's, then again, then once more, petitioning the FBI to please reunite the family. Finally, one night late in February 1943, as Henry climbed the front stairs of the tenement, the odd odors of embalming fluid and Mr. Kratz's cigarettes rising from his dirty clothes, he could hear loud voices coming from the apartment. Henry bounded up the stairs on frightened legs, and found two men in black suits and gray felt hats. They were FBI agents. As soon as Henry entered the parlor, they turned to him with serious frowns and Henry's hands began to shake with panic.

"Who are you? What's going on here?" Henry asked, glancing at his mother, who was sobbing on the worn-looking sofa, looking stricken. Timothy, in his blue pajamas, was beside her, looking back at him, terrified and wondering.

"They said we're leaving tonight," Timothy, whispered.

"Who's leaving?" Henry asked, staring at the blank-faced men.

"Your father's been interned. You've got ten minutes to pack what you need," one of the agents announced grimly.

"Where are we going?"

"We're going to send you to be with your father, kid. Now grab your things and hurry."

Henry, helping his mother to her feet, turned and ran into the tiny room he shared with his brother. Finding the large yellow suitcase beneath his bed, he began piling all the clothes he could fit, lifting armfuls from his and Timothy's dresser drawers, as his mother, still standing confused in the parlor, kept on sobbing.

"Mother," he said, holding her hand. "Go get your things. We're going to see Father."

His mother's face did not brighten. She only shook her head and asked:

"What did he do? What did he do to us?"

Henry left her standing there and ran to her room, finding as large a traveling bag as he could and taking whatever looked necessary—shoes, dresses, a coat, underwear, he packed them up, hurrying to place the brown bag by the front door.

"Where are we going?" Timothy asked, sitting on the sofa, afraid to look the strange men in the eyes.

"You're going somewhere safe. It'll be okay," one of the agents said. "Now go help your brother out."

Timothy nodded, helping Henry close the enormous yellow suitcase, which they dragged to the front door together. Henry looked around the dreary apartment in a panic, searching for anything else his family might need, but the taller of the agents, glancing down at his watch, said:

"Okay, it's time. You got a train to catch." He reached down and grabbed both suitcases, the tiny family following, marching out into the quiet, unfamiliar whispers of the city street.

• • •

MORE THAN THREE DAYS later, Henry climbed out the wide door of a troop transport train and stepped into the dry heat of a nearly empty Texas town. Holding hands, the two boys shuffled quietly behind their father, whose wide, strong arm braced their mother as they marched slowly along, following the line of internees before them. It had turned out that their father and uncle had been held in Chicago all that time, in a converted warehouse with other German- and Italian-born suspects. Henry's uncle Felix was a bachelor, and because of this he was sent to another internment facility somewhere within the snowy borders of Wisconsin. Henry, still deeply shamed by his father's cowardly betrayal, refused to look him in the eye, and so he stared outward at the blank plains of silent brown earth, the horizon a single line bisecting the blue sky.

"Where are we?" Timothy asked.

"Somewhere in Texas," Henry whispered.

"Why did they bring us here?"

"Because we're German."

Henry glanced around and saw family after family, all disheveled and heartbroken, their small bundles and suitcases packed tightly with their possessions, some wearing the only set of clothes they owned, climbing out the open door of the train, blinking at the wide blue sky. Their faces were all the same as his father's and mother's, long and gray, their eyes sadly sunken into the flesh. Their lives had been torn from them, like a beating organ, and they did not know how to carry on, other than to be silent and to obey the orders shouted at them.

A guard with a rifle directed the families onto several transport trucks. Henry sat beside his brother in the truck bed, turning to watch his father as the vehicle slowly pulled away.

"How long will we be here, Dad?" Timothy asked in a whisper.

"I don't know. They can do what they like to us."

Henry turned and saw his mother was crying once again.

"Will we be put in jail?" Timothy asked.

"I don't know," their father said. "We can only wait and hope they treat us better than they have."

Henry turned away from his father and looked at the other families, who, like his, sat huddled together and whispering. Perhaps a half hour later, maybe more, maybe less, the truck began to slow, and the flat, nearly invisible horizon of gray earth began to brighten, turning green. Henry stared from the back of the truck at the fields of verdant leaves, unsure what he was seeing, until a young girl across from him shouted it out: spinach. There were irrigation ditches cut back and forth and troughs of fresh water and workers walking along the wide fields and then the farms were gone and the earth became gray again. Finally, after almost an hour, the truck slowed to a halt. Henry turned in his seat and saw the shadow of an enormous fence, guarded by dozens of soldiers. The transport trucks slowly drew past the gate, stopping a few moments later, one beside the other, nearly five trucks full of interned families. The families stepped from the trucks no longer tethered to the world around them. What would happen to them? What sort of life would they be allowed to lead? And everywhere, only silence, and the shadows of young men in uniforms, wielding guns.

Henry could see there were houses, gloomy, rectangular-framed wooden bungalows, much like the shape of the homes back in Chicago. He smiled when he saw them, then stopped because he saw there were no trees. There were no trees anywhere and no birds either and the sun had become very hot suddenly. He noticed he had sweated through his one clean shirt. A man in a military uniform climbed down from one of the transport trucks, lifted his helmet off, wiped at his sweaty forehead with a white linen handkerchief, and then donned his helmet again. He looked around at the sad faces and said to the dirt:

"Welcome to Crystal City, Texas. This is a detainment facility for interned families of foreign nationals. You will be staying here for some time but please remember, this is not your home. This will never be your home."

HENRY, NOW FOURTEEN, terrified by his unfamiliar surroundings, had stopped talking. Crystal City was divided into two large sections, one set of facilities for Germans, one for the Japanese, with both groups of detainees under heavy guard at all times. The young man did not like the feeling of being constantly watched, the long shadows of the soldiers crossing and recrossing the narrow streets. In Crystal City, there was no place to be alone, no place to hide. The sun hung close to the earth, its terrible heat piercing everything. It left no secrets untouched, no quiet places to sit and stare and dream. Though the German children had their own elementary school and high school, with its very own school newspaper, marching band, and sports facilities, Henry found no books to his liking in the school's library, no drugstore where he could go buy the latest issue of *Justice Society of America* or *The Airship Brigade*, no empty alleys to pretend he was somewhere else. In the stark landscape of the internment camp, everything was plain and lifeless. There was nothing to be excited about, no adventures to be had, no reason to talk. And if it was his father who had cost them their home, whose easy laughter and convincing lies had forced them to be sent to this awful place, then Henry would prefer not to speak at all. Having decided his father really was a coward, a crook, a spy, he gave up saying anything to anybody.

AND SOON HE found he could no longer daydream. The world of Crystal City was all flatness, as if the real world, the world of the little tailor shop and his delivery job, were only memories now. The family's "home" was very nice, a small, square-shaped bungalow with a small kitchen and a room for his parents and another for him and Timothy to share. But there were no skyscrapers on the horizon. The spectacular clouds had vanished from the reaches of the sky. All was dull and sun-bright now, an empty world without shadow or fog or dimension. There were no gray moments of twilight, no dark gangways, no snow-filled alleys to explore, nothing silver or striking or imposing along the skyline to help the boy imagine what might be possible instead. Each night, as Henry lay in his cot, the soldiers marched back and forth along the perimeter of the fence, their footsteps echoing colorlessly. The footsteps of the soldiers then became the footsteps of the G-men in Mr. Miner's stairwell, then the sound of his friend Mr. Miner, leaping from the open window. Henry, terrified in bed, found he could not sleep. He could not fly up and over the wire fence using make-believe; he could not dream an escape for himself because he could not dream.

ONE DAY, stalking along the outside circumference of the camp, counting his footsteps as he went, Henry looked up and watched three transport trucks pull into the administration area. He saw several Japanese families being escorted from the trucks, their bags set down in the gray dirt as they took in the hopeless angles of Crystal City. As he stared, he caught sight of two tiny girls, twins, their dark eyes and dark hair luminous in the Texas sunlight, each holding one of their mother's hands. One of the girls was in a blue dress, the other's was purple, and as they looked around at the plain rectangular buildings, the tall wire fence, the young men in uniforms hustling back and forth with their rifles, they did not cry or flatten or sink with dismay. The two twin girls, together, leaning over in the dirt, began to write something, using the tips of their fingers, drawing a picture, scribbling something before their mother tugged gently at them and they followed the rest of their family toward the Japanese section of camp. As soon as the families cleared out, Henry, still counting his steps, searched among the footprints and marks made by the heavy suitcases, until he found what the two twin girls had drawn in the dirt.

It was a picture of two birds, their pointed beaks touching, as if to kiss. Inside of each bird was a single Japanese word, a letter perhaps. Henry stared down at the strange little drawing in the dust and wondered if maybe it was a secret message left for someone to decipher. He soon decided it was the two girls' names, written in the dust to mark their new home. He looked down at the two tiny birds until he had memorized their shape, then continued on, counting his steps until a guard near the gate told him to move out of the way.

LATER THAT WEEK, Henry quietly sought a place to be alone, in hopes that by being alone—out from under the watchful eyes of the bored soldiers and the difficult glare of the midday sun—he might once again be able to daydream. The young man searched the dusty circumference of the camp, until he finally discovered a small, unlocked utility shed—twenty or so yards behind the administration building—which was filled with tools, shovels, brooms, and gardening equipment. It wasn't very dark but it was incredibly hot. Climbing over a pair of sawhorses, Henry could feel his entire body shivering with sweat. Slowly, he closed the door and sat in the corner, the shed lit by the bright sun streaming through the gaps between the metal sheets overhead. Henry closed his eyes and immediately he was in a submarine, moving undetected, several leagues beneath the surface of the murky ocean. Just outside the submarine's hull was a squid, perhaps, or a school of vibrant, translucent fish, their strange skeletons visible through their shimmering skin. Perhaps he was all alone, searching out the lost city of Atlantis, or transporting secret weapon plans to the British, while in the clouded waters above, a Nazi gunship searched for him, depth charges at the ready: *"All engines stop. We are surrounded by a Wolf pack but fear not."* Or better still, he was miles and miles above the surface of the earth, in the airship X-1, speeding off toward several thousand uncharted galaxies: *"Prepare yourself, Airship Brigade, for intergalactic flight! Five-four-three-two-one! All systems go!"*

Henry hardly realized he was speaking aloud to himself, his voice high and unsure and scratchy. Just as he imagined a breech unexpectedly erupting in the airship's hull, poisonous space vapor leaking into his lungs, the storage shed exploded with light, and Henry, startled from his daydream, let out a high, strange-sounding cry.

"Who's in here?" a low voice mumbled. "Hinkley? Is that you? I can hear you whispering, you wing nut. It's me, Doug."

Henry, hiding behind the rack of shovels, could see a young

man in uniform, his handsome, broad face broken in a smile.

"Hinkley? You better hop to. The lieutenant is looking for you. We got a truckload of rations to unload."

Henry held in his breath, closing his eyes, his heart beating hard in his chest.

"Hinkley?"

The young soldier stepped into the shadows, reaching out a hand. When the soldier saw Henry huddled there—a pale young man with a narrow face, mouth mumbling in frightened whispers—he went for his rifle, dropping the gun awkwardly at his feet. Henry saw the gun fall and cried out as the rifle discharged, the round ricocheting inside the empty shed, the sound muffled by the noise of transport trucks passing by. The soldier, just as frightened, grabbed the gun, and stared down at it with surprise, seeing his mistake.

"Wow. Sorry about that, kid," the soldier said. "The safety wasn't on."

Henry nodded, still in hiding behind the tools.

"Are you okay?"

Henry muttered something, his body still trembling.

"Well, what are you doing in here, kid, in the first place?" the soldier asked.

Once again Henry could not speak. His mouth moved but the sounds that came out were only faint whispers, the ghostly outlines of words.

"Well, come on out of there, kid."

Henry nodded and hurried past the young soldier, whose eyes were bright and whose face was flushed with sweat.

"You shouldn't be back there. Someone might get jumpy and shoot you or something."

Henry nodded again.

"Yes . . . ," he muttered.

"What's a matter? You don't understand English?"

Henry shook his head and then pointed to his mouth.

"You don't speak English or something?"

Henry nodded again. The soldier smiled a little with comprehension.

"You go to the school? The German school here? You talk German?"

Henry shook his head no, then whispered:

"I was . . . just scared. I'm . . . I'm . . . okay."

The soldier smiled a little wider and then looked down, embarrassed for poor Henry. "Well, you shouldn't be back in there all by yourself, kid. Someone might get the wrong idea and think you're up to no good. Now, what was it you were doing in there all by yourself?"

"Nothing. I was just . . . I was just . . . nothing," Henry muttered, unable to catch his breath. He looked down and saw that his knees were still shaking.

"Well, you better go on home now before my lieutenant comes along. He's not likely to believe you weren't up to some kind of mischief."

"Thank you," Henry whispered, nodding once, then again, then a third time. "Thank you," his voice unfamiliar in his throat.

The young soldier laughed as Henry hurried away, still in a panic. As the boy turned, he looked at the name on the soldier's green uniform, seeing it stitched in block letters: FAULK. Lying in his unfamiliar bed that evening, whispering to himself, Henry remembered the soldier's kind, surprised face and dreamt that the two of them were best friends already.

．　．　．

HENRY BEGAN TO FOLLOW PFC Faulk after that, shadowing him in secret at first, as the young soldier hurried from his position on guard duty to escorting new internees to their quarters, then, in the dark, hurrying back to the rectangular gray-brick barracks for a few hours of sleep. Not long after their first meeting, Private Faulk would catch sight of the strange, silent, bright-eyed boy skulking behind him, trying to be sneaky, but always stumbling or tripping or staring blankly for too long. One afternoon, while Private Faulk stood guard near the rear entrance of the camp, he glanced over and saw Henry hiding a few yards away, around the corner of the dispensary building. The boy seemed to convince himself of something, before he hurried over to where Private Faulk was positioned and handed the young soldier a small piece of paper. Just as quickly, Henry hurried off again, hiding in the shadows of the dispensary once more, watching as Private Faulk unfolded the note. *Thank you for not ratting me out.* Private Faulk read the note once more and looked up and saw the boy grinning behind his hand. Private Faulk, only a young man of nineteen himself, folded the note back up, glancing around to be sure his lieutenant was nowhere in sight. A few moments later, the boy hurried toward him again, handed him a second note, and then quickly disappeared, running awkwardly back toward his family's bungalow. Private Faulk pulled at the corners of the note and looked down and saw what the other young man had written. It said, *You are a true friend.*

WHEN HENRY WAS NOT hiding in the shadows, following Private Faulk around the compound, he usually lurked near the Japanese side of camp, staring through the wire at the boys and girls running up and down the dusty street, giggling, playing tag, their voices high and unfamiliar, their laughter something distant and dazzling, and still only a few yards on the other side of the fence. He would stand there for an hour or two, looking for the twin Japanese girls. They usually sat in the shade near their mother, resting in front of their tiny bungalow, sometimes gently brushing each other's hair. Other times, walking along the fence—the fence which did not limit movement between the Japanese and German sides of camps, but discouraged it by offering only a narrow open gate—Henry would see other drawings the twin girls had etched in the dirt: two butterflies, two elephants, two horses, each decorated with the strange Japanese characters. Henry, dreaming himself into a comic book story, imagined they were asking for his help, asking to be rescued. Once, he saw them drawing in the dust only a few feet from him, kneeling together on the other side of the fence. He waved to them, and slowly, in unison, they returned the gesture, moving their small hands with graceful apprehension. The next day, he left a note for them as well, a drawing of two girls with bird wings for arms, placing the folded paper in the crook of the wire fence. When he returned later that afternoon, he was elated to see the note was gone, and a drawing of an enormous apple had been scratched in the dirt. Soon, almost every day after that, Henry was leaving them drawings; strange monsters, underwater cities, maps of other worlds. If he happened to see the two twin girls kneeling beside the fence and if he called out to them, they would ignore the sound of his voice, afraid of approaching the wire perhaps, or possibly preferring the silence of the secret game they had all invented. Once he found a miniature paper crane, another time a paper butterfly, and still another time a tiny white paper flower, all left in between the crooks of the wire fence. Henry guarded this collection of paper objects, hiding them beneath his narrow bed, taking them out late at night to ponder their intricate, unknowable meanings.

ONLY A FEW WEEKS later, Henry was hiding in the equipment shed pretending he was piloting a test rocket deep into the heart of a volcano when Private Faulk slowly opened the shiny silver door. The light from the late Texas afternoon cut through the shadows of the shed, revealing the shape of Henry hiding beside a stack of concrete mix. Private Faulk marched inside the equipment shed carrying a worn-out-looking portable radio beneath his arm. He slipped off his helmet and struggled to find a cigarette inside his depressed-looking dungarees. He lit it, exhaled, and gave young Henry a worn-looking smile. "Hinkley and me found it last night. There's a whole pile of junk kept in this building on the other side of camp, near the Japs. Movie projectors, radios, all kinds of stuff. We figured if no one was using it, we might as well, you know, get some fun out of it ourselves. We'll see if the battery's any good." The private gave the dial a turn and listened as a Gene Autry song quietly rose to life. Private Faulk took a long drag, then, remembering himself, offered the boy a cigarette of his own, but Henry, unsure what to say or do, just shook his head, staring down at his worn-out shoes.

"Well, sure, I'm Doug, by the way." He extended his hand and gave Henry's a quick, lively shake. "What's your name there?"

"Henry," he murmured. "Henry Casper."

"Well, Henry Casper, pleased to meet you. You ain't from Texas originally, I'm guessing."

Henry shook his head.

"Where you from, then?"

"Chicago."

"Chicago? Well, hey, that's something. You're an awful long way from Chicago, aren't you?"

Henry nodded.

"Well, sure. What grade are you in at school?"

Henry shrugged his shoulders.

"You don't know?"

"I'm supposed to be in eighth but they put me in the seventh because I missed so much school back in Chicago."

"Oh, well, how are the teachers here? They treat you okay?"

"There's a marching band," Henry whispered. "We didn't have a marching band at our old school."

"Well, that sounds all right. What about your family? You got any brothers or sisters?"

Henry nodded. "Two brothers. One's in the army. The other's sick. He doesn't go to school all that often."

"Well, you make sure *you* do. When the war's over they're going to need all kinds of engineers and scientists and architects to rebuild everything. You pay attention in school now and you'll be able to do what you please. Let the rest of these slobs worry about having to go off and shoot each other."

Private Faulk stubbed out the remains of his cigarette, then turned and gave the radio's dial another slow turn. Static hissed from the speaker, through the tinny notes of a trumpet solo, past a report from the Armed Forces Network, and then, almost magically, came an excited voice:

ANNOUNCER: *Good evening, ladies and gentlemen, and youngsters alike. WGN Chicago and the Pennsylvania Coal Company are proud to bring you the continuing Adventures of the*

Airship Brigade. Pennsylvania Coal Company, the one with the blue flame. Episode Twelve: The Secret Origins of the Airship Brigade, Part Two. *Young Alexander Lightning, teenage boy, raised by his widowed mother, Margaret, in the prairie town of Fairfield, Oklahoma, makes an amazing discovery in the family's abandoned barn with the help of his boyhood friend, Hugo. There, the two chums find a mysterious radio-ring hidden in the hayloft, which young Alexander soon realizes has been left there by his missing father, Doctor Lightning. Alexander accidentally switches the ring on, transmitting a secret signal across the boundaries of the universe, and within moments, a sinister silver rocket ship lands in the Lightnings' vacant cornfield. The rocket ship has been sent from the dastardly Planet X, and soon a platoon of robot soldiers march from the rocket to invade the quiet Oklahoma town, in search of the powerful and mysterious radio-ring. Alexander and Hugo hide in the barn, unsure how to save their lonely little burg. Alexander cries out for help, holding the ring in his hands, desperate for sudden bravery. And just then . . .*

ALEXANDER: Look, the secret ring is beginning to blink. It's . . . flashing. It's maybe a message of some kind.

HUGO: I don't know, Alexander, maybe you shouldn't fool with that again.

ALEXANDER: Gee whiz, if only I knew Morse Code. Oh, no, what's that?

ANNOUNCER: *From out of the blue, a splendid golden zeppelin has appeared just over the cloudy midwestern horizon, drawing nearer and nearer, hovering just above the roof of the small red barn.*

ALEXANDER: Oh, gee, what awful planet has this ship come from?

ANNOUNCER: *The golden zeppelin issues forth a strange sound and begins to land. Three odd forms slowly climb out: the first, Doctor Jupiter, a dashing-looking gentleman with a gray Vandyke beard and monocle. The second, Doctor Jupiter's sixteen-year-old daughter, Darla, a gorgeous brunette with big brown eyes and a winning smile, follows, lifting off her glass space helmet. The third, Tor the Man-Ape, an enormous brute, hulking, hairy, mysterious, appears with a dangerous-looking ray gun. They see the terrified young men, Alexander Lightning and his best friend Hugo, and decide to approach, the doctor raising his hand in an offering of peace. Alexander, still frightened, finds a pitchfork and points it at the trio nervously, while Hugo, always afraid to fight, hides in a heavy stack of hay.*

ALEXANDER: Who are you? What do you want with us?

DOCTOR JUPITER: We come with amity in our hearts. And a grave sense of hope. You must be Doctor Lightning's young son, Alexander.

ALEXANDER: How do you know my father?

DOCTOR JUPITER: I'm afraid there's no time to explain everything, young man. All that you wonder will soon be revealed. You must trust that we've been summoned here, by the magical radio-ring, to do whatever we can to assist you. It seems the Robot Legion of Planet X is determined to make short work of your charming little town.

ALEXANDER: They look unstoppable.

DOCTOR JUPITER: Unstoppable by normal means, yes.

But as you'll soon discover, we are anything but normal. Darla, my dear, prepare the X-1 for flight.
DARLA: Yes, Father. Will the young earthlings be joining
us?
DOCTOR JUPITER: But of course.

HENRY CASPER HAD NOT moved since the radio broadcast
had begun. He sat staring at the glowing green transmitter,
sweat and joy spread across his face. Private Faulk, smoking
silently, also listened with a most serious attention. And yet,
at that moment, the radio, rickety, warped with age, failed,
ending the episode some three full minutes before the writers
and actors and the Pennsylvania Coal Company had intended.
Private Faulk, frustrated, pounded on the receiver once, then
again, but it was no good. Annoyed, Private Faulk switched the
radio off and lit up another cigarette, the lighter flickering like
a meteor in the blossoming night.

"Well, you know they all got out of it somehow," Private
Faulk muttered. "They always do. That Doctor Jupiter always
got some sort of plan. But damn, wasn't that a good episode?
I never heard that one before, did you?"

Henry shook his head excitedly. "They're my favorite. *The
Airship Brigade*, I mean," Henry stammered.

"Mine, too. Well, I'm going to see if Hinkley can fix this
thing. If it works, we can listen to it tomorrow night, how's
that?"

Henry nodded, beaming, his feet nearly floating above the
ground, an endless, speculative joy rising from his heart. He
followed Private Faulk out of the dingy equipment shed, down
past the rations building, where the young soldier began to
whistle the familiar Glenn Miller ditty "Moonlight Cocktail."

There, in the dusty divide between the soldiers' barracks and the rows and rows of small, shadeless bungalows, the stars now appearing in the open Texas sky, Henry knew he had found more than a friend: in those spectral stories of cloud-pirates and spacecraft, the boy had seen a brief, unavoidable glimpse of his greatest dream. Somehow, he knew he had to fly.

SOME NIGHTS LATER, walking back from the equipment shed, lost in a dream world of make-believe cosmic flight, Henry failed to notice his own father leaning against the wire boundary fence, sharing a cigarette with Ernst Horner, a man Henry had feared at first sight. With his dark eyes, narrow chin, and jagged, unhealthy teeth, Ernst Horner had the crude features of a comic book villain. And yet, he always had some small token, a dull-looking plastic toy or piece of hard candy, which he would offer Henry, his bony face gently parting in an ugly-looking smile. Mr. Horner was known around the German side of camp as a criminal and thief, a smuggler and liar, a *Verbrecher* who ran a kind of black market for luxury items—extra rations of milk, meat, nylons, razors, even glossy movie magazines. Henry's father, with his cunning and quick, deft hands, had gotten involved with this man, assisting him in his schemes. Together, Henry's father and Mr. Horner had already broken into several equipment sheds, plundering what they could from the various camp stores. Len, with his agile fingers, made short work of the clumsy locks they encountered, and soon he discovered theft to be a much more lucrative pursuit than the dull, repetitive stitching and steaming of the tailor shop. As proof of his guilt, Len had hidden a stockload of stolen kitchen utensils beneath both of his sons' beds. Len's swift hands were also of use in slipping the wary-looking camp guards a small but necessary percentage of their profits—passing a sentry near the gate's opening, Len's hand would dart out and quickly return, a sudden contented smile appearing on the young soldier's face as he stared down at his palm, counting out the loose bills gathered within.

Standing in the dark of that early evening, leaning near the taut wire fence, Henry's father motioned lazily for his son to approach. Henry stopped dead in his tracks. He slowly walked toward his father, staring down at his own dusty shoes. Len grabbed his son firmly by the shoulder.

"Here he is, my son, the quiet one. Mr. Horner here says he has seen you talking to the *Japanisch*, is that true?" his father asked with a sharp smile.

Henry shrugged his shoulders and hoped his silence would end the awkward interrogation.

"They are a vile, vile bunch," Henry's father whispered. "They're trying to rob the food from our mouths, do you know that, Henry?"

Henry slowly shook his head.

"They've been trying to sell things to our own people. They have been coming through the fence, selling things on our side without Mr. Horner's permission."

"Well, if I were you, a young man, I'd stay as far away from them as I could," Mr. Horner said with a grin. His grin was like a bad odor, something unfamiliar, unwanted, and greasy.

"So you stay away from them, do you understand, Henry?" Len whispered. "Sometime soon, very soon, there's going to be trouble. You keep away from them and that side of the fence."

Henry nodded and then hurried off, holding the corner of his shoulder where his father's unkind grip had been. A few moments later, mumbling to himself, he bumped into Private

Faulk. He stared up into his friend's eyes too upset to say anything, and stumbled away in a cloud of confusion.

ON THE LAST NIGHT of April, the two young men—the youthful soldier and Henry Casper—were both huddled in the shadows of the equipment shed, both of their hands placed on the radio—Private Faulk's fingers adjusting the tuning knob, moment by moment, like a scientist, compensating for each flicker or twitch of sound. Henry turned the antenna slowly, both of them captivated by the latest *Airship Brigade* story. Henry was silent, afraid, worried, wondering if he ought to mention to Private Faulk his father's and Horner's threat. But the quick fear in his heart made thinking and speaking difficult. Inside the metal hull, the temperature was almost unbearable. Outside, the early evening heat had sent the citizens of the makeshift city in search of shade. Henry's younger brother, Timothy, refused to leave his metal-frame bed. As the sun began to sink, Henry and Private Faulk listened to the static-filled broadcast of the latest *Airship Brigade* episode, tweaking and turning the antenna and worn knobs, shaking the old radio when nothing else seemed to work:

ANNOUNCER: *Tonight's adventure:* The Secret of the Moon. *The valiant Airship Brigade, led by young Alexander Lightning, narrowly escapes the onslaught of the Japanese air pirates. Losing them in an enormous maze of storm clouds, Alexander bravely pilots the X-1 zeppelin out of peril, soaring through the outermost reaches of earth's atmosphere.*

ALEXANDER: Wow, Darla, that was close. I thought those nasty air pirates were going to sink us for sure.

DARLA: I wasn't worried for a moment, Alexander. I just knew you'd fly us to safety.

ALEXANDER: Then how come you're holding my arm so tightly?

DARLA: Well, maybe I was scared, just for a little bit.

HUGO: Girls sure are funny, aren't they, Alexander?

DOCTOR JUPITER: And to think, the people of the Secret Volcano City will now be safe. You've done well once again, Alexander. I know your father would be quite proud.

ALEXANDER: Gee, thanks, Doctor. Hey, look at this! Our atmospheric indicator is giving us a strange reading.

DARLA: What does it say, Alexander?

ALEXANDER: We must have flown into an Arctic air current of some kind. The controls! They're all locked up.

DOCTOR JUPITER: Did you try the mechanical override, my dear boy?

ALEXANDER: Yes, none of the controls are working. It's as if we're being pulled by an invisible force of some kind.

TOR: Tor afraid.

HUGO: Me, too, Tor. Alexander, it feels like we're caught in a spin!

ALEXANDER: There's no need to be afraid. But for now, everyone prepare themselves for a crash landing.

ANNOUNCER: *The X-1 buckles and lurches, hurtling from the sky, spinning as it nears the frozen surface of the uncharted Arctic below. The airship quickly picks up speed as it falls helplessly towards the earth.*

ALEXANDER: Brace yourself for impact, everyone . . .

The radio began to hiss, the transmission now lost. Henry, horrified at the thought of missing the ending, began to shake the antenna violently. Private Faulk tweaked the tuning knob, and then, just as suddenly, from somewhere along the internment camp's perimeter, a loud, powerful siren began to sound. Private Faulk, startled, looked up, standing hurriedly, opening the metal door of the equipment shed.

"An air raid? It sounds like it's an air raid or something," he muttered to himself. He flung on his helmet and grabbed his rifle, which had been resting against the shed's unlocked door. Lifting his left hand to his eyes, squinting in the direction of the strange siren, the young soldier saw what it was.

"It's a fire. There's a fire near the storehouse."

Without glancing back, Private Faulk hurried off toward the shouts and clamor of panic. Henry, looking down at the useless radio, crept close to the equipment shed's door and watched as the storehouse, one of the largest buildings in this part of the detainment facility, instantly broke out into a bright explosion of red-yellow flames. The hastily built structure, mostly wood and canvas, filled the twilight sky with a striking black cloud of ash. Henry gaped at it, still safely hidden in the shadows of the metal equipment shed. A dozen soldiers, then a dozen more, began passing buckets full of water to each other in a long line, from the nearest well to the borders of the fire, but it was of little use.

In only a few moments the fire had engulfed the storehouse, and now, seething with flames, the blaze began to spread. The nearest building, set aside for administrative offices, was another impermanent wood structure, and beside the administration building was the first line of family bungalows, stretched out along the Japanese side. One by one, each of the buildings began to smoke, the heat igniting the cheap boards, the awful crackle of split wood, the stink of melted plastic, the sooty smoke of the burning camp blowing through the air. Henry, terrified, watched as the administrative building collapsed, one of its walls falling forward, like something out of a silent movie, crushing four or five soldiers in a wave of deadly flame. The rest of the structure folded like a house of cards, the ceiling and other walls tumbling sideways, toppling the bungalow next door. Japanese children rushed from the adjacent houses and began to scream as fathers and mothers hurried them to safety. The soldiers hooked up a hose to a distant water tank, but, undermanned, untrained for such a catastrophe, they were unable to contain the fire. Four or five Japanese girls, trapped inside one of the burning bungalows, began to scream. Henry, hiding in the shadows, could not make out their words, but felt their awful terror as the buildings turned into bright white flames.

As the nearby houses began to burn one after the other, Henry watched through blurry eyes as the first of the wounded soldiers was pulled from the wreckage. There were four of them altogether, all coal-black and blistered, covered in ash, dragged from their places beneath the burning wall. One of them, his bluish eyes the only color in his face, choked, gasping for air, clutching at his own throat. As he was carried away, his darkened helmet came tumbling off; Henry could see that his blond hair, recently shorn, nicked above his ears, looked exactly like Private Faulk's. The soldier's fingers tugged at his windpipe, while his other hand dragged in the dirt. Henry gasped, then backed away, cowering in fear. It had been his father, him and Mr. Horner, who had done this, he was sure of it now. With his quick hands and hasty little laugh, Henry could almost see Len standing there, hidden somewhere in the shadows, entirely faceless, the tiny fingers of his hand clasping and unclasping each other with vulgar pleasure.

And then, from somewhere, a frightening scream: a Japanese mother, held back by her husband and two American soldiers, began to wail as their bungalow was quickly engulfed in flames. Henry did not need much time to recognize the woman's sharp-looking face: it was the mother of the two twin girls, who, it seemed from her baleful screams, had somehow become separated from her two tiny daughters. Henry closed his eyes as their house tumbled apart, a cloud of dust and ash rising high from the pile of twisted lumber, climbing past the woman's sore voice, past the low-slung stars, higher and higher, the two girls, surely ghosts now, drifting up farther and farther away, past the solace of the empty sky to the bright, familiar light of the moon.

IT WAS TWO DAYS later, when the fire had finally been defeated—half of the Japanese section of camp had been destroyed—that Henry, reading the official announcement that had been posted near the camp's gates, saw the truth in typescript on a pulpy white page: Private Douglas Faulk of Beaumont, Texas, along with seven soldiers and twenty Japanese detainees, was dead. Henry, standing behind the long silver fence, watched as the construction brigade used bulldozers to clear the wreckage. Seeing the disastrous remains, Henry once again thought of his father, of what he and Mr. Horner had done, imagining his tireless, scheming hands, trying to forget his drawn, featureless face.

AFTER ANOTHER WEEK of not spotting the twins, Henry was sure that they, too, were dead. Henry's world, the world of his imagination, had been razed overnight. The war, which had roared for years now in lands both distant and impossible, was strangely close. Henry's dream of flight, of airships and imaginary planets, had all been ruined by what he had so long ignored on the covers of newspapers and in the peaked, frightened transmissions of the radio.

A FINAL IMAGE, remembered so many years later, spun from the sadness of that awful night. One evening, Henry, a month or two after the fire, stood staring through the wire gaps of the fence at the demolished buildings, when he spotted a giant white moth. The creature was hovering just above the wreckage, and then, like smoke, it was gone. It soon reappeared, alighting gently right along the wire fence. Henry stared at it, surprised by its enormous size—certainly it was as big as his hand, or even bigger—its delicate white wings silently flapping, its antennae nervously twitching, the minute, dull hairs along its rounded back, the segmentations of its lower half dazzlingly apparent. Henry watched the creature for a long time, studying it. He was pretty sure it was watching him as well.

"You are the King of the Night, aren't you?" Henry whispered.

The giant moth seemed to flap its wings as a dignified response.

"You're on the side of my father. And the Nazis. You and Mr. Horner and him. You killed my friend? You killed those two girls?"

The moth quickly went still.

"I'm going to kill you and end this war once and for all," he murmured, then slowly, as slowly as he dared, he leaned over and grasped about blindly for a rock. Still keeping careful watch on his foe, Henry raised his hand back and threw, without taking aim. The tiny rock struck the fence with a dull ping. Given a sudden moment to escape, the frightened moth flew high into the darkly lit night, its wide shape quietly vanishing.

AFTER THE TERRIBLE events of that April, Henry returned to his silence, growing over the next two years into a tall, awkward shadow. By early spring 1944, the Casper family, like a number of other German families interned at Crystal City, had been offered a choice: further internment or repatriation, whereby the family members would be sent across the Atlantic, back to Germany, in exchange for American prisoners. Afraid of what the future would hold for him and his family in the States—other than further shame—Len quietly agreed to be sent back to Germany. Henry, now sixteen, finally broke his silence. He demanded that he be left with the family in the adjacent bungalow, the Worsteins, an elderly couple from Buffalo, New York, who had been charged with sedition. Len, acknowledging his son's fierce resentment and ignoring his wife's protests, left the boy in the care of the Worsteins, bestowing on Henry the last of the family's remaining possessions—some photographs and a lovely black suit, which Len had stitched from black market linen. Henry refused to wear it. Then, like so many other figures in the young man's life—Mr. Miner, Private Faulk, the twin girls—his family disappeared, crossing on a ship named the *Gripsholm*, returning to a country that was soon to vanish itself.

IT DID NOT UPSET Henry Casper to be alone in the least. By then his father had become a shade, a villain, a shadow, a coconspirator in his fabulous nightmares. His mother and younger brother, Timothy, had also disappeared from his attentions. Lost in his own imagination, Henry ignored their familiar faces until, like those dramatic moments atop his bicycle back in Chicago, or hiding in the equipment shed listening to the failing radio, they were gone as well.

EIGHTEEN YEARS OLD NOW, having finished his last two years of high school in the internment camp with exceptional grades—the camp remained in operation for two years after the official end of the war—his teachers remarking upon "how committed, how astute, how clear-thinking" he had become, Henry applied for entrance into the Air Force but was denied. He returned to Chicago, finished an engineering degree at the University of Illinois, where he received a modest scholarship, and soon after, he gained an entry-level position at a midlevel aeronautics company. Henry quickly rose through the ranks on the strength of his wildly inventive sketches. He radically reimagined the first modern jet fighter, with wings, landing gear, and nose cone all borrowed from his own childhood ideas of space rocketry.

HIRED BY MCDONNELL DOUGLAS at the age of twenty-six, Henry moved to their headquarters in St. Louis and maintained his composed silence well into his courtship of Violet Brecht, a second-generation German girl who worked in the company's administrative offices and shared with Henry a fondness for silence, and also epic adventure movies. One year later, in 1955, the couple were married at city hall in a very quiet civil ceremony.

. . .

A YEAR AFTER THAT, in 1956, as a new war was beginning overseas in Asia, their first and only child, Jonathan, was born. By the boy's fifth birthday, it was obvious there was something quite wrong: Violet, having baked a cake in the shape of a lovely blue sky, with mountainous clouds of white frosting, watched in horror as the birthday boy collapsed, falling from his chair, landing on the tile floor, crushing his blue paper party hat.

To Whom It May Concern,
There is no such thing as a Good War.

To Whom It May Concern,
You were silent when frightened which is not the same
as being brave.

To Whom It May Concern,
*   You did not say goodbye to your mother or father or*
brothers. And then they all disappeared. You did not hear
from them again.

.   .   .

THISBE LOOKS UP and sees her grandfather has finished writing. He folds each white page into its own envelope, then licks each gluey flap, firmly pressing it closed. Finally he searches his bureau drawer for a stamp, scribbling down the same address on each letter. When he is finished writing, he hands the envelopes to his granddaughter without so much as murmuring a word.

"Would you like me to mail these for you?" she asks.

Her grandfather nods curtly. She takes the envelopes from his hands and then stares down at him shyly. "I'm sorry I chickened out," she whispers. "Please don't be mad at me. I'm just not good at doing things I'm not supposed to."

Henry nods, still refusing to look her in the face.

"Well, maybe we can try again tomorrow? I can come after school, and we can try then. Or if I can't make it tomorrow, maybe the day after that?"

Henry nods, glancing up at the soft symmetry of his granddaughter's young face.

He nods at her and then gently kisses the back of her hand.

Further Comments of a Questionable Historical Importance

A GLORIOUS WHITE HORSE COSTS BERNARD CASPER his life. His hands bound with rope behind his back, a gray blindfold covering his beady gray eyes, he is led to the center of town by a group of German soldiers, who disregard the enormity of the event, smoking their cigarettes, cursing, spitting, and joking loudly. Bernard's clubfeet, badly malformed, drag bare in the mud. As a prisoner convicted of sedition, he is marched through the dirty street toward the town square—a collection of cobblestones and weedy roses—where three other traitors have already been executed, shot in their heads and hearts and stomachs, all left bleeding near the town's only statue, a terrible rendering of King Wilhelm in limestone, the seditionists wilting at his whitened feet like so many dead flowers. It is fall 1869. The Franco-Prussian War carries on. The townspeople of Wissembourg, a grimy little hamlet along the French and German border, come to their doors, parting their threadbare curtains to watch the prisoner stumble forward, tripping as he goes, shoved back and forth between unclean, rough hands, cowering at the filthy language of the young

German soldiers. The prisoner knows he is about to die. He
has urinated on himself once already.

Figure 3: A horse

AT THE CENTER OF TOWN, the prisoner's back is shoved
against the great stone base of the statue and a cigarette is
placed hastily in his mouth. The soldiers forgo the courte-
sies of a more formal execution—their bearded lieutenant is
drunk, busy elsewhere in a whore's bed, unconcerned with the
rigorous virtue of a seditionist's death—and ask if the prisoner
wants his blindfold removed or not. Bernard says he does. He
says he would like to see the sky before he is to be shot. A
young soldier, once a musician, a violinist with nimble fingers,
unties the prisoner's blindfold very carefully.

Another group of soldiers, also drunk, drag Bernard's
gigantic white horse up the street, the horse struggling and
whinnying, before they kick it and tie the skittish animal to
the statue of the king. Bernard Casper frowns, lowering his
head. The horse, once his, then sold, will now be his partner in
death. It begins to clomp the muddy earth, equally frightened.
Bernard sees the horse's breath in the early morning air, twin
clouds of blue smoke. The horse does not seem to recognize
him. A sergeant with a round face and a silver saber approaches
Bernard slowly. With his serious demeanor, he does what he
can to try and invoke some sense of ceremony.

"Is your name Bernard Casper, sir?"

"*Ja.*"

"Is it you who sold this horse to a French officer, thus aiding his escape?"

"*Ja.*"

"Is there any evidence you'd like to offer at this time that may clear you of this crime?"

"*Nein.* It was only a mistake, a terrible mistake. It happened because I do not know which empire we are subjects of. One day it is the Germans, the next it is the French. One month we are told to fly a flag of one color, the next month it is something else. I sold the French officer the horse because I had had enough of not knowing which country I would be in when I awoke each morning. So I decided, once and for all, it would be France."

"And in doing so, in declaring allegiance with the French, you have provided aid to our enemy. For crimes against the king, you have been sentenced to death. Do you have any final words?"

"*Nein.*"

"*Nein?*"

"*Nein.*"

The sergeant nods, raising the saber, marching stiffly toward the group of seven soldiers. He lowers the saber and the soldiers form an inelegant line, raising their rifles to their glimmering eyes. The sergeant raises his saber again, pointing at the horse. "*Zuerst, das pferd,*" he announces, turning to face the unstill animal. Bernard closes his eyes too late. The sergeant's saber drops, and the hollow echo of seven shots ring out, the great beast rising in its final moment, so much like a statue itself, rearing up as if to climb the clouds of gun smoke directly into the sky and then it falls to its side. The horse snorts once or twice more, its head unmoving against the muddy ground, its one visible eye blinking once, then again, once more, before a cloud of steam slowly rises from its open wounds.

The sergeant lowers the saber and turns toward the prisoner, muttering, "*Und jetzt der mann.*" The soldiers reload their rifles, some quickly, some clumsily, and turn and face Bernard. Bernard Casper, now shivering, has begun to weep. He weeps without embarrassment. His cowardice is well known. In this moment, it feels like a gift. The sergeant raises his saber. It looks golden in the sudden light of the sun. The saber falls. Seven shots ring out, all at once, each round delivering certain death. But one, a single bullet, tears through the gray wool of Bernard's pants, cutting hard across the bones of his hip, puncturing what has always been most important to all men, his scrotum, then continuing on, the bullet screaming through the open doors of a barn, cracking the front windowpane of the Edel family, the town's only tailors, passing through a gray cloth curtain to where a young girl named Elsie Edel is, at that moment, precariously balancing on the edge of a zinc bathtub. The single shot pierces the soft fruit of her navel and impolitely imparts her womb with the impossible mystery of life.

Though the wound is not very deep, it is this, this second and more final act of cowardice, that results in the mysterious birth of a boy who, by many accounts, never would have been conceived if not for his father's first act of treason. Elsie Edel, choosing the disgrace of the dead over the disgrace of the living, gives her child the name Jacob Casper. The town watches as the boy grows quietly into manhood, following closely at his mother's unsullied skirts. No one is surprised when, at the age of five, it is revealed that both of the boy's feet are hopelessly clubbed.

Sixteen

On Wednesday morning, at the Museum of Natural History, Jonathan confides in the life-sized models of aquatic animals in the World Under the Sea exhibit:

"She's leaving me. If she hasn't already, then she probably will anytime now," he whispers, staring up at the giant humpback whale. "I blew it. I really screwed it up bad this time. And I lost the grant. And the French found a live specimen. And now my life is total shit." The enormous purple giant squid does not seem moved by the news. Fixed there, in the shadows of the closed exhibit, it does not even seem to be listening. Jonathan sits on the bench and stares up; he is the only moving shadow in a room full of white sheets covering displays that have yet to be finished.

"I am a mess. I really am. I am a fucking mess. I mean, I'm not even supposed to be in here. The museum canceled my research hours. They asked for my fucking key."

Some minutes later, an odd jingling echoes down the tiled corridor. Jonathan straightens up, trying to comb his greasy hair with his fingers. He looks like hell. The bags beneath his eyes are sunken and black. His blond beard is tangled and uncooperative. He has been wearing the same yellow and red T-shirt for the past three days. Roger, the security guard, ambles down the hall and smiles, taking a seat beside Jonathan on the small wood bench.

"Professor."

"Roger."

"Thought I would find you down here."

"Yep."

"I heard they asked for your keys."

"They did."

"How did you get in this morning?"

"I didn't give them back."

Roger nods, scratching his hairy, tattooed neck.

"I think I'm supposed to get those keys from you."

"Probably."

"Do you want to give them to me now or do you have to clean your lab out?"

"No. I cleaned it out yesterday."

Jonathan sighs and reaches into his pants pocket, finding his key ring. He unthreads the museum's three keys and hands each—one, two, three—to Roger, planting them in his pinkish palm.

"I'm really sorry about this," Roger says.

"Me, too, Roger. I'd been working on this project for fifteen years now. More than fifteen. Like eighteen. It's hard to just watch it all turn to shit."

"What happened anyway? Did you get fired or something?"

"No," Jonathan says, smiling. "Not yet anyway."

"Oh."

"We lost our funding. So . . . well, we can't afford to keep our space here."

"That's too bad. You were still studying those squids and everything?"

"Yep."

"What are you going to do now?"

Jonathan leans forward, sighing again. "I don't know, Roger. I really don't. You got any suggestions?"

"Nope." He scratches his neck again, uncomfortable with Jonathan's gloominess. "Do you want to get high?"

"Okay, Roger," Jonathan says, almost inaudibly. Roger reaches into the front pocket of his blue uniform, finding a stubby joint. He lights it and takes a long drag and hands it to Jonathan, who stares at the joint for a moment, studying it. A small wisp of smoke rises from the lit end, up and up and up, curling around the innumerable tentacles of the giant squid hanging overhead. Jonathan closes his eyes and takes a long drag, feeling the same cloud quietly surrounding him, the cloud expanding and growing, until he is only just a suggestion, a puff of smoke, a figure of breath himself.

A FEW MINUTES LATER, Jonathan shows up late to his History of Paleontology 101 class and finds the enormous lecture hall mostly empty. There are only about nine or ten students out of a class roster of fifty. He does not despair. He accepts the lousy turnout as another insult in the ongoing depreciation of his life. He smiles to himself in grief, then sets his briefcase behind the beige podium and begins sorting through his notes, hoping to stall. Maybe five or six more kids will show up. But no one comes. Jonathan glances up at the small, bright, clean faces of the students who have bothered to attend his class this afternoon, hoping some of them will seem eager, willing, wanting to learn. But no: they hate him. It is obvious now.

The girl with too much makeup on in the front row is filing her nails. A boy wearing an iPod is singing along to himself. A girl in the back of the hall checks the time on her cell phone and yawns again. Jonathan looks over the empty seats and then opens his mouth to speak, but nothing comes out. He lowers his head, grabs his briefcase, and then races out.

JONATHAN SITS in the Peugeot in the garage behind his house, staring at the empty spot where his wife's car ought to be. Jonathan can almost make out the shape of the Volvo station wagon, of where it should be, of what it ought to look like, imagining it as a series of invisible, angular dashes:

Instead there is only a blank space, a background of dull, repetitive concrete bricks, a pattern of chipping mortar, of small cracks, a cobweb triangular and menacing in one corner. There are boxes upon boxes, stacked high atop each other, some ready to fall over. Somewhere within those dilapidated cardboard shapes are all of Madeline's books from graduate school. There is a box somewhere in that stack that contains her field notes from Ecuador—a six-month research trip to study the social behaviors of migratory birds. There are the goofy letters and flaky love notes that Jonathan wrote to her while she was away, a note folded to look like a heart, another that was supposed to look like a bird. And somewhere within those notes are the words, the feelings, the vanished glow, the panicked urgency, the wonderful, needful alarm, the proof of love, the thing that really matters. If Jonathan had the right kind of oscilloscope, if he had an X-ray machine or a magnifying device, maybe he could discover where he went wrong, where the awkwardness, the factitiousness began, where he started to follow the evolution of a prehistoric species more closely than the three people he should have been observing. Jonathan sighs, staring at the evidence before him. It is one of those incalculable, extraordinary moments when, in adult life, like in the field of paleontology, the physical proof is so undeniably clear. In those dusty, duct-taped boxes, somewhere beneath all this clutter, are the invisible, interred remains of the relationship with his wife. In the blank space where Madeline's car should be is the overwhelming enormity of what Jonathan has been missing.

INSIDE THE EMPTY HOUSE, it seems that his daughters have also vanished. Jonathan pokes around, calling their names, searching for their book bags sprawled somewhere on the floor, their shoes kicked off in the middle of a room, for some sign, some note, but no, there is nothing. He checks his watch. It's almost four o'clock. He paces around the house once more, picks up the phone, finds there are no voice messages waiting for him, hangs up the receiver, putters around, then takes a seat in his gray chair in front of the television. Jonathan flips through the channels slowly, then, suddenly remembering, he searches out CNN, leaning forward in his seat, muting the noisy chatter of the blank-looking host, a woman with dark hair and a square jaw. And then he sits there waiting, ignoring the news of the latest conflict in Palestine, of the war in Iraq, of the upcoming presidential elections, he sits there biting his fingernails, uninterested, until finally a purple icon of a squid appears in the small headline box above and to the right of the host's head: SEA MONSTER IN CAPTIVITY, the box reads. Jonathan quickly unmutes the television. It's not much, really, only a ten-second story: there are a few shots of Dr. Albert and his stupid-looking goatee. There's one quick shot of what appears to be a giant squid held in an enormous tank, then footage from *20,000 Leagues Under the Sea*. Jonathan squats before the television set and when the program flashes back to the footage of the squid, floating silently in its glass prison, Jonathan places his palm along the screen, trying to cross the impermeable void of static and electrons, to feel the cool glass of the gigantic aquarium against the flat of his hand. And then, just as quickly, the next story is being reported, the woman's expression unchanging, the headlines behind her a blurry field of text Jonathan does not care to understand. Once again, CNN, with its sound bites and tabloid format, has missed everything. When he has knelt before the TV long enough, when he is sure there will be no more mention of the giant squid for at least another hour, Jonathan stands, calls his wife's name, and listens to the keen silence. Returning to the kitchen, Jonathan glances out the tiny kitchen window, standing there wishing that he was not so appallingly alone. He watches the sun begin its descent as the final traces of light cause the faintest, farthest clouds in the west to glow.

Seventeen

A. On Wednesday, the cloud-person seems to be lost.
Today Madeline has not gone to work. She has followed the
cloud-person all day long. But the cloud does not seem to be
following Madeline's map. Madeline very nearly causes an accident as the Volvo lurches around a slow-moving minivan. The
cloud seems to have forgotten the rules. It is zigzagging now,
from the lake to Hyde Park, then veering recklessly, the wind
carrying it quickly toward the north side of the city. Madeline
is frantic, honking her horn, banging on the steering wheel,
she does her best to avoid the traffic, but the cloud seems to
be drifting north, crossing over the high buildings of the Gold
Coast. Madeline tries to watch it and the road at the same time.
She glances in the rearview mirror and sees her two suitcases
and her travel bag. By now she has packed everything: all of
her clothes, shoes, photographs, all of her toiletries, anything
she thinks she might need if she finally decides it is time to just
leave. The suitcases sit silently in the backseat, waiting. They
are waiting like Madeline is waiting, though Madeline suddenly believes she might no longer be waiting for anything. She
thinks maybe she has already made her decision. Maybe she

is just waiting for the right moment now, for an opportunity, maybe for a chance to say goodbye. Maybe that is it. Maybe she is waiting for someone to notice she has been missing, just so she can say goodbye, and then, and then that will be it. Traffic has stopped moving along Lake Shore Drive, and Madeline, panicked, watches as the cloud continues to hurry off without her. Madeline begins to honk her horn, but the line of cars does not respond. The cloud-figure does not slow down. Madeline murmurs, "Wait . . . wait . . . please don't go . . . don't be an asshole . . . just wait," then throws open the driver's-side door and, leaving the Volvo stranded there, parked in rush-hour traffic, she begins to follow on foot. The cloud drifts higher and higher until it is only a faint impression, and then its gone, once and for all.

Eighteen

AMELIA FINISHES THE BOMB ON WEDNESDAY MORN-
ing. With the Internet's instruction, she has built an explosive
device that runs on a simple timer—the stolen watch, which
will, in turn, trigger the explosion of one densely packed length
of metal—the toy airplane, filled with the mixture of clipped-
off match heads, taken from the professor's cigarette case, and
the black fireworks powder. The bomb is silver and its wires
are red and white. It looks amazing. It somehow looks exactly
as Amelia had always imagined.

Staring down at it, preparing to place it inside her book bag,
Amelia is now too afraid to touch it. The Internet has warned
that pipe bombs are the most unstable of explosive devices,
that the gunpowder or match heads might suddenly ignite
from the slightest, most minuscule amount of friction, and
that a number of would-be terrorists are killed every year by
unplanned, amateurish explosions. Gently wrapping the device
in a small cloth towel and then an old gray sweatshirt, she carefully, slowly, fitfully—holding her breath—places the bomb in
her book bag, and then gently zips the zipper up, once more

afraid to breathe. She lifts the bag upon her narrow shoulders. The bomb does not go off. It does not destroy the second story of her parents' house, it does not kill anyone or cause unnecessary collateral damage; the bomb, perfectly assembled by Amelia, does what it's supposed to at this point, absolutely nothing. Though her heart is throbbing in her thin chest, Amelia is quite pleased with herself. She has gotten through this first, difficult, nerve-wracking phase of the operation without dying. She is not an amateur. The rest of her plan is going to be easy, or so she whispers to herself, staring at the shiny reflection in the mirror before her. With the book bag sagging on her shoulders, Amelia nods once more to herself, and then cautiously places her black beret on her head. She looks exactly right, a missionary with black eyeliner, a revolutionary poster girl—she imagines, years from now, an independent film starring someone like Winona Ryder, but younger, portraying this exact, amazing moment. Saluting her reflection, Amelia then turns from the mirror and marches vigilantly down the stairs.

WITH THE PIPE BOMB resting only a few centimeters from her spine, Amelia decides to skip breakfast. She ditches her sister at the end of the street and walks carefully down the empty tile hallway of her school, trying not to jostle her backpack. At this time on a Wednesday morning the school is almost completely deserted. She stands before the abandoned student newspaper office. THE MIDWAY, it says in silver letters along the glass window of the wooden door. Amelia glares at the faded lettering, feeling betrayed even by this, the newspaper's middling, uninspired title. She finds the office key in her book bag, careful to avoid upsetting the explosive device.

She glances down the hallway once more to be sure she isn't being watched, then unlocks the door and sprints inside, barely breathing.

Inside, the office looks like it always does; it's a complete mess. Mr. Wick has left the wrappings of yesterday's lunch on his desk: a crumbled-up, half-eaten cheeseburger from the cafeteria, some molten-looking french fries, and an empty cup of chocolate pudding. *No wonder this newspaper is so useless*, Amelia thinks. *How can it be anything but a reflection of the small, infantile minds who carelessly throw it together?*

Amelia glances up at the round clock that hangs above the office's two computers. 8:49. She has eleven minutes to plant the bomb and hurry to her first-period class. Amelia tenderly slips the book bag off her shoulders, and then, as lightly as she can, she places it on the photo editor's desk. Black plastic tooth by black plastic tooth, she unzips the bag and then slowly reaches inside. She grasps the bomb's heavy wrappings and carefully lifts the explosive device out, placing it on the desk before her. She looks up at the clock again and already another minute has gone by. She must plant the device and get out of the office before Mr. Wick shows up at nine o'clock, still half asleep, powdered donuts and giant coffee from Starbucks in his enormous, unwashed hands. She nervously looks up at the clock again. 8:50. Unsteadily, Amelia begins to unwrap the device. One of the lead wires is caught on a stitch of the sweatshirt's fabric. She begins to panic. Her neck immediately erupts with red welts, her forehead bristling with sweat. *Okay. Okay. Okay. Breathe, breathe.* All she has to do is pull the stitch from the wire without detaching it and setting the explosive off in her hands. 8:52. She breathes deeply, scratches the hives on her neck and left shoulder, then tries to breathe again. She places her hand over her unsteady heart and sighs, then takes one more deep breath, closes her eyes, and lightly tugs on the sweatshirt's hem. The thread breaks free, the bomb does not explode, and Amelia glances up at the clock once more. 8:54.

Holding the pipe bomb as far from her chest as her slender arms will allow, she hurries over toward the advertising desk, vacant these last two months since Patsy Walker, the advertising editor, quit. Amelia slowly places the pipe bomb in the unlocked top drawer of the black metal filing cabinet, gently setting the timer for 11:00 a.m., when she knows the student newspaper office will be deserted, as that's when Mr. Wick has to teach his journalism seminar for juniors and seniors, and all the other student editors are busy in their own classes. The timer beeps once, twice, then a third time, and Amelia nervously slides the drawer closed. She finds the key to the filing drawer on her key ring, slips it into the silver-colored lock, and double-checks it to be sure the cabinet cannot be accidentally opened. There. 8:59. She sighs, grabs her book bag, heaves it onto her shoulder, stands behind the office door, glances through the window, which by now reveals a hallway full of sleepy kids, then walks briskly among the unknowing masses, stepping quickly toward her first-period civics class.

AMELIA IS UNABLE to concentrate on anything that whole morning: she bites at her nails, scratches the odd blisters on her neck and arms, and keeps glancing up at the clock. It is 10:47. When Mrs. Dennison calls on her in her third-period physics class, Amelia has no idea what the question or the answer might be. From Mrs. Dennison's expression of disbelief on her rotund, pasty face, Amelia can tell that her teacher is both delighted and disappointed. "I'm surprised, Amelia," Mrs. Dennison says, now smiling. "I thought you had all the answers."

"Sorry, Mrs. Dennison," Amelia says with a false laugh. "I think I'm developing lactose intolerance. I'm having serious medical issues at the moment."

"Do you want to go down to the health office?"

"No, Mrs. Dennison. I'll try to persevere."

Mrs. Dennison smiles and nods, then goes on with her physics problem, something about the law of inverse reaction. Amelia hasn't taken a single note in her notebook, which lies open to an empty page in the middle of her desk. From the corner of her eye, Amelia glances up at the minute hand once again as it crests toward the top of the hour. She feels like she herself is about to explode. She thinks of Mr. Wick, sitting there dopily behind his desk, eating his powdered donuts, unaware of the danger only a few yards away. *Maybe today is the day he decides to go over the photo layouts. Or the day he accidentally falls asleep. Oh, shit, what if he's in there napping right now? What if I made a mistake?* Amelia immediately imagines the sound of Mr. Wick's primitive snores. A swell of panic begins to vibrate through her chest. She tries to jot down the formula Mrs. Dennison has written on the blackboard but the letters and numbers all look completely unfamiliar to her. *What does any of this mean? What does physics have to do with how people live? Isn't it just another expression of white masculine power, trying to tyrannize the natural world? Just like Mr. Wick. Mr. Wick. Mr. Wick. If the bomb goes off and Mr. Wick dies, accidentally, well, that will be one less spineless white male to repress an entire generation. But what if it's someone else? Like Max? Or Heather? Or someone you can't even think of, like a janitor, some poor working-class father with three children to support? What if you accidentally kill an innocent janitor? No. No one's going to be hurt. Why are you even thinking about this shit right now? Just stay calm. Imagine yourself as a poster, as an actress in the small-budget movie of your life. Be fearless. Try and imagine this moment as being important.*

When Amelia has finished copying down the formula, she looks up, watches as the black minute hand slides closer to the numeric 12 at the top of the clock. It is 10:56. Something in her chest is screaming. It can't possibly be her heart. She is sweating. Her forehead feels slick. She glances from the blackboard to the clock again. It is 10:57. For some reason, she is raising her hand right now. For some reason, she is speaking. She is saying that she needs to go see the nurse. The words, simple, without inflection, tumble from her tongue as she stands and takes the hall pass from Mrs. Dennison's chubby hand. Already she is running down the hall. She is flying down the tiled stairwell, sliding around the corner, her thin legs moving as quickly as they can, hurtling her small body toward the school newspaper office at the end of the hallway. The clock in the middle of the hall reads 10:59. She lunges for the doorknob. The door to the newspaper office is open. Mr. Wick, his fat face full of white powdered donuts, is sitting behind his desk, reading through a pile of new student stories. He mutters her name in surprise, choking a little on a donut as she dashes toward the subscription desk. She unlocks the filing cabinet drawer without responding. The bomb lies before her, a patchwork of wire and leftovers: matches, a wristwatch, a toy. Without another thought, Amelia pulls the green lead wire, immediately disconnecting the timer. She glances up at the clock. 11:00. The bomb does not explode. The newspaper office is silent, except for the awful chewing of Mr. Wick at his desk. The school bell begins to ring. When it does, its unpleasant drone vibrates along with the shaky tone of Amelia's heart and she very nearly collapses. As soon as the bell has finished its trebly announcement, Amelia shoves the filing cabinet drawer closed, her knees shaking, her hands shaking, her heartbeat still pounding vainly in her ears. She steadies herself against the subscription desk. Mr. Wick looks up from his papers and asks what it is she's doing. Amelia turns then, and with as much false confidence as she can muster, she says, "I was looking for my notebook. I guess it must be in my locker." Mr. Wick nods. Amelia turns the small silver key in the lock then slips it into her pocket. She decides she will have to return after school to get rid of the bomb, as she's shaking too much to try and do it now. Amelia takes a long, deep breath and, miraculously, she somehow manages to stumble out without fainting.

FOR THE FULL five minutes between classes, Amelia stands before her locker, not sure what it is she's supposed to be doing. She is searching for something, a book maybe, unsure as to what class she's supposed to be heading to next. The second bell clangs loudly above, announcing her tardiness. She does not hear it. She is staring at the photos she has pasted in her locker, photos of Che, of Fidel, of Marx. Their somber faces all frown with disapproval. *What just happened? Why did I fail? Maybe the newspaper office was a bad idea—of course I'd be suspected. It's better, in the end, that I backed off. Or is it? Maybe I am only lying to myself right now. Maybe this is exactly what every coward in history has ever thought. No, I'm no Weatherman. I'm no Patty Hearst. I have tried to stage a revolutionary moment and I have completely blown it. I'm a failure. I'm a phony.*

Two boys—freshmen, probably—hurry past Amelia, one of them colliding with her left shoulder, knocking the stack of unsorted books from her arm, scattering them all across the hallway. The boy shouts an apology from over his shoulder and keeps on running, while Amelia stops, bends over, and scoops up her belongings from off the dirty tile floor. For the first time in as long as she can remember, she does not curse out loud. Instead, a soft pattering of tears begins to trickle from her eyes. This crying jag is only the latest of her unending, secret failures. Before she trudges off toward her next class, already tardy, she stops and itches her reddened neck. Mr. Hansen, her English teacher, will definitely give her shit for being late again. At the door to the classroom, Amelia distractedly glances down at her nails and sees, along her fingertips, there is blood.

AFTER HER CLASSES have ended that Wednesday afternoon, after ditching the bomb in the dumpster near school, Amelia waits in the university faculty parking lot, once again hoping to see Professor Dobbs. She does not care if it is pathetic, her coming up here every day after school to try and find him. Instead, she sits beside his lustrous Saab, thinking up different excuses for running into him. But, of course, he does not show. Maybe he is avoiding her. Maybe that's why he never gave her a way to get hold of him, no cell phone number, no email, nothing. Maybe he saw something about her, something she can't see in herself, something predictable, something desperate and incredibly weak. Maybe he carries on with students like this all the time and, in the end, she is only a plaything to him, a piece of soft plastic, a disposable product. But at the moment she is just too depressed to be angry. Still she waits and waits and waits, and when it finally gets dark, when she checks her watch and it reads 6:00 p.m., when she has finished imagining the young professor fucking some undergraduate student—someone just like her but more dynamic, more self-aware—she stands, exasperated, and begins hurrying home. Usually Amelia does not like to walk at night by herself. Most of the time she feels that she is being followed by someone menacing—a maniacal sexual predator or an FBI surveillance team. Amelia often believes she is more important than she actually is, and that secretly, behind every corner, every parked car, every tree, someone, some important observer of history, is almost always watching. But today is very different. Walking home, defeated, her book bag slung low across her back, limping sadly beneath the bare arms of the autumn trees, she does not imagine herself as an image in some future history book or a reenactor in the documentary of her life.

AFTER AMELIA GETS HOME, after she kicks off her shoes and collapses onto her bed, she stares up at the photograph of Patty Hearst on the wall above her bed and something in her heart goes sick. No. She is no revolutionary. She is a coward. She is done trying. She is done pretending. Like the rest of America, like everyone else she knows, she is giving up. She is done trying to do something great. She is done trying to change things for the better. She pulls herself to her feet and seizes the photo from the wall with one quick swipe, splitting it down the middle as her blue eyes begin to swell with tears. She rips the image again and again until it is a dozen tiny pieces of colored paper, until, like her, it has become nothing. When she has finished, she snatches the torn pieces from the floor and quickly shoves them into her bottom dresser drawer. There the pieces lie—inconsolable, inconsequential—a sad hum rising from her collection of other tragically useless objects.

Nineteen

AFTER SCHOOL ON WEDNESDAY, AFTER CHORUS PRAC-
tice has ended, Thisbe pedals down the shady twilight streets,
down the Midway to her block, and then walks her bicycle
around the side of the house to the garage. Thisbe opens the
garage door and is jubilant to find her mother's Volvo parked
there. She runs inside the house but her mother is nowhere
around. She finds her father hunched over a stack of maps and
documents in the den, and says hello. Her father nods, without
looking up, and whispers, "I'm going to see Grandpa tonight.
If you'd like to go, I'll be leaving in an hour or so."

"Is Mom home?" Thisbe asks.

Jonathan looks up from his work for a moment, and then
nods, without a sound. His eyes meet his daughter's and Thisbe
feels an exquisite sadness for her dad. She smiles at him, then
turns and runs up the stairs as quickly as she can. She knocks
loudly on her parents' bedroom door, calling her mother's
name, but no one answers. She gives the doorknob a turn and
finds it is locked. Why would her mother lock it? What's going
on in there? What's her mother so afraid of anyway? Thisbe
knocks once more and then begins to back away, unsure of

why her mother won't answer. She sits silently beside her parents' door for an hour or two, then gets tired and wanders off toward her room.

AROUND TEN OR eleven that night, Thisbe gets hungry and traipses downstairs. All she finds in the refrigerator is spoiled milk and some wilted celery. She finally uncovers some old crackers and munches them dryly in her mouth. She heads down the hallway to watch television and finds her mother sitting there in the dark, looking messy in her robe, staring out the window into the shadowy backyard.

"Hi, Mom," Thisbe whispers.

"What are you doing up, sweetheart?"

"I had a bad dream that I didn't have any arms. And then I was hungry. And then I had to go to the bathroom. And then I couldn't go back to sleep."

"Me neither," her mother sighs. Thisbe sits down beside her and offers her some crackers. Her mother nods and quietly nibbles along the cracker's salty edge. "These are pretty stale," her mother whispers.

"Yeah," Thisbe says with a grin.

They both chew in near silence, mother and daughter, staring through the window at the dark shapes moving as shadows in the backyard. Thisbe glances over at her mother's face and mutters, "Mom?"

"Yes?"

"Are you . . . are you planning on leaving us?"

"Oh, Thisbe," her mother says with an unsure smile, shaking her head, her dark eyes looking sad and full of uncried tears, glowing in the faraway light from the kitchen. "I would never. Never. I just . . . it's just hard for me to be here right now. Your father and I . . . well, we . . ." Her mother smiles again, sadly. "We just don't know what to do with each other."

"He loves you. I know he does."

Her mother smiles again.

"Thank you, Thisbe. But it isn't that."

"What is it?"

Her mother fingers a thread that has come unloose from the corner of her robe. "It's complicated. Your father loves me but he's also in love with his work. I feel like I'm always in competition with it. And he wants me to give up a lot of things to take care of you guys but he doesn't want to give up anything himself. And he can be so selfish . . . sometimes he can act like we're not even here. I know he loves me but I'm afraid it's because he needs me to take care of him. I don't know, honey, like I said, it's very complicated and I just don't think it should be all that complicated."

Thisbe nods, chewing another stale cracker.

"Oh."

Her mother nods, too, staring back out the window. She then turns, her smile big and beaming. "What if you and I, what if we take the day off tomorrow?" her mother asks.

"And do what?"

"I don't know. We could go shopping. Or get some lunch in a fancy restaurant or something."

"I don't know," Thisbe says. "I have chorus after school. And a test in English. And then I'd have to get the homework from someone and I don't really know who I could ask."

Her mother nods, touching Thisbe's knee.

"Well, you're definitely your father's daughter," her mother says with a smirk.

Thisbe's face goes red for a moment. She realizes, too late, that she's hurt her mother's feelings. She shakes her head and says, "I mean, I bet I could find somebody. Or I'll just make up the test on Friday. It's no big deal."

"Are you sure?"

Thisbe nods.

"Okay, don't tell your father."

"What about Amelia?" Thisbe asks, hoping her mother will not invite her older sister as well.

"Amelia will probably want to go to school instead."

"Probably."

"Okay?" her mother asks.

"Okay."

"Okay, now, why don't you head back up to bed? We'll have a nice girl's day tomorrow."

"Okay," Thisbe says, quickly kissing her mother's cheek. She grabs the empty box of crackers and stands, picking crumbs off of her pajamas. She starts off down the hallway and then turns, thinking, staring down at her feet, unsure of something. She thinks of Roxie, of missing the chance to see her, of once again lying with her in the field.

"What is it?" her mother asks.

"Nothing. I just . . . well . . . maybe . . ."

Her mother smiles. "It's okay if you think you should go to school instead. We can go out together some other day."

"Are you sure?" Thisbe asks.

"Sure."

"Okay," Thisbe says and hugs her mother again. "Thanks Mom," she whispers, then rushes off, climbing awkwardly up the stairs. Her mother sits in the dark, staring out the window, looking for the answer to something, anything.

Twenty

ON WEDNESDAY NIGHT, THE NURSING HOME STAFF informs Jonathan that his father may be nearing the end. He has refused to speak or eat anything for two days now. That evening, the nurses do not bother Jonathan when he arrives after the visiting hours have ended. Jonathan thanks them for this small, thoughtful concession. When he walks into the darkened room, he sees his father lying there in the white hospital bed, the old man now hopelessly small and delicate. His thin eyelids flutter as he sleeps, his mouth whispering dull, indistinguishable noises. Jonathan takes a seat in the uncomfortable blue chair beside his father's bed and carefully takes hold of his father's limp hand. "Hello, Dad," Jonathan whispers, but his father does not seem to notice. Jonathan softly squeezes Henry's palm but there is no response. The nurses have left the television on to keep the old man company: a history program about the Wright brothers flashes from the TV set in the corner. Jonathan leans over and stares at his father, murmuring the single word, with the soft appeal of a question. "Dad?" But there is still no answer.

Jonathan squeezes the tiny hand, the skin, the knuckles so

weak, so brittle. "Dad, don't go. I need you. Please." The eyelids flicker but do not rise, do not open.

"Dad. Please. I need you. Dad?"

His father is silent, breathing heavily. One of his eyes opens, then another. He glances up at his son and then smiles.

"Please, Dad. I think I've made a terrible mistake."

His father's lips move without sound.

"The girls, and Madeline. I think I've lost them, Dad. I think I've lost them and now I don't know what to do. You're the only person who I can talk to."

His father's eyes blink and his lips continue to move soundlessly. There are only two words left, two words that remain before he vanishes for good. He wants to speak. He wants to use these two remaining sounds to help his son, but he is unable. They are gone. All the words he has ever known have disappeared—along with the clothes he has given away, the photographs he has discarded, the fantasies of flight, the old and unsure memories. Henry turns on his side, facing his son, then motions toward the nightstand. There beside a disposable plastic cup is his notebook and pen. Jonathan grabs them and carefully places them in his father's hands. Struggling to open the book to a blank page, Henry slowly scribbles a single straight line, then a dot, then a wavy line, then a dot, then one more straight line, ending with a third dot, three marks that aren't words at all, only a feeling, not even a single sound:

!?!

Jonathan stares down at the scribbling and shakes his head.

"I don't know what that's supposed to mean, Dad. I mean, Dad, she's leaving me. Madeline's leaving me. What should I do? What should I do, Dad?"

Dad?

Henry hears the single word *Dad* again and again. The single word resonates a long way, somewhere through the distance of ten, then twenty, then nearly forty years, the sound reverberating in Henry's weak ears, a solitary echo making its way down an empty, carpeted hallway toward the den in the back of the house in St. Louis, where Henry, sitting on a pale green sofa, does not answer. It is an afternoon late in 1966 that Henry would prefer not to remember. And yet he is now remembering it, hearing that particular word resonate with uncertainty again and again.

"Dad?" Jonathan is calling out faintly. The boy throws his book bag on the yellow linoleum kitchen counter and then calls out once more. He listens for his father's voice but instead he hears a boom and the tremble of a jet screaming across the rounded rectangle of the television screen. "Dad?" he shouts a second time, but again, there is no answer. Jonathan pours himself a glass of milk, then one for his father, and, carrying them both as carefully as he can, he shuffles toward the racket coming from the television room.

"Dad?"

His father, Henry, thirty-eight years old, sits in his place at the end of the sofa, with his unbuttoned white shirt, a dark blue tie hanging undone around his neck. There is a glow of sadness about him, surrounded by the dark wood paneling, the pale sofa, and the yellow shag rug, making the flesh of his hands and face look lifeless and ill. From the ashtray resting near the sofa, Jonathan sees his father has been sitting there for quite a while, a pyramid of stubbed cigarettes crushed on top of each other. Jonathan hands his father the glass of milk. Henry accepts it gratefully without a word. Jonathan takes a seat beside him and asks, "What are you watching, Dad?" but Henry does not answer.

On the television screen is the four-thirty news, and there is a story about the war in Vietnam being broadcast. Jonathan knows better than to ask questions while his father is watching the news, especially when it has to do with the war. Henry Casper sits quietly, his security badge from R and D—Research and Development at McDonnell Douglas—still pinned to the pocket on his white shirt. The television groans as a burnished silver F-4 Phantom drops a payload of napalm over the small gray and brown and green village of Trang Bang. Something important breaks in Henry Casper's heart. The F-4 is his plane, one of the planes, a plane he has helped to design and build.

"Dad?" Jonathan whispers, but his father is faraway and silent.

An orange and red fireball engulfs an outcropping of trees and grass in one combustive show of flames—knocking the glass of milk straight from Henry's trembling hand. There are two small girls, twin sisters, both naked, running from the flames, the clothes burned right from their skin, and all Henry can do is sit there on his sofa, thousands and thousands of miles away and begin to weep, quietly, regretfully, without surprise. His empty hands reach out toward the absolute distance of the television screen. Though Henry, in his position as an aeronautical designer, had worked mostly with the nose and wing design, on paper it had only been a drawing, a picture, a problem to be solved. On the TV now, the young girls are on fire, their mouths agape, shaken with all the fear of the world—*why has he done this to them?* He reaches out, ignoring his ten-year-old son, falling to his knees, placing his hands against the television screen. He is asking them to forgive him now, asking them to please listen, to know how awful he feels now, how small, how sorry. But there is no reply. Jonathan, upset, keeps repeating the word over and over again, "Dad? Dad?" until Henry turns, not recognizing his son's voice, hoping it is the girls calling out to him, hoping, in their final moments, that they will forgive him. When he turns and faces his son, he sees they will not.

Or maybe there were no twin girls on the television screen at all. Maybe it had been a photograph or an article in a magazine or a story someone had mentioned at the office. Maybe the afternoon did not happen exactly the way Henry now remembers it. Maybe it does not matter—the order of events, the actualities, the facts. Maybe the image, real or not, transmitted across television waves or simply imagined, was enough.

After that day, after watching the F-4 burn an entire village in a few static fractions of a second, Henry Casper will surrender himself to the television for another three months, waiting for the young Vietnamese girls to reappear. After using up his vacation time and one long month of an unscheduled medical leave, he will be fired by McDonnell Douglas. During those lengthy afternoons, he will only leave the television room for an hour or two, staggering around the house, looking for something to fix, a loose doorknob, the front porch railing. One day he finds Jonathan hiding in the familiar safety of his tiny bedroom. He spends hours watching his son glue together the wings of a model dinosaur, the chassis of a model race car, the nose cone of a model airplane, which the boy will hang with fishing line over his bed. At night, tucking Jonathan in, Henry will glance at the shadows of the winged dinosaurs and airplanes hanging over his boy's head. He will understand then that he will never be forgiven for what he has knowingly or unknowingly been part of. He will kiss his wife Violet good-night and return to the television room to watch the final news broadcasts of the evening, the stations signing off sometime in the night, the familiar static echoing from the room, the electric red, white, and blue of a flag waving in the darkness.

WITH THE LIGHTS off then, the television set now silent, Henry unwillingly begins to imagine that which he wishes he did not have to. He watches ghosts—those of the two twin girls—and others who are nameless, faceless, hundreds of them, all burned beyond recognition, as they crowd him in the tiny television room. They stand awkwardly amid the matching furniture, their stares vacant, like fallen stars or moons, all of them softly aglow. Somewhere among the phosphorous dead is Private Faulk, somewhere there are other familiar faces, all sad, resigned, his father and mother, his younger brother, Timothy, his older brother, Harold, killed in action, all of them are quiet, and yet they do not let him rest. They hover beside him in the darkness, the glow of their bodies shifting from blue to white. The only thing that quiets them is the noise of the television, its own light fierce, impossible to ignore, overpowering. Even after the last broadcast, Henry will sometimes turn the machine back on, the soft static clouding the glow of the dead with fields of impenetrable, electric snow.

THREE MONTHS AFTER his breakdown, Henry does not care what is on television during the day, as long as, at any moment, he can stand, sigh, check the knot in his robe, and cross the room to change the channel, searching for breaking news of the war in Vietnam. Violet, his wife, who seems to love him a little more since he has fallen apart, brings in trays of iced tea and small sandwiches for him. Jonathan, who sits near his father's feet, watches whatever his father watches, news programs, nature programs, shows about American history. Together, they are silent, Jonathan doing his fourth-grade homework, lying on the yellow shag carpet, watching his father with curious dismay, Henry waiting for a message, an answer from somewhere beyond the screen that will let him live with a clear conscience again. But it does not come. It never seems to come.

TOGETHER, DURING THOSE months, father, fired from his job, and son, who is often quarantined from school with his mysterious seizures, watch *The Courtship of Eddie's Father*, *The Brady Bunch*, *The Price Is Right*, cartoons like *Yogi Bear* whom Jonathan dearly loves, and early evening broadcasts of *Batman*, with Adam West as the caped crusader. *Batman* is their favorite show to watch together. Violet has sewn a fairly accurate Batman cowl for Jonathan, who wears the mask around all the time, even when he goes to bed. Sometimes, with the mask on, he will sit on the sofa beside his dad, dividing his attention between watching the show and watching his father's smile, gauging his dad's reactions out of the corners of his small blue eyes. Sometimes, after a particularly good episode, his father will stand, patting his boy on the head, leaving the television room for an hour or so. Spying on him, following his father throughout the house, Jonathan will see his father standing behind his mother in the bedroom hallway, his arms wrapped around her middle, both of them whispering. Sometimes his father will make a telephone call to some unknown party. Other times his father will walk to the front window and stare out, muttering small realizations to himself: "Looks like the Penneys got a new porch. Good for them. Good for them."

AT THE AGE of ten, only a few months before the introduction of the antiseizure medication, Jonathan begins to fake seizures at school. Taking a cue from his father's heartbreak and glad to be kept at home, Jonathan sits beside Henry all day, silent as he stares at the television for a glimpse of forgiveness that will not appear. Jonathan fakes seizures as often as once or twice a month. After each episode, he is kept home for several days, or up to a week at a time. His parents, both reasonable, or mostly reasonable, are terrified to send the boy back to class until a thorough assessment of his health can be made. A boy from Jonathan's grade, Billy Anderson, brings his schoolwork by. Together, Jonathan and his father travel from specialist to specialist, returning home weary from the white institutionalized medical offices. Jonathan will sometimes wear his pajamas all day, quietly playing in his room, building his dinosaur models, reading an abridged version of H. G. Wells's *The Time Machine*, waiting until he hears the electric buzz of the television suddenly flicking on, the sound of his father waking up.

• • •

IN SECRET, while Violet takes a better-paying job at the telephone company, father and son watch hour after hour of television in silence, Henry searching the commercials, the game shows, the cartoons, for the shadows of the wounded Vietnamese girls. Once he thinks he sees them in a detergent commercial. Another time, he is almost positive that the girls are on a children's show. Finally, they both appear as contestants on *The Price Is Right*. The girls do not jump up and down. They do not seem happy. They are both wearing the same white dress and they are no longer burning. They are ghosts. They have been trapped in this perfect world of luxury cars and vacuum cleaners and sparkling stereo equipment. They do not seem angry, only very, very sad. They do not win anything. They stand beside a row of products, their heads down, their eyes entirely dark. They are barefoot. They do not want to be on the game show, but because they are now ghosts they have no choice. The world of television, of reruns and repeated images, is the world of lost spirits. Henry, nervous in his spot at the end of the sofa, cannot watch it anymore. He gets up, cinches his robe, and switches the channel. It does not seem to matter. Now the two ghost girls are standing in the background of *Kojak*, dressed as underage prostitutes. Henry switches the channel again, and this time they are on *Happy Days*, a pair of odd-looking bobby soxers. He gives the knob another turn and all of a sudden the landscape of the moon appears—it is footage from an observatory telescope. The two ghosts have vanished somewhere in that distance, in that vast blackness. Henry watches the screen suspiciously, each flicker of movement, each white pixel, but no, now they are gone.

Henry then flips through the channels, finding a rerun of

Batman, the garish outfits, the bright exaggerated sets, no sign of the lost girls anywhere. They are still out there somewhere, though, Henry is sure of it, trapped with all the other ghosts he has ever known, waiting patiently up there on the moon now, where everything always goes when it is forgotten.

Taking a seat back on the couch, Henry turns and looks over at his son, who is busy with a stack of homework. He gently places his hand on the back of the boy's neck and says, "Don't ever be afraid to say you're sorry."

"Dad?" Jonathan asks, his eyes looking up from his spelling assignment.

"When you foul something up. Don't ever be afraid to say it was your fault. You'll live a much happier life that way."

"Okay," Jonathan says, shrugging his shoulders, staring down at his homework.

"Don't you wanna watch Batman?" Henry asks his boy.

"We've seen that one before. It's Catwoman. She steals a golden cat."

Henry nods. "I have a hard time keeping them all straight, I guess." He looks over at his son and smiles, seeing the boy's hand, so small, busily writing out his assignment. Henry taps his finger against his knee, wanting to say something more, to let the boy know how proud he is of him, for not giving up, for hanging in there, for trying to face whatever keeps happening to his little head, but all he can figure to say is, "Well, you can always count on Batman."

"Yeah."

"Where's your mask? How come you're not wearing it?"

"I can't wear it and do my homework. It's too hard to see out of."

"Well, sure. I get it. You need any help with what you're working on?" Henry asks.

"Nope."

"Well, if you do, all you have to do is ask."

"Okay."

"Jonathan?"

"Yes?"

"Never mind, kiddo. You just do your schoolwork."

"Okay."

Henry watches his son for another moment or two and then whispers:

"Do you understand why I had to quit my job?"

"Dad?" His son's face is small and confused.

"Do you know why I haven't gone to work in so long?"

Jonathan shakes his head, embarrassed for some reason, and looks down at his schoolwork. "No. I guess not."

"It's only that sometimes . . . sometimes it takes courage to do something, and other times it takes courage to not do something. Does that make sense to you?"

Jonathan nods, still unsure, wanting to please his dad. His father reads this in the boy's bright eyes.

"You're a good boy. You know that, don't you?"

Jonathan, his face red from hearing his father's words, does not turn. He only shrugs, staring down at his schoolwork.

"You're the best thing I ever did," Henry whispers. "The best," and then, feeling the boy's embarrassment, he nods and stares off at whatever's playing on the television.

ONE EVENING, after a particularly good episode of *Batman*, feeling unusually happy—the televised image of the burning village only a distant, foggy dream—Henry hurries out to the garage, his son secretly following. Jonathan, hiding at the edge of his father's yellow Cougar, sees his father struggling to pull down a large cardboard box from a high shelf, marked with a great painted x. Jonathan blinks, watching as his dad tears open the taped cardboard flaps, fumbling through its contents, some old magazines, a few record albums, some photographs, a fraying black suit.

"This was a suit your grandfather made," Henry says. "It doesn't look like much but it's all I've got left of him."

Jonathan nods silently. From within the suit jacket's lining, a brown spider emerges, narrowly escaping. Henry and his son watch the tiny creature hurry off, disappearing into the shadows of the gloomy garage. Henry's eyes do not leave the spider, not for a long time, and then, with a thoughtful turn in his eyes, he looks down at his son and murmurs, "Jonathan?"

"Yeah?"

"I hope you forgive me someday."

The boy's face goes white, as he's unsure of how to respond.

"For what, Dad?"

"For what? For quitting my job. For leaving us in the lurch. For being a coward. Will you forgive me someday?"

"Oh." Then, without thinking, the boy mutters, "Sure, Dad."

"We always have to try to forgive the people we love. I think it's the bravest thing we can do. When the time comes, I hope you will."

Jonathan is silent for a few moments and then whispers, "Okay, Dad."

"Okay," says Henry, smiling. He begins to rummage through the box again and seems to find what he's looking for.

"What's that?" Jonathan asks.

"Comic books."

"Wow," Jonathan whispers, astonished. On the covers are spacemen, werewolves, superheroes, some he recognizes, like

Superman and *Batman*, some he doesn't, *The Airship Brigade, The Flash, The Green Lantern, Hourman*. They are struck in valiant, noble poses, fighting it out with cruel-looking villains, performing incredible feats of strength.

"*The Airship Brigade*," Henry mutters, handing an issue to his son. "Now this one was always my favorite." He taps the cover twice, then goes on searching through his childhood belongings. Jonathan flips through the miraculous stories, Alexander Lightning piloting his zeppelin bravely through the sky, rescuing a silver-skinned princess. Henry lets out a low whistle and lifts something from the box. It is a tattered record album, red and black and yellow, a great golden zeppelin crossing a silver moon. Henry is grinning, staring down at it, elbowing his son lightly.

"What do you think of this?" he asks, but Jonathan just shrugs.

"It looks okay."

"Okay? Do you know what this is?" His father turns the record sleeve over and taps it with his forefinger twice. "It's a V-Disc. From during the war."

"Oh."

"It was a radio program from when I was a kid. I used to listen to it all the time."

"Oh."

"They used to play the stories on the radio. They'd record it on records, you know, some of their best adventures. That's what we got here: *Mysterious Islands in the Sky*."

"That's cool."

"Cool? Kiddo, you don't know what you're missing. Come on, let's go check it out. Grab those other records there. Good. Okay, let's go."

Jonathan, holding the comic books and records to his small

chest, looks up, and for the first time since he can remember, he notices his father is beaming.

FATHER AND SON are sitting in the front parlor beside the outdated Sears stereo. The needle makes contact with the rough grooves of the old record and instantly produces a sound. It is like a magnificent storm has suddenly swept itself into the room, lightning and wind echoing from the hi-fi's speakers. Then there is the theme music, horns and strings announcing, "*The Continuing Adventures of Alexander Lightning, teen commander of the undefeatable Airship Brigade!*" A thunderbolt hisses with fiery electricity through the speakers. "*Episode One Hundred:* Mysterious Islands in the Sky," the announcer Pierre Andre shouts with flair and dramatic promise. Jonathan smiles at his father, who winks, turning the treble down on the hi-fi, then hurrying back to his seat.

ANNOUNCER: *WGN Chicago and the Pennsylvania Coal Company are proud to bring you the continuing adventures of the Airship Brigade. Pennsylvania Coal Company, the one with the blue flame. Episode One Hundred:* Mysterious Islands in the Sky. *Young Alexander Lightning, teenage boy and supreme commander of the Airship Brigade, has found himself captured, along with his closest companions—his best friend, Hugo, Tor the Man-Ape, the intelligent Doctor Jupiter, and his darling daughter Darla—all held hostage on the strange floating cloud city of Xenon. Their miraculous airship, the X-1, has suffered incredible damage, seemingly beyond repair. Young Alexander, terrified for his life, finds himself trapped, his wrists harshly bound, as he is forced to face the Evil Cloud Emperor's unimaginable wrath.*

EMPEROR: Your puny world has caused me turmoil for much too long. After I am done disposing of you, Alexander Lightning, I will turn my Inviso-ray machine on your helpless planet.

ALEXANDER: As soon as I get myself free, you'll pay for what you've done. Earth will never fall victim to your cruel plans.

EMPEROR: Brave words, Alexander Lightning. Without you to protect it, your world will soon be decimated. For one precise blast from my Inviso-ray will leave your planet in absolute panic, rendering all things on your puny earth completely invisible. Chaos will reign supreme, and soon, with my cloud army, I will easily conquer what remains, plundering what I please.

ALEXANDER: Do what you must with me, but leave our planet alone!

EMPEROR: Kidnapped scientists of earth, prepare the Inviso-ray.

SCIENTISTS: Yes, Emperor Xenon. We will do as you command.

ALEXANDER: Why do those scientists obey your commands?

EMPEROR: It is mind control, dear boy. Using this telepathic helmet, I can command anyone I wish to do my bidding.

DARLA: Do you really think he has the power of mind control, Father?

DOCTOR JUPITER: It's possible, my dear. You saw how easy his cloud-army did away with our airship using their powerful ray cannons. I'm afraid their technology is much more advanced than ours.

TOR: Tor frightened. Tor no want to see jungle destroyed.

ALEXANDER: Mind control or not, friends, Tor is right. We can't let the emperor go through with his evil scheme. I think I have a plan.

EMPEROR: Guards! Escort our prisoners to the Coliseum of the Unfathomable.

GUARD: Yes, Your Majesty.

EMPEROR: Now you will see what we do with uninvited guests, my dear boy.

HUGO: Where do you think they're taking us, Alexander?

ALEXANDER: I'm not sure. I don't think it's for ice-cream sundaes. Look, they're bringing us into a coliseum.

(The roar of an angry crowd erupts from the record.)

DARLA: Yes, look, look at all of the people. Who are they?

DOCTOR JUPITER: I'm afraid they're not here to cheer us on, my dear.

HUGO: This is all my fault. If I hadn't been trying that stunt with the X-1 . . .

ALEXANDER: Nobody blames you for what happened, Hugo. It was an honest mistake. Who knew what was going to happen when we followed that mysterious air current?

DOCTOR JUPITER: It now seems it was just a trap to bring us here all along.

(A terrible shriek echoes from the distance.)

DARLA: Gosh, Alexander, what was that?

ALEXANDER: I don't know. We mustn't be afraid. We've faced worse before, I'm sure of it.

DOCTOR JUPITER: Yes. Just remember the Enchanted Sands of the Mad Sultan.

DARLA: And the Blind Bandits of the Himalayas.

ALEXANDER: And the Air Pirates of Monrovia.

EMPEROR: Prepare the Unfathomable!

ALEXANDER: That doesn't sound very encouraging. Doctor Jupiter. Do you have any ideas?

DOCTOR JUPITER: I'm afraid not, Alexander.

ALEXANDER: Tor, do you think you can free yourself from these terrible cloud manacles?

TOR: Tor not think so. Too strong for Tor.

ALEXANDER: Well, if we can't use our brains, and we can't use our brawn, all we have left is our bravery.

DARLA: What are you going to do, Alexander?

ALEXANDER: Just use a little earth gumption, that's all. Tor, as soon as they open that monster's cage, I want you to try and distract it. Doctor Jupiter and Darla, see if you can find a way out of here. Hugo and I will do our best to put a stop to that Inviso-ray machine.

DOCTOR JUPITER: I will do all I can, Alexander.

ALEXANDER: We'll see how terrible this Unfathomable creature really is.

(The Unfathomable howls, drawing closer still, as a thematic swell of violins marks the end of the episode.)

ANNOUNCER: *Will Alexander Lightning face the Unfathomable and survive? Will the Evil Emperor of Cloud City complete his terrible scheme? Will the Airship Brigade free*

*themselves and save the earth in time? Tune in tomorrow night
for the exciting conclusion to* Mysterious Islands in the Sky.
Tomorrow's episode brought to you by Ovaltine.

FATHER AND SON, sitting on the sofa together. Father and
son, listening to the needle slide through the final silent groove,
skipping for a second, before the record arm abruptly retracts.
The fifteen-minute episode is now over. Father and son with
a secret between them, still imagining the world above, the
mysterious islands in the sky, the Unfathomable. Jonathan
leaps to his feet and flips the record over, replacing the arm,
and, sitting there staring at the spinning shellac, both of them
silent. They manage a kind of stillness, a dreamy quiet where
their thoughts of their own individual futures—as clear as the
voices from the radio program—beam as bright and undam-
aged as rays from any distant galaxy. Father and son listen to
the radio show, listening to each other think.

"Dad, will people ever live on the moon?" the son asks.

"I think so," the father says. "I'm quite sure of it. Would you
like to go visit there one day?"

The boy nods, without having to think. "As long as I don't
have to go alone," he says.

"No," the father says. "One day, you and I'll go. We'll make
a regular trip out of it. How does that sound?"

To Whom It May Concern,
There is no such thing as a Good War.

To Whom It May Concern,
You loved your son too much to tell him how much you
loved him.

To Whom It May Concern,
You did not fly to the moon. It was a dream you were
too afraid to ever pursue.

• • •

AT A HALF HOUR past midnight the nursing home is eerily quiet. Between waking and sleeping, between memory and dream, Henry's eyes slip open, a startled breath escaping from his lips, a single word appearing along the brine of his teeth: *Moon. Moon. Of course,* he thinks. He is falling, falling, falling, the moon slipping farther and farther away. He is drifting helplessly toward earth. Henry struggles for a second breath, unsure where he is exactly. His arms and legs feel cold and stiff. He turns and sees someone sitting in a chair, breathing deeply beside him. Henry does not recognize the other man's face. He begins to panic, stirring beneath the stern white sheets, but no sound escapes his mouth. He cannot talk. He cannot yell. All he can do is blink.

BESIDE HIS FATHER, Jonathan has fallen asleep. At first he does not notice that he is still holding his father's hand. The television is still flickering silently. Jonathan squints, placing his palm against his eyes, and then he looks down at his father's tiny, wrinkled hand. He kisses it. His father is not quite awake, not quite asleep, his eyes blinking nervously, his breath slow, aggravated, but deep.

"The moon," his father suddenly whispers, sure of the importance of these two final words. The old man's eyelids twitch a little, the lashes short, his father's lips muttering, murmuring oblique words as he dreams.

"The moon?" Jonathan asks, but his father does not respond. He watches Henry's face, his lips, for another word, another sign, but nothing else comes. Finally, Jonathan stands, yawning, then switches off the television. He stretches, pulls on his

jacket, whispers goodnight to his father, and steps quietly out
of the room.

JONATHAN FINDS HIS Peugeot parked in its spot at the far
end of the empty nursing home parking lot and sits in the
driver's seat, silent, tired, more sad than he has ever been in his
adult life. He looks up at the glare of the yellow streetlights,
rising there just above his car. There is something moving
there, a flash of something that appears and then disappears
just as quickly. Jonathan blinks, leaning over the steering wheel,
staring up toward the small circles of fluorescent illumination,
and there, there is actually something moving up there: moths,
dozens of them, a cloud of gray and brown, the dust from
their wings making tiny flecks of darkness somewhere among
the bright shape of white and yellow light.

Twenty-one

ON THURSDAY MORNING, ONLY A FEW HOURS LATER, Jonathan awakes to find his daughter Thisbe standing over him, crying. Lying on the sofa, Jonathan is incredibly confused at first, looking up into his daughter's wide, panicked eyes, her small pink mouth slightly agape. When Jonathan sits up, asking her what is the matter, he is aware of the world spinning, the entire den trembling, his daughter's face slipping out of focus, becoming soft and fuzzy.

"It's Mom," Thisbe says again. "She left us. For good."

Jonathan scratches at his beard, sighs, and then tries to understand.

"What time is it?"

"Six. In the morning. I got up because I heard Mom's car leaving. You know how it makes that one sound?"

"Yes."

"Well, it made that sound. And when I got up, she was gone."

Jonathan nods. "Let's not get excited. Let's take a look around first."

Together they climb the stairs, then walk quietly down the

hallway. They stare into the master bedroom without saying a word. Both of the bedroom closets are standing open, as are a few of the dresser drawers. Most of Madeline's clothes and shoes are gone, plastic hangers lying on the floor or resting uselessly on the bed. Her suitcases have been taken as well. Jonathan stares at the empty space where his wife's clothes should be, at the spot where the suitcases ought to be standing, his eyes trembling with tears, his pulse pounding loudly in his head.

"What are we going to do, Dad?" Thisbe asks. "What are we going to do?"

At first Jonathan does not answer. He only stares at the unmade bed, at the empty dresser, at the bedroom which he has not slept in for almost three weeks now, and finally, finally his heart decides it has had enough. *Enough.* Jonathan throws on some clothes, grabs his keys, hurries out to the garage, gives the car a start, backs up, and decides he is going to do something about what is happening to his life. You bet he's going to do something: he is going to find his wife. He is not going to wait around, hiding. He is not just going to sit there and watch things fall apart anymore. Where can she be? Logically, there's only a certain number of places. He drives down the Midway, then to Lake Shore Drive. His first thought is Madeline must be at work and that the Volvo has to be parked in the lot at the research facility, but when he arrives there, he finds it is not. At this hour of the morning, the lot is empty. He thinks about heading inside, down to her lab, to try to talk to a few of her colleagues, but the doors are locked and no one seems to be around. He knocks on the glass doors once, then twice, then hurries back to his car. The Peugeot speeds away, or as close to speeding as it can go, back onto Lake Shore Drive, circling the shady streets of Hyde Park, looking for the familiar-looking

Volvo in the parking lot of any restaurant that might be open this time of the morning—maybe the Pancake House—but there is nothing. He travels past a few motels, then a hotel, but again, there is nothing. Nothing. Jonathan searches alone in the early morning light, until the sun begins to travel past the clouds of the easternmost sky. It is now glaringly obvious to him that Madeline is not, will not be returning.

BY THEN IT IS almost nine a.m. At this time of the morning, there is an unbelievably long line in the drive-through of McDonald's. Jonathan waits patiently, wondering how much longer all of this can go on, how much longer before he decides to just give up and disappear as well. When it is his turn to pull up to the plastic brown speaker, a tinny voice asks, "Welcome to McDonalds's, may I take your order?" but Jonathan has no idea what he is even doing there. He orders a number three breakfast meal and pulls up to the drive-through window, staring up at the early morning sky, the clouds like mountaintops, like a vast and rumbling sea, the view from the Peugeot's window exactly like a map of oceanic topography. The kid from the drive-through window, the same kid with his abundance of unhealthy purple zits, announces the amount due. Jonathan searches in his wallet, hands the boy a few bills, collects his change, and waits for his meal. The tiny glass window of the drive-through swings closed and Jonathan glances up at the sky again. Suddenly a switch is thrown somewhere in his brain. His heart immediately reacts. The clouds overhead, white, stunning, slowly moving, have begun to sharpen, the inexact edges become angles, the feeling, the awful stuttering of his heart, his hands now going numb. He tries to tap on the drive-through window but no one is there. All of a sudden his legs have disappeared, his toes going cold, his feet, his breath is now far away, a distant sound beneath the rapid, upset beating in his chest. A cloud seems to separate itself from all of the others at that moment, and Jonathan is unable to fix his sight anywhere else. He cannot remember the last time he took his phenytoin. As he struggles to breathe, a car behind him begins to honk. In this moment, a flash of single images echo in his brain: Madeline, his daughters, his father, the empty lecture hall, the model of the squid at the museum, his father, who would tell him exactly what to do at this moment, Madeline, whom he would like to cry to, to ask forgiveness from, to be saved by, his mother, his daughters, then Madeline again. Jonathan begins to cry in desperation, twitching, his tongue curling up into the back of his throat. He falls forward against the steering wheel, the scream of the Peugeot's horn the uninterrupted message of his terrified heart. *Madeline*, he thinks, reaching for a hand that is not there. *Where are his arms now? Why can't he say anything? Where are the girls? Why doesn't anyone hear him?*

Jonathan, adrift in that unquestionable profundity, can taste salt in his mouth. He struggles to stay awake but, seeing the great cloud bearing down upon him, he knows there is no escape. As its enormous shadow falls upon his face, he tries to shout, but the cars honking their horns are much too loud. The pimply-faced boy leans out of the drive-through and taps on Jonathan's window. Jonathan can see the boy's fingers there, separated by the thick pane of glass. He can even make out the boy's greasy fingerprints, which are now smudged along the Peugeot's window. A stranger's fingerprint, that small detail, that impractical, momentary beauty, makes Jonathan smile. The boy from the drive-through window is now dialing 911. He is tapping on Jonathan's window and telling him this, but Jonathan cannot hear anything but his own heartbeat. He has collapsed now, lying sideways, falling into the emptiness of the passenger seat. The cloud hangs there in the air, crossing the seam of the old windshield as Jonathan does his best to keep breathing. As he loses consciousness, Jonathan begins to recall the dull words of Dr. Roberts—the discouraging neurologist from his childhood, the gray-bearded specialist whose aversion therapy was so painfully unsuccessful—attempting to explain his incredible findings in a 1961 article in the *New England Journal of Medicine*:

. . . and although epilepsy is a common neurological disease, our understanding of why it occurs is often lacking. In the case of subject 23-2400, we know the occurrence of petit mal–type seizures are caused by a specific visual trigger: the unlikely shape of a cloud. Distinct from other similarly diagnosed patients however, the effects of light and motion do not provoke any reaction in the patient, nor do tests of other comparable shapes, noted in trials 13A, 13B, and 13C, in which visual representations of a mountain, a river, and a lake were introduced. The initial experiment 12F has been repeated in three successive trials with precisely the same results: when presented with an illustration of a cloud, the autonomic nervous system is instantaneously engaged, heart palpitations, sweating, then tremors occur, concluding with the patient losing consciousness. The obvious question for us as researchers has become one of specificity: What is it about this particular shape that causes such a strange reaction in this patient?

Upon initial study, it appears that the subject's response is a divergent, sympathetic nervous system reaction, an exception to the Fight or Flight response as first described by Walter Cannon in 1915 and the General Adaptation Syndrome as later noted by Hans Selye in 1936. Ongoing research suggests that the cloud itself represents an autonomic fear of complexity, and that this unusual neurological response to a terror-stimulus is simply the survival instinct of a species that inhabits a world which has, over such a short period of time, become much too complicated. Further studies may prove that this reaction is actually an inheritable trait passed from one generation to the next, as the less aggressive of the human species who chose flight over fight are now more likely to reproduce, resulting in what Richard Aldwin has named "the heredity of cowardice" (Aldwin, 515). The longer human beings exist, it seems, the less likely we are to choose to be brave.

The emergency room is mostly empty at this time of day. The paramedics—young handsome men in blue jumpsuits—joke with Jonathan, who has begun to recover. They ask him if he has taken any narcotics recently. Jonathan tells them he wishes he had. His heart is still beating much too quickly. He adjusts the oxygen tube that they have inserted in his nose, trying to breathe deeply. The paramedics roll him on a gurney through the automatic sliding glass doors, leaving him in a little curtained bed in the back of the emergency room. A young nurse with cold hands takes his pulse and his vital signs and says everything looks pretty normal. Someone is screaming behind another curtain nearby. Jonathan closes his eyes, his heart slowly returning to its usual beat, his breath coming easier. He begins to feel the blood in his hands and feet again. His legs do not feel so distant. Before a doctor can come in and evaluate him, Jonathan stands, buttons his shirt back up, finds his brown jacket lying on the floor, and quietly exits through the sliding glass doors. He unsnaps the plastic bracelet from his wrist and puts it in his pocket. He hails a cab and takes it back to where the Peugeot is parked in the McDonald's parking lot. He sees he has been given a ticket for leaving his car unattended, abandoned there by the paramedics in a corner of the lot, but he does not remove the orange paper from his windshield. The radio in the car crackles with static and Jonathan switches it off, preferring the sudden silence and his own labored breathing.

WHEN JONATHAN GETS HOME and pulls the car into the garage, he sees the Volvo is still gone. Backing into the garage beside Madeline's empty spot, he holds his hand over his heart and finds a white EKG tab left stuck to his chest, then another, then another. He sits there, holding the steering wheel in his hands, and thinks, *I have ignored everything important around me. I have made my life a stupid, empirical, factual thing. I've forgotten what it means to be happy or unhappy. I have been so narrow-minded that I've forgotten to look around at the rest of the world: I've been in a kind of fog for years and years.* He climbs out of the car and goes to find his wife, knowing what he wants to say to her now, how badly he wants to apologize, to convince her of his love for her, knowing none of it will be easy.

OF COURSE, Jonathan does not find Madeline. She has vanished completely: no note, no sign, no message to be read in the arrangement of her shoes near the back door, because all of her shoes are gone. Jonathan sighs aloud into the empty stillness of the house. Where are the girls? Certainly they should be home by now. But no. It's four p.m. and there's no one. Nothing. Jonathan retreats to his bedsheet tent in the den. He climbs inside and stares at a black and white wedding photo of his missing wife. In the photo, Madeline is wearing a strapless dress that does not exactly fit, the cut a little low along the bustline, but she looks elegant, with tiny flowers in her hair.

She is laughing at something, holding her dress up with one hand and her bouquet in the other. Madeline. She is smiling a smile Jonathan does not quite remember, a smile before a certain kind of impatience set in, a certain kind of frustration, a certain kind of indifference. The smile, in its perfect lightness, with her one dimple on her left cheek, is the most lovely, unfussy thing Jonathan has ever seen. Its shape, and the whole of the rest of Madeline and Madeline's face, are now gone, somewhere else: missing. Where is she right now? Where has she gone? It is Thursday, October 28, 2004, 4:35 p.m., and it feels like the world is ending.

As the evening wears on, Jonathan climbs out from the fort and decides, fuck it: he will get high. His daughters are still not home. And there are some rolling papers in the drawer of the oak desk, and a little baggie of very dry weed, hidden in a dense volume of Coleridge's "Kubla Khan," Madeline's idea of a joke. Jonathan does a terrible job of rolling a joint, it looks bunched up at one end and the paper keeps coming unwound. But, finding an old blue plastic lighter in his desk, he lights it anyway and inhales deeply. His lungs contract and expand, his heartbeat slowing lazily. Uncoordinated thoughts drift through his head. He finds himself sitting on the floor in front of the television, eating a bowl of frozen strawberries, flipping through the channels with the sound off, admiring the shape of everyone's mouths. When he gets to CNN, what he sees nearly causes him to choke.

It is footage of the prehistoric giant squid: *Tusoteuthis longa*. Floating in an enormous blue tank, the creature looks pale white, its innumerable tentacles reaching out, drifting behind it like listless seaweed. The animal does not look well. In fact, it looks terrible. A close-up reveals its huge, alien eye, bubbles hurrying past as the squid drifts aimlessly in its tank. Jonathan grabs the remote control and turns up the volume.

"Scientists are reporting that the prehistoric giant squid they captured five days ago has died. Researchers are still trying to determine the cause of the creature's unexpected death. At the moment, they believe the animal may have suffered a severe shock when it was removed from its natural habitat."

The camera cuts to footage of Dr. Jacques Albert behind a small metal podium, his hands folded before him as if in penitence. He looks exhausted. Jonathan climbs from his chair, then across the carpeted floor, placing his face as close as he can to the television screen. The Frenchman is answering questions from the press, saying, "Yes. At four o'clock this morning, the specimen emptied all the ink from its ink sacs. We feel that the great animal did this in a final attempt to remain hidden, as it is a creature that prefers the solitude of the ocean, unaccustomed to captivity and the interaction of other species. By seven this morning, I was informed that the animal was . . . deceased."

Dr. Albert, speaking in a philosophical tone, stares beyond the camera and the lights, removes his glasses from his thin face, and then leans into the collection of five or six microphones, looking grim. "What we have learned in the short time we have been able to study this magnificent creature is nothing short of amazing. Although this one specimen has expired, there is great promise in our study of its DNA, which will affirm what we have long suspected . . ."

Jonathan crushes the power button on the remote and falls on his back. He stares at the tiny lines and cobwebs along the ceiling; his perfect dream of discovering that great animal alive, of one day observing it, of coming to know it on a scientific and even personal level, has now disintegrated. There is now no hope of him being the one to come up with a simple answer, to find a single, unified conclusion. With the squid's death, it has all been crushed, left dead floating in an enormous saltwater tank. Now even this, his idea, his plan, his wish has disappeared, vanished, poof! Like everything, like Madeline, like his father—or at least very soon. Yes, science teaches us everything: where we come from, what we share with the world and the universe. It shows us the entire, impressive fabric of all creation, Jonathan thinks, lying there before the blank television screen. It tells us everything, all the secrets we ought to know, everything except the most complicated, the really difficult things.

Twenty-two

A. On Thursday morning, just before dawn, the cloud-figure returns. Lying in bed, staring through the bedroom window, Madeline discovers that the figure has finally come back. She sees it standing there in the backyard, unmoving in the top of the highest trees. Then, slowly, it begins to step away, climbing apprehensively just above the telephone lines. She glances over at the alarm clock and sees it is not even six a.m. She gets dressed without worrying about what clothes she is now wearing before she rushes downstairs, out to the garage to start the car.

B. In the Volvo, Madeline circles around Hyde Park, following the cloud-figure, who seems lost. It steps without any sense of direction across the early morning sky. Madeline does not know what to do. Crossing among the other low-hanging clouds, the cloud-figure stumbles toward Fifty-fifth Street, then races back to Fifty-sixth Street, ambling above the tallest branches, back and forth along Cottage Grove Avenue. The sun has just begun to break across the sky.

C. It is Thursday morning, five days before the presidential election. Like the world, like the country, the cloud seems unable to make up its mind.

D. After nearly five hours of following the figure, Madeline pulls away from where the cloud is circling, and rushes into a fast-food restaurant to use the bathroom. When she returns, the cloud is still there, moving from treetop to treetop, describing the same route along the hazy sky. Madeline stares at it, waiting for the figure to make a decision of some kind. But it doesn't, it seems totally incapable of moving on.

E. After another seven hours, Madeline falls asleep, watching the cloud-figure stand solemnly in the tree limbs on a narrow side street. Shifting the station wagon into park, she closes her eyes, putting her legs up on the passenger seat.

F. When she wakes, it is dark out. It looks like it might start snowing. The sky is gray and ominous. She switches on the radio and it reads 9:49 p.m. The news on NPR is unpleasant, several dozen dead in the Gaza Strip. She switches off the radio and glances up through the windshield and sees the figure moving restlessly from one tree to the next, back and forth and back again.

G. Finally, she understands: it is pacing.

H. The cloud-figure is walking back and forth. Seeing it now, Madeline switches the Volvo off and hurries beneath the figure on foot, glancing up through the trees at the odd shapes the stars make in the dull gray sky.

I. The cloud is pacing back and forth, directly above one of the university's libraries. Fog from the lake hangs above the grass as Madeline crosses a stretch of lawn and stands before the unlit building. Closed. Of course. She checks her watch again but it seems to have stopped working. It reads 3:25 p.m. She looks up and sees the figure stepping back and forth, anxious, as if making some grave decision, and then, slowly, as if descending a staircase, the cloud-figure begins to sink, first just a foot or so, then more, gradually, gradually, until it is walking just above the threaded grayness of the evening mist.

J. Madeline rushes toward the cloud as it pushes its way into a field of fog. Madeline, her heart beating nervously, follows, seeing that the haze is a city of its own, rising up and down, with phantom trees, and misty buildings, and a long, narrow field made of silent gray clouds. To the west, there are some other shapes. The enormous library has strangely faded behind the bank of gray, and Madeline is startled to see there is a group of other cloud-figures: rows and rows of them rising up from the fogginess, glinting and ephemeral, glowing from the distant starlight. Madeline watches her cloud-figure join the others until it finally disappears.

K. The other cloud-figures also seem indecisive. Watching them shift and move back and forth, Madeline sees their feet and hands and shoulders almost shapeless, swirling in place. The stars overhead have mostly gone black, a few silent glimmers of light cutting through the cloud-figures' chests, their bodies made briefly clear, their hearts suddenly visible. Something happens then, with the moon and the stars streaking over the cloudy figures. A blur of light, circles of gold and blue and silver intersect, and something behind Madeline begins to glow as well.

L. Madeline turns and what she sees is inexplicable. There is a moment of absolute stillness, as if the sun itself has just set behind her, and the heat of the thing causes Madeline to shout, closing her eyes and turning away. There is a countdown ringing in her ears, like a loudspeaker in a dream.

M. 10-9-8-7-6-5-4-3-2-1.

N. Then a new cloud, great and darkly shaped, rising above all the others, fills the evening sky. "Reproduction factor k of 1.0006 . . ." the cloud-figures all raise their hands in exaltation. A loudspeaker hisses from somewhere with unfamiliar words and static: "The Italian navigator has landed in the New World." A second voice, trembling along invisible telephone lines asks, "How were the natives?" to which the loudspeaker responds, "Very friendly."

O. Almost immediately then, Madeline sees the cloud-figures begin to disappear, one by one, vanishing like ghosts. Next the eerie evening fog begins to dissipate, until there is only one figure left, the one Madeline has been following all this time: standing there, high in the topmost branches of an elm tree, it stares out at what was once Stagg Field, at the remnants of Chicago Pile #1, both of which are now gone, now only another university building, now only a library.

P. Madeline finally understands what she has seen: it has been a test. *This is the spot right here*, she thinks. *All this time* *and I forgot. It's been here, right here, all along and I forgot. Here, right here*, she thinks. The world's first controlled nuclear reaction. December 2, 1942, 3:25 p.m., happening beneath the empty western grandstand of this field, that moment kept still in time, relived again and again and again, the thoughts of those brave, intelligent men and their doubts, all of their immeasurable fears and reluctance, burning, lingering there in the air, in the trees, in the grass, in the colorless stretch of sky. Madeline sees the cloud-figure standing there, his movements no longer anxious but now just incredibly weighty, ponderous, sad, stepping from branch to branch, tree to tree, as if it is measuring and remeasuring the terrible consequences of this decision, perhaps the worst decision in history. *Why?* it seems to be asking, wavering there above the trees, uncertain, as temporary as a ghost. *Why did we do what we did? Why did we believe this was necessary?* Madeline begins to back away, watching as the field slowly starts to fade into darkness, the cloud-figure growing more and more opaque. *Why did this happen?* it whispers soundlessly. *Wasn't there some other way? Didn't we realize we might end the war and condemn the world at the same time? Why didn't we see that there was no science on earth, no idea, no experiment, no device, to keep people from hurting each other? And why didn't we see that this thing, this creation, would only make things worse?*

Q. Watching the cloud-figure slowly fade into nothingness, Madeline begins to tremble. She does not want to be here. She wants to be at home with Jonathan, with her daughters, she wants to hear them arguing with each other and laughing. She does not want to be here, like the cloud-person, having made its terrible decision, now lost, now lonely.

R. Madeline looks up as the figure vanishes into the trees.
She stands there for a few moments before she realizes it is
gone. She finds her car parked in a tow zone, searches for her
keys in her coat pocket, and drives off toward home in a frenzy.

**S. When Madeline looks up again, pulling to a stop at a
traffic light, she realizes it is morning.** The sun has begin to
peak in the east and there is a soft glimmer of dew along the
Volvo's windshield. She switches on the radio and discovers it
is already 8:00 a.m. Somehow it is Friday morning.

**T. The election is only four days away, or so the radio
broadcaster claims.** Madeline turns off the radio before she
can hear any other bad news.

**U. Madeline parks the Volvo in the garage and sits behind
the wheel for a few moments in the dark.** She is trying to
understand exactly what has happened. She glances over and
notices that her husband's car—the red, rusting Peugeot—is
gone. She switches off the engine, takes a deep breath, opens
the car door, and steps toward the house, her entire body
trembling.

**V. Thisbe is eating her breakfast in silence at the kitchen
table.** At first she looks up at their mother with doubt, and
then, soon enough, she is beaming.

"You're back," Thisbe says with a dimpled smile, blinking
her sleepy eyes.

"I am," Madeline says, frowning a little, taking a seat beside
her at the kitchen table. "Where's your father?"

"He's gone. He went to visit Grandpa."

"Where's Amelia?"

"Still in bed," Thisbe whispers.

"Still in bed?"

"She said she's not going to school today. She said she's giving up."

"On what?"

"On everything."

"I see," Madeline whispers, finally realizing, in this moment, exactly what her absence has meant.

"Are you back for good?" Thisbe asks, setting down her spoon, glancing up suspiciously.

"I think so." Madeline watches her daughter's face for any sign of anger or dismay. There is none, only her two, mismatched dimples gleaming brightly. "How do you feel about that?" she asks.

"I don't know. Pretty good, I guess."

"Good."

"But . . . but you guys shouldn't keep doing this to us," Thisbe whispers. "I mean . . . you're supposed to be our parents. You're supposed to be in charge of things."

"You're right. It isn't fair. And I'm sorry."

W. Madeline leans over to take her daughter's hand but Thisbe pulls it away. All at once, her daughter's face is shiny with tears. Thisbe tries to cover her eyes with her hands, but it is hopeless. She is crying hard now, her shoulders awkwardly trembling.

"It's okay," Madeline says. "You're okay, I'm so sorry, I'm so sorry, honey, shhhh." She stands, wrapping her arms around Thisbe's shoulders. "Shhhhh. You're okay. We're all going to be okay."

X. Madeline presses her lips to her daughter's forehead.

Y. Thisbe closes her eyes, trying not to cry anymore.

Z. Madeline closes her eyes and tries to do the same.

Twenty-three

BY EIGHT A.M. FRIDAY MORNING, AMELIA HAS RESIGNED herself to a life of absolute mediocrity. She lies in bed upstairs, considering how best to go about it. Maybe she'll only eat at fast-food chains from now on and become grotesquely obese. Or no. Maybe she'll stop worrying about being taken seriously as a young woman and start dressing like the sluts on MTV. Or no. Maybe she'll get rid of all her French records and start listening to the garbage on the radio. Wow. Anything is possible now. Amelia stares up at the cracks in the ceiling above her bed, these cracks and lines that, as she squints, seem to resemble exactly how she is feeling. *I've been kidding myself all along. Everything I believed in has turned out to be nothing.* She listens to her sister slam the front door, hurrying off to school, and immediately a nervous ache begins to fill her chest. She is going to miss her classes again, and because she's kind of mean—she knows she is but can't help herself—no one will share their notes with her tomorrow, and then she'll fail civics and history, and then she'll have to spend all summer making up stupid classes that she should have passed in the first place. But it really won't matter then. Because at that point, she'll still be here, lying in this very bed. Amelia is imagining how long it will take for her legs to atrophy when, all of a sudden, the door opens and her mother barges in.

"Why aren't you getting ready for school?" her mother asks.

"What are you doing in my room?"

"I came to see why you aren't downstairs yet."

"Because I'm not going to school. I'm done. I quit."

"You're quitting school?"

"I'm quitting everything," Amelia announces.

"Really."

"Yes. I'm not going to try and do anything meaningful anymore."

"Why not?"

"Because it doesn't matter. Everything turns out to be totally pointless. It's like everybody, everything in this world is so mediocre and no matter how hard you try, nothing ever changes. And I . . . I can't do anything about it. Everything I try turns to shit," she hisses, and then, against her will, she starts crying. For the first time in months, in years, in almost as long as Amelia can remember, she closes her eyes and begins to weep, wiping tear after tear from her eyes, embarrassed by this very childish display of emotion. "I don't know even know why I'm crying," she whispers. "It's stupid. It really is."

Her mother stares at her face. There is something there in her mother's eyes, the same hesitancy, the same doubt. Just like her daughter, she does not know why everything seems so weird and wrong with the world today. Madeline takes a seat on the bed and places her hand on Amelia's arm, smiling softly.

"Amelia?"

"Yes?"

"I want you to know that I think you're right. The world

does seem like a terrible place right now. But I'm going to tell you something because I think you need to hear it: you've become a very negative person. And I don't know if it has to do with me and your father, or if it's the other kids in your classes, or if it's what happened with the school paper, but you've become very critical. Of everything. I don't know when it happened—you used to come home from school so excited about whatever you learned that day, and now, now, you wear this look all the time. Like nothing makes you happy anymore. And I happen to think that seventeen is too young to be disappointed by everything."

Amelia frowns, unable to look at her mother. She begins crying again, covering her face with her hands. "I got demoted at the school paper," she hisses. "They made me the fucking Culture Vulture."

"They did?"

"Yes. They did."

"Well," her mom says with a short sigh, "you're going to have to show them you aren't going to be ignored. You're going to have to use this new position to do something great. Okay? Now take a deep breath," her mother says, rubbing Amelia's cheek. "Okay. Do you want to go to school or not?"

Amelia nods her head, still crying. "I guess."

Her mother grins at her and then says, "Good. Do you want a ride?"

"No."

"No?"

"No. I'm all right now." Amelia wipes at the corners of her eyes and then whispers, "Are you back to stay?"

"I am."

"Okay," Amelia says, almost silently.

. . .

ACTUALLY, AMELIA has bigger things than her mother to worry about this Friday: her first column as Culture Vulture is due this morning and she hasn't written a single word of it. She decides to ditch her first-period civics class and to try and write it in the library. At the back of the research room, she finds an out-of-the-way cubicle that doesn't have a lot of graffiti on it. She takes out a sheet of lined paper. She puts her pen to the page and begins writing without thinking. She is going to try to take her mother's advice. She is going to try to use her stupid column to show them what she can do. She starts off by writing, *How We Are Slowly Killing Ourselves Through Our Dependence on Corporations*, and then she begins to outline the destruction of American democracy as it correlates to the rise of national corporate chains:

People always want what's familiar. That's why everyone likes McDonald's and Pizza Hut and Starbucks. Because they're brand names and you can go into any McDonald's anywhere in the world and order the same thing. Which is a total bonus for some people. The fact that McDonald's uses gross, substandard ingredients and is like poisoning everyone in the country doesn't matter. People hate anything that's not familiar, anything where you might have to actually decide and think. Even if it's not good for the other people around them, or in other communities. Or the environment. Every time a Starbucks opens up, all the local coffee shops go out of business. And that puts people out of work. But it happens again and again. One day soon, when the corporations have taken over, and the world is like this completely monotonous, American suburb, where everyone looks the same, and talks the same, and thinks the same, and eats the same food, and practices the exact same religion, and everybody lives in the same kind of house, and listens to the same stupid music, well, we're all going to be sorry. Or probably not. Probably we won't even notice. We'll be too busy watching the same show on TV.

Amelia smiles reading over the last line, proud of what she has written. She stands, finds an open computer, types it up, prints it out, and, before first period has even ended, she places it—with a derisive smile—in Mr. Wick's donut-specked hands.

AT LUNCH, while Amelia is sitting alone, staring down at her stupid tuna sandwich, William Banning, in his preppy blue sweater, takes a seat beside her and slips the draft of her column at her from across the Formica lunch table.

"Mr. Wick said we can't run this."

"And why the fuck not?" Amelia hisses, throwing down her sandwich.

"Because you're supposed to be writing about like cultural events. Like television and movies. This doesn't have anything to do with that."

"I mention television in there. In like the last line."

"Well, he said we can't use it."

"Because I actually expressed an opinion? Because it's not the same old stupid Culture Vulture crap? 'TV is great. Isn't pop music so awesome?' I don't think Mr. Wick had anything to do with this. I think you didn't want to run it and so you're blaming him."

William frowns, his lean face going temporarily red.

"I just don't think it's your best work."

"*You* don't think it's my best work? What the hell do *you* know about good writing? You're not even a writer. They just brought you in because I actually have something to say."

William looks down at the sheet of paper and nods, then looks up, pushing his glasses against his nose. "I just think . . . well, it's like everything you write is so one-sided. You don't ever write about . . . like other people's ideas. All it is . . . is like one long complaint. I don't know. I mean . . . I just think you're smarter than that. I mean . . . well . . . like anyone can tell how smart you are, but like . . . it just doesn't take a big IQ to do this kind of stuff."

"What the fuck do you know?" Amelia can feel a wave of hives pushing to the surface of her skin.

"I know, well . . . there's like some interesting points here . . . but you never like . . . consider like the opposite opinion. Like, well, ask me what I think about like Starbucks."

Amelia rolls her eyes, shaking her head, then looks across the table at William.

"Okay, fuckface. What do you think about Starbucks?"

"I like it. I mean, it's really good coffee. And they have a lot of different kinds. That's why people go there. Because it's like . . . good. And they use fair trade coffee. And their part-time workers get health benefits."

"Big deal. It doesn't mean they have the right to like monopolize everything. I mean, that's like saying America is awesome so we should like take over the whole world. It's like the evils of capitalism. It's all like . . . gluttony and greed."

"I think it's more like human nature. Like, I mean, well, there was just as much greed in the Soviet Union, right? Communism is just as flawed." William shakes his head, staring down at the draft of the article. "I don't know. Maybe people hate places like Starbucks because it's all over, not because it's good or bad. It's because it's easy to hate it. It's like easy to hate something faceless . . . because it reminds you that you're not all that special. I mean, like you know, Wal-Mart or whatever, everyone shops there. I think . . . I think that's a lot more interesting. The fact that, like in secret, everybody loves Starbucks."

Amelia frowns, looking down at her draft. "I wouldn't know. I've never even been there," she says, frowning.

"But you wrote about how much it sucks."

"I don't care about the coffee. I care about the idea," she whispers.

"I just think . . . well, like it's weird to live in America and like pretend, you know, that you don't live in America. Like you're somehow . . . outside of it. Like the fact that you wrote your anticorporate essay on an Apple computer. Or like drank a Diet Coke while you were writing it. That's what seems really interesting to me. Like, I mean, have you ever read Plato?"

Amelia shakes her head.

"No?" he asks again, surprised.

"No."

"My dad, he teaches humanities at the university. He lent me the *Parmenides*, it's pretty impossible to understand. But there's a lot in there about paradox. Like how opposites can't function without each other."

"I know about that," she lies.

"Yeah, maybe if you wanted to check it out, I could lend it to you. It's pretty good."

"I mean, sure . . . whatever."

"Cool. So do you think . . . do you want to rewrite this?" he asks, looking down at the piece of white paper.

"I don't know. Maybe. If I have time."

"Cool," William says, looking around, suddenly realizing how close he is sitting to her. He stands, patting down his hair in the back.

"Yeah, cool," she says and watches William Banning slowly walk away. She notices he is like a camel, no, a giraffe, he is slow and thoughtful, and much more intelligent than Amelia had ever thought. She looks down at her essay and smiles, remembering how he had said she was smart. She looks over his handwritten notes, then, finding her pen in her purse, she hurries to answer some of his blue-scribbled questions on the page.

AFTER THAT, Amelia once again rushes over to the parking lot of the sciences building to see Professor Dobbs. She has a number of things she would like to discuss with him. She finds his Saab parked in its usual space in the faculty lot. She stares at her own reflection in its driver's-side window for a second, fixing her hair, putting on a quick dash of pink lipstick. She gives her armpits a quick sniff and, satisfied, checks to make sure her butt looks okay. It looks okay, but only okay. She leans up against the car, but then she decides that makes her look too young, and so she stands there, shoulders tensed, trying to find some body position that makes her look older, more refined than she actually is. When Professor Dobbs strolls out nearly half an hour later, briefcase in his hand, wearing a handsome corduroy jacket and dark pants, his reddish brown hair parted impeccably along the left side of his head, his chin jutting ahead slightly as he walks, Amelia's eyes lock on a lithe form walking beside him, her arm in his arm, the two of them laughing. The girl—or woman, Amelia is unsure of her age—has beautiful long brown hair. She is dressed very stylishly in a cardigan, sleek-looking pants, and fancy shoes. Amelia, seeing the other woman's shoes, realizes she is not a girl at all. She is someone older, someone with a job. When Professor Dobbs turns from his laughter and sees Amelia waiting desperately at the car, his smile all but disappears. For a moment he glares at her, and then, composing himself, he widens his grin, falsely, as the fabrications begin to wheel in his brain. By the time they reach the car, Professor Dobbs has the whole scenario figured out. He's jolly, unexpectedly, happy to call Amelia's name with a grin. "Amelia, hello, how are you? This is Professor Winthrop."

Professor Winthrop nods, extending her hand without a smile. "Please, it's Alice."

"Alice," Professor Dobbs says, correcting himself.

Amelia shakes the woman's hand and frowns. Is it her skinny little waist? Or carefully plucked eyebrows? Amelia would have no idea how to even go about such a thing. Is it her jewelry? The way she stands so confidently, undisturbed by this stupid young girl waiting at the professor's car? Is it her breasts? Could it be that the professor is just as mindless as the boys in her high school when it comes to these things? Is it all as simple and stupid as a pair of tits?

"We were just on our way to an interdepartmental meeting," Professor Dobbs says, obviously lying. "I hope whatever questions you had about class could wait until next week? If not, why not send me an email this weekend?"

Amelia, a spate of red hives blistering along her neck, silently nods. She steps aside, watching them climb into Professor Dobbs's car. She hears the engine start up, watches the automobile as it speeds away. She stands in the parking lot alone for some time, quietly ignoring the red sores throbbing all along her hands and face. As she walks home, her hands begin to tremble uncontrollably, her blue eyes filling with tears. She lets out a howl, a single sound that is not a word at all, unless it is all words, all feelings, the sound of her heart combusting, the noise of it echoing in the empty space of the faculty parking lot. She staggers back toward her house. Suddenly she wonders if anyone will be there when she gets home, if, for once, just this one time, there might be someone she can talk to.

Twenty-four

ON FRIDAY AFTERNOON, THISBE GOES TO CHORUS PRACtice a half an hour early: she pretends to be practicing the piano, but really she's desperately hoping to see Roxie. She is wearing her sister's glittery eye shadow and pink lip gloss. She has fixed her hair three times already. With her fingers on the dusty piano keys, she closes her eyes and begins to pray dramatically:

Oh Heavenly Father, please forgive my stupid, stupid actions and grant me a reprieve from the stupid, stupid thoughts that I am having. Please don't let her come. Let her quit chorus or maybe make her move away. Don't let me ever see her or talk to her or be close to her again. Let me be normal. Let me be like everyone else. Don't let her be nice to me. Let her be totally mean. Let her spit in my face. Let her burn my hair and stab my eyes out with a hot poker and let her shoot hot arrows into my throat and thighs and stomach cavity. Do not let me have any feelings for her. Do not let me imagine the feeling of her lips . . . No. Give me some tropical disease instead. Give me some incurable illness like leprosy or malaria or gangrene. Let both my arms fall off and all of my teeth rot and let maggots crawl out of my veins. Let birds peck out my eyes and spiders make their cobwebs in my lungs but do not let me think of being in love, dear Lord. Do not let me think of love.

When the other girls arrive, noisy, giddy, jostling, Mr. Grisham hands each of them that afternoon's sheet music. The chorus forms a half-moon around him and Thisbe notices the empty spot where Roxie's bright face should be, but isn't. She keeps glancing at the stupid clock on the wall, missing her cues for chord changes, watching as three-thirty comes and then silently slips away.

In the middle of "Miss Otis Regrets," her fingers start to feel clammy and uncooperative, splayed like claws across the black and white keys. Thisbe, without a word, stands and rushes out, past dopey-faced Mr. Grisham, past the half-ring of startled chorus singers, who immediately begin to whisper and snicker, through the wooden door, down the yellow-tile hall, collapsing in an empty stall in the girls' bathroom. She begins to cry right away, not even knowing why, not even bothering to wipe the tears from her face. She kicks at the dirty floor, then the stall door, then tears the roll of toilet paper from its roller, flinging a loose, wide sheet of it into the air, before covering her face with her hands, kneeling beside the commode, gritting her teeth in fury. When she has stopped crying, she washes her face, marches down the hall, past the musical recital rooms, past the door where she can hear Mr. Grisham making clumsy work of the piano as the girls sing "In My Life," past the front double glass doors, to where her bicycle is locked up. She is not sad anymore, just angry, and she is not even sure why she is angry, only that she feels incredibly betrayed. She unlocks her bicycle and begins to pedal off—where, she isn't sure, just around. She pedals up and down the silent tree-lined streets, hoping to see Roxie walking alone or riding her own bike.

Thisbe glances in store windows and stops at the café on Fifty-fifth Street, but in her weak, busted little heart she knows all of this is hopeless. She has no idea what Roxie's phone number might be or where she actually lives. She has no idea where Roxie goes when she's alone.

THISBE GETS AN IDEA and pedals back down her street into the garage. She finds Roxie's guitar case standing upright in the corner. Thisbe searches through it, finding a phone number on the inside of the black cardboard lid. Running inside, she grabs the cordless phone, rushes to her room, and dials. After three rings, she hears a voice, coarse, perturbed, unapologetic, which she knows has to be Roxie.

"Hello?"

"Roxie?" Thisbe asks, her hands clammy again.

"Yeah?"

"It's Thisbe. From school."

"Oh."

"I didn't have your number. But then I found it in your guitar case."

"Okay."

"I was worried because I didn't see you at chorus practice."

"I'm not doing chorus anymore."

"Why?"

"I'm just not."

"But why didn't you tell me? I was waiting for you."

"It's not a big deal. I just decided today that I was sick of it."

"What about your history grade?"

"Mr. Grisham can fuck off. I hate the chorus. I'd rather fail."

"But then you're going to have to take his class during summer."

"I really don't give a shit."

"Why are you so mad?"

"I'm not mad. I just don't know why it's any of your business."

"It's not. I just thought we were friends."

"We are. But I don't like people butting into my business."

"Well, I'm not. I just didn't see you at practice and I thought you were sick or something."

"I'm not sick. I just didn't want to go."

"Oh, well, do you want to meet somewhere? You can come over and we can write some songs together or something."

"I don't think so. That's kinda boring."

"Why are you being mean to me?" Thisbe asks, her hands beginning to shake.

"I'm not being mean."

"Yes, you are."

"Whatever."

"Well, do you want to do something or not?" Thisbe asks.

"I think I'm just going to stay here."

"Oh. Well. I guess I'll see you in school tomorrow."

"Sure. Whatever."

"Okay, well, 'bye."

"'Bye."

Thisbe hears the dial tone after the lines disconnect. She stares down at the phone, then, without thinking, she quickly dials Roxie's number again.

"Hello?"

"Roxie?"

"Yeah."

Thisbe notices the way the other girl sighs when she says

yeah, as if Roxie can recognize the tremor of her voice, as if she knows what Thisbe is about to say.

"It's Thisbe again."

"Yeah."

"I . . . I just . . . why don't you want to talk to me?"

"I just have other things to do. I mean, it's like it's no big deal."

"I know, but . . . are you . . . did I . . . do something wrong?"

"What?"

"The other day? Did I do something wrong?"

"What? No. I mean, it's no big deal. Listen, I have to go," Roxie says, though both of them now know she is lying.

"Don't you . . . don't you want to be my friend?" Thisbe asks, but her words are too weak, too lame. They fly awkwardly through the telephone wires, their meaning disappearing somewhere along the way.

"You're being weird," Roxie whispers, like there is someone else in the room, a boy or her mother maybe. "I'm going to go."

"Wait . . . ," Thisbe whispers. "I just . . . I don't know what I'm supposed to do. I've never done any of this before, with anyone."

"I have to go," Roxie says again, and this time Thisbe knows that Roxie has decided never to talk to her again. The other girl says goodbye and then hangs up and Thisbe sits there, cross-legged on her bed, listening to the dial tone buzzing in her ear. She switches the phone off and wonders if God is watching her now, and what He might be thinking. She stumbles down the stairs, back to the garage, and pedals off on her bicycle. It is just past four o'clock now. There has got to be an evening mass somewhere at five. She does not know how long it will take to ride there but she decides she has to go to the big cathedral downtown. She will go there and light a candle and kneel in the silence and be surrounded by simple, holy things: crosses, and stained-glass windows, and statues of saints. What she needs now is to confess, to tell God and the world the truly horrible things she is feeling. With her feet on the bicycle pedals, she rides as quickly as she can, humming "Miss Otis Regrets" as she dodges late afternoon traffic on her way to the lake along the bicycle path.

IT TAKES THISBE more than an hour on her bike: exiting at Chicago Avenue, then heading west—taxicabs screaming past, tourists and shoppers rushing across the street, ignoring the flashing stoplights—Thisbe does not know where the cathedral is exactly, and once or twice she circles the same block, hoping to find it. Turning left down State Street, a smile crosses her reddened cheeks as soon as she spots its magnificent sand-colored stone and blue-bronze spires rising high and majestic into the sky. She finds a parking meter and locks her bicycle up, then straightens her skirt and fixes her hair, which has begun to come undone. She marches up the stone steps toward the great wooden doors, already beginning a Hail Mary as she grabs the great gold handle, but the door refuses to budge. Thisbe tries again, with no luck, then grabs the handle of the adjacent door, but finds both of them are locked. She places her ear up against the thick ornate wood and thinks she can hear singing. There is someone in there singing, without her. She rushes down to another set of doors, then another, finding all of them locked tight. She has begun to sweat, from the long bicycle ride and her anxiety, and still she is sure she can hear singing. Why won't He let her be saved? Thisbe begins to knock quietly on the door, then louder, then louder. Tourists and residents passing by stare at the strange girl in the gray skirt banging on the cathedral doors. "Hello?" she pleads, "Hello?" but no one seems to hear. Finally, trying the center doors once more, she knocks as loudly as she can, and then she can hear the lock begin to rattle and turn, and the door beside her unexpectedly squeaks open. An old man, with a gray jump-suit on and an enormous ring of keys in his hand, pokes his head out and frowns, gray eyebrows knotted above his empty blue eyes. "Why are you banging on these doors? Don't you know this is a church?"

"I thought . . . it's not open? I mean, why are the doors locked?"

"We're shampooing the rugs."

"Well, if I could only come in for a few moments . . ."

"The church is closed until tomorrow morning. Nine o'clock mass."

"But I only need to come in for a minute or two."

"Come back tomorrow, young lady."

"But I heard singing?"

The old man squints at her, then smiles. He opens the door a little and points to a large utility cart full of brushes and screwdrivers and vacuum heads, where a large silver radio is blaring an aria.

"I can't just come in . . . for a few seconds?"

"You're too young to have done anything that can't wait till tomorrow," he frowns, then nods, and pulls the enormous door closed. Thisbe hears the lock turn and the music begin to fade. Taking a seat on the stone steps, she begins to glare at the busy people walking around, as if they don't mind that the end of the world is coming.

•   •   •

ON THE WAY BACK south to her neighborhood, Thisbe decides to go to the secret field by herself. She hopes Roxie will be there, hiding in the waist-high weeds, and the thought of holding her hand, and the feeling of lying beside her again, are too powerful to ignore. She pedals faster now and gets to the field just as the sun has begun to set. Leaving her bike in a dark green thicket of grass, she climbs up the path, feeling the wind and dry flowers rubbing against her bare knees. She runs toward the secret spot, sure for a second that she will see Roxie there, smiling, stretched out on her back, but no, it is empty; maybe there will be a note or some letter or something, anything, a sign from the other girl, but, looking around, Thisbe sees she is alone, and that there is nothing, nothing but the music of the air wandering through the prairie grass. Frowning now, she takes a seat, then lies back in the stiff gray and green and brown thistles. She closes her eyes, her ears cupped by the soft, pleasurable silence of early evening. *Why wasn't the church open? Why didn't He want me to be forgiven?* Thisbe opens and closes her hands, grasping at the dry grass, wondering, *Why have a church at all if God isn't going to be around to see you when you need Him? Why? Maybe . . . maybe because it isn't as simple as just going to church to find Him. Maybe because it's all a silly idea anyway. Maybe because He's not hiding in that church in the first place. Maybe He doesn't like to be kept on the inside of things or put in boxes or Bibles or prayers or churches. Maybe, if He is really real, maybe He's alone here, waiting in this field, and all He really wants is for me to think about Him. Maybe He doesn't care about me being a martyr at all. Maybe He only appears when I'm happy. Maybe He wants me to sing even though I'm bad at it. Maybe He wants me to sing because it makes me feel happy and that's all He really wants for me anyway.* Thisbe places her hand on her chest, then, moving it, she places her palm above her belly, to the exact spot where Roxie first touched her, and then, drawing in a breath, she tries to sing. What she sings is "Ave Maria," and her voice, unsure, tremulous, frightened, rises through the field grass as invisible and weak as the wind. Pressing harder on her diaphragm, she tries again, this time letting her lungs ring, like two golden bells, not caring who might hear her, sure no one is listening anyway. This time, the sound is a little stronger, a little more careless, spiraling up from her open mouth. Once more, she tries to sing a solitary note, and, as she holds it, the sound suddenly takes flight, reaching the lowest of the low-flying clouds. Thisbe holds in her diaphragm, her eyes closed tight. Like a kite, the note quickly soars up, and then so does she, the single note rising in her chest like a balloon. Now she is truly flying, her feet leaving the ground, floating on her back, her eyes closed tight, her song lifting her closer and closer to the clouds, until finally, fighting against her breath, she begins to descend. When she alights on the grass, she begins to laugh, opening her eyes, glancing at the world, looking out past the small field, the thistles gently brushing her face and hair.

Twenty-five

ON FRIDAY MORNING, JUST PAST SIX A.M., THE RETIRE-
ment home is mostly quiet. Some of the unlucky residents
are wandering the halls murmuring to themselves, while the
rest of the unfortunate congregate in the recreation room to
watch an assortment of morning game shows. Henry Casper
slips out of his red robe, pulls on the jacket of the frayed black
suit, then the pants, working the tie over the collar of his white
pajamas. When he is finished dressing, he wheels himself over
to the radiator in the corner of his room, and reaches one
thin hand behind the dirty metal pipes. After a moment, his
pale fingers find what he is searching for—a small white paper
flower—the only object that seemed too important to discard.
Gone are all the photos, the old letters, all of his aeronautical
drawings. The rest of his memories are filed in his top bureau
drawer in separate envelopes by date and year. Henry gently
cups the paper flower in his hand, looking down at its intricate folds, then slips it into the inner pocket of his suit coat,
deciding he will take this final memento with him to Japan.
When nothing else remains, when he has finished gathering
what's left of his courage, when he is all but ready to vanish,

he wheels himself across the tiny room and finds his silver radio on top of his bureau, which he carefully places in his lap. Pushing himself across the hall, he places the radio beside Mr. Bradley's bed, nodding to the frail-looking man, whose thin eyebrows rise, acknowledging this thoughtful gift. Then Henry is off. He turns the wheelchair around, glances at his black digital watch, which now reads 6:34 a.m., and begins rolling himself as quickly as he can down the long, tiled hall. By then he has become completely invisible.

BEFORE THE DAY NURSE at the front desk understands what is happening, before Jeff the orderly, pushing the metal food racks through the glass doors, can turn and appreciate the velocity at which Mr. Casper is now traveling, Henry's left wheel screams loudly as he skids to a stop near the door. This is followed by the tremendous clatter of Henry ramming himself as hard as he can against the meal trays, knocking the metal rack on its side, pre-warmed breakfasts spilling everywhere, leaving the glass security doors wide open. Without any trepidation this time, Henry wheels himself into the closest elevator, presses the *Door Close* button with a grave authority, then salutes once to the day nurse who is running around from behind the front desk. Only a few seconds later, Henry is wheeling himself rapidly through the lobby. He sees the thick-necked security guard near the front door holding the yellow telephone to his ear—the guard having just been alerted. Henry cuts left, passing unobserved down the side corridor, pulling himself through a pair of unlocked double doors, speeding past the kitchen and the laundry, where at the end of what seems like an endless hallway there is a sudden explosion of daylight.

. . .

ONCE HE IS THROUGH the service doors, once he has wheeled himself down the narrow alley, he is as good as gone, stopping for a moment at an unmarked corner, raising his right hand to hail a cab. The cabbie is unfamiliar with English, preferring, like Henry, the gravity of silence. Once he is safely installed in the backseat of the cab, once his wheelchair has been prop-erly folded and shoved inside the trunk and the taxicab is in motion, the cabdriver glances in the rearview mirror, asking for a destination in a thick Eastern European accent. Henry, scrambling among the pockets of his black suit jacket, finds a small slip of paper, then hands it through the narrow slot of the divider made of bulletproof glass. The cabbie glances at it, puzzled for a second, and then nods. What Henry has drawn is a sketch he has made hundreds and hundreds of times: an uncomplicated form, one long cylinder with two wings and a raised tail—the simple, solemn shape of an airplane.

Final Comments of Limited Historical Importance

THE ICE IS TOO THIN TO CROSS. IT IS LATE SPRING of 1630, when naval officer Jean Caspar, a third-class officer aboard a French vessel from the colonial *Compagnie des Marchands*, decides to shoot himself in the head.

Lost in search of a new trade route through the uncharted Arctic, the vessel ran aground nearly eight months ago on a fierce peninsula of ice. Now a storm cloud looms lazily above the lopsided mainmast as Jean stares up into the gray sky and howls, the sound echoing infinitely in the empty northern expanse. He treads along the ice-strewn deck, following an improvised system of ropes; the hull of the ship has been split into numerous parts, and so requires the curious to cross back and forth, from bow to stern, starboard to port, using several intertwined lines of snow-covered hemp. Following the ropes down a darkened passage, he finds himself alone in the main storeroom beneath the deck. Here a number of wooden crates have been hastily torn apart, some carrying glittering crystal tea sets, others glowing with magnificent silver serving plates, while the rest of the cases are now pyramids of warped and broken timber. The provisions themselves are long gone.

Figure 4: An ear

STOPPING ONLY ONCE on Allumette Island to trade with the Algonquins, the officers and seamen traveled north and soon discovered that they were unprepared for the desperate climate and its terrible weather, and one by one they began to die. Jean Caspar, standing there in the vacant storeroom, is the last man alive on the vessel, a cruel joke none of the other sailors would have enjoyed. For it is Jean Caspar, with his failing liver—congenitally malformed, ineffective, responsible for Jean's bright yellow skin tone and strange ammoniac odor—who ought to have been the first one dead; it ought to be his body that is now frozen in the makeshift mausoleum in the second storeroom.

But the first to go was Captain Louis Nicollet. Captain Nicollet had insisted on toting the crates of expensive tea sets and serving plates to swap with the Chinese and Indians, instead of stowing extra provisions. Jean Caspar did not argue with this poor decision, for he believed—in his spirit and bones—that it would be through the sole deployment of beauty—with the exchange of their superior French silver, their polished gold carafes, their spectacularly handsome jewelry—that the French would soon take command of the rest of the globe. *To be a king, one must wear a cape and gold crown,* Jean reasoned. *It must be the same the world over. In these primitive places, in these small worlds of sadness and dirt, there must be a tireless hunger for something beautiful, something beyond their miserably common lives. As soon as these lost souls learn the exquisiteness of the French language, of our poetry, song, and dance, the planet will be a much more enlightened place. Beauty, indescribable beauty, will conquer them all.*

Unaccustomed to such drastic cold, however, unable to survive on such notions of pomp and beauty, the captain froze to death while setting up a croquet set on the flat isle of snow surrounding the ice-locked ship. Several other sailors soon followed, their bodies, one by one, filling the secondary storeroom.

Jean Caspar, nearly fifty years old, watched able-bodied seaman after able-bodied seaman succumb to the deadly, unfamiliar frost. The remaining officers all took sick and then died, leaving the inexperienced, cowardly Jean in charge. Instead of directing the rest of the survivors to forge ahead or to search for safer ground, terrified of both the native Inuits and the strange mountains of ice looming in the distance, Jean Caspar gave no orders, and barricaded himself within the captain's empty quarters, where he decided to devote the rest of his time to silent prayer. There he hid, examining the captain's collection of antique rosaries, pleading with these exquisite icons for salvation. The other shipmen, distraught, marked with the black mouths and bruised skin of scurvy, soon turned to barbarism, killing each other in a matter of days. Jean Caspar, thinking of his lovely wife Iris and his two daughters back home in Avignon, listened with terror to the howls and cries from beyond the heavy door of the captain's cabin. Several gunshots, the sounds of flesh upon flesh, a scream for mercy—all echoed within the strange whiteness of those empty spring nights.

Within a few days, it has all grown very silent. Jean, glancing up from the tent of his folded hands, stands, pulls on his cap and decides it is in the best interests of the ship, the crew, and himself to take a look.

Quietly shifting the captain's heavy armoire from its place in front of the door, holding the captain's flintlock pistol in his hand, Jean Caspar follows the rope through the abandoned ship, searching for life. There is none. Two men, Baudin and Monod, lie beside one another, their necks split, blood frozen like a thousand pennies surrounding their heads. *Rich men*, Jean thinks gravely. He steps slowly over their corpses and finds Chardin with his right hand missing, having bled to death, lying near the foremast. The last, Isidore Duperrey, a bright-eyed boy of nineteen or twenty, has been stabbed several times in the chest. In his frozen grip there is a crucifix, the wooden cross split from the wretched cold. Jean places his hands against the young man's eyes to gently lower his lids. He would like to grant him the kind of peace that he, as an inexperienced and cowardly captain, could not offer the young sailor in life, but the skin is too cold and will not give. Death and this awful clime deny the guilt-stricken officer the chance to make a final gesture of apology. It is this particular insult that forces Jean Caspar to do what he has already been planning, not yet mentioned in any of his silent prayers. Like some of his men, he will meet his end by his own hand, with the quick and surgical certainty of lead.

Fearing that the Inuits will do something savage to him when they discover his body, Jean decides to climb up the splintered mainmast, hoisting himself up to the lookout's perch. He surveys the empty wasteland of the north once more, before he closes his eyes and asks for one final forgiveness. He puts the captain's pistol to his right ear and fires one time.

Before the lead shot makes a decisive rearrangement to the

interior cavity of Jean Caspar's skull, the cowardly officer imagines this: a great, singularly luminous cloud, rising from the
distant mist, moving with such force that it must be directed
by providence. The cloud glows with a luminous silver sheen.
Jean Caspar, having already pulled the trigger, the lead having
not yet made its way through the quiet mass of his brain, stares
at this cloud and, at once, realizes he is in the presence of some
great, unknowable entity. There are a thousand questions he
would like to ask it, all the puzzles that arise over the course
of the life of a man, and yet, with the pistol forced against his
right ear, the shot already traveling up the barrel, he knows it is
too late. He does not regret the great silence, however. For as
the magnificent cloud hangs above him, its contours drawing
dark lines of shadow upon his face, he realizes the wondrous
brilliance of so many possibilities, of so many questions never
to be answered, a world of infinite probabilities, of infinite
promise. Jean has the harrowing, joyous excitement of what a
supplicant must feel upon first meeting God: soon his brain is
filled with a new, astounding, inexpressible glow. It is exactly
as he always imagined it: absolute, unadulterated beauty. And
then the cloud fades, vanishing into unfurling mist, a vapor-
ous haze. Now a second cloud forms around Jean's head, its
fog filling his mouth and ears and throat. It may be the gun
smoke. In that moment, then, the lead does its appointed duty.
The sound of the shot is swallowed by a gust of wind and the
shifting of the ship, entrenched in the unending formations of
ice. Then there is silence. Then the cloud disappears, drifting
elsewhere.

Twenty-six

ON FRIDAY MORNING, JONATHAN WAKES UP TO THE
sight of white sheets hanging over his head, then sighs, crawling out from under the makeshift tent. He wipes his eyes with
the back of his hand, checks his watch, then begins to get
dressed. It's just past seven a.m.—and visiting hours at the
retirement home begin promptly at eight. After that he has his
afternoon class. And then a departmental meeting. Jonathan
lurches into the bathroom and washes up. He stares at his face
in the mirror with both disappointment and a little disgust, his
beard looking like some horrible undersea growth. He opens
the medicine cabinet. There, on the bottom shelf, is the orange
plastic vial of pills. He looks at the label for a few seconds,
twists off the white plastic top, and places a single silver pill in
the palm of his hand. Today he will not flee from that which
is uncomfortable or difficult. Today he is going to try his best.
When he is dressed and ready, Jonathan leaves a short note for
the girls on the kitchen table: *Went to visit Grandpa, class, then a
Meeting at School. Eat some Breakfast, See you Tonight.* He stumbles
around the house looking for his car keys, finds them, and
staggers into the garage. The garage. The Volvo is still gone.

He gazes at the empty gray space for a moment, then crawls into the Peugeot and starts it up. While he is backing his car into the alley, he pauses once more, still imagining the shape of his wife's missing car, of her behind the wheel, the shape of her mouth, of her eyes, of her face, then slowly he drives off.

As JONATHAN PULLS the Peugeot into the parking lot of the nursing home just past eight o'clock that morning, he can see that there's been some kind of trouble. A police cruiser is parked out front and, near the entrance, two nurses are arguing with a uniformed policeman. Jonathan tries to hurry past them, but Nurse Rhoda, her large hoop earrings dangling above her pink scrubs, stops him with a frown.

"Your father took off again," she mutters.

Jonathan is stunned. "No."

"Uh-huh. And he can stay gone as far as I'm concerned. We were all worried about him. We all thought he was at death's door."

"How long ago? When did you notice he was missing?"

"Well, he ran poor Jeff over and then he disappeared. It was about an hour ago, I guess."

Jonathan makes quick, heartfelt apologies to Rhoda and the rest of the nurses and then runs back to his car. The Peugeot refuses to start. As the engine whines and stutters, Jonathan closes his eyes and murmurs, "Don't do this to me, please don't do this to me," then tries the ignition once more. The engine finally gives, spinning dully to life, and Jonathan speeds out of the parking lot, hurtling down the boulevard as fast as he can, flying toward the expressway.

· · ·

O'HARE INTERNATIONAL AIRPORT looks like a city on the moon, full of glossy metal and plastic buildings; the structures extend out in odd, cubist directions and at unusual angles. It also looks a lot like a maze. Jonathan searches for the short-term parking lot, and when he is unable to find it, he pulls up in front of one of the departure terminals, putting on his blinkers, and hurries from the vehicle. There is no way to know what airline his father might try and take. He could be at any one of the other terminals, and even running as fast as he can, it might take hours to find the right one. And by then his father might be gone. Jonathan pauses, trying to breathe. The busy passengers rush all about him pulling their baggage, signs and electronic monitors glow in his periphery, people kiss hello or goodbye, children cry. *Who are all these people and how can it be that they are all alive on this planet at the same time?* Jonathan thinks, before turning back to retrace his own steps. *Okay, where is he? Where would he be?* Jonathan turns once more and hurries up to the next available ticket agent. He smiles at the dark-haired woman, wiping a sweaty palm against his forehead.

"Can I help you?" she asks.

"I'm looking for my father. I'm afraid he might be lost."

"Do you want me to contact security?"

"I don't know. I'd like to try and find him myself first. But maybe we should."

"Sir? Would you like me to contact security?"

Jonathan turns, shaking his head, following his steps back outside again. He stops and looks over at his car: the windshield has already been decorated with two bright orange parking tickets.

"Okay, Dad, where are you? Where did you go?"

And just then Jonathan remembers his father's last escape attempt: Japan. He rushes back inside, up to the same service counter, and asks the same ticket agent what's the next flight from Chicago to Japan.

"There's one at around noon, and another this evening."

"Nothing before that on any other airline? Can you please check that?"

"Just a moment," she says, typing the computer keys thoughtfully.

"There's one leaving in half an hour from United."

"Where's that?"

"The International Terminal. Terminal Five."

"Where am I?"

"Terminal Three."

"Okay, how do I get to the International Terminal?"

"You can walk or take the tram."

"Which way is it?"

The ticket agent smiles, then points outside, to her left. Jonathan returns the woman's smile, shakes her hand, then flies off, his lungs on fire, his whole body trembling.

AT THE INTERNATIONAL TERMINAL, Jonathan tries to explain to one of the security guards the specifics of his father's situation, but without a ticket he is not permitted anywhere beyond the lobby. Jonathan tries to speak with another security guard but he, too, only reiterates the simple rule: no ticket, no entrance beyond this point. In a frenzy, Jonathan hurries over to the ticket counter, checking his watch every few minutes, then purchases a one-way ticket from Chicago O'Hare ORD to Tokyo, Japan TYO for $1,827.10. He puts it on his credit card and hopes, somehow, some way, it will be refundable, knowing in his heart that it will not. Because he is traveling alone, without any baggage, with a one-way ticket, because he is sweating profusely, the security officers take him aside to search him more thoroughly, and when he has finally passed this final hurdle, Jonathan is almost completely out of breath. He glances down at his ticket, searching for the gate number, M15, then he limps toward it, trying to breathe slowly, his face sweaty, his knees weak. He feels like he might faint at any moment, the fluorescent lights swimming all around his head. "Okay, just a few more gates," he whispers to himself. "Just three more, two more, one more, there, there," he gasps, hurrying over to gate M15.

But he does not see his father in the crowd. Jonathan lets out a sigh and stumbles into one of the uncomfortable gray plastic chairs, dropping his face into his hands. Overhead, the electronic voices repeat dizzying information about changed flights and gates, and Jonathan, having failed, thinks he might begin to sob. By now he realizes he will not make his afternoon class. It will be the third time he has canceled this semester. When Jonathan lowers his hand from his eyes, fighting back the accumulated tears of failure after failure, he spots an old man in a wheelchair, staring out the large square window at the enormous airplanes parked just beyond the glass, the sounds of their engines a constant drone, a kind of song maybe, the old man not staring off at the airplanes themselves so much as their shapes, the ideas they suggest, dreaming of what they might somehow become.

Jonathan rises, catching a few small tears with the corner of his sleeve, then steps beside his father. He places one hand on the old man's shoulder, startling him for a moment. As his father turns, wheeling the chair around, Jonathan sees his expression isn't one of dismay, of disappointment, it's a look of surprise, of sudden, pleasant joy.

"Dad? What are you doing here? You scared us half to death."

His father frowns, then smiles, clutching his son's hand.

"I can't let you get on that airplane, Dad. I wish I could, I wish we could let you go, but we can't. You know we can't."

His father does not stop smiling, still grasping at his son's hand.

"Dad. Why do you keep doing this to us, Dad?"

Jonathan's father squeezes his hand, then points at Jonathan's heart, then at his own, suggesting something Jonathan can't even begin to guess.

"What? What are you telling me, Dad?"

His father repeats the gesture, tapping Jonathan's chest, then his own, pointing out the window at the open blue sky.

"What?"

He repeats the same gesture once more, very slowly.

"You want me to go with you?" Jonathan whispers.

His father nods, proud that this most secret of messages finally makes sense.

"I can't do that, Dad. I can't. I have the girls, and Madeline is still gone, and there's work. I wish I could, I really do, Dad, but I can't. Okay? Okay. Come on, let's go see if they towed my car yet. Maybe I can find a pay phone to call the nursing home and let them know you're all right. Okay, come on, Dad, let's go."

But his father doesn't respond; he only turns to stare off at the planes taxiing back and forth outside.

"Dad. We have to go."

His father does not make a movement or a sound.

"You're not going to talk to me? You're not going to answer me?"

His father refuses to look at him now, his bright eyes on the curves and lines of the mammoth airplanes outside.

"Dad, please, say something."

But there is only silence, silence and the noise of a thousand people hurrying all around them.

"Dad. Say something. Tell me I'm an awful son, I don't care. Just say something."

Only silence, only the myriad human sounds of the airport.

"Dad? Dad, why do you want to make this hard for everybody? It's hard enough . . . I mean, with what's been happening in my life, I don't know why you want to make things so difficult for me. Jesus." Jonathan looks away and then murmurs, "Come on, Dad, let's go."

His father slowly frowns, staring up into his son's face, quietly realizing the apprehension and pain he has been causing. He reaches out one emaciated hand and gently touches his son's cheek, then mutters a single word, a single sound, and in speaking it, he hopes to say everything he has been too afraid to murmur, everything he has kept to himself—from the early silences of his long-ago childhood, to the unspoken quiet of their relationship as father and son, all of the shame, all of the loss, of having done nothing worthwhile, of having been part of something horrible, worse than criminal, something brutal and thoughtless and destructive, of having built nothing that mattered, nothing important—and then, seeing his son, he understands he is wrong. What comes out then is hard to hear, inexact, a little weak—the sound of the invention of which he is most proud.

"*Jonathan.*"

Jonathan smiles softly, feeling his father's shrunken hand against his face. "Dad?"

"Jonathan," his father repeats, looking up into his son's face. "Jonathan. Jonathan." And that is all. Father and son stare at each other for one moment longer, then the son stands, touching his sleeve to something in the corner of his eye. He steps beside his father, gently pushing the wheelchair forward, down the long tile hall, past the food court and magazine stands, out past the lines waiting before security, the word still resonating in the air, its actual meaning imprecise and unimportant now.

ONE OF THE RAREST of modern phenomenon then: the Peugeot has not been towed. Jonathan stares at the number of orange tickets it's accumulated in his absence, a whopping ten altogether. He helps his father into the front seat of the car, folds up the wheelchair and slides it in the back, then turns to make sure his father has buckled himself in.

"I'm sorry, Dad. I wish I hadn't found you. I really do. But I did. And I couldn't live with myself if I didn't know where you were. I'm sorry, Dad, I really am."

But his father does not seem to have heard, his grayish green eyes having gone hard, his face stern, his gaze rapt, staring at the planes taking off and landing. Finally, as they pull back onto the expressway, his father again breaks his vow and quietly whispers, "Thank you for coming to find me."

ON THE CAR RIDE back to the retirement home, both Jonathan and his father are silent. His dad stares out the window at the city moving beside them, the identical-looking houses, trees, cars vanishing as quickly as they appear. Soon they are returning to Hyde Park, soon the familiar University of Chicago campus is in view, then it, too, is gone, and finally, there, in the corner of the windshield, is the bleak-looking rectangle of the South Shore Nursing Home. Jonathan pulls into the parking lot, shuts off the engine, and begins to unbuckle his seat belt. Just then, his father places a weak-looking left hand on his son's wrist, then slips his right beneath his black suit jacket. From within the suit's worn lining, his father retrieves a folded piece of paper, carefully placing it in his son's hands.

"What is this?" Jonathan asks.

His father smiles for a moment, then holds a finger up to own lips and whispers, "Shhhhhh," before turning to unbuckle the seat belt, not speaking another word.

AFTER JONATHAN HAS finished explaining everything to the nurses, when he is done apologizing to the nursing home's director, when his father is once again installed in the same gloomy, semiprivate room, Jonathan kisses his dad's forehead once, then rushes off, down the elevator, across the parking lot, and back to his car. He checks his watch: he's late again. He'll have to hurry if he's going to make the one o'clock faculty meeting. Surely they are expecting him to attend. There will be awkward questions and serious reprisals for his having canceled as many classes as he has. Twelve thirty-five p.m. He has just enough time to go home and change and get ready for the end.

WHEN JONATHAN IS ALONE a few moments later, sitting in the front seat of the Peugeot, he starts up the car, glances through the back windshield at the wide blue sky, and then, without knowing why exactly, he puts the car back into park.

He digs through the front pocket of his windbreaker, finds the note from his dad, and stares at it. It is nothing. Nothing. Jonathan, baffled, finally sees that it is a small paper flower. He is both surprised and confused, staring for a moment at its puzzling white shape. *What is this supposed to be, Dad?* It's something so odd, so precise, so out of place, this small paper blossom. *What is it? Is this supposed to be some kind of sign?*

Clutching the flower in his palm, Jonathan begins to smile. *It is a secret message*, he quietly thinks. *It's an apology.* He begins to inspect the tiny bloom, studying it like a fossil, like a pen from his beloved prehistoric squid, and what he sees now is how old it is, how worn the paper looks, how intricately folded, how brilliantly complicated it is: lines intersecting lines, each bent to a perfect slant, each in its own thoughtful place. What Jonathan feels next is an odd sort of wonderment at the paper flower's certain and uncertain angles, at the curious complexity he now holds in his hand. And then he thinks: *It's beautiful. It's beautiful because it's complicated. Because there's not one thing. There's not one thing that makes sense of everything.*

AND SO IT HAPPENS: as Jonathan pulls the Peugeot into the garage late that Friday morning, he is startled by the shape of the old Volvo parked there. He stares at it with unequaled gratitude for many, many moments. He once again memorizes its shape, its color, the odd smell of the engine, its nicks and scratches and dents. He stares at the passenger-side tire that needs to be inflated, at the silver trim that has begun to dangle from its place, and everything that makes that car his wife's car, each microscopic detail, and feels grateful for all of it. Jonathan climbs out of the Peugeot, hurries toward the house, pauses, turns, reaches into his pocket, finds the white paper flower resting in the cup of his hand, and then places it beneath the windshield wiper of his wife's rusty-looking car.

As JONATHAN RUNS into the house, he can hear Madeline moving around upstairs. It is way past twelve and the girls are in school by now, so it has to be Madeline. She is alone in the house with him, she is back, at least for the moment, maybe only home to take a shower or do a load of laundry. Because of this Jonathan must act quickly, and the thought of quick action terrifies him. He stands there in the kitchen and wonders what he should do, and how he should proceed, the sound of the clock on the wall now synchronized with his awkward heartbeat.

Each footstep from above, each creak of the bedroom door panics him, and still he is unable to decide what to do. He wishes he had the words, the courage to walk upstairs, to tell her what is in his heart, to say, *Although I have ignored you, our love, and the world around me, I am profoundly sorry. I am now ready to resume our love. I am ready to do right by you and be with you again. I am begging, kneeling here. Please.* But these words are only intimations, only feelings which he cannot, does not know how to speak. He stands there, staring up at the ceiling, and feels defenseless, as if he is dying.

And then, without another pause, without any more deliberation, he climbs the stairs as quickly as he can. He passes the mirror in the hall and tries not to glance at himself but it is impossible to ignore how terrible he looks. He looks like a serious mess. His hair is sticking up in back. His blond beard is uncombed, with unruly white tufts trailing out along his chin. He has been in the same T-shirt and blue jogging pants for days. He tries to arrange himself, tucking his T-shirt into his pants, then, deciding against that, he untucks it. He checks his breath by blowing into his palm and trying to smell it. The results are uncertain. He clears his throat and after a few moments of painful indecision he steps through the bedroom door, and finds Madeline standing there in her gray robe, her hair wrapped up in a towel. She has just gotten out of the shower. Her neck is still dappled with moisture. She is brushing her teeth. She sees him and is startled for a moment. She is nervous and silent and soft-looking.

"Hello," Jonathan says.

"Hello," she says, glancing up from the bathroom sink, her mouth filled with white foam. She looks gorgeous, a whole other woman, a stranger. Every part of her seems to be far away and graceful and unyielding. He does not know if he should try and touch her. He thinks of rushing toward her and kissing her but is afraid. He is afraid she will stop him and say the words he cannot bear to hear right now. So he begins to smile, unsure if he should be smiling. He wants to be mad for some reason. He wants her to know how worried he's been, how he has been feeling like he's been split wide open, how his life has suddenly stopped making sense, but all he thinks to do is stare at her. He says, "I have to go to school now, for a meeting. But maybe we can talk later, if you want to." He says, "We've missed you. We really have. I have." He does not say what he would like to. He does not say he is nothing without her. He is too afraid that she will not understand. That she will think he is weak, which he is. He is afraid she will not see how hopelessly in love with her he is, and always has been, for as long as he can remember. He wants to apologize for being so selfish, so ungrateful for her, for the girls, for their love. He wants to tell her he has been doing some serious thinking. He wants to tell her the prehistoric giant squid is dead and that his dream of knowing the answers, of seeing the simplicity of the universe, of solving the big questions, has died along with it. He wants to tell her she doesn't need to worry. That things have changed. That he has realized something. That he is thinking different thoughts now, but he does not know what is supposed to happen next. He is desperately trying to think of some happy ending, but all he can do is stare at his wife from across the tiny room. He smiles at her and then turns and rushes down the stairs, into the den, to find something to wear, something that does not reveal how upside down everything has become. He settles on a blue shirt and a pair of jeans and prays someone else at the meeting will also be dressed so informally.

AT THE DEPARTMENTAL MEETING that Friday afternoon, Jonathan shows up late, feeling clammy, beads of sweat glistening on his narrow forehead. There is no inquisition. There is no talk of his dismissal. Instead, he is asked what he thinks of the new course catalog. There is a debate about whether the cover photograph on the course catalog is as appealing as it should be. There are also some questions about the catalog's font, if it is as readable, as inviting to students as the administration believes. When someone asks Jonathan what he thinks, he is surprised and looks up from the gloss of the shiny mahogany table, incredibly relieved. "I really don't have an opinion either way."

His chairperson, Abigail, frowns at him from the head of the table and then announces, "Okay, let's take a five-minute break, everyone. Jonathan, if you wouldn't mind, I'd like to have a word with you."

The other faculty members cough and nod, slowly exiting, pulling themselves up from their comfortable seats. Jonathan does not move. He looks down at the university's brochures or course catalogs or whatever they are, and waits for the conference room to be empty. Before he can begin the lengthy apology he has already prepared, Abigail stands, straightening her pants suit, and then hovers beside him.

"Jonathan?"

"Yes."

"I need to know what's going on with you. I had two students in here today complaining that you've been late to class and that you've canceled three times this semester already."

"I'm sorry. I've been . . . well, the truth of the matter is . . ." Jonathan scratches his beard, unable to look his chairperson in the eye. He stares out the shiny glass windows at the tops of the black walnut trees outside. "Did you ever think, when you were younger, that your life would be so hard? Didn't you think things would make sense, that it would somehow be easier the older you got?" Jonathan asks.

Abigail smiles, touching his hand.

"Maybe. I'm afraid I don't remember what I used to think. It's all a kind of blur to me. I do know, well, I've come to value those little complexities. I believe it was Kant who said—"

"Hmmmm," Jonathan says, frowning.

"If you need some time off, I can arrange a grad student to take one of your classes. There's nothing to be embarrassed about."

Jonathan shakes his head, looking up into her green eyes. "No. I just . . . I've just been a little lost. My father . . . and other things. It's just sometimes hard to get a hold on everything. Do you know what I mean? It's like a million things all coming at you. It's hard to know where to look sometimes."

Abigail smiles, touching his hand again. "Welcome to middle age," she says with a grin.

AFTER THE THREE-HOUR meeting, Jonathan rushes into his office to call the nursing home and to ask about his father. The nurse puts him on hold for five actual minutes and comes back to tell him that his father is okay, he's resting, though he's been given a sedative to help him sleep. Jonathan says he will be there as soon as he can. The phone begins to ring again as soon as he hangs it up. He stares at it, momentarily afraid. He does not believe it can be good news. It rings once, then again, then a third time. Finally Jonathan answers, his hand trembling.

"Dr. Casper?" comes the nervous voice.

"Yes?"

"This is Ted, your grad student. And Catherine. She's standing next to me."

"All right."

"Dr. Casper, we tried you at home but your wife said to try you here."

"Okay. Fine."

"Dr. Casper, they think they spotted a giant squid about thirty miles south of Hawaii. It's probably not *Tusoteuthis longa*. It maybe looks like *Architeuthis dux*, but still, there's no way to know. I mean, either way this might be a great opportunity to get data from a live specimen for a comparison study. There's a film crew down there now with video. The first moving footage of a giant squid in its own habitat."

"Hawaii?"

"It's in American waters, sir. The French will need a couple of days to get the permits. Catherine and I could get on a flight tonight. There's still some money in the budget from the university."

Jonathan holds the phone, his heart vibrating.

"Well, what do we do, sir?" Ted asks.

Jonathan stares out of his narrow office window at the cloudy afternoon sky, then softly begins to say the few words he did not believe he ever would.

Twenty-seven

A. As Madeline is lying in bed that Friday evening, she thinks she hears Jonathan come home. There is the noise of the lock turning as he opens the back door, the sound of him tiptoeing across the kitchen, and then the quiet of him sneaking down the hallway toward the solitude of the den. For some reason, her heart begins beating rapidly, much too fast for no real reason. She holds her breath, listening to him moving about, setting down his briefcase, taking off his jacket, the sounds echoing up through the heating vents. She is almost sure that she can hear him slip off his shoes, one after the other, and then there is nothing, no sound, only silence from the floor below. What is he doing down there? There is the creak of his feet on the threshold at the den's door—is he pacing? Is he trying to make up his mind to go hide in his fortress or not? And then, almost at once, she can hear him creeping up the front stairs, down the hall to their bedroom, where he finds her, sitting up in bed. Jonathan clears his throat and whispers a hello.

"Hello," Madeline says.

"What are you doing?" he asks.

"Waiting for you to come home, I guess."

"You were?"

"Yep."

Jonathan smiles a little, his blue eyes twinkling, as he loosens his shirt and slips off his sweater.

"How is your dad doing?" Madeline asks.

"He's okay," he says. "Not so good, I guess. I think he's maybe getting towards the end. He's just . . . I think he's given up."

"I'd like to go see him . . . I mean, I didn't know if you want me to, but I'd like to."

"When we got married, he said getting you to fall in love with me would be the best thing I ever did."

"He was right."

Jonathan smiles again. "I wanted . . . I wanted to just tell you . . . that I was sorry . . . That I know how difficult I must be to live with. That I've been in a fog. I . . . I know it can't be easy. I know sometimes, well, most of the time . . . all of the time, I've been too focused on my work. I know I've been kind of thoughtless. But I just wanted to tell you I think you're pretty amazing, putting up with me and taking care of the girls. I mean, to be honest, I don't know how you do it. I wouldn't even know how. I just wanted to let you know that none of it matters if I don't have you. I'm not afraid of how hard it's going to be, to convince you, to make this work. Because I don't want anything, really, besides you. I guess . . . I guess that's it for now. I have other things I want to tell you but I guess that was the most important thing. So, well, thanks."

Jonathan pauses, then thinks about crossing the room to

where she is sitting, he thinks about trying to kiss her, but only nods again, before turning to walk away.

"Would you like to sleep in here tonight?" Madeline asks, not meeting his eyes.

"Would you like me to?"

Madeline nods, not saying the word.

"What are we going to tell the girls?" Jonathan asks.

Madeline wrinkles her nose and then frowns. "I'm going to tell them that we're both fucking crazy."

Jonathan nods and slips off his shirt, then his pants, and crosses the room to the bed.

B. When Jonathan climbs into bed, the two of them finally lying together again, they do not make love. Jonathan, exhausted, puts his arm around his wife and presses his face against her back. Within a few moments he is asleep. Smirking, Madeline listens to him begin to snore, then, trying to follow his breath, feeling the weight of this odd man against her, she finally closes her eyes, too.

C. On that cloudless Saturday morning, Madeline wakes up and sees Jonathan lying beside her, then decides that she's probably going to end up loving him forever.

D. It might be as easy as all of that. He is lying beside her in the bed, his face buried in the pillow, his arm is flung over the top of his head. She can hear him breathing. She thinks he looks perfect like that, like a boy, and then that's all there is. Beneath all of her thoughts and worries, beneath the complication of conflicting identities and needs, maybe it's as simple as loving the way some other person looks when they're sleeping.

E. That Saturday, strangely, is like almost every other Saturday ever. Jonathan goes to visit his father that morning. He returns saddened, but soon he is back to work in the den, following his grad students' updates from Hawaii. Madeline speaks to her research advisor, Dr. Hillary, to explain her recent absences before she vacuums the house, singing selections from the Beatles' *White Album*. Amelia is up in her room busy with her school assignments. Thisbe pedals around the neighborhood on her bicycle sighing because she's bored again. The only difference today is the prevalent feeling that, at any moment, any of them—father, mother, daughter, or sister— might vanish. They are all very careful and polite, glancing at each other curiously out of the corners of their eyes. They watch a movie together that night, all of them spread out in front of the TV. It is Thisbe's pick, *The Song of Bernadette*, which everyone tolerates silently.

F. The next morning, when Madeline opens the front door, she finds the Sunday paper, and realizes that today is Halloween. The late autumn weather is crisp and bright, the sun shining low in the east, orange and red and yellow leaves are glowing in the trees. Madeline stands on the front porch for a few moments and tries to decide if she is going to dress up to answer the door to give out candy to the neighborhood children or not. She decides she will, and begins searching through the house for something to wear.

In the basement, Madeline finds an old witch costume for herself and a caveman outfit for Jonathan. She climbs back upstairs, puts on the witch outfit, which is a little tight in the middle and the butt, but it makes her boobs look pretty great, then wakes Jonathan with a kiss. "Boo," she says.

"Happy Halloween," he says.

"Did you remember?" she asks.

"I don't think so. I thought about it yesterday a little, but I guess I forgot."

"Do you want to hand out candy to the kids?"

Jonathan rubs his beard over and over again, then wipes the sleep from his eyes and says, "Why not?"

"It's almost eleven o'clock," she says. "I bet they'll start coming around noon."

"Okay," he murmurs, letting his head fall back on the pillow.

"Jonathan!" she shouts, placing his costume at the foot of the bed.

G. Together they hand out candy to neighborhood kids all afternoon. There are only about two dozen or so, but Madeline likes to watch Jonathan do his little routine: standing behind the door, slowly opening it, so that it appears to open on its own, then leaping out, shouting in some indecipherable caveman language. Most of the kids don't even get scared, though one, just a toddler, starts to cry and Madeline is happy to be able take her hand and comfort her, before dropping a Reese's Peanut Butter Cup into her orange, pumpkin-shaped bag. Afterward, Jonathan and Madeline lounge around in their costumes, wondering if any older kids might come by that evening, but none do. At one point, sitting on the sofa, staring out through the parlor windows, Jonathan and Madeline are watching the sun set, when Amelia steps into the room and sees her father, dressed as a caveman, sleeping with his feet in her mother's lap. Amelia squints, inspecting the unfamiliarly familiar situation, and smirks, her mother's kind of smirk actually, before strolling back into the kitchen.

H. On Monday morning, Madeline asks the girls if they want a ride to school. Both of them say yes. When she goes to the start the car, she finds a tiny paper flower placed beneath her black windshield wiper. She lifts the wiper blade gently, then holds the paper flower in her hand, staring down at it with a soft blush and a curious sense of surprise.

Jonathan: I thought I had you figured out.

"What's that, Mom?" Thisbe asks, but Madeline smiles and slips the flower into her purse without an answer. As she pulls up in front of the school, Madeline wants to tell her daughters that things are going to be okay with her and their father. She doesn't know how to put it exactly and she can feel them getting ready to run off, but before Amelia can leap out, Madeline puts the Volvo in park and says, "Girls, I'd like to talk to you about your father for a minute."

"We know, you're like all in love again," Amelia says, rolling her eyes.

"Okay, but, well, I just wanted to say—"

"Mom, I'm going to be late," Amelia whispers, rigid in the front seat.

"No, you're not," Thisbe says from the back, shaking her head. "We got like an hour."

"Well, I actually have things to do. I'm supposed to be doing stuff for the paper."

"BS," Thisbe whispers. She glances at her mother in the rearview mirror as Madeline tries to continue.

"I just wanted to say that I'm sorry for making things difficult for you both. It's just that we're trying to figure things out . . . and . . . I hope when, or if, you guys decide to get married, you never have to worry about things like this. But it's just that . . . it doesn't usually work out so easy. It's hard sometimes but we're going to keep trying."

"Okay," Amelia says, her hand on the door handle. "Can we go now?"

"Okay, I guess," Madeline says, stammering a little, wondering if she should say anything else. "Okay, well, have a great day."

Before she finishes her sentence, Amelia has opened the door and has taken off. Thisbe, slow, dressed a little sloppily in overalls, leans forward and kisses her mother's cheek. "You have a great day, too, Mom," she says, and then, finding her book bag, she follows, disappearing into the small, colorful constellation of kids. Madeline watches them both go, then puts the Volvo back in drive, and rushes off.

I. On the way to work, Madeline listens to NPR and remembers that the presidential election is tomorrow. She doesn't know what to expect. The polls are pretty close and she's afraid that John Kerry, as thorough as he was during the debates, might have struck people as too wooden, without much of a personality. She's afraid of what will happen if George Bush gets reelected. She doesn't think it will be the end of the world, just that it will be very, very bad for everybody.

J. At work that Monday, Madeline finds two more dead pigeons, murdered, lying there at the bottom of the enclosure. Madeline inspects their bodies inside the lab and again finds they're both females. That's eight dead birds altogether. There's no way she can hide this. When Laura, her assistant, shows up with coffee an hour later, Madeline lets her know what has been happening.

"Raped?" Laura asks, her thin eyebrows raised in shock.

"Then murdered."

"Why?"

"I don't know. I'm pretty sure it has something to do with the dominant males being removed."

"Yeah, but why?"

"I don't know."

The two of them spend the rest of the morning inspecting the animals, finding nothing else out of the ordinary, nothing abnormal, no signs of infection of any kind, nothing unsettling about the enclosure itself, no external forces that they think might be causing this strange behavior. Finally, Madeline presents the case to Dr. Hillary, her research advisor. Dr Hillary, his beard as dense and as white as chicken feathers, sits in his leather chair, nodding, staring at the top of the point his fingers make pressed tightly together. When Madeline finishes reading her notes, Dr. Hillary nods, then grimly asks, "And why do you think your birds are committing murder?"

"I really don't know. I mean obviously it has to do with us removing the older, more dominant males."

"Yes, but why would that cause such upheaval, such bizarre behaviors?"

"I don't know," Madeline admits.

"You've seriously upset those birds' hierarchy, no?"

"Yes."

"And the results have been quite drastic."

"Yes."

"And you don't know why."

"I know the how but not the why. I thought removing the more aggressive birds would result in less aggression."

Dr. Hillary smiles, rocking back and forth in his chair.

"So what you found is that without the older, dominant males, the younger, beta males became much more aggressive, aberrantly aggressive, no?"

"Yes."

"And why do you think that happened?"

"Because the dominant pigeons keep order."

"It would seem so."

"That still doesn't explain the rape, and then the murders."

"Let me redirect you, then," Dr. Hillary says. "How do pigeons mate?"

"What do you mean?"

"What kind of process do they have?"

"They have a dance."

"What kind of dance?"

"Well, the male bows to the female several times, then he blows out his neck feathers, puffs himself up, starts circling the female. Then he might spread out his tail feathers and drag them around. Then if there are other males present, he'll try to separate the female from them by chasing her. Then the female, if she's willing, will slip her bill into his and they'll begin bobbing their heads, then after that the male climbs on the female's back and— "

"So there is a ritual, no, a kind of dance, as you said?"

"Yes."

"I am willing to bet that none of the males that you have in that cage are following the important steps of that ritual dance. I believe, if you were to study them, you would find the males try to mount the females without any kind of dance, as you call it, and the females, unsure of how to proceed without the ritual, think they are in danger and fight off the males' advances. I think the males then, frustrated, after some time simply peck their prospective mates to death."

"It still doesn't explain why."

"Where did you learn about how the world works?"

"School," Madeline says with a shrug. "Then grad school."

"And what about role models? Your parents, for example. Certainly as a child, perhaps as a teenager, you saw them as dominant influences as well."

Madeline, eyes wide, feels herself begin to smile. "The males weren't there to teach them the dance."

"The dominant males were not around to establish order. Or to pass on their knowledge."

"Wow."

"Wow, indeed," Dr. Hillary says. "So . . ."

"So if I return the older, dominant males . . ."

"Then I think you have a very interesting study on your hands."

"Thank you, Dr. Hillary."

Madeline shakes his hand and sprints back downstairs to the research labs.

One by one, Madeline reintroduces the red-tagged males back into the experiment's population. There is no noticeable difference at first. One of the older males flies around, searching for a roost. It squabbles a little with a yellow-tag male, using its larger size to force the smaller bird out of its large box. Madeline makes a note of this and wonders what this sort of thing might say about the world of human beings.

K. At lunch, smoking in the front seat of her lab assistant Laura's car, she does not make eye contact with Eric. He is acting strange anyway, all nervous and twitchy. When they finish their smoke break, heading back inside the poorly lit research facility, Madeline leans beside Eric and says, "I need to talk to you for a minute." Eric looks shocked. He pushes his glasses farther up his nose and nods as Laura strolls back to their lab module. Madeline does not know what to say, only that she has to say something. She clears her throat, then shifts her weight from foot to foot, then simply says, "Eric, I don't know if you were unsure or not, but I'm married."

Eric nods, running a hand through his uncombed hair, sighing. "Okay, I know, I mean . . . I really apologize. It was just one of those things."

"Yeah, you just can't do that because you think it's okay. Because it's not."

"I'm sorry, really."

"Just don't do that again. Ever."

"Sure, okay, I just . . . well, sure. I'm sorry."

Madeline nods, marching off, the sound of her shoes against the concrete floor sure and steady. She smiles a little to herself as she walks away, a little proud maybe, a little more certain than she has been in some time.

L. Before she heads home that evening, Madeline checks on the birds once more. Two of the three reintroduced males have found nests. The third, a broad, granite-colored fellow with a slightly hooked beak, is too busy chasing a passel of newly introduced females, which Madeline finds pathetically charming.

M. In the Volvo, on the way home from work, Madeline begins to cry. But it's okay, it's the good kind of crying. As she's searching for a CD to pop into the player, NPR plays a report about Private Daniel Harkins, the soldier in Baghdad, who was captured and who has been held captive for nearly three weeks. He has been released. Madeline turns up the radio and the professional monotone of the NPR reporter repeats, "Private First Class Daniel Harkins has been released from his captors in the capital city of Baghdad. He's being flown to a medical facility in Germany, where he'll be given time to recover from his traumatic experience before returning home to North Carolina . . ." The report then goes on to mention that fifty people have been killed by a car bomb in Basra. Madeline switches off the radio as she pulls the Volvo into the garage. In the dark, with the automatic garage door sliding down, she frowns at herself for being so weepy.

N. On Monday night, nothing all that interesting happens. Madeline and Jonathan sit on the couch and watch a special on the worst storms of the century. While they're watching TV, Madeline keeps sneaking glances at her husband, making sure he's okay. He's taken his antiseizure medication, that much is obvious. She looks at him again and smiles. She does think he's still kind of handsome, maybe a little too serious, a little too self-involved, but he really is pretty nice-looking. She holds his hand and it feels okay, it feels like it means something. And then, without lifting his eyes from the television set, he does something pretty terrific. He squeezes her hand once, then again, a secret code, just to let her know that he knows she is there, that at that particular moment, he is thinking of her and her only.

O. At work the next day, the covey of pigeons is perfectly silent. There are no dead birds. The red-tagged dominant males each roost in their own corner of the pen. When some of the less dominant males, the yellow-tags, begin to fuss, one of the red-tags always swoops down and begins squawking. Madeline makes a note of this in her book but isn't sure what it means exactly.

P. Maybe it actually means dominance is some kind of natural state. *Oh, shit*, she thinks. *What the hell does that mean for the world? What does that mean for the rest of us who really don't love the idea of being dominated? What if we really don't want to be part of a dominant empire? What the hell do we do then?* Madeline considers these questions as she drives home from work. She stops at a church two blocks from her house to cast her vote. She does it quickly, punching a hole for the judges based mostly on whether they are female are not, and if there are no female candidates, based on whether they are Democrats or not, and if there are two female Democrats, then she decides based on the way their names sound. After that she quickly heads home.

Q. That Tuesday evening, Madeline sits beside Jonathan and watches the election returns. Thisbe lies on the floor, working on her math homework, glancing up at the television every so often. Amelia just can't keep still.

"I'm supposed to be writing something about the election for the school paper, but I can't watch," Amelia confesses. "If John Kerry loses, I'm going to totally kill myself. Or move to Canada." But she takes a seat in the puffy white chair for a while, scrawling some notes to herself in a little yellow notebook, then gets up, then goes and makes some popcorn, then comes back, sitting on the edge of the sofa. Thisbe watches her sister bouncing back and forth around the house and smiles, shaking her head. She turns to her parents and asks, still lying on the floor, "Did both of you guys vote for John Kerry?" Madeline smiles and nods, as does her husband, who also winks.

"Oh," Thisbe whispers.

"Who would you have voted for, honey?" Madeline asks.

"I dunno. George Bush, I guess."

Her sister, Amelia, sighs, looking glum. "That is so stupid."

"What?" Thisbe asks. "It's my imaginary vote, I can vote for whoever I want to."

"George Bush is only like the worst president of all time."

"I don't think so. I think he just isn't as good a talker as that other guy."

"Did you even watch the debates?" Amelia asks suspiciously.

"Yes. We had to watch them in history class."

"And?"

"I guess I liked the president. The other guy, he was too hard to follow. His answers were too long. It was like he talked too much instead of just saying what he thought."

Amelia rolls her eyes. "Well, thank God you don't get to vote."

Thisbe shrugs her shoulders, returning to her math home-work, her left leg rising and falling as she scribbles mathemati-cal figures on lined paper, the world on the television screen before her being quickly transformed by similar equations.

R. Things don't look so bad for John Kerry at first. All the New England states vote for him, and the maps, on the differ-ent news channels, show a large block of blue as it gradually appears in the northeastern corner of the country. Most of the Midwest and South vote for the incumbent president, and just as quickly, those parts of the map glow bright red.

S. Madeline can't help getting her hopes up as she watches: Illinois, then Michigan, Wisconsin, then Minnesota, all flash bright blue.

"Wow, this is gonna be close," Amelia whispers, trying to do the electoral math in her notebook.

"It looks like it," Jonathan says. "I hope it doesn't get decided by Florida again."

"No, Florida is already red."

"We'll just have to see what happens," Jonathan says.

T. By eleven o'clock, almost all of the votes are in. Once again, the country is completely divided: the southern Midwest and the South have voted for the Republican, the Northeast, northern Midwest, and the West have voted for the Democrat. The entire presidential election hinges on the state of Ohio. Ohio? Why Ohio? Ohio, like the silent, anonymous heart of the nation, located center and to the left, Ohio will, in the end, decide the fate of the country, the world, maybe even the universe. Some reporters mention that there are voters still waiting in line, even at this hour. What can be going through their minds? What kind of questions are they asking themselves as they stand there waiting to decide? Or probably their decision has already been made and, standing there, impatient, waiting to be heard, they stare ahead and wonder why something so simple as punching a hole or marking an X or touching a screen has to be so difficult. Maybe that's the real question anyway. Why so much concern about the election in the first place, when, in the end, it is only another contest between two Ivy Leaguers? Why does it matter who wins when the results, no matter who is named president, will probably be the same? *Because it does matter*, Madeline thinks. Because among the things the two men share, there is a world of differences, significant, immutable differences. It is not a small, simple, meaningless decision. Madeline, pacing around the kitchen with nervous energy, finally steps outside, wishing she had a cigarette. She walks quietly into the backyard, her bare feet in the grass, looking up at the sky, at the tops of the trees, searching for the strange, indecipherable shape of the cloud-figure, but it has gone for good, Madeline knows, peeking up there once more: there is nothing. Only the moon, and the swaying trees, the telephone lines, the shadows of the garage, the sky full of clouds continuing their movement east.

U. "Okay, well, goodnight anyway," Madeline whispers and steps back inside.

V. At one o'clock in the morning, the news channels all begin to report that the state of Ohio is now red. By then the girls have both gone to bed. Madeline, sitting beside Jonathan folded up on the couch, flips from channel to channel, hoping to see a different answer, but no, no. From the local networks to the cable channels, each one claims the same thing, their maps all swiftly transformed, the absentee ballots and electoral arithmetic summarily counted, a winner finally announced. A televised photograph of George Bush appears on all the channels, almost all at once, and, flipping through, Madeline feels like a terrible mistake has been made.

"I think that's it," Jonathan whispers sleepily.

"Why?" Madeline mutters. "Why? Why did people vote for him?"

Jonathan shakes his head, then sighs. "You can never underestimate the power of fear."

"Is that what you really think?"

He nods again. "I do."

Madeline sighs, still staring at the TV. "I guess you're right. That's what they did. They tried to frighten people—with the war and terrorists and gay marriage—and it actually worked. It actually worked."

Jonathan kisses his wife's forehead and then stands. "Are you ready for bed?"

"I don't think I can sleep," she whispers.

"I don't think so either." He scratches his beard and then straightens his shirt. "I guess I'll go do some work for a while."

"Work?"

"I guess." He leans over and kisses her lips softly, then her forehead again, and says, "Goodnight." He stretches then, strolls down the hallway to the den. Madeline flips through the channels for another couple of minutes and then switches off the television. She straightens up the parlor, then the kitchen, putting away some dishes, then leans against the counter, sulking. "Forget this," she says, marching down the hallway to the den.

W. When Madeline finds Jonathan sitting in the den—the professor scanning a map of the ocean—she slips off her shoes and places her hands over his eyes, standing behind him.

"Hello there," he says.

"Hello there," she says.

X. When they begin to kiss, Madeline remembers why she loves her husband in the first place. It is precisely because he is a mess, because he is a dreamer, because he is afraid. It is because he needs her so badly, that he kisses her so softly: it is because he doesn't want to lose her. She has almost forgotten how it feels to be touched so gently, to be treated like something surprisingly precious, knowing, in the end, that this other person needs you just to keep on living.

Y. This is a good enough reason to keep kissing.

Z. As they keep on kissing, and kissing, things do not seem all that complicated.

Twenty-eight

IT IS WEDNESDAY MORNING, IN THE MIDDLE OF THIRD period, when Amelia realizes her history project is due tomorrow. She has absolutely no idea what she is going to do, only that it will end up being the most mediocre history project of all time, ever. Standing at the front of the classroom, Mr. Anson, her history teacher, declares that each student will be required to present their projects to the class, and they will do so alphabetically, starting tomorrow, Thursday morning. Amelia frowns, her neck beginning to itch, already feeling nauseous. She glances around the room and sees that there is only one boy with a last name that starts with the letter A—Bob Antwerp—and only two kids with the letter B. Amelia closes her eyes, sulking, as Mr. Anson, his brown mustache twitching, reads off her name. "No more than ten minutes for each project, ladies and gentlemen. I want focused, thoughtful responses to the historical issues you've decided to explore. Think about how that particular historical issue affects the world you know today." Amelia considers her awful first attempt, the cruddy movie she made, then her second, the cruddy protest with the cloud costume, and sighs, more hopeless than ever.

. . .

At lunch, Amelia sits alone, gazing down at her vegetable enchilada, wondering how she's going to come up with an acceptable history project in only a couple of hours. Shit. As she's contemplating the grotesque food in front of her, William Banning takes a seat across from her and says, "Not too appetizing, huh?"

"It's the only vegetarian dish they have. It tastes like ass."

"It's probably pretty bad for you."

Amelia nods, sighing again.

"I really liked the piece you gave Mr. Wick this morning, about the election. I liked the part about people voting for Bush because he avoided being too complicated. Like how he just kept repeating the same things over and over again and that's what people really wanted to hear.'"

Amelia grins, quoting from her column: "'*People don't want answers, they want bumper stickers.*'"

"Yeah. That was really sharp."

"Thanks."

"I was wondering . . . you know, the student council has elections coming up. Maybe . . . would you be interested in like running for something?"

"I don't think so," Amelia says with a frown.

"Oh, well, I just wanted to ask. I mean, I'm sure you're busy with a bunch of other things. I just wanted to . . . well, thank you for like . . . not . . . well . . . for being cool about the newspaper. I mean like I'm sure somebody else in your position would have probably quit, and you're the only one writing anything of any value and so, well, I just wanted to say thanks . . . and if . . . well, I dunno. Good luck with your . . . enchilada."

Amelia, blushing, looks down at the awful assemblage of folded tortilla and cheese. "I have to do a project for my history class," she mumbles. "It's due tomorrow and I really don't know what I'm going to do."

"Whoa," William says with a smile. "I didn't think you were one of those people who waited until the last minute to do anything."

"I'm not," she says. "I just . . . I wanted to do something really awesome. But it was like . . . everything I tried seemed so obvious and dumb."

"What is your project about?"

"I don't know. I wanted to do it about communism. And like how capitalism is like ruining everything. I wanted to make a movie but it came out like shit."

"Oh."

"I don't know. I just wanted to get the people in my class to think about being consumers and everything. And like how it's like affecting all these other things. Like pollution and global warming and all of that. But it just seems too preachy, I guess. Like there was all this voice-over and it was way too obvious."

"Yeah," William says with a nod. "I get it."

"I wanted it to be all arty, you know. Like subtle, but I don't know how to do that."

"What if you just showed pictures?"

"What do you mean?"

"Like what if you made a movie without any sound or anything? Or maybe just some music and you just showed pictures."

"Yeah, I don't know," she says, but already the great wheels in her mind have begun turning.

"Well, I'm supposed to be in Latin," William Banning says. "See you later."

" 'Bye," Amelia says and doesn't like how giddy she feels.

AFTER SCHOOL, Amelia once more finds her way to the university parking lot, searching for Professor Dobbs. Immediately she sees he is not alone again. There he stands, flirting with a bevy of bright-eyed coeds, answering all their questions with a smile, winking at them, his hands touching their arms and their shoulders and their backs. Fifteen minutes later, Professor Dobbs says goodbye to the last of them. A girl with braces practically gushes as she holds her class notes against her chest, skipping off.

With his arms full of student papers, Professor Dobbs struggles to open the driver's-side door of the Saab. Amelia, ducking between two parked cars, watches as the young academic accidentally spills his classwork, cursing to himself, dropping his keys beneath the car. "Schadenfreude," Amelia whispers, nodding to herself, then wonders if that's the right word for the situation. It doesn't really matter. She walks over to where Professor Dobbs is kneeling, collecting his fallen papers. When he sees her shoes, he looks up from them to her legs, to her waist, to her chest, to her neck. When he reaches her face, recognizing the disappointed frown, he quickly becomes panicked. He holds the manila file folders against his chest, scrambles for his keys, trying to smile, trying to disappear into his sedan as swiftly as possible.

"Amelia, what a surprise, I didn't, well, I didn't see you in class again today and, of course, I was afraid—"

"I'm not in your class," she whispers.

"Oh." This information seems to momentarily relieve the

young professor, who carelessly tosses his students' work onto the passenger seat. "Well, I was just hurrying off to a meeting again. It was nice running into you like this but—"

"I want you to know that I think what you did to me was wrong. I've thought about it and I think you should know that."

"Well, I'm sorry to hear that, Amelia. I mean, of course you're entitled to your beliefs and feelings, but both of us are adults and no one forced anything upon anybody."

"I've decided you're part of the problem," Amelia says with a frown, her black beret casting a strange shadow over the professor's feet. "You and everybody like you. Just because you have a little power, you think you can treat people like . . . things. But you can't."

"I'm very sorry you feel that you've been mistreated, Amelia. Perhaps I misjudged you. I thought, of course, that you were adult enough to understand the nature of the relationship. If I've done anything to—"

"I was standing over there, thinking of maybe fucking up your car or something," she murmurs. "But now I just feel sorry for you."

The professor, unsure what else to do or say, nods, then climbs into his vehicle. He starts the car and begins to back out of the lot. Amelia stands there, staring sadly as he goes, before she simply turns away.

WHEN SHE GETS HOME, Amelia finds her younger sister in her room again, lying on her bed. She's too tired and too depressed to even yell at her. She throws down her book bag and mumbles, "Move over," before crashing onto the mattress.

"Your bed is so much better than mine," Thisbe says.

"It's like the same exact bed," Amelia mutters.

"Well, it feels better."

"What are you doing in here?"

"I dunno. Just thinking."

"Why can't you do that in your own room?"

"I need to ask you a favor."

"What is it?" Amelia asks.

"It's kind of crazy."

"What is it?"

"I need you to go to the retirement home tomorrow with me."

"Why?"

"I need your help to do something. I can't . . . you're just good at dealing with people."

"But what do you want me to do?" Amelia asks. Her younger sister turns and whispers her plan in her ear. It is a secret, Thisbe says, then, when she is finished whispering, she climbs out of her older sister's bed.

THE MOVIE AMELIA makes for her history class that night is called *The History of Clouds*. Like William Banning suggested, it's mostly just single images, some still images, some moving, with a simple sound track over them. Amelia picks a song from an American band with a French-sounding name, Le Tigre, "Cry for Everything Bad That's Ever Happened," and edits the images to the instrumental track. The film is pretty simple: it begins with a long, single shot of a cloud, which turns out to be a brightly lit galaxy swirling in the ocean of purple-black space, then cuts to a cloudy shot of earth, closing in farther and farther until there's an amazing wide shot of a bank of clouds over the Arctic, which she steals from *Koyaanisqatsi*, and then it cuts to some other borrowed footage, of clouds pouring out from a steam train, then a shot of a field of black clouds above an old coal factory, then a series of shots of clouds from various power plants, then the clouds above the Los Angeles skyline, hazy and dim, and then there are several shots of clouds of black and gray above a bombed-out Baghdad before, finally, the short film ends with a shot taken from Amelia's front yard, staring up through the trees at the sky overhead. When Amelia finishes editing the final sequence, she starts the movie over and watches it again. It's okay, not great or perfect or anything, nothing too spectacular, but at least it's something. At least, instead of just repeating the same old stupid history report, instead of doing the same old thing, she has tried to do something serious, something with some kind of meaning.

WHEN AMELIA WAKES UP Thursday morning, she takes a shower, brushes her hair, gets dressed, eats breakfast, puts her books in her book bag, double-checks that she has the DV tape, then grabs her black jacket and beret. All at once, looking down at the simple circle of fabric, she decides she does not want to wear it. Instead, she brushes her light brown hair once more, then grabs the beret and tosses it into her bottom dresser drawer, placing it on top of all the other mass-produced junk she has collected. She stares at the beret lying there for a moment. Everything is quiet. Everything is still. Everything is perfectly silent. Amelia then closes the dresser drawer and hurries down the stairs, feeling a little unsure without the beret on top of her head, but why not: it's just for today.

Twenty-nine

BEFORE SCHOOL ON THURSDAY, THISBE IS EATING HER cereal and staring out the kitchen window, at the sun, at the sky, at the world quietly beginning its day while she has to get ready to go to the worst place on earth: school. Across the table, her older sister is munching loudly, scanning the morning paper's headlines for something to be mad about. This morning Thisbe is too tired to gloat about the results of the recent election. She stabs at the remaining golden puffs of starch getting soggy in the golden white bowl of milk, wondering what she is going to say if she happens to see Roxie today. Maybe Roxie will act like nothing is wrong. Maybe she will rush up to her in the hall and smile and tell her what her crazy mother made for dinner last night or go on about some silly idea for a song. Or maybe not. Maybe, with the rest of the school hurrying along, the bell for the next class echoing above their heads, she will rush right past Thisbe, acting like she doesn't even know her. That would be the worst thing in the world, Thisbe decides. If she came up and said something mean, that would be okay. *If she acts like I don't even exist, like she doesn't even know me, well, that would be the worst thing ever, of all time.* As Thisbe considers this, she notices a flash of white slowly moving across the sunlit grass of the backyard. It is her neighbor's cat, Snowball. Thisbe smiles suddenly, setting down her spoon, then hurries to the door with the cereal bowl full of graying milk in her hand, stepping outside as quietly as she can, while Amelia, still reading the paper, continues mumbling to herself. Squatting down on the back porch steps with the bowl, Thisbe makes a few soft kissy noises, clapping her hands against her thighs. The cat freezes where it stands, sniffing a wilted azalea bush. Thisbe gives a short little whistle, then snaps her fingers. Snowball squints its bright blue eyes, suspicious, but, smelling the delectable bowl of sugary milk, the cat creeps along the border of the backyard, tense, its tail raised, its pink nose twitching. Thisbe makes a few more kissy noises, though at this point it's unnecessary. Snowball stalks through the grass, sniffing, until its mouth is gently lapping at the rim of the bowl, and Thisbe, so gently, so carefully, begins to run her fingers along the back of the cat's soft head. Snowball does not seem bothered, now completely entranced by the bowl of milk. Thisbe softly caresses its pointed white ear.

Dear Heavenly Father, Thisbe says silently, closing her eyes, *let the world be as nice to me today as this cat. Please do not let anyone utter a harsh word or give me a dirty look for being a spaz. Please do not let me drop anything while I am walking down the hallway. Please do not let certain people pretend that I do not exist. And please do not let anyone I love die anytime soon, at least until I am in my thirties. Through Christ, Our Lord, amen.*

The cat, having finished the milk, its rough tongue flicking against the empty bowl, glances up at Thisbe as she scratches beneath its chin. Then it is off, just a quick flash of white fur disappearing behind a thornbush, and Thisbe can hear her sister shouting.

. . .

THISBE WALKS DOWN the school hallway with her eyes almost completely closed. She is partly pretending she is a blind martyr, and partly trying to avoid seeing Roxie. As she is knocked about by the older boys and girls, excusing herself each time she bumps into somebody, she can almost feel Roxie somewhere among that mass of hurried, anxious bodies, watching her. She can almost sense the strange electric current traveling from the other girl's eyes and mouth, her lips, careening down the hall to where Thisbe steps so clumsily, trying to avoid being seen. By third period, Thisbe realizes how dumb she looks, and as she hurries all the way across the building to her math class, it finally happens. Roxie, in a blue sweater, her blond hair looking styled and spiky, comes around the corner from the next hall, talking to some other sophomore, a girl with sharp features and gray bags beneath her heavily mascaraed blue eyes, just as Thisbe is rushing in the opposite direction. Every part of her body feels weak. Her breath falters, her heart betrays her, beating as loud as a plea. Thisbe almost stumbles, crashing into two older boys in front of her, as Roxie, definitely noticing her out of the corner of her eye, decides to pretend she does not, continuing to talk very excitedly to this new girl, this girl with the dark circles and makeup and slutty-looking blouse. Thisbe, fighting back a sob, feels Roxie's shadow pass over her own; the entire world—of unnamable countries, of thousands of people, of millions of catastrophes, including all of the students at this lousy school—slows down for a single second as they pass one another, both of them silent, both of them pretending not to have seen the other's stilted, awkwardly feigned nonchalance. These two bodies pass in such close proximity, elbows, maybe for a moment, coming within millimeters of each other, electrons, neutrons, protons, things immeasurably small finding one another for that solitary second, then, having made contact, somehow changing, the larger world growing silent now as they drift apart, one moving down D hall to the east, the other moving down D hall to the west. In that painful moment, Thisbe searches for something in the other girl's eyes, some glimmer, some glow of recognition, but finds only stony greenness. What does not happen in those following seconds is the end: Thisbe does not collapse, she does not die of an asthma attack, she does not faint or stab herself in the heart with a No. 2 pencil. For as awful as the moment is, it is soon over, and Thisbe, placing one foot after the other, finds herself still alive, still breathing, sad, heartsick, despondent—yes—but stumbling on weak legs to her next class.

AFTER SCHOOL, Thisbe does not go to chorus practice. She explains to Mr. Grisham, in the hallway between sixth and seventh periods, that her grandfather is really sick. She uses the term "way sick," as a matter of fact, and when the phrase comes out of her mouth, she smiles to herself, thinking she sounds exactly like her older sister. Mr. Grisham nods attentively, then, without any previous indication—no hand on the shoulder or further verbal cue—he throws a long, nervous arm around Thisbe's neck and gives what is, surprisingly, a very gentle hug. "We'll all be thinking of you," he says and then releases her and strolls off to teach his music class, the awful echo of poorly fingered oboe notes already squawking from his room. *It is not a lie at all*, Thisbe tells herself. *We are going to see him.*

. . .

WHEN THISBE OPENS the front door of her house, she finds her older sister is already home, already a little impatient. Thisbe reminds herself that what she's planned is almost impossible to do alone. The two girls chat about school for a moment, Thisbe puts her book bag on the kitchen table, even though her mother has asked her not to do this a hundred times. She grabs a glass of water and gulps it over the sink, something her older sister, Amelia, thinks is uncouth, then finishes it with a healthy, "Ahhhh," and wipes her mouth with the back of her hand. Without another word, the two sisters, separated in age by almost four years, the older girl, a little taller, a little more savvy, refined, her makeup simple but thorough, in a dark sweater and jeans, the younger, her brown hair darker in a ponytail, in her gray coat and gray skirt from school, a smudge of something at the corner of her mouth, no makeup, her eyebrows in desperate need of tweezing, or so the older one thinks, together, silent, not so much different at all, the familial resemblance in the color of the hair, in the shape of the nose, slight and narrow, the thin mouth, the rounded eyes, the two girls exit their home before either one of their parents returns from work, afraid of having to explain where they are now headed. Together, they walk briskly down to Fifty-fifth Street, find a cab, and take it south, passing the dreary-looking shopping centers and run-down homes until some twenty minutes later they are there, ready to lie, to do a strange kind of misdeed. They sign both of their names on the register of the retirement home, taking the elevator to the third floor, walking demurely down the hall, or as close to it as they can. They find their grandfather watching television in the quiet confines of his room.

. . .

WHAT HAPPENS NEXT happens in near silence. Thisbe searches through her grandfather's dresser for some clothes, Amelia, a little stronger, tries to help their grandfather out of bed. It is rough going at first, on her own. The old man's purple, swollen feet and spindly little legs do not seem willing to bend. Their grandfather smiles at them kindly the whole time and does not ask for an explanation. To him, perhaps they are two other girls, twins, their nearly identical faces and dark hair, something from a dream or a memory. He is happy to see them, with their voices and dark eyelashes, with the softness of their hair and hands. He knows, somehow, that they have come to save him.

"I'm not so sure about this," Amelia hisses over her shoulder. "I can't get his legs to move."

"We need to get his wheelchair."

"Great. Where are we going to find that?"

Thisbe twitches her nose, surveying the room. "Go ask the nurse for one. Tell her we're going to take him for a walk."

"What if she says no?" Amelia asks.

"That's why you're here. That's why I asked you to help. You're good at being pushy. I'll get him dressed."

Amelia rolls her eyes and abandons her grandfather at the bed, placing his legs back beneath the starchy sheet. Thisbe has found a pair of large gray pants, a button-up sweater, and a blue stocking hat. Very gently, she begins to work the pants up her grandfather's narrow legs, over his pajama bottoms, buckling them at his hipless waist, then she slips on a pair of dark socks. Leaning him against her equally thin frame, she works the sweater over his hospital gown. By the time Amelia returns with the wheelchair, its left wheel squeaking loudly as it rattles down the hall and into the room, Thisbe has their grandfather dressed. Yes, he looks like a madman, yes, he is totally disheveled, his gown tucked into his pants, the sweater buttoned up wrongly, everything looking enormous on his wilted body, but he hasn't tried to stop them yet. He now sits leaning against Thisbe, his hazel eyes glowing.

"I found a bunch of wheelchairs at the end of the hall," Amelia explains. "I don't think anyone noticed."

"Good. Help me get him into it."

Together, they lift their grandfather from the bed to the wheelchair. When he is settled, he makes a little sound, like a sigh, and then, turning, he reaches up to place his papery-thin hand against Thisbe's cheek. Thisbe smiles, fits the stocking cap over her grandfather's head, then takes the two handles of the wheelchair in her hands. Before they cross the threshold into the tile hallway, Amelia, glancing down toward the nurses' station, whispers, "I don't know if this is such a good idea. I mean . . . I don't know why we're even doing this."

Thisbe, undeterred by this last-minute hesitation, pushes the wheelchair into the harsh lights of the hall and answers, "Because we are." Together, they walk behind their grandfather, the wheels of the chair squeaking with each full revolution, closer and closer to the octagon-shaped nurses' station. "If they say anything, you have to talk," Thisbe says. Amelia nods, sizing up the three nurses buzzing at their desk. Step by step, they move down the hall, the wheels giving a squeak every few seconds. They are passing the desk, the nurses laughing with each other about something. One of them, a heavyset black lady in a pink smock, gives Thisbe a suspicious look, which Thisbe, immediately, without having to think, returns with the most angelic-looking smile she can form with her lips, still pushing the wheelchair along. "How's Mr. Casper today?"

the heavyset nurse asks, and before Thisbe can stutter a half-
formed response, Amelia has hit the security door button and
says, "We're just taking him for a walk around the block." The
glass security door opens and the two girls pass through, the
sound of the elevator arriving bringing an end to that particularly uncomfortable conversation. When they hit the bottom
floor, Amelia stumbles out of the elevator, then through the
front doors to the street, where she hails a cab. Thisbe, smiling
at the security guard as she passes, meets his question, "Taking Gramps for a walk?" with a single nod, before rushing
her grandfather through the glass doors and finally outside.
Already Amelia has gotten a cab: it's waiting near the end of
the block, its taillights flashing bright red as it idles. Amelia
opens the back door and helps lift her grandfather into the
backseat, as Thisbe climbs around the other side and keeps
him upright, before buckling him in.

"Okay, so where are we going?" Amelia asks, but Thisbe
just nods, taking her grandfather's hand, making sure he is
properly bundled up. The taxi driver, a young fellow in an
orange and green dashiki, helps Amelia fold the wheelchair up,
then he opens the trunk and places it inside. Amelia joins him
in the front seat, before he puts the cab into drive and asks,
"Where to?" in a distinctly African accent. Thisbe tells him
their destination and the driver nods, enters something into his
fare computer, and pulls away into traffic. From the backseat,
staring out the window, Thisbe sees the autumn sky is cloudy,
overcast, dismally gray. The sun, hidden behind a heavy cast
of cumulus, does not offer much in the way of encouragement. As the cab winds its way north and east, Thisbe silently
wonders if what she has done is the right thing. Beside her,
her grandfather breathes heavily, glancing with wonder at the
world flying by.

. . .

TOGETHER, ON THE paved path along the eastern edge
of the great lake, the two girls push their grandfather along,
the wheelchair moving a little uneasily against the November
wind. The lakefront park, and its wide field of grass, green
only a few weeks ago, now looks drab, the lake itself choppy
with gray waves. Thisbe pulls the stocking cap down over her
grandfather's ears as they trudge along, past the yellowed stone
fieldhouse, past the athletic field, past the end of the paved
walkway. Thisbe has to turn their grandfather around backward, pulling him up the slight muddy embankment, past the
spot where she and Roxie had ditched their bikes only a few
weeks ago. Up and through the weedy prairie grass, once yellow and brown, now dark, nearly black, Thisbe pulls at the
handles, stepping backward. Her older sister pushes from the
front of the wheelchair, their grandfather silent, smiling at
the unyielding margins of the cloudy sky, to the spot where
she was certain she and this other teenage girl had somehow
flown. She takes a rest for a moment, breathing deeply, the
cold, cold November air burning her lungs, leaning against
the sturdy frame of the wheelchair. Her older sister looks
around, unimpressed, and asks, "Now what?" her eyebrows
tilted above a face full of doubt. The field grass, though mud-
died, is still tall. It sways wildly back and forth with the great
gusts of wind rushing along the lake. Thisbe itches her nose,
then grabs her grandfather's hand and leans in close to his
fuzzy ear, whispering only a few words, which her older sister
cannot hear, but very quickly their grandfather smiles wider,
then closes his wrinkly, sunken eyes. Thisbe, kneeling beside
him on the muddy ground, still grasping his tiny hand tightly,
closes her eyes as well. Amelia, annoyed now, shaking her head

to herself, knows it will be she who will be blamed for this, the sound of her father's and mother's voices already echoing in her brain. When the sun climbs out from behind a massive patchwork of clouds, Amelia has to cover her eyes with her hand to ward off the glare. The wind works its way through her hair and, turning, she searches for the familiar shapes of her sister and grandfather, which, just for the moment, seem to be somewhere they should not be, dozens of feet up in the air. When the sun disappears again, only a moment or two later, the wind startling itself into submission, Amelia lowers her hand, glancing back at her sister and grandfather, and finds them both on the ground, beaming.

ONE MONTH, two weeks, and some fifteen minutes later, in the final seconds just before he dies, Henry Casper will still be smiling.

FOR YEARS, Thisbe will later think of that one moment in the field as the only time she was ever sure of anything in her life.

Thirty

IT IS JANUARY ALREADY AND SOMEHOW THE WORLD has not ended. Through the windshield of the Volvo, Jonathan watches as the snow drifts through the air, dusting the top of the angular trees in perfect whiteness. Beside him, Madeline is singing along with the stereo, a song by John Lennon. In the backseat, Amelia is mostly quiet, staring out at the neighborhood as it flashes past in a parade of gray and white. She is reading *Parmenides* by Plato, on loan from William Banning, and she looks down at the pages with a certain fascination and a wide-eyed feeling of confusion and delight. The backseat, however, is missing its other occupant, Thisbe Casper. Jonathan notices this absence again when he glances in the rearview mirror. His youngest daughter has gone to the auditorium early, to get into costume, to put on her makeup, to be nervous, to stand behind the curtain of the empty high school theater, and to smile at the thought of singing onstage. Above the trees of the near-empty street, the sky is full of clouds: they move and tumble like set pieces, shifting silently as the Volvo speeds along the wet Hyde Park thoroughfare.

Figure 5: A cloud

The family finds a parking spot close to the auditorium's entrance, then they take three seats near the back, in the second-to-last row, as Thisbe has requested, as far as possible from the flood of lights, so that when she glances up from the last line of the chorus, she will not see her parents and her sister and suddenly lose her nerve. The auditorium begins to fill up quickly. The band, mostly juniors and seniors, in formal black jackets owned by the school, begin to tune their instruments. Jonathan takes Madeline's small white hands, warming them, as Amelia passes each of them a simple white program: *Gunga Din*, it says. *A musical, as adapted from the Kipling by J. R. Grisham.*

BACKSTAGE, THE STUDENTS help each other with their makeup and costumes, and Thisbe, with her eyes closed, grins, her dimples visible, as a girl named Marcie dabs a smear of rouge across her cheeks. "Hold still," Marcie whispers, giggling.

"I can't," Thisbe says, and laughs. "It tickles."

Marcie shakes her head, beginning to laugh, too, and as the other girl's fingers gently outline her faint eyebrows, Thisbe feels like she just might die. Behind them, in a narrow half circle, the other girls in the chorus, all portraying nameless British sergeants, practice their opening song, borrowed from Kipling:

It was "Din! Din! Din!"
With the bullets kickin' dust-spots on the green.
When the cartridges ran out,
You could hear the front-files shout:
"Hey! We need ammunition, mules, and Gunga Din!"

Mr. Grisham dashes past, muttering, "Five minutes. Five minutes, everyone!" and Thisbe blinks, overcome with excitement, nearly ruining her mascara.

HER PARENTS, SITTING in the second and third seats in the second-to-last row, begin to clap before anyone else, as soon as a rushed-looking Mr. Grisham takes the stage. Amelia, folding her book closed, turns to them and says, "You guys are so lame," and after some brief remarks, with admonishments about cell phones, the director exits, and the band begins to play. The music is rousing, exotic, a little out of tune and a little off-time. Jonathan is still holding Madeline's hand. They will hold each other's hand throughout the entire performance. They will proudly watch as their daughter, Thisbe, a captured Thuggee, commits suicide, overacting a little, but with ferocious commitment. When a spotlight accidentally falls from the rigging during the second act, smashing against the stage, the whole auditorium will echo with anxiety and concern and useless worry, but Madeline will turn to her husband and roll her eyes. Then she will smile. It will be a secret message and will mean at least one million different things. Seeing it, unsure of the message exactly, Jonathan will, in his heart, say *yes* anyway. After an unscheduled intermission, during which the damage from the fallen light is assessed and quickly cleaned up, the play will awkwardly resume, without much excitement or poetry. It will keep going, for half an hour too long. Jonathan will continue to watch the play, though after his daughter's performance he will begin to daydream about a number of other things: his father's death, only a week or so before Christmas, which came quickly and without much warning, just as his dad seemed to be doing a little bit better. Jonathan's eyes will begin crowding with tears, thinking of his father lying in the hospital bed—his small hands and narrow face so gaunt, so distant already— and he will quickly try to think of something, anything, else to keep himself from crying. He will begin going over the early chapters of a book he plans to write about the evolution of defense mechanisms in prehistoric animals, or he will start planning another grant proposal for the Hausman Institute, this one about the biological imperative of flight versus fight, or maybe he will return to his considerations regarding the new data accumulated from the squid discovered off the coast of Hawaii. What wonderful thoughts roam through his head before he looks down and sees his wife's knees, beneath white-colored nylons, dimpled with beauty. Hidden behind the fabric, with the lights from the stage playing off of them, they look like two flowers. Or two apples. Or two mountaintops. Jonathan will stare at them absentmindedly for the remainder of the play. After the curtains are drawn and the last note sung, the audience, composed of parents, siblings, and teachers, will do what they can to stifle their disappointment and weariness. When they all exit the theater, their station wagons, minivans, sedans, and SUVs will all be blanketed in perfect white snow. A father will gently sweep the snow from the windshield—the station wagon's engine running, the heat turned up as high as it will go—staring inside at his family, each of them smiling, each of them content, for the moment, safe, for the moment, happy. The father will stand in the snow and wonder if the world will ever be as simple and as lovely as this again, this moment, this. With snowflakes in his hair, on his shoulders, in his beard, ignoring the weather, he will climb into the Volvo and ask if anyone would like to maybe go get some ice cream. The rest of his family will groan with disinterest but it will not matter. They will get ice cream and then argue with happy voices about the daughter's first play.

FOR NOW, THOUGH, the lights in the auditorium go dim. The dark red curtains slowly open, the crowd of parents and siblings and teachers politely hushing one another. Thisbe, waiting in the wings of stage left, repeats the first line of the first song to herself, over and over again. The lights come up onstage and the audience begins to clap quite loudly. The actors begin to take their places, the music fades, and then what follows is both astonishing and quite ordinary.

Acknowledgments

ALL MY LOVE AND GRATITUDE TO Koren and Lucia. Many, many thanks to Sylvie Rabineau, Maria Massie, Tom Mayer (one of the best editors I've ever had the chance to work with), Johnny Temple (for his support and encouragement), Johanna Ingalls, Todd Baxter, James Vickery, Jon Resh, Cody Hudson, Todd Dills, Mickey Hess, Todd Taylor, Sean Carswell, Dan Sinker, Jonathan Messinger, Chris Abani, Felicia Luna Lemus, T Cooper, Randy Albers, Sheryl Johnston, Donna Seaman, Quimby's Books, the Hideout Chicago, and the Columbia College Fiction Writing Department. I am also indebted to the scientific work of Temple Grandin, Neil Shubin, and Phil Eyden, whose astute research greatly informed the writing of this book. Thanks also go to the *New York Times* for their material on American internment during World War II. A very special thanks to Arthur D. Jacobs, Major, USAF, Retired, whose archival work for *The Freedom of Information Times* concerning his experiences in Crystal City, Texas, proved to be invaluable.

picador.com

blog
videos
interviews
extracts